GW01271848

For many years Aiden J Harvey has been a professional entertainer working in many facets of the industry, within which he enjoyed a decade of particular success throughout the 1980's, appearing on numerous hit television shows as well as television spectacular productions including 'Live at the Palladium' and 'Live at Her Majesty's'. In addition, he is extremely proud to have entertained our armed forces in war zone circumstances in the Falklands and the Middle East.
He now turns his creative talents to writing; 'ACE' being his first work being brought to the reading public.

For my cousin Alec Goldstone

Also for Gary Edwards, for his tireless work on my behalf and endless belief in my work!

Aiden J. Harvey

ACE

To DEBS
Enjoy the read!
[illegible]

AUSTIN MACAULEY
PUBLISHERS LTD.

A CIP catalogue record for this title is available from the British Library.

ISBN 978 184963 744 2

www.austinmacauley.com

First Published (2014)
Austin Macauley Publishers Ltd.
25 Canada Square
Canary Wharf
London
E14 5LB

Printed and bound in Great Britain

Prologue

South Africa, 1940

The summer heat had been practically unbearable, soaring at some points during the day to a sweltering 120 degrees Fahrenheit (45 degrees centigrade). Even an hour after the sun had set in the South African sky, a sticky humidity prevailed. A bead of sweat broke away from his temple and journeyed down over a boney cheek. Employing a handkerchief, he dabbed his furrowed brow, whilst his thin lips, discharged his instructions from behind where he had told her to be seated.

"Proverbs sixteen and seventeen ... chapter sixteen." He said; her nervous fingers flicked through the pages of the good book until she found the passage. He angled his tall wiry body over her and whispered into her ear.

"Now render unto me, the Lord's message child."

She licked her lips and began,

"The preparation of the heart in man, and the answer of the tongue, is from the Lord.

All the ways of man are clean in his own eyes; but the Lord weigheth the spirit.

Commit thy works unto the Lord, and thy thoughts shall be established.

The Lord hath made all things for himself; yea, even the wicked for the day of evil." The tone of her voice had a graceful quality, and for someone as tender in years as she, the text was delivered with a degree of eloquence, indeed, he had taught her well.

So close was he now, she could feel his breath on her shoulder. Although somewhat perturbed she read on.

"The heart of the wise teaches his mouth and added learning to his lips.

Pleasant words are as honey-comb, sweet to the soul, and health to the bones."

Outside the house, storm clouds had begun to dominate the skyline.

The wooden chair, in which she was sitting, creaked as his hands took some of the weight from his upper body, allowing him once more to stand upright. He walked slowly around the chair, his eyes remaining focused on her, while her voice echoed around the walls.

He was a highly respected man in these parts, a bastion of white middle-class society. It was even said by some outsiders that he treated his black workforce with more regard than they deserved, and without question he had been charitable towards her, he had rescued her from a wretched existence which would have resulted in probable starvation or sickness and disease for which there was little or no medication for people like her. Since she had arrived at the house two years earlier, she had been well fed, clothed and heartily glad to have a roof over her head. In addition to these favorable deeds, his God-fearing instructions had guided her towards salvation. The same man was responsible now for her heart to pound with a flurry beneath her firm, youthful breasts over which a palm vigorously explored, kneading her flesh inside the dress that he had feverishly unbuttoned just moments before. His other hand held her firmly at the nape of the neck as he wrenched her from the chair. Her discordant breathing fluctuated in an effort to control her frenzy under his dominant persuasion. This lustful encounter was consummately unexpected by her and, though her limbs felt leaden she made an attempt to escape these uninvited advances, but it was futile against his superior height and strength. He tightened his grip at the back of her neck and smiled down upon her dark countenance.

"Don't fight me," his grip tightened once more, "Did I not give you sanctuary child!" He hissed, and a strong pungent smell of whisky invaded her nostrils, this coupled with a sour stench of sweat emanating from the man's armpits added to her repugnance. Again she strived to free herself from his vice-like grip, managing this time to escape the man's sinister clutches, she turned to run, but in her effort to do so felt the dress tear away from her shoulders and with one mighty tug on the material he sent her spinning like a rag doll to the wooden floor, where upon landing, her head collided with the solid surface with a sickening thud, rendering her momentarily insensible and oblivious to his next contemptible maneuvers. In a tempestuous fluster he ripped off the remains of her clothing, and then callously entered her. In the short time that it took her to regain consciousness the deed had been executed.

PART I

Chapter One

King – Monaco, Southern France 1982

They had met when she and her former school chums made one of their frequent weekend visits to the bright lights of Monte Carlo. He had impressed her instantly on that first chance encounter. He was tall and though he had a rather prominent nose, he was, she considered, endowed with striking good looks and at the time she considered him to be refined and certainly not without charm. To crown these presupposed attributes he was evidently fairly rich. This impressive culmination certainly helped the eighteen year old to do something that she had never previously done on her excursions to the Metropolis, and that was to miss her last train home, knowing full well that it would cause her parents some distress. After her friends had reluctantly departed to catch their only mode of transport home, giggling on their way at their friend's impetuosity, her newly acquainted companion invited her to dine with him at his favorite restaurant and she accepted gleefully.

The Restaurant L'Escale appeared to be full on their arrival, but, she was once again impressed when the Restauranteur on recognising her tall male friend immediately showed them to the only table with place settings for two in the entire establishment. A thought crossed her mind *'had he pre-empted all this?'* She told herself not to be so silly. They ordered the house speciality, Fruits de Mer, to accompany the exquisite compilation of fish; they drank several replenished glasses of Batard Montrachet Grand Cru, the flavours of which combined perfectly with the ambience within the popular eating house. Their conversation was made in English, which she spoke fluently and was accompanied by a soft sensual tonality which would arouse any red blooded male and cause a wimp to run for cover. He had a clipped South African timbre that carried itself through in his attempts at the French language. They agreed that with her proficiency with English they would communicate in that tongue. Throughout the meal they chatted constantly. She had not been counting, although she figured that from their first meeting tonight, his unfortunate nervous tic had been evident on at least four occasions, this time being the fifth. The twitch itself was not overly obvious, but the motion that acted in accordance had, Danielle thought, an almost cocksureness about it. She assumed that this was his way of camouflaging his self-consciousness, and served to endear her even more towards him.

"Irwin ... Irwin what?"

"What?"

"What is your surname?"

"King."

"King, yes, it is a very noble name and you are from South Africa, no?"

"Yes."

"Ah yes, this is why we speak in English together, your French is atrocious Monsieur." She confirmed and they both laughed at her boldness. Once their laughing had subsided King leaned in closer to her.

"Mademoiselle."

"Please ... call me Danielle ... Danielle Marie."

"Well, Danielle Marie, that's a beautiful name to go with a remarkably beautiful woman."

"Girl ... I have only recently developed these." She said cupping her breasts, causing King to look about him to see who might have caught sight of her little provocative motion. She smiled at his slight embarrassment and countered.

"Monsieur, I am French and very proud of my body."

This was true, although Danielle was something of a late developer at any rate physically. She was first aware that her physical emergence had changed at an alarming rate when she was sixteen. At first she had been uncomfortable with her newly formed curves and conscious of men scrutinising her form, especially on the beach that she frequented in the summer months. Whereby, at that time, being something of a tomboy cursed her full and dancing bosoms for being so involuntarily mobile whilst she merely strolled along the sands. Whereas only twelve months previously she could run around unheeded, invisible to the gathering of young males.

"It pleases me that you find me attractive." She confessed and went on,

"I have my mother to thank for my complexion."

"She must be quite something then." He said smoothly.

"She is, though unpretentious, and when she was my age, she was the belle of my village."

"So tell me ... where do you come from, or should I say, where do you live?"

"Not far from here, Villefranche, do you know it?"

"Yes." King said though he had never heard of the place.

"It is very picturesque." Danielle said proudly.

"From my house, which is quite modest, on the Rue de Poilu, I have a magnificent view of the Port De La Sante and as a small girl I often comforted myself that although at that time my family was poor, only a princess could afford such a panoramic view."

"Sounds wonderful." King agreed.

"From that same spot I would often daydream of how it must have been when Villefranche was founded by the Count of Provence in 1295, his name was Charles D'Anjou. I learned this at my school."

"Did you learn your English there too?"

"Yes, you may think me boastful, but I passed all my exams."

"You have beauty and brains."

She countered his advances with an assured smile, though she was becoming aware that the wine was starting to take effect on her.

"Yes, I am very proud of my little port town with its narrow streets and evocative names, it has changed very little since its restoration to France in 1860 from the Dukes of Savoy."

You make it sound very romantic," he said, hiding the fact that he was beginning to get a little bored so he made an attempt to change the subject.

"And what about your father, what does he do?"

"What does he do?" Danielle said slightly confused by the question.

"His work ... his profession?"

"Ah, well now, my father has done many things, he is a very proud man, a characteristic you might say of his original vocation."

"A proud man you say?"

"Yes, Monsieur very proud, and in my eyes a very fine man." Danielle announced with elation.

"I'm intrigued." King said. A momentary thought flashed through her mind, she was not sure, but she did detect an air of sarcasm in his tone? She dismissed the notion as quickly as it had occurred and resumed.

"Until I was twelve years old, unfortunately I did not see nearly enough of my Papa because of his work, you understand, you see he was a fisherman."

"A fisherman?"

"He even had his own trawler."

"Interesting."

"Do I recognise a little mockery in your voice, Monsieur King?"

"No, no ... I'm sorry if I ..."

"No need, I, like my father, am also proud, perhaps a little too proud, no?"

"It's to your credit that you have inherited some of your father's plucky nature." He declared skillfully.

"Thank you."

"So, how does your father make his living now Danielle?"

"He cans fine fish. He sold his fishing boat and now he has his own factory."

"Your father shows fortitude, where does he distribute his goods?"

"All over."

"All over where?"

"France ... in restaurants, cafes and shops."

"Not abroad?"

"No, though I know that he has aspirations that one day ..."

"Maybe I can help him." King said, and contemplated on what a good cover canned fish might make one day for his own dealings overseas. For the first time that evening a silence fell between the two young people. Danielle drank the remainder of her wine and said.

"You have not told me what you do."

"Shipping."

"Ah, maybe then you can help my father, no?"

"If I possibly can, then I will, trust me, I will look into it."

This was indeed turning out to be a wonderful evening, the dashing young man sitting opposite her, with the olive complexion and coal black eyes, perhaps could help her dear Papa and hopefully might want to get the opportunity to date her again. Her youthful eyes sparkling in the candlelight, transmitting her natural sensuality. He smiled confidently back and said.

"Come, I will get the bill and drive you home to your house."

"Merci ... thank you for tonight, it has been truly wonderful."

"I hope that your parents are not going to be too angry with you for missing your train." King lied skillfully, for his design presently was on how he was going to bed this sexy young brunette, he smiled and said,

"We must do this again."

"That would nice ... but please, on our way back to Villefranche, can we stop at Le Jardine Antoinette?" She enthused.

"Yes ... of course."

The Ferrari wound its way along Boulevard de Belgique towards the magnificent gardens.

"Stop here." Danielle prompted and King eased the car to a halt. She opened the door and climbed out, then stooped down through the open door.

"Come ... please." She said eagerly, and pushed the door shut. King duly obliged her request and climbed out of the sporty red car.

"Up there." She said pointing up the hillside beyond Le Jardine Antoinette. They both lifted their gaze to where Danielle was indicating. There, stood a magnificent white mansion house, highlighted by an abundance of floodlights, the structure had huge arched windows and doors. On the second floor a grandiose balcony swept along for a third of the length of the property's exterior face.

"It basks in year round sunshine. It is the house of my dreams, it is magnifique."

Danielle turned and indicated to the Tennis Club de Monaco situated directly behind where they were standing.

"It was from there I first saw this house, I was playing in a school tournament and could not take my eyes off the place, I convinced myself that the view from up there on that terrace must be fit for a princess, like home from home, no?"

It took thirty five minutes for them to make the journey back to Villefranche and on arriving outside her parent's house Danielle thanked King once again and said,

"Where are you shipping to next?"

"Tomorrow I will be leaving for Central America."

"Well, Irwin, may I wish you Bon Voyage."

"You may, and I will call you on my return."

"I look very much forward to then, tell me, do you live in Monte Carlo?"

"Yeah ... that is, I have been residing for the past few months at Hotel du Louvre and now I'm thinking about purchasing some real estate over there when I get back from my trip."

"Very grand." Danielle substantiated, with a smile that displayed perfect teeth. Then she did something else that she had never done before. She kissed a man on her first date. He responded vigorously, their tongues wrestled and explored, her heart began to thump beneath her breast. He placed a hand gently between her soft silken thighs, at first she resisted the motion, her breathing quickened, while her conscience tussled with her wanton needs under his skilful coaxing, persuasively stimulating her to comply with his progress.

"We can make love on the beach, come let us go there." She said breathlessly into his ear. King put the car into gear and sped through the labyrinth of small roads, following Danielle's directions. On reaching the cove, they wasted little time disrobing each other, yearning to stimulate their desire. The night was warm; their flesh aglow in anticipation, their naked bodies entwined and became one under the stars, to the dulcet resonance from lapping waves that gently beat out time harmoniously with the rich golden sand. Something else ensued on that night that had not happened previously, Danielle Marie lost her virginity. She would also tell herself in time to come that she should have caught the last train home.

King did however; keep his promise to Danielle to help her father, (though it was not until some seventeen years after he made that pledge.)

Danielle's father disliked Irwin King intensely, for the man had stolen away his only daughter and the filthy swine had put her in the family way at such a tender age. Sure, he had had the decency to marry her but, in his eyes King was something of a tricky parcel which, when opened up contained an unsavoury surprise. Now here he was defaming him and his hard work over the years.

"I am right then in assuming that your business is on the brink of bankruptcy?" Irwin King pressed.

"That is a ridiculous assumption."

"Is that so?"

"How would you know that?"

"Let's just say that I know."

"It is true that my canning processing business is going through a lean time, but ..."

"Don't goad me." King interrupted, "I will waste no time with hypothesis old man, besides I did promise your daughter some time ago that I might help you."

"Danielle does not know of ...?"

"No."

"I beg of you please, do not inform her of my misfortune."

"I have a proposal for you ... you and I will go into business together, what do you say?"

"Never!"

"Then go bust, see if I bloody care."

The old man licked his lips nervously. This detestable individual had him by the balls and was beginning to squeeze him into agreeing. King continued.

"I would like to use your ... our business as a blanket for the transport of some of my own consignments to several ports of call."

The old man said nothing but continued to listen with apprehension to his terms. The younger man's South African accent beat on at him.

"This way you will pull yourself out of the shit and may even put you back in the black ... how many staff do you have?"

"Five."

"Sack them."

"What?"

"You heard me, get rid of them; I will supply the people that we need for our little enterprise."

"I don't understand, these people have worked for me for ..."

"I have no room for sanctimonious thoughts old man; all you have to do to begin with is instruct the new personnel how to operate the canning machines."

This conversation had taken place only two days previously and already the plant was in operation with its new workforce in place. At first in his ignorance the old man thought it ridiculous to can plain flour, but was sickened to the stomach when he ascertained what the product actually was. The whole undertaking was done behind locked doors and was completed and ready for shipment within just less than two days. Each large tea chest contained several dozen tins of the white powder, with bogus labels advertising fish contents. The tins surrounding the extremities of the large containers did accommodate the products apprised, pending any would be attempt to investigate the merchandise.

"Now, we load up the trucks and take the goods to your new cargo vessel." King announced, passing over the appropriate documents.

"My new cargo vessel?" The old man said thoroughly confused.

King just gave him a crooked smile.

Chapter Two

Danielle Marie (Present Day)

Danielle Marie King pouted her generous lips and applied the finishing touches of colour to them with a subtle shade of lipstick. Satisfied, she then placed the golden bullet shaped instrument into a Juan designed silk lined handbag. Through the ornately framed mirror her dark brown eyes toured the facial features in the reflection. The once long brunette mane was now cropped short and displayed the graying of maturity, although it still held a natural healthy radiance. Her petite Gallic looks belied her age and she was confidently aware that despite the fact she was in her late thirties, the eyes of admiring males and females fell upon her form wherever she made an appearance. It was the eyes of her husband that were on her now, observing her whilst she adjusted her shoulder pads discretely affixed inside the Christian Dior two piece suit which she had acquired a week ago and had chosen to sport for this part of the day. She then finished off her light application of make-up.

"Why don't you try using a trowel?" Irwin King said sarcastically from the doorway of the en-suite bathroom that they shared, albeit situated between their individual bedrooms. He held a black tom cat in one arm clutching it to his naked chest, whilst with his free hand he stroked the feline's glossy coat. The cat purred ecstatically at its' master's tactility. On noticing the animals' presence in the room Danielle frowned, then endeavored to turn a blind eye and said,

"I have got a number of things to acquire and prepare for Jean Paul's homecoming today."

"What is this?" he said churlishly and loosened his hold on the tom cat, allowing it to drop deftly onto the marble floor. "My son is coming home here, and I know nothing about this?"

"He called late last night from Florida, I telephoned the casino to tell you but they said that you were busy."

King had indeed been busy last night, though not at the casino.

"Who took the call at the casino?" he enquired.

"Monsieur Dupont, he asked me if it was an emergency, and when I told him that it could wait until the morning he told me that ..."

"He told you what?"

"That you were busy playing the table."

King was fully aware of this, since Dupont had rang the room at the Hotel American to inform him of his wife's request to speak to him. In return he had scolded the Casino Manager for disturbing him for such futile reasons. In fact, the true basis for his abrupt response was that his 'bondage session' had been interrupted. In order to make it physically possible to inform Monsieur Dupont of how inconvenient his phone call to the hotel room had been the high class hooker, held the receiver to King's ear for him. When the phone conversation had been concluded, she replaced the receiver in its cradle and returned to the task in hand and proceeded to spank her clients' rear, "That's it" King had cried out "Just on the arse ... not where it can show."

A wave of repulsion immersed from the pit of her stomach. Danielle's eyes welled up and a lonely tear flowed lazily down her cheek. She wiped it quickly away smudging the newly applied mascara; she looked directly into King's eyes.

"You bastard" she choked through gritted teeth.

King's guts somersaulted momentarily, though a calm expression concealed his thoughts. How could she possibly know....? Dupont?

"You disgusting animal" Danielle wheezed, trying hard to repress the nausea and loathing within her. Wearing nothing more than a pair of boxer shorts and a conceited smile, King stepped pompously towards her rubbing his naked chest, which only added to her repugnance. She wanted to run, but found herself completely stupefied by the sensation of his sinuous body rubbing against her. Recognising how petrified she was King crouched down slowly until his face came level with the top of her thighs.

"Now which pussy should I stroke I wonder"

"Just take the thing away from me" Danielle pleaded. King gathered the tom up from between her ankles and embraced it, then whispered into the cat's twitching ear, "You should learn from your master, not to go places that you are not wanted." Then he strolled over to the large arched patio doors, opened one of them and sent the fur bearing tom onto the sizeable balcony to take its daily tour of inspection over the small, yet resplendent grounds. Danielle sneezed three times in quick succession. Her aversion to the moggy had cause to irritate her breathing and on looking into the mirror she saw that the whites of her eyes had a smattering of pink to them, it would be a good twenty minutes or so before the itching would subside and mollify.

"Such vanity .... honestly," King declared mockingly.

"Merely pride in my appearance, mon amour, the only vanity around here is located between your legs," Danielle responded with equal contempt. Their marriage was a facade and had been for several years now, yet when in public together they were the toast of the town at whatever paradise like locality they might be. The guise was moreover performed with flourish for their son, Jean Paul. She walked over to the grand arched windows and took consolation in contemplating that her expectations all those years ago of the white mansion house on the hill were well founded, the view over which she gazed now, was quite magnificent, overlooking Le Jardine Antoinette and beyond to the Port de Fontvielle and the rich blue of the Mediterranean. King had acquired the property on his return from Central America as a matrimonial home for himself and Danielle after being shocked at learning that his then, one night stand had fallen pregnant.

"I'm sorry that the cat caused you such consternation, why don't you have a drink to calm your nerves down ... or is it too early in the day for you?" King said cynically. Danielle licked her lips, 'One day at a time' she said in return to herself.

"You know .... alcohol could ruin your looks if you're not careful" he pushed. Danielle did not react though she felt enraged by his brutality for he knew only too well that she had been dry for six months now. Six months, two weeks and three days to be precise, and no thanks to him and his derisive tongue. There was a polite rap on the bedroom door at which Danielle turned her concentration back to straightening her jacket along with her posture before responding with, "Oui, entree."

The door opened smoothly and an immaculately garbed coffee coloured female entered the room and gave Danielle her customary open kindly smile, accompanied with,

"Bonjour Madame Danielle"

"Bonjour Floss"

"It is a beautiful morning; would you like to have your breakfast on the terrace today?"

"Just coffee Floss thank you."

King re-entering Danielle's bedroom from the bathroom while busily fastening his robe, roared, "Where are my bloody newspapers this morning?"

"They are in the drawing room Mr. King, sir." Floss replied.

"Well, I want them on the terrace pronto"

"Yes Mr. King sir"

"And I want steak and eggs sunny-side up"

"Yes Mr. King ..... on the terrace sir?"

"No ... on a bloody skate board ... of course on the terrace, now get out."

Danielle looked on at the somewhat aged face, etched in lines that could tell a host of stories with regard to the King dynasty, but to this day had remained honourable and silent. Danielle's heart went out to the woman as she shut the door behind her.

"You heedless bastard" Danielle seethed.

"I'm already a bastard twice in one day, eh?"

"However did I marry such a distortion?"

"What's wrong with you, you have to raise your voice every now and again to keep them on their toes."

"Don't be ridiculous, Floss has been a servant to you for most of your life, looking after your self-centered aims and wants .... My god – don't you have any compassion?"

"What are you asking me? That I should allow them to think themselves equal to me ... why, without my father and now me .... Floss and her bloody half-wit brother would have nothing ... nothing I tell you ... no food ... no roof"

"What about dignity, what about ... their dignity?" Danielle enquired.

King's face flushed red with malice.

"Bloody dignity ... shit ... how many times ... shit ...now where I come from for blacks to have dignity as you call it, is a new concept, and I for one don't bloody buy it."

"Then buy this" Danielle heard herself say. The adrenaline sped through her and her heart beat accelerated beneath her breast. She was going to reveal her intentions, and this time she would acquaint her design utterly sober, and if he flipped and went into a rage then this time she felt sure that she would be able to escape his vicious clutches, unlike last time when so slow with the dissipating effects of alcohol she didn't see the first blow coming, just a benumbing sensation around the left side of her face. To accompany his fit of sheer petulance, King had threatened to ruin her father. The day after these events came to pass Danielle Marie decided to strengthen her resolve and gave up drinking. As powerful and fiendish as her husband might be she would not allow him to hurt her father. What did her dear Papa ever do to cause such malice? It was only an idle threat to intimidate her ... wasn't it?

'I want a divorce' was all she wanted to say, but another rap at the door halted her progress.

She would tell him she decided when her son returned to his conquests after his visit.

"Your car is ready Madame Danielle," Floss announced from the doorway.

"Thank you Floss, forget the coffee," and with that she was gone.

Chapter Three

The Overlord

Irwin King employed a wooden cocktail stick to remove the last annoying piece of meat from between his teeth, he then picked up one of the morning newspapers from the table and perused its pages, not really digesting a great deal of the information before him, until his eyes locked in on the sports page at a small article accompanied by a picture of his son. The editorial headline read; 'KING OF JUNIORS TO COME OF AGE'

Underneath the photograph of the handsome young man, it announced that Jean Paul King, the seventeen year old Junior French Tennis Champion, will next year be doing battle against the best of them when he aims to start his campaign in Melbourne, Australia for the start of the Grand Prix circuit in late December. Speaking from his Fort Lauderdale camp after completing a hat-trick of victories in American tournaments, the young Monaco born hot shot said, 'I have some satellite tournaments to compete in against some considerably tough opposition, but I will be concentrating on making my bid for the Australian Open and to do that I must continue on winning.'

Jean Paul's coach, American Brad Holding, appraised his protégé by saying he has already proved himself as being the best junior singles player in the world and this year he has matured into a stronger player both physically and mentally, he has superb stroke technique, speed and mobility and the right attitude to be a champion, he just believes that he can't be beaten. Take it from me, he will make it to Melbourne and the next year will see him displaying his talent in the heat of the Louis Armstrong Stadium of Flushing Meadows, New York, on the red clay at Roland Garros in Paris and the grass of Wimbledon. I am confident that in the near future Jean Paul King will be the world's top pro tennis star. The last words from the budding world number one *'Bring on Goliath for David is ready.'*

King looked up from the report and smiled for this latest disclosure only confirmed something that he already knew, that his son was going to become a tennis champion. That is where his ambitions are, so therefore, that is what he will be. Jean Paul's dogged determination was one characteristic that he had inherited from his father's personality, and that dogged determination had certainly aided Irwin Kings' development of financial success, even if that was only part of the ingredients he used to achieve it.

As far as the outside world was concerned, King had made his fortune by way of his dexterous trading on the stock market and his astute administration in the buying and selling of property. Indeed, some of this was true, but the money that was initially instrumental in his early transactions had blood on it, but the mask that King wore was foolproof and durable, his mercenary past could not and would not ensnare him, or so he thought. His mind began to wander, and his thoughts echoed back to him of that day twenty years ago when he had his first bloody encounter in Belize.

Another tropical mosquito infested night finally surrendered to the dawn of another day over Central America. From a cavity in the compact of a small roadway, a land crab (given that name because its ancestors had long ago turned their backs on the ocean for warmer and much dryer climes), clawed and scurried along in search of a tit bit to ravage and drag back down a murky hole that was the crustacean's home along with thousands upon thousands of its kind that thrived in this particular habitat.

Irwin King checked the time on his watch; his instructions were scheduled to arrive at the quay by twelve noon, only another half an hour to go. He angled his lean wiry six foot two frame in an effort to afford his eyes to browse over the perspective from a small window on the third floor of the Bellevue Hotel. Just beyond the width of the narrow road between the waterfront and the confines of the hotel, a wooden jetty secured the moorings of a dozen or so small boats that bobbed around in the water. Ten metres along the quayside away from the small pier, three young local boys were diving in and out of the begrimed water with a brash and carefree disposition, much to the horror of a gathering of on looking white tourists, whom no doubt had been strictly informed as Irwin himself had been, that to be foolish enough to bathe in the water within the channel of the Belize city bay would result in certain death by poison from its pollution, or at the very least an agonising paralysis that would be permanent and was completely incurable. King looked on and observed that a couple of the white visitants were digging into their pockets and rewarding the three foolhardy boys, as they doubtlessly considered them to be. The facts are, however, that the youngsters' behavior was to the contrary, for they went about this enterprise on a daily basis for twelve months of the year. It might be, therefore, that the youngsters believed that they were being given the money for their daring exhibition of aquatic prowess. Moreover, it was well known locally that the young trios along with many other citizens were immune to the perils that the water and its impurity embraced. An outbreak of excitement suddenly erupted as one of the young boys jumped up out from the water, his eyes were round like saucers with obvious shock, pointed a finger towards the small pier where he had just been swimming. The three boys along with two of the gathering made their way along the quay to the jetty.

King turned and slowly made his way down the stairs of the hotel and out into the overwhelming heat of the day and walked towards the gabbling mob looking down on the body which had been wrenched out of the water, with the help of the three boys and some rope. The corpse was then turned over onto its back across the jetty. King recognised the dead man's languid face. He had been in the company of Carlton Watt the day before, along with another man charting out a strategy to relay the shipment of narcotics from one of the small islands several miles off the coastline of Belize to a European destination. King had been under direct orders from the top to make sure that the cargo was reduced by 76 kilos, which was coincidentally the approximate body weight of one, Carlton Watt. The sound of police sirens filled the air across the bay.

"What happened to the poor guy's eyes?"

King overheard one observer saying, and he turned and walked idly back towards the Hotel.

'Crab fodder' King said to himself, and reflected on how the two unseeing eyeballs resembled marbles when they rolled down the black hole into the grateful claws of a lurking land crab.

His private phone rang out breaking through his envision and back to the present, it rang three times then cut off, after a few seconds it rang again, this time King picked up the phone. The Italian voice on the other end incorporated its customary genial tone.

"Ciao, come sta?"

Bene, gracia e tu?"

"Bene ... bene, I am happy for you ... now I will be mooring in Marbella for twelve hours only, scheduled from 11 am tomorrow, you understand, no?"

"Yes."

"Prego ... please, I would like for you to join me on board 'Bella Cristina' and take lunch with me, perhaps I can tempt you to some of my best vino to make for nice occasion, no?"

King thought instantaneously about Jean Paul's party, though he did not contemplate turning down the Italian's offer.

"I will be there."

"Gracia, bene ... don't let me down, no? .. ciao."

"Ciao." King said in conclusion before the line went dead and he reflected upon the certainty that nobody lets Agnazzio Bennetti down. Jean Paul's birthday incontrovertibly would take a secondary standing of importance this year. For although Bennetti was King's mentor, by turning down his invitation, the likelihood would be, that he might never see next year.

He resumed with the cocktail stick, diligently picking away any remnants of food that may still be lurking between his teeth. A split second of excessive enthusiasm made him flinch and curse at the same time. The acrid tang of blood from the negligible nick in his gum mingled with the aqueous fluids inside his mouth. Once again his mind reeled back in time.

He recollected his initial confrontation with the Latin Overlord, Bennetti. The invitation for the two to meet had been initiated on King's arrival in Belize. The coded instructions originally expressed that on entry to the country, he should immediately make his way to the Bellevue Hotel and await further information regarding business moves, etc. Confident with the arrangements and after walking through passport control untroubled, he made his way through the crudely assembled terminal building and out into the blazing afternoon sunshine, the brightness of which caused him to grimace. He sighed and put down his suitcase on the pavement, then reached into his pocket for his sunglasses. Before he had chance to place them on his nose, a thick West Indian voice from a metre or so said,

“Put dem away man, you won’t be needin dem.”
“What?” King said, turning to where the man’s words had emanated.
“Your name King man?”
“Who wants to know?”
“De Boss, him want to see you.”
“Boss ..?”
“Yeah man, de Boss .. him want you to cum wid us.”
“Oh .. and if I don’t want to?” King answered assertively, the sobering sound of the hammer of a gun being pulled back into an engaged position directly behind him, weakened his resolve somewhat, it was not just the torrid heat from the sun that resulted in his armpits instantly venting their uneasiness. Right at this moment, he sincerely hoped that his bowels would not display a similar apprehension to the situation.

The man behind King nudged the gun into his back, and grunted something that King did not comprehend.

“Me think man, you cum wid us now, dig?” The shiny faced West Indian said with a smile that displayed a mouthful of slovenly kept molars, beckoning King towards their vehicle.

“And don’t forget your suitcase man!” He added walking towards the rear door of the Land Rover.
“Get in de back man.”
“Where are we ...”
“Shut de fuck up man, just get in!”

King stepped up and did as requested of him, then sat down on the hard wooden bench seat that ran along the side of the vehicle’s interior. The West Indian climbed in after him, followed by a disheveled man whom King presumed to be South American, he had an unshaven chin and dark depraved eyes, that did not leave King for one moment, neither did the gun in his hand waver from its target. With a nod of his head, the malicious looking Mexican gestured to his accomplice, who closed the vehicle’s door behind him, then the Espanic took up a position directly opposite their captive.

“Told you you wouldn’t need sunglasses.” The West Indian chortled, while in one swift movement, threw a black bag over King’s head, he struggled in retaliation, albeit for a brief moment, the gun pressing hard into his ribcage acting as a deterrent against any further combat on King’s part.

“Now put your hands behind your back!” The West Indian ordered.
“Hmmm?”
“Just do it honky,” he chided.

King obliged without a word, and a pair of handcuffs were pressed tightly around his wrists, pinching into his skin with the final click. The next sound that he could ascertain was that of one of the two men moving towards the front cab. He surmised that it would not have been the silent Mexican, for his mind’s eye advised him that the man’s arrogant gaze was still focused upon him along with the pistol. The sound of his own blood pumping, thumped vehemently inside King’s skull. His perception had been accurate, the west Indian’s words instructed him from the driver’s seat.

"You give us any hassle man .. and we got stuff to knock you out, dig?" The sound of the man's hand banging on the steering wheel expressed his annoyance.

"Do you dig man!"

"Yes .. I dig .." King corresponded, but his thoughts differed grossly to his response, *'If I come out of this you bastard I will feed you to the fucking fish!'* The Land Rover's engine started up and pulled away with a jerk, the sudden motion resulting in King falling to his left and bouncing off the bench seat onto the floor, he instinctively made an attempt to climb back, in an instant the unmistakable impression of the gun pressed through the hood, hard against his temple, halting any progress.

"You stay on the floor, gringo .. and don't make a move or I blow your brains away .. comprende?" The Mexican rasped in fractured English, although on this occasion King understood implicitly the Mexican's declaration, as if it had been delivered by an old Etonian. Then without notice the wheels crashed into a large pot hole, then another and another, tossing the sturdy army vehicle around over what had become a lunar-like road surface. The terrain over which they travelled did not alter for half an hour or more during which time King had been pitched and thrown around like a football. As suddenly as it had eventuated, the ride returned to a comparatively smooth regularity. King inwardly sighed appreciatively, though by now his ribs ached under the bruising that the turbulent excursion had procured. Underneath the metal shackles his wrists were raw and the bitter taste of his own blood filled his mouth. *'If I get out of this alive I will'* .... his thought was interrupted by the vehicle coming to a halt, and the engine being turned off. His eyes searched frantically underneath the blackness of the hood. The only faculty remaining in his favor that might possibly give him a clue as to what may present itself to him next, was his hearing, but a chilling realisation shrieked inside him, his ears had become evidently indifferent to their capabilities due to the clamour that had been so predominant throughout the violent jaunt that he had endured. He was at the moment unceremoniously aware of another of his own human senses. At first it was quite a pleasant sensation, a feeling, warm between his legs, then swiftly growing cooler along with the contemplative recognition of what had occurred.

"Hey gringo ... you pissed yourself, you dirty shit." The Espanic voice bellowed, then, suddenly the other aches and pains throughout his body were neutralised instantly when the Mexican's foot collided with King's testicles, a horrid nausea seized his guts. He was oblivious to an ensuing blow that caught his benumbed head and beneath the blackness of the hood a flash of brilliant white exploded behind his eyes, he was now unaware of the rear door of the vehicle being opened, or the domineering voice of Agnazzio Bennetti discharging his order to the two kidnappers.

A voice was groaning from somewhere far away and coming closer. 'Water' the voice craved, the utterances were even closer now. His eyelids flickered open then closed again for a moment, the moaning compelled him to open them again, he blinked in an effort to focus in on the face that looked down over him *'were the features above him those of a woman? surely not, the groaning came from male vocal chords.*' He was only aware of the fact that the whining had emanated from himself when the water she tendered him passed through his dehydrated lips. The woman's features steadily clarified, King's eyes left her momentarily to scan the room, he lifted his head off the pillow, but the throbbing between his eyes beckoned him to lay back once more. He looked up at the woman's dark Latin eyes.

"Can I get you anything ... you hungry?" She said with an Italian inflection.

"No ... thanks."

"You have been out for sixteen hours."

"What?"

"You sleep like a bambino."

"Where am I?"

"Everything is OK."

"OK?"

"Si .. my brother would like to see you when you feel up to meeting him."

"Your brother?"

"Yes, Signor Bennetti."

"Bennetti?"

"He is ... the Boss, anyway, I go now, you just ring the bell here if you want anything, no?" With that she turned to leave the room.

"There is something I want." He said gruffly.

"Yes?"

"I want to know about those two junky brained bastards that hoodwinked me." He grouched.

"They are like dogs, they do as they are told."

"Then tell me something, Signora."

"Signorita." She amended. *'I don't wonder'* King mused, and hoped that she wasn't a mind reader.

"Does the Boss ... your brother always treat his guests to a tour of the Belizean jungle and throw in a bloody good hiding into the bargain?" He challenged, unable to conceal his indignation.

"What makes you think you travelled through jungle?"

"It's true that I was not able to take in the landscape with my own eyes, due to the blindfold, and the closest I got to any vegetation was my travelling companions. But I don't know, I guess I put two and two together, the Land Rover, the rocky track, or was it all just an elaborate ploy to screw me up and leave me totally disorientated?"

"It would be as well for you to take some advice, Mr. King, don't ask too many questions." She said through tight bloodless lips before turning towards the door. Before she opened it up to leave she swung around and said in conclusion.

"And do not challenge Signor Bennetti's logic, it could be very bad for your health Mr. King." With that she vacated the room to leave the solo occupant to his thoughts.

Two hours thereafter the woman returned to escort the captive to his initial appointment with the Boss. They walked from what appeared to be a capacious villa through a luxuriant tropical garden, which eventually opened out to a spacious area that accommodated a swimming pool and a tennis court. Between the two amenities was an arrangement of comfortable tables and chairs equipped with parasols.

"You sit and wait." The woman said, shepherding him to a chair.

"You can watch the game till my brother is ready to speak with you."

He sat down, thankful for the umbrella's protection from the mid-afternoon sun, however, there was nothing to defend him against the abundance of parasitic insects that flourish in that part of the globe. He looked on while the two men thrashed their way around the tennis court. King speculated that by their cavalier mannerisms the participants were ostensibly Italian, though he knew instantly which one of the two was Bennetti. The man had indisputable charisma, his hair looked as if it had grayed prematurely giving him a defined distinguished air. King guessed at the time that Bennetti was in his late thirties or early forties. Despite that, his maneuverability was likened to that of a man half his age. He obviously was also blessed with a good metabolism, ensuring him a lean stalwart physique.

Bennetti at no time acknowledged his abducted guest during the time he was on court. After which, what was more unsettling for King was that 'the Boss' and his tennis friend totally ignored his presence when they finally decided to make their way to the pool to cool off. He had been enraged by this conduct, but was aware that it would be absurd to raise any objections. He was astute enough to understand that he, Irwin King, was merely a pawn in the game. He swatted yet another harassing insect that had come to rest on his face and cursed in a low whisper then sat back, awaiting the inevitable meeting, with some trepidation.

After his swim the Italian dismissed his tennis opponent and sauntered over to where King was sitting. At first King did not know whether to be amused or perturbed by what happened next. The Italian discarded his towel rendering himself totally naked. His eyes were on King. *'Was he expecting a reaction?'* King pondered. Without a word the man sat himself down opposite him. His eyes never left King's. There he sat unprotected from the elements, the insects and, King contemplated even an attack from King himself, and yet the man maintained an intense aura of self-confidence and control.

"You look uncomfortable .. what's the matter with you, did you never see a naked man before?" The Italian taunted.

"No .. I mean, sure, it's just ..."

"Relax, I have nothing to hide from you, this is my way of saying this is me, Agnazzio Bennetti, but you ... you can call me Signor Bennetti, no?"

"This is a rare privilege Signor Bennetti, I am .."

"Cut the crap, just listen to what I have to say is all I ask, capiche?"

King shifted uneasily in his chair, he saw the madness in the Italian's eyes for the first time.

"I want for you and me to be friends, it will be in your best interest." He added and the crazed expression on his face abated as rapidly as it had appeared. King was now convinced that 'the Boss's' reputation was not a fabrication, his palpable mood swings were infamous.

"I have a proposition for you." He continued. "I need for someone to step in the shoes of a departed member of my empire, I think the shoes maybe fit you, no?"

"I'm listening ... Signor Bennetti."

"Bene ... good, you learn quickly, this is good, now tell me Irwin ... you don't mind if I call you Irwin?"

"No."

"Tell me Irwin, how ambitious or should I say ... how greedy are you for great wealth?"

"Very, I guess."

"Yes, I have found from experience that a man will do anything, and I mean anything for money, no?"

"To an extent."

"There are no barriers, greed is infinite believe me, I know, I think that you will serve me well." Bennetti said adamantly, while at the same time massaging his scrotum. This aberrant display caused King's skin to crawl, but he hoped that his repugnance was not visible on his face. He fought hard to control his body language and in response he spoke as evenly as he could muster.

"Can I ask you Signor Bennetti, what your proposition .. your ..."

"Let me explain." The Italian cut in, King wanted to run, but he knew for certain that with the wink of an eye he would be gunned down by Bennetti's army of marksmen continually on duty to protect the drugs baron.

"Understand this Irwin, there is no turning back, you have to commit yourself to me, and in return for your loyalty to Agnazzio Bennetti you will be rewarded handsomely, you understand, no?"

"It appears I have little choice Signor Bennetti."

"Bene .. bene, you will be a good student, I am happy for you." The Overlord grinned, albeit briefly, his dark eyes impulsively hardened and narrowed.

"You mess with Agnazzio Bennetti just one time and you are a dead man, like the guy whose shoes you are going to stand in, that fool he lose his head, capiche?"

"I understand."

"Good, now we understand one another, you listen good to me. From now on you are in charge of transportation of merchandise. For the operations to run smoothly you need to do all the things I now tell you ... on your return to France from your next assignment, you will set up a cover to protect the organisation. To inquisitive eyes you will be .. respectable man of business, I will set this up along with the laundering of money, when necessary. This is clear so far .. ?" King nodded his head, but his instincts told him that there must be a catch. He was not prepared for the first stumbling block.

"You will marry as soon as it is possible, this will clearly aid our purpose."

"Marry?"

"This will help for good disguise for you ... but your wife .."

"Wife? .. but Signor Bennetti, I'm a gamophobic."

The Overlord's laughter pierced the air. It had an oddly feminine quality that caused the captive to cringe.

"I have an aversion also to matrimony." The Italian remarked between his sniggering.

"But this is because I like my vice versa .. you understand the joke, no?"

King managed to smile feebly back at Bennetti's derisory jibe, and as abruptly as it had come about the Italian's laughter ceased. His facial expression altered in a dramatised fashion as if his skin was made from rubber. He looked towards King now with condescending eyes.

"Your future bride, whoever she might be will learn nothing of your dealings."

"But this is preposterous, why would I need to be married to follow your orders and carry out transactions?"

"Insurance."

"Insurance?"

"Of course, your wedding gift to your bride will be a joint offshore bank account. Only difference with this account will be that it will be in a company name over which I have ultimate control. This way, Agnazzio Bennetti have his insurance, capiche?" He affirmed. King said nothing while the Overlord continued with his arrangements, making dramatic use with his hands to dispatch his desires. He went on.

"I hope you chose your wife well Irwin, because when you make vows in the House of God, those vows will never be broken, I am Catholic and, in the eyes of our Lord and the Holy Spirit, it is a sin, you understand, no? ... I say, you understand?" He pressed.

"Yeah .. yes."

"Bene ... good, Irwin, I am happy for you."

King knew that he would have to capitulate to these and any other requests or orders that Bennetti gave to the then, young Irwin King. He simply had no say in the matter. The twelve foot high fence that entwined the drug baron's villa and gardens served as a reminder to the futility an attempt at escaping the man's clutches would bring. From this day on, he would not be in command of his own life, nevertheless King was going to try out an experiment with the Overlord.

"Can I ask a question Signor Bennetti?"

"Go ahead .. feel free."

"The two bums who brought me to your house!"

"Yes?"

"What are they to you?"

"They are what you say ... just bums."

"Well .. what I'm about to tell you .. you're not going to like Signor Bennetti."

"Oh?"

"One of them .. the West Indian."

"Yes?"

"He said .. he said, that he'd seen pictures, photographs, of your sister."

"What are you saying?"

"I overheard him saying that he had seen some pictures of your sister .. how can I put this? .. well your sister, in an unchaste pose." King said, selling the fabricated story with skilful conviction. Bennetti's tanned face lost some of its colour.

"You say that little shit has .."

"I can't prove anything, he said he had destroyed the evidence, apparently the photos were very explicit, he said something about, .. well, it was hard to hear over the noise of the engine, you understand but ..."

"What?"

"He said the pictures showed your sister masturbating." King announced. Bennetti's eyes filled with rage and he began to rant and rave in his native tongue, he flicked his upper teeth with his thumb vigorously. King looked on, his face concealed his glee. He had the baton now, the Overlord was doing the singing. The part of the tune he was awaiting finally came as Bennetti's temper subsided enough for him to say.

"Now you have a chance to prove your loyalty to me, no? .. before he die, take out his eyes."

"It would be my pleasure Signor Bennetti." King advocated, marking up in his thoughts a homerun in the mind games match, although he was not anticipating Bennetti's final sortie.

"You like tennis?" The Overlord said, recovering swiftly from his indignation, replaced now by a composed manner.

"Tennis?" King responded somewhat confused.

"It is my second favourite sport, we maybe have a game sometime ... but tonight I have other plans, capiche?" Bennetti said with a mawkish smile, furthermore, his hand once again toyed around the area of his own penis. He raised his eyebrows in readiness of King's reaction to his solicitation. Repulsion gripped King's guts, his mind had been flummoxed by the Italian's allurement.

"What would my future wife say?" Was all King could think to say. *'What was her name again?'* his conscience brooded, *'Danielle ... yes, that was it, Danielle Marie.'*

Chapter Four

Monte Carlo

Floss' older brother, Solly had on many occasions pulled the car up outside the grandiose Hotel de Paris to collect his Boss, Mr. King, or Madame Danielle. He would often behold the magnificent alabaster structure and make provision for his imagination to browse around its exotic interior. Well today, thanks to Madame Danielle's invitation to join her, he was going to allow his imagination to rest and his eyes to confirm the decor for sure. Before he and Madame Danielle ascended the eight highly polished marble steps at the front of the hotel, Solly looked up above the great wooden swing doors and the four magnificent pillars to the superbly sculpted figures of two naked women standing with open arms, as if to welcome all who call. A wave of panic swept momentarily through him.

Why did Madame Danielle need him, Solly, a mere servant to her household to accompany her on this second rendezvous with the other party? The initial meeting between the man and Madame took place two weeks previously and Solly had been ordered to secrete any knowledge of the man or the encounter she had had with him. Solly had duly obeyed her command and, although he only saw the man briefly on the steps of the Hotel de Paris that day, he recognised him from the assignation some years ago. His dark skin had aged somewhat and he now sported a grey beard that merged in with the silvery hair on his scalp, but Solly could not quite put a name to his face, although he did recall that at that time it was his master who held conference.

Danielle and Solly entered through the swing doors into the grand entrance hall. A tall middle-aged bespectacled man approached them, and enquired,

"Madame King?"

"Yes"

"Don Lawrence" he said in a clipped English accent. He stretched out a hand, Danielle quickly got on with the formalities and Lawrence requested her and Solly to follow him to 'somewhere a little more private.'

They entered a somewhat modest room that did not concur with the rest of the hotel.

"Ah, Madame Danielle, please come in and take the weight off your feet." the bearded man said standing up from behind a large desk. His rugged black face softened when he smiled and regarded her approach towards him.

"You've already met Mr. Lawrence" he continued in his American drawl that Danielle had not quite been able to pinpoint the origin of up to now.

"Drink?"

"No thank you" Danielle licked her lips. One day at a time she told herself and said,

"Please can we get on?"

"Sure ... sure why don't we, Mr. Lawrence take the stage."

Lawrence lifted up a small attaché case from under the table, placed it on top of the desk and flicked it open.

"May I firstly thank you Solly for agreeing to attend this meeting today."

Solly felt confused but remained silent.

"It is extremely important you understand," Lawrence went on, "That we clarify a number of fait accompli for my clients." He motioned a hand towards Madame Danielle and the man whom Solly recognised.

"Yes sir."

"Anything discussed here is strictly confidential and will not be revealed to anyone outside these four walls, is that clear Solly?"

"Yes sir." Solly answered and felt the palms of his hands grow cold with sweat.

"Now I want you to cast your mind back some eighteen years or so," Lawrence continued. Solly was now aware of the reasons for his required presence within the resplendent hotel. A wave of panic rushed through his veins, for, hadn't he been sworn to secrecy by his Boss, Mr. King, never to breathe a word? He was unable to disguise his anxiety through the contours of his aged facial features. Recognising his discomfort, Danielle patted his gnarled hand.

"Relax Solly, it'll be fine."

"Yes, Madame Danielle," Solly said unconvincingly.

"Now .... we want you to recollect the events of a particular month of that year.." Lawrence continued and Danielle's mind hurtled back to that November virtually two decades ago.

Monaco, Southern France
November, 18 years earlier

'She should have booked herself into a hospital as her housekeeper, Floss, had suggested. If things were to go wrong as they obviously were now.' The pain returned, she cried out louder this time, for the spasm possessed a more steady formidable reprisal this time and tore through her like a huge corkscrew. Did she love her husband enough to endure this? She didn't think so.

"Don't push this time" Madame Danielle's doctor implored.

"I have to," she cried, "I have to!"

"I am going to give you a sedative to help us."

"Us ... us!?"

The steady hand of her housekeeper mopped Danielle's anxious brow. She looked up at the kindly face that regarded and tended to her and it was gradually becoming a blur, the dark features had lost definition though continued to comfort her affirming that, "Everything will be fine .. just fine Madame Danielle."

"We have a problem," she heard her doctor pronounce from somewhere in the room. The voice seemed to reverberate around the walls.

"Problem ... problem?" and she slipped into a dark abyss.

It was Floss, who had called him by telephone to give the news that his wife's waters had broken and that she was about to go into labour, some six days earlier than expected. Fortunately, he assured himself everything that money could hire or buy had been provided for the birth of his first son, it will be a boy he irrefutably told himself. Indeed, the bedroom had been virtually converted into a hospital ward with all the instruments needed for any event ... well almost any.

He had chartered a flight to haste a fast journey to his home in the South of France.

He walked through the glass doors from the airport's main concourse. Solly donned his cap and opened the door to the rear of the silver Mercedes. King's thick south African accent gave out Solly's orders.

"Let's go, and don't spare the horse's boy."

"Yes, Mr. King, Sir."

The car pulled away smoothly and Solly did not disobey his boss's orders, the horses were not spared, and King was delivered swiftly and safely to his residence, whereupon arrival, he was ushered to the drawing room by Floss to meet his wife's physician.

"I got here as quickly as I could Doctor .."

"Well, I am happy to inform you Monsieur King, that for seven hours and twenty minutes now, you have been the father of twin boys."

"Twins .... boys?"

"Yes, it took me by surprise also, one of the little fellows had been playing hide and seek with his brother. Medical technology is on the verge at the moment of introducing a scanning machine that ..."

"I want to see them." King interrupted.

"Yes, yes of course, although Monsieur King your wife has had a rather unpleasant time of it all. But thanks to your very capable housekeeper and some very good equipment, pulled through with flying colours. I am afraid though, your wife is rather weak and I have left strict instructions to your members of staff not to disturb her under any circumstance. She needs rest."

"I want to see the boys!"

"Yes .... of course Monsieur, but .."

"But what?"

"I have been monitoring their progress."

"What ... is there something wrong?"

"No, no they are perfectly fashioned, indeed very handsome babies."

"Then what is the problem?" King said with an air of agitation that took the doctor by surprise. Doctor Pettett looked up into the eyes of the tall man and paused before saying,

"You see Monsieur, the twins are not selfsame ... they are not identical you understand?"

"You can tell that already?"

"Oh yes, yes quite definitely," the ageing doctor went on "This is a truly fascinating case, I personally have never encountered one like it, although I did read some time ago in one of my medical journals of a case somewhat similar, although ..."

"Spit it out old man for pity's sake," King said displaying further impatience at what he considered to be the Doctor's dithering manner. Doctor Pettett mused that he would need to employ a level of prudence on his patient's husband if he was to avoid the indignation he was sure would come from this man when given the truth of the situation. He took in a deep breath before saying.

"I will try to explain a tangible reason for the circumstances we find ourselves witness to in this case." The Doctor explained, rubbing his brow with his hand before continuing, "But please Monsieur, for a moment or two, it would be to your advantage to be attentive while I attempt to analyze my theory on this phenomenon, then, when you have been presented with the facts as I see them, of course you have every right to call for a second opinion."

The frown on King's face deepened further, though he did not speak, he concluded that he would permit the fossil faced fart just one more minute, he looked at his watch and then back to the Doctor. In his mind's eye King visualised himself kicking the old-timer firmly between his decrepit legs, and crushing his grizzled balls. The scowl on King's features gave way to a thin smile.

"You see." Doctor Pettett proceeded, "Dizygotic twins are non-identical, fraternal for want of a better word implies, these twins develop from two separate zygotes .. in other words, separate entities."

"Can we get to the point man." King pressed.

"Yes ... there are ... you understand Monsieur King, two ova and two sperm, so the boys therefore are genetically contrasting individuals ... no more alike than other siblings."

"For fuck's sake man, how many more times, what are you telling me?" King stormed, visibly shaking the older man, who closed his eyes endeavoring to compose himself. He appreciated the fact that for his services he was being rewarded quite handsomely although, at this very moment he was beginning to regret the undertaking. He scratched the skin on his thinning crown and said,

"Do you have any Afro-Caribbean ancestry?"

"What?"

"Does your wife?"

"No!?"

"Then ..."

"What are you trying to say man, that I have fathered black babies?"

"No Monsieur."

"Then what the bloody hell are you saying?"

"That one of the new-born has black pigment tissue, Monsieur."

"Bloody impossible man ... How can that be?" .

"Well, Monsieur King ... in the hope of not sounding callous, .. to put it in layman's terms, one of your children is what is colloquially known as a throwback."

"If one of the children is black then it doesn't belong to me." King spat ungraciously.

"But Monsieur, surely ... "

"Who besides you and I know about this?"

"Well, ... your housekeeper and myself of course were the only .... "

"And my wife?"

"Why no Monsieur, as I said, she needs to rest ... she is totally unaware of the whole episode, you see, I had to sedate her."

"So she doesn't know that it is twins that she has given birth to?"

"I doubt it, although mother's intuition is a factor that you cannot write off." Doctor Pettett looked at his watch, "Your wife, Monsieur King, I think will be coming out of her tranquillised condition very soon, you can perhaps inform her then of, ... "

King rang the service bell impatiently interrupting the doctor's flow. He pulled out a cigarette from a Marlborough packet and lit it, drawing the smoke deep before exhaling loudly. There was a polite rap on the Drawing Room door and Floss entered.

"Yes, Mr. King, sir."

"How is our patient?" the Doctor asked before King could speak between his second puff at the cigarette.

"And, congratulations once again, Floss, you really are a very good nurse." Doctor Pettett confirmed.

"Thank you Doctor Pettett, Madame Danielle is still resting sir, she ...."

"Good, now take me to them." King said extinguishing his cigarette.

The three of them climbed the grand staircase without speaking, then entered the bedroom. The head of the huge bed was encompassed by a variety of monitoring machines. Danielle lay with her eyes closed in a deep impenetrable sleep. Her dark hair was unfurled around the salmon-coloured silk covered pillow. The twilight emitting from the arched window, bathed the soft contours of her face. On one side of her bed a crib of generous size lodged the two new-born boys, positioned with their heads at each end. Their eyes were closed enjoying the first hours of tranquility since their traumatic arrival into the world.

King turned on a light situated above the crib, then eyed the small faces within, one of the babies stirred, King's gaze remained on the wriggling infant as if transfixed. The minute dark features twitched as his eyelids fluttered expressing discomfort, the small toothless mouth opened up to release a blubbering cry.

"He's hungry for mothers' milk," Floss announced, lifting the tiny bundle from the cot. "Madame Danielle will be coming too shortly, so ..." Doctor Pettett began to inform them.

"No." King cut in abruptly, "Take it downstairs with you and feed it a bottle."

"But."

"No buts, do as I say."

"Yes, Mr. King, Sir."

"I don't want my wife awake yet."

Floss obeyed his orders and left the room holding the baby tightly against her bosoms. King looked into the crib at his other offspring, this time he managed to smile.

"We asked you here Solly, to confirm for my client and more importantly, Madame Danielle, the existence of a twin brother to her son, Jean Paul." Don Lawrence urged. Solly's mouth curved into an unpersuasive smile, his upper lip quivered and his heart thumped hard inside his chest. 'How could these men possibly know?'

"A twin?"

"Yes Solly, a twin."

Solly shifted in his seat. His stomach was in knots now and he was finding difficulty in breathing evenly. 'How could they know?' he asked himself again, 'and why wait all these years to fetch it back to the surface?' Danielle recognising Solly's dismay, took his hand in the hope of reassuring him that she was on his side.

"Take your time Solly." she said softly. Although when she had been informed of this revelation, two weeks previously, by the man seated behind the desk she was utterly devastated and ready to blame everyone and anyone for this disgraceful deception that caused her so much pain and consternation. She had treated their meeting with suspicion, especially when the man refused to give her his full name, only his initials, L.T.H., he had been in contact with Danielle on two occasions before that first meeting, requesting the utmost confidentiality, especially in respect of her husband, and that it would be in her best interest that they meet. She recalled his first words the day the two met,

"How well do you know your husband?" he asked in his American drawl.

"What kind of a question is that?" Danielle had responded.

"Because Madame, I'll get straight to the point, are you aware of his scurrilous deals and undertakings over the last twenty years?"

"Enlighten me Monsieur"

"I have good reasons for detesting him, Madame."

"Why is he accountable for this animosity towards him, Monsieur? .. And how can this possibly be in my best interest, as you put it?"

"In answer to your first question, Madame, thanks to Irwin King, I have just spent seventeen years behind bars." He combed his fingers through the curly silver hair on the top of his head and gave a wry smile.

"I had a head of goddamn dark hair when I went in there, I had time to watch every strand turn grey."

Danielle looked at her wristwatch and recognising her impatience he responded,

"For fifteen or more years of my sentence I was eaten up dreaming up ways of getting to him and getting even, and since getting out, I learned something else about King that helps me detest and loathe him more than mere words can say, but it was something that the Doctor said to me before he ...."

"Doctor?" Danielle cut in.

"Pettett, ... Doctor Pettett, remember him?"

"Of course I remember him, he brought my son into the world .... poor man, he was found dead the very day after Jean Paul was born, it was thought to have been suicide at first but,..." Suddenly she had realised who the black American was that she was sitting in the same room and conversing with,

"My God" she gasped, "You ... grey hair or dark hair, and the beard, it's you!"

"Yeah, but before ... listen, the whole thing was a set up."

"All the evidence needed was found at your apartment."

"Sure, it was planted."

"And the witness, the man who saw you leave?"

"Let me explain .. look, what I'm going to tell you now is the truth."

"Why should I believe you? You were found guilty in a court of law and brought to justice." Her words echoed around the room, unnerving her and causing her veil of composure to fail her. She wanted to run, away from this madman. *'What was she doing here?'*

"What motive would I have to kill Pettett?"

"Drugs .. you were a junky."

"Another fabrication."

"Monsieur, I really don't have time to listen to all this, you have served your time as they say, so that is that, now if you will excuse me?"

"What I'm about to tell you Madame, involves you."

"Me?"

"Yeah, now please all I ask is that you just sit there, relax and listen."

"Relax?" She gave a lame laugh and shifted in her chair. He offered her a cigarette, she accepted one and he lit it for her, she was one of the rare breeds of people that could do, or do without cigarettes, but right now she felt she needed one. He put the lighter into his jacket pocket and proceeded to embark on his story.

"That night, King told me by phone to go over to Pettett's home, he said he wanted me to collect a package."

"A package?"

"Sure, it was nothing unusual, see in those days I was a kind of 'go for' used by the Ring. I was used to call on all kinds of folk, from hoods to Politicians and high ranking dudes, I had even collected from Doctors before, so nothing strange about that. Difference was, this time, I was informed by King that the back door of the house would be open and the place would be unoccupied. I was just to walk in and pick the parcel up off the dining table."

"Did you say these things in Court?" Danielle enquired.

"Hell no ... the Ring would have hanged me by the balls."

"Better I think Monsieur than doing seventeen years in jail?"

"No Madame, it would have been castration first then total mutilation."

"Who are these people ... this Ring as you call it?"

"They're an enigma ... all I know on that score is, I used to take my orders directly from King, and whatever job I was given to undertake, his ass was always covered."

"They protected each other?" Danielle probed almost impassively.

"Yeah ... see, I don't know how many guys there are at the top of this organisation, but King's right up there with the big boys, making the big bucks, and boy has he diversified since I've been in the slammer."

"So ... do these faceless people not scare you?"

"Shitless .. now, where was I?"

"The parcel on the dining room table."

"Ah yeah, you see that's just it, there was no parcel. I searched the whole goddamn dining room and there was no parcel. Then I heard this guys voice groaning in the next room and I got kinda' panicky, as I was about to turn to leave, there was the Doctor standing in the doorway looking straight at me, and let me tell you, his eyes told me he was not on this planet. He called for me to help him and with that he just slumped like a sack of shit onto the floor. I rushed over, but there was nothing I could do for the old timer and realising that, I was just about to beat it as fast as my legs could carry me then, he spoke his last words to me, he may have sounded half pissed but I understood what he said as clear as a church bell. He told me that King had been round his house and pumped him full of heroin ..."

Danielle stood up from the chair and turned to leave.

"Please, hear me out ...." he pleaded. She came to a halt at the door and turned,

"Really Monsieur, why would he want to kill the surgeon who aided the birth of my son?"

"Sons Madame."

"Sons, Monsieur?"

"You see, apart from your housekeeper and her brother, I believe that he was the only witness to the fact."

"Yes .... I was under sedation so ... what are you trying to say?"

"What I'm saying Madame, is that eighteen years ago you gave birth to twin boys."

"Impossible ...... where ..... how dare you ..." She was filled with panic and confusion. This man was crazed, her mind became a maze of bewilderment and her womb ached. She fought to mollify her nerves and controlled her facial muscles enough to force a smile.

"Monsieur, are you trying to tell me that this baby died at birth and I am not aware of this fact?" she said with an air of sarcasm.

"No, Madame."

"Then where is this child, where was he taken?"

"Where was your husband after the birth, did you see him when you came to?"

"No .. he was called away on business."

"And your housekeeper?"

"Floss, she was with him ... it did seem odd at the time, although I had two very capable nurses looking after me, to replace her, I was so excited about Jean Paul, you understand, that I didn't take much heed. In those days you see, I didn't ask questions."

"But things have changed since, Madame?"

"Yes, ... yes, they have."

"Then I take it that you and your husband are ..."

Monsieur, I have not come here to discuss my conjugal situation with you." Danielle cut in. He held up a hand to quell Danielle's annoyance and said,

"It's just that, once the fire beneath the cauldron is lit, then I think it would be in your best interest to get your pretty ass out of the kitchen, is all I'm saying."

"That, I think is for me to decide!"

"Point taken ..... Ok, now, Madame Danielle, do you recall where your husband went on ... business that day?"

"No, as I told you ... I didn't ask questions."

"I believe he ... your other new-born son was taken to England, Madame."

"Ridiculous ... why ... what motive would he have to take the new-born baby there? Really Monsieur!"

"Because I know he had had some business to do there, but I think it gave him the opportunity to get the kid as far away from here as he could think of without ..."

"Are you saying then, that there was something ... something wrong with the child?"

"No, Madame."

"Then once again I challenge you to tell me what possible motive would he have to...?"

"The other twin was as black as I am," he cut in, "and we both know about your husband's preconceived notions on that score."

She could not help it, her laughter echoed around the room. *'This man is a total nutcase'* her thoughts gibed. Hickman's expression remained unchanged by her outburst, his eyes continued to hold contact with hers. *'Could a madman's gaze display such candor?'* she asked herself, before apologising.

"Monsieur, my husband is, I do believe, capable of many things, but, to frame you for murder ... and ... and ... the abduction of his ... my child?"

He said nothing, but his eyes remained fixed on hers. *'Should she believe these preposterous allegations?'* Her heart raced, her mind grappled with the bad tidings presented to her. She knew and understood Floss' loyal attributes, and was aware of her fearfulness of King's predominant temperament. But she could not comprehend how her housekeeper and soul mate could live with this deception, *'did her husband have something on her to trade for her silence?'*

"Can you prove this Monsieur?"

"Yes, but I would ask you not to approach your housekeeper on this matter ... not just yet at least."

"Why shouldn't I?"

"We don't want alarm bells going off or any cause for suspicion. So I want you to act as normal as possible from the moment you walk out the door."

"Very well,... although, Monsieur, it will be very difficult for me to do, considering the gravity of all this, coupled with the thought that you believe that I have a son somewhere whom I have never even set eyes on, causes me great distress."

"Yes, I'm sure it does .. but in the meantime between now and our next rendezvous I will start the ball rolling and start the search for your boy, if ... that's ok with you?"

"Of course, if he is out there then we must find him." Danielle pressed, now she was going to lay the bait, she put her hand into the silk lined bag and pulled out a cheque book and pen. To her astonishment, he did not bite.

"Don't worry your head about money, Madame, I have resources enough to cope with this little enterprise" he assured her.

"May I ask you then, what do you plan to gain from all this?"

"To bring down King's scuzzy little business stone by stone and maybe, just maybe, get down to the foundations and find the Satan's champion, the man who the guys involved in the mob call the boss."

"This all sounds very sinister."

"The Devil looks after his own, but with God's help we will vanquish the no good son's ..." He announced vehemently, and the passion in his tone gave Danielle cause for concern. He smiled from across the table.

"I know what you're thinking, I'm some kinda bible basher, a fanatic, or Billy Graham with a tan." He prompted.

"No ... I ..."

"Well, let me put you at your ease. Sure, I believe in God, and I have those avaricious men who relish in their power to manipulate people, by bending the rules of common decency and spitting in the face of our creator to thank for my salvation and love for the lord."

"Monsieur, I respect your passionate ideals, but suddenly I find myself in the middle of all this."

"Like I say, when you feel the time is right, get out of the kitchen."

"Monsieur, you bring me all these painful disclosures and simply sit there and tell me that when things get hot I should run for cover, this is not in my nature. I need to know more."

"Then know more you shall, we will meet in two weeks from now." He confirmed.

"I have one more question before I leave this room and reflect upon what has been said today."

"Sure, fire away."

"You must understand Monsieur, that I do not discriminate towards other human beings merely because of the colour of their skin, no?" She said straightening herself in her chair, she went on, "What I am saying Monsieur, is that my family has no history as far as I know, of Asian, Caribbean of African blood, so how can this be that I have mothered, though up to now I have only your word on this, that I am the mother of a black twin son?"

"These things happen, and they are happening now in life more than ever before, one thing at a time Madame, seek the truth and you will find!" He said and stood up from his chair. Danielle climbed from her seat and they shook hands, she was pleased that his handshake was firm, although not excessively so and that there was a warmth within his grip.

"When we next meet, I would appreciate it if you would bring along with you your housekeeper's brother." He had said in conclusion and set the date and the time for their subsequent engagement.

Solly was looking forlornly towards Danielle now.

"Madame Danielle ... I promised Mr. King, sir, that I would never speak of this to anyone."

"I'm afraid Solly, that the cat's out of the bag, so to speak, thanks to our friend here" Lawrence informed him gesturing a hand towards the American.

"I'm sorry Madame Danielle .... so sorry." Solly choked and the tears flowed down his face. It was several minutes before Solly was able to find a modicum of composure. Still clutching his hand Danielle whispered,

"No-one's blaming you Solly .."

Holding an immaculately white handkerchief he stared unblinking into Danielle's eyes, then wiped his sodden face.

"He was so beautiful Madame Danielle ... so beautiful."

The last two weeks had been hell for her, concealing not only her thoughts and uncertainties, but also camouflaging her feelings. Only once between the time that dragged so slowly between these meetings did her resolve falter albeit for a fraction of time when she almost, so nearly confronted Floss. But now the wait had been worth enduring and she wept.

Once she had recovered her composure, for the ensuing twenty minutes Danielle was embroiled with a deluge of detailed accounts gathered together by Don Lawrence and the American with regard to what, until now, she believed to be her recent private life. To add further to her discomfort, some of their disclosures dated back somewhat further.

"Were you aware Madame, that your father's company was accursed with cash flow problems twelve months ago?" Lawrence affirmed. Danielle fought hard to bridle the anger building within her. *'How could they know anything about her father's business, that she did not?'* She took in a deep breath before replying.

"No ... my father never mentioned it to me."

"Way I see it, he was left with two choices," the American said. Danielle raised an eyebrow and stayed silent. He continued, "Either go bankrupt or find someone willing to help him out of an insurmountable situation."

"This is preposterous, he would have informed me."

"I'm sure he would have, but I think you know better than me of his dogged pride,"

"I grant you that my father is rather stubborn, though he is a rational man in business."

"Yes ... that may be so but, your father was given two goddamn choices, and in choosing to surrender to your husband's cash handout, he found himself staring into the mouth of a treacherous shark. I'm sure I don't need to tell you, that once a shark bites it don't let go 'til it's taken a piece of you with it."

"I do not think that my father would allow himself to be exploited in any way." Danielle countered defiantly, though her thoughts denounced her words, reflecting on how under the weather her Papa had appeared on the last few occasions she had been in his company. Concealing this fact, she went on,

"Besides, since my father has acquired orders from abroad, he has ..."

"Oh yeah, I was just coming to that, the purchase of the ocean-going vessel!?"

"Yes, that has been utilised for deliveries of his products abroad ..."

"And so it was, used that is, to deliver consignments to other countries, although the cargo wasn't necessarily always products that he would normally transport."

"Monsieur, my father is a respectable business man."

"Was."

"Was?"

"Was, 'til King came into the frame. He gave your father the money required to blow away the wolves at the door in exchange for shipments of merchandise that he wanted delivering."

"What merchandise would that be?" She enquired, suppressing an unwelcome chill that suddenly descended upon her very bones. The American's eyes momentarily moved away from Danielle and glimpsed over at her companion. She recognised his muted prompting and concluded that Solly had heard more than enough at these proceedings and requested him to leave the room and wait outside in the car for her, before he did so, he was once again reminded of the confidentiality required from him. After he had closed the door behind him and before continuing with the minutes, Lawrence turned to Danielle then said,

"I trust that he will keep all this to himself?"

"Yes ... most definitely" she replied, confidently then added, "It would not be through him that my husband would learn of today's liaison."

A temporary hush fell upon the compact walls of the room. Danielle was conscious that if King did find out about these activities, then it would not be only Solly that she would have to look out for. The suppressed apprehensiveness of her husband's latent iniquitous past was coming towards her now like a steam train without brakes and something inside her ghoulishly beckoned the onslaught of hearsay to keep coming, she scolded herself for her inquisitiveness and right now she could really use a drink. *'One day at a time'* she deliberated in defiance of her hankering and heard her own voice intervene on her thoughts and the brief silence within the room.

"Merchandise .. is it .. was it .. illicit materials?"

"You scored a bull's-eye."

"My father's boat .. he is involved?"

"When King says jump through the goddamn hoop."

"Please, I beg of you, this is not true."

"I'm sorry."

"What ... guns ... drugs?"

"Let me put this to you, King has made mega bucks out of human misery, he thrives on it. To begin with, he will probably use the vessel to ship drugs, crack, cocaine, marijuana maybe, but now he deals in the lowest trade of all. See, with narcotics it's kinda like shifting the buck, you don't actually see the results of your dealings first hand, but the reprobate now has sank to the most deplorable depths of all."

"What can be more deplorable than drugs?" She reasoned through her now dry lips. She was aware that her composure was beginning to splinter. *'Her father involved in the drugs trade, or something more sinister, but what could be more sinister than drugs?'*

The American cleared his throat and his ebony face took on a look of severity.

"Are you aware that ... slavery remains to this day the largest source of labour in the world?"

"Slaves ... mon Dieu, non."

"And that there are more slaves than the entire work forces of North America or Western Europe? It's estimated that global profits are annually one trillion US Dollars greater than the value of all American currency in circulation last year."

Danielle closed her eyes, unable to absorb the horror being bestowed upon her this day.

"Fortunately, for your estranged son, King wasn't trafficking in humans at the time the kid was born or ..." He declined from finishing the sentence, identifying her demeanor noticeably collapsing at his affirmations.

"I'm sorry, all this must be pretty hard to take in, I've been kinda callous in dealing out this unwelcome deluge of chickenshit."

"What will become of my father?"

"I ain't the law, so there ain't nothing I'm gonna do, gonna hurt him."

"Poor Papa, he must be living in hell."

"His hands are tied as I say."

"And slavery ... those poor people." Danielle said sincerely, "What can be done?"

"Well, Madame Danielle, I feel that life and God has channeled me into this undertaking, I might not be able to stop this widespread exploitation, but I'm sure as hell gonna try."

"This is all so macabre ... even at the expense of my father, who must by now be on the edge of insanity, I am surely on your side Monsieur, if this is the case then God forgive us."

"I can't guarantee your father's safety, but we can in one way protect him."

"How?"

"We certainly cannot take any more chances or underestimate your husband Madame, so I suggest that any future meetings between the three of us should be arranged by you. We will furnish you with several contact numbers before you make your departure. We will also rely on you to determine the locations that you would like those rendezvous to take place."

"That is ... " The American added, "If I assume rightly that you want us to find your estranged son for you?"

"Yes ... yes, I do Monsieur Hickman, that is your name isn't it .. Larry Hickman?"

He raised his eyebrows then smiled warmly. Danielle mused that it was not the kind of smile that one would receive from an ex-convict, or a murderer?

"You'll have to forgive my reticence in not giving my full name ... you see, if I'd done that in the beginning then ..."

"No need to explain," Danielle cut in. She was now loaded with questions and not a great deal of time left of this engagement to fire them.

"Monsieur Hickman, besides your involvement in the murder of my physician .. "

"I told you, it was a set up."

"I am sure that in time I will doubtlessly learn the truth, but for now, how do you propose to locate the whereabouts of my ... of my son?"

It felt odd to her to be speaking of a son, whom had not even suckled her breast, let alone got to know her as his mother. But she could only hope that since this ascertainment, one day she would be able to reform an allegiance with him.

"Don has been busy these past weeks preparing a pathway towards that goal." Hickman announced and beckoned Lawrence to continue. Lawrence gave out a small cough and looked over his spectacles towards Danielle and said.

"You will undoubtedly appreciate Madame, that this undertaking has been not unlike entering a labyrinth" his English accent echoed off the ceiling giving his voice a semblance of a right wing British Politician in the House of Commons, it also bestowed a patronising quality that Danielle did not endear to, though, nevertheless felt she wanted to trust. His resonant voice continued.

"After many hours of analytical labour sifting through documents and pockets of information here and there from various official buildings .."

"Official buildings?"

"Yes Madame, do not be concerned our secret is safe, I merely frequented Government offices, hospitals, libraries and of course orphanages. Please do not be troubled, there were no names involved at any time."

At this moment it was not names or secrets that troubled her, it was guilt that tormented her, '*orphanages*' she brooded at the thought that the poor unfortunate boy may never have found a home.

"Are you OK Madame?" Lawrence enquired.

"Yes ... yes ... please do go on .."

"I have narrowed it down to eight possibles."

"Eight, you say?"

"Yes, three in and around the Greater London area, two in Leeds, one in Manchester and one in Coventry."

"These are all cities, what if..."

"Madame, I can assure you that my investigations have been extremely thorough. Each of these eight males were orphaned or abandoned within the month of November that year, I excluded baby boys with sisters or brothers, initially there was nine."

"Nine?"

"I'm afraid ... that one was unfortunately stabbed to death in his early teens, on a Manchester street amidst a gang feud."

"What if he .. I could never forgive myself." Danielle said with sincerity and prayed that the deceased mobster was not her offspring.

"No heed in speculating at this time."

"No .. no, please continue."

"I have .. that is, Mr. Hickman and I have taken the liberty, to save time you understand, to send each of the eight candidates a letter of introduction and within the correspondence suggested that it would be in their best interest to reply to a box number. Now on my return to London tomorrow, I will endeavour to make preparations for all, bar two of the aspirants to visit my London office."

“Is there a problem with the two that cannot make a visitation?”

“You could say that Madame, one is in prison for armed robbery and the other one is in a drug rehabilitation clinic .. but if need be ..?”

“One moment Monsieur Lawrence,” Danielle interrupted, a sudden thought caused a small rush of adrenaline to colour her cheeks. “My son has a very rare blood group ... my son, Jean Paul .. so surely, probably?”

“Yes ... yes, this will indeed aid our exploration, I’m sure.”

Chapter Five

The Newcomer (Manchester, England – Seventeen Years Earlier)

The journey home from school was never a dull one for Jack Sharpe when he was in the company of his two favourite 'chums', Davy Simpson and Gary Whitney. For, to begin with, the three boys shared the same hobbies and interests. In an animated fashion they would chew over their thoughts and ideas on their walk home and this warm late August evening was no exception. Each of them displayed as much bravado along with as much wisdom (as three fourteen year olds were able) as they discussed their hypothesis of what was their favourite subject, the female anatomy.

Davy kicked a small stone and the three friends studied its journey as it danced vigorously for some fifteen metres before ricocheting off a lamppost with a 'ping' into the cobbled street.

"In off the post," Gary remarked before Davy probed

"Hey lads, have you seen the knockers on Maria Cantwell in class four B?"

He held two cupped hands in front of his chest in an exaggerated fashion.

"Nipples like chapel hat pegs" Gary agreed.

"She'd never drown that's for sure" Jack added, then continued, "Mind you, I've heard it said that she has seen more shagging than a copper's torch."

The three youth's laughter echoed loudly around the narrow thoroughfare. Jack rounded off the day's discussion relating to the aforementioned subject matter by telling a few 'dirty jokes'. Davy and Gary chortled and clapped their hands together in approval.

They continued in a similar juvenile vein until they reached the end of the street and entered through the open iron gates to Greenbrow Park. This was one of the few bits of green grass and trees to be found in Trafford North and the boys enjoyed their daily stroll through, using it as a short cut to their respective homes.

Greenbrow Park stood in four and a half acres of council owned land, with a six foot high iron spiked fence running around its length and breadth. Inside, adjacent to the perimeter a host of mature trees do their utmost to soften the stark metallic presence of the rusting iron fence. Inside the park, a play area with slides and swings for young children, with a small man-made pond situated symmetrically in the parks' centre. There were a variety of trees dotted about throughout, ash, cedar elm, conifer and four enormous oaks that are said to have been there since Cromwellian times. Some nicely maintained rose gardens in the summer months added a splash of colour to the landscape.

Jack inhaled hard the sweet aroma of freshly cut grass, this was one of his favourite smells in all the world (not that he had travelled anywhere further in the world than Southport on a day trip) but he was sure that there could not be anything more delightfully aromatic than the smell of freshly mowed grass.

"They are putting together some more new tennis courts over there" Davy said, pointing to the far end of the park where only last year two new concrete courts had been laid.

"Grass courts," Davy added.

"How do you know?" Gary quipped.

"Harry Cunningham told me, and he should know, cos he plays tennis, so he's bound to know."

"Tennis? – it's a game for Nancy's," Gary blurted.

"What do you know?" Davy prodded.

"I know not to wear a pair of white girly shorts, and get the piss taken out of me, that's all"

"Come on Gary, I reckon that tennis is a great game, don't you Davy?"

"Yes Jack, I thought that Wimbledon was really neat this year."

"Wimbledon?" Gary gushed, "That's all posh folk noshing strawberries and cream, you two will be joining the bloody county set next". Throughout this little revelation, Gary pushed the tip of his nose up with his forefinger.

"All that's changing now, it's not just folk with lots of brass that play and watch tennis these days." Jack reasoned

"Yeah," Davy agreed, "Look at that Arthur Ashe, he won Wimbledon the other year. He made it to the top against all the odds, and he wasn't brought up posh."

"Not to mention the fact that he wasn't white" Jack augmented.

"OK, point taken."

"Besides, it's just that," Jack continued, "Like you Gary, being brought up around here I had never set eyes on a tennis court, apart from on the telly that is, but now those new courts over there have given us the chance to play the game and I'm itching to get a racket and have a go."

"Me too, I'll give you a game sometime Jack," Davy enthused.

"Grass courts did you say Davy?"

"Aye, they'll be ready for next year, they say."

"Do you fancy a walk over to take a gander?"

"Count me in!"

"But we only live over there" Gary said pointing towards the gates ahead of them, just beyond the spot that the annual November bonfire ritual takes place. Jack and Davy turned and started to walk in the direction of the new courts. Gary hitched his satchel higher onto his shoulder, shrugged submissively and called after them,

"Hang on, wait for me."

As the trio drew closer they saw two young girls unlock the side gate, with a squeal it opened and they entered onto the concrete courts. By the time Jack and his friends reached the criss cross wire fence surrounding the playing surface the two youthful females had started to hit the yellow balls over the net to one another.

"They look quite useful," Davy commented.

"I told you it was a bloody girl's game," Gary quipped.

"You tell Bjorn Borg that, I bet you a hundred quid he's a millionaire since he won Wimbledon. You tell him that it's a girl's game," Jack challenged.

"Bjorn Borg? Well he looks like a bloody girl for a start off, with all that long blond hair and all that"

"Give it a rest Gary."

"Football's my game, it's a man's game, I'll stick to that thanks, you won't catch me ponsing about in a pair of bloody white shorts shouting fifteen love or whatever it is they say to one another, not bloody likely."

Jack could hardly bring himself to take his eyes off her. She seemed to float around the court as if on air. Her natural athleticism made her every move, her every swing of the racket look effortless. The girl possessed a natural olive complexion. Her legs and arms contrasting against the spotlessly white tennis dress she adorned that day. Her shiny blonde hair danced and shimmered in harmony with each change of step and positioning of her body.

"Jack," Davy said for the second time and this time gave him a nudge.

"Eh?"

"No chance."

"What?" Jack said and was then suddenly startled by a wild shot from the other end of the court that smashed against the fence in front of him, he had been standing with his mouth gaping. He swiftly attempted to return his facial expression back to normal, his eyes met hers for what seemed like an endless moment and he felt his cheeks tingle as he blushed in a way only an adolescent can.

"Who is she?" Jack said in a low whisper.

"Forget it, you've got more chance of plaiting fog," Davy answered in a quiet voice.

"Are you ready to start?" Jack heard the blonde haired girl say.

"Rough or smooth Mary?"

"Rough."

"It's smooth, I'll serve first."

The two girls changed ends and as they did so Jack turned to Davy again and whispered, "I haven't seen her around here before."

"She lives up on Dale Road in one of those big Victorian houses." Davy announced quietly in return.

"Lived there about a year." Gary cut in, with gusto.

"Shhh!" Jack prompted.

Gary duly obliged and, lowering his voice continued,

"She goes to Central Grammar School, bit too up-market for you Jack, besides she's got to be all of eighteen."

Jack watched as she served her first serve. He was surprised that a girl could hit a tennis ball as hard as she did, and Mary at the other end was going to struggle to win a game, let alone a set off this blonde haired beauty with the perfect smile, Jack thought to himself.

The three boys watched the first set giving the odd cheer of encouragement here and there. The blonde haired girl beat Mary 6-1, and Jack thought that she had let her friend, Mary, take that one game so as not to break her confidence.

"Bloody hell, look at the time" Gary spluttered, looking at his watch,

"I promised my mum I wouldn't be late, I've got to look after our Doreen while she goes to Bingo – I'm dead meat."

With that he turned on his heels and ran. Jack and Davy each wore a broad grin on their faces as they watched Gary ungainly trundle off across the field towards the other end of the park. His white shirtlap hung out and flapped in the breeze over the seat of his grey trousers, whilst he tried repeatedly to secure the satchel to his shoulder and at the same time cantering over the turf.

"It's time I got back too" Davy announced.

"Right" Jack said and he turned to look back towards the courts where the two girls were busily fighting out another rally of shots. Jack once again became transfixed as he gazed at the blonde's strong but feminine legs, as with each strenuous move they obeyed and pumped into action. A trace of perspiration had by this time enveloped over the surface of her soft olive skin, causing her limbs to glisten sensuously in the early evening sunlight.

"I'd eat her sweaty socks," Jack said to himself.

"Are you coming?" Davy enquired.

"I think I already have."

"Stop drooling, come on let's go."

"Hang on a second."

"Unlucky, Mary," the blonde haired girl called, "It was just out, that's forty-fifteen."

She walked over towards the fence where Jack and Davy were spectating to retrieve a few loose tennis balls.

"You're a pretty good player" was all Jack could think to say.

"Thank you" she replied and smiled. Her eyes stayed with his a little longer this time. Jack's face tingled and the hairs on the back of his neck stood out, again his face reddened. He puffed his cheeks and blew out a soft sigh, to somehow stop his heart from pounding so hard. She turned around and walked confidently back to the baseline to set herself up to serve by bouncing the ball on the floor.

"See ya," Jack squeaked through the criss cross wire fence. Without looking back in his direction she said,

"Yes – Bye," and served another ball at her opponent.

Jack turned reluctantly towards Davy who was already walking slowly on ahead. He put on a little trot to catch him up. Jack drew up alongside and fell into step with him.

"I think I'm in love," Jack said catching his breath.

"Aye, but I wouldn't let Harry Cunningham see you ogling at her like you did, he'd knock your block off."

"Harry Cunningham?"

"Yeah, he's head boy at Central Grammar, and that's his bird."

"I'd risk a good hiding just to hear her say new balls please. Anyway, how do you know so much about her, I've never seen her before?"

"Her name's Helen, that's all I know."

"I'm going to marry her one day!" Jack heard himself say. (Some years later this came true).

The two friends finally reached the corner of Argyle Street, came to a halt and stood conversing, Jack mimed a tennis shot with his right hand.

"So that's it Davy, I'm going to delve into my savings come Saturday and buy me a racket," he enthused.

"I'm OK, I've already got one, it's in the attic somewhere, it's a good one too, a Dunlop like what you see at Wimbledon."

"Brill," Jack agreed, and the two boys said their farewells.

On reaching the front door of number forty six, Jack pulled out the yale key and before he could insert it into the lock, the door opened and his mother's face beamed down at him from the top of the well polished step.

"Where have you been Jack lad, me and your dad have been on pins, we've got a surprise for you."

She stood to one side and allowed Jack to step over the threshold into the hallway where he halted and looked back at his mother while she poked her head out of the door and glanced up the street quickly left and then right before closing the door behind her.

"Go into the 'Best Room', your dad's in there waiting .. go on," she pressed.

It must be important Jack thought, the 'Best Room' was only ever used at Christmas or when they had relatives round from Basingstoke.

Jack opened the door to the room and entered. His father was standing in front of the unlit fireplace and on seeing Jack he smiled. Then, in a low quiet voice said,

"Come in lad, and sit yourself down, your mam and me have got some good news."

"Yes, sit down on the sofa Jack" his mother said in a whispered voice, while at the same time quietly closing the door.

"Has this room been bugged," Jack whispered back mockingly to his parents.

There was something different about the 'Best Room' today Jack mused sitting down on the rarely used sofa. It wasn't the fact that the dustsheets had been removed from furniture, or the spray of assorted flowers that had been arranged and put into his mother's favourite vase, which stood proudly on top of the sideboard, there was something different about its atmosphere.

"Talcum powder?" Jack said and sniffed, then he inhaled once more.

"I can smell talcum powder."

"Shhh" his mother beckoned, "Keep your voice down, you'll wake the baby."

"What baby!?"

"Over there lad" his father indicated with a nod of his head to the farthest corner of the room.

"Your dad and me....we've adopted a baby, and you've always said you would like a little brother or sister."

"Is it a boy or a girl?"

"A boy," Jack's parents enthused simultaneously.

Jack stood up to make his way over to where the crib was standing.

"Aye lad, go and say hello to your little brother."

Jacks' mother was about to say something but his father held up a hand in a motion to stop her continuing.

"Go on Jack," his father said. Jack obeyed and walked over to the tiny cot and looked inside.

"Well?" his father said. Jack lifted his gaze up from the baby, then looked over to where his mother and father stood smiling broadly and linking arms.

"He's a big baby," Jack commented.

"Well that's because he's eight months old lad," his father said.

"And..." Jack hesitated.

"Well?" his mother prompted.

"What's he called?"

"His name is Arthur"

"Arthur? ... that's ... an ace name ... that's what I'll call him, Ace!"

"Well?"

"He's black," Jack said finally.

Chapter Six

Ace in the Pack – Manchester, England – Present Day

The relentless rain came down in torrents over the narrow streets and alleyways of Trafford North. The yellow street lights tried in vain to lift the November early evening gloom. The guttering that ran along the base of the rooftops belonging to the terraced houses gushed out the excess water loudly onto the shining pavements below where in turn the manholes and the grids swallowed and gurgled with what seemed a perpetual thirst. Arthur or 'Ace' as his brother had nicknamed him years before, carried a sports bag over his right shoulder and held tightly onto the two toggles that were connected by string to the hood of his Manchester City Stadium coat. His head was bent forward and his back slouched to umbrella himself from the weather. He smiled to himself as he thought that he must resemble to any would be observer, one of those matchstick men in an L S Lowry painting.

He approached the end of the street and looked around for traffic, saw that it was clear and crossed over. As he did so, the delightful aroma of freshly cooked fish and chips wafted by way of his nostrils, causing the juices in his mouth to flow and his stomach to rumble.

On reaching the corner where the welcoming brightly lit 'chippy' stood, he peered through the open doorway. Queuing at the spotless stainless steel counter were two elderly female customers who turned their heads and nodded with a "Good Evening", in response to Arthur's jovial "Evening All". The man busily serving behind the counter looked up and gave a broad smile in Arthur's direction saying "what'll it be Ace, the usual?". The usual being Steak and kidney pudding, chips and oceans of rich brown gravy. The thought of it made Arthur drool. He chuckled and answered "Sorry Mike, not a chance, not while I'm in training." The proprietor turned to his two customers and poked his thumb in Ace's direction.

"Honestly, some of these young ones don't know what's good for them."

The two old ladies nodded in agreement.

"Anyway Mike, I've got to cut along – see ya," Ace said with a wave of his hand. The man behind the counter returned the gesture with a "yeah, see you Ace, hey let me know when the next tournament is, I'd like to come and watch.."

"Right you are Mike."

On reaching the main Manchester/Sheffield road the rain had begun to ease off. Arthur turned left towards Belle Vue. It was ironic he mused that they should call this part of the world by that name, observing the vista before him.

A sheet of tabloid newspaper danced in the wind high above the busy main road, a sole empty Coca-Cola tin rattled along the pavement rolling blindly to and fro. The evening commuter traffic laboured along with a slow perpetual drone. An odd early November 'Guy Fawkes' firework cracked and flared lighting up a small part of the sky with a flash of colour for a second, then vanishing into the dark Manchester night forever.

Arthur swung around on himself and walked backwards for a few paces hoping to spot the transport he needed to embark making its way in the oncoming traffic. In the distance he could make out the bright upper deck of two buses, he squinted slightly in an effort to focus in on the destination and numbers displayed between the top and lower deck but was unable to do so. His trainers squelched as he turned back around and walked towards the bus shelter that stood thirty metres ahead. He hitched his sports bag closer to his shoulder and allowed his mind to wander as he made his way to it, and for the umpteenth time today his thoughts went back to the letter that he had received that morning, the dispatch was signed simply, a friend.

The splash of a wheel hitting a puddle alongside him and with it the loud blast of a car horn made Ace bolt upright and turn his head rather too quickly to his right causing a slight click in his neck, that was swiftly followed by an unpleasant burning sensation. On seeing the red Ford and its driver, he immediately forgave them both for the brief panic that they had caused him. He opened the passenger door and climbed into the seat placing his bag between his feet, he pulled back the hood of his coat then rubbed the back of his neck vigorously and shut the door with his left hand and at the same time thrust his open right palm onto his brother Jack's open left hand, there was a loud clap when the hands connected on greeting one another with their familiar five high routine. Jack put the car into first gear and turned on his indicator then moved off slowly.

"Nice to see the old reflexes are still there Ace."

"What?"

"Well, when I pipped the horn there I think you broke the World High Jumping record."

"I'll take the smile off your face – I'll send you the cleaning bill."

Jack laughed as he manoeuvred his way back into the traffic, as he did so the rain once again began to fall in heavy droplets, thudding hard on the roof of the car, he turned the windscreen wipers on. Ace turned to his brother.

"So how's things?"

"Just fine."

"Anything come up on the job front?"

"Not yet, but something will." Jack smiled, though his brow was slightly furrowed.

"Yeah bro, something's bound to turn up."

"So much for a lengthy successful career in showbiz eh?" Jack said, with a hint of irony, and Ace knew that in recent months, his brother had been going through a comparatively lean time. Since relinquishing a steady position with a local company, in favour of applying himself as Manager of a gifted young rock band, it was to Jack's utter dismay, that he learned of a recording company persuading the young musicians to relinquish their ties altogether with him. Initially he had been filled with embitterment towards the recording people for their deplorable business methods, and obviously deeply hurt by the young group's disloyalty. Now, he was simply angered by his own stupidity.

The car pulled up outside a large brick building that was grossly marred and discoloured by the passing of years and stood as a monument to the soot and grime of old industrial Manchester. Above a doorway was a bright fluorescent tube of light that had been manipulated to spell out the name 'Bettabody's Gym'. Arthur lifted his sports bag up on his knee and said,

"Oh, by the way Jack, I got a letter this morning. I'd like you to read it and give me your thoughts."

"Sure, who's it from?"

"I don't know, it was just signed, a friend."

Jack pursed his lips and said, "Have you got the letter with you?"

"No, I left it at home on the top of the fireplace."

"OK, how long are you training for tonight?"

"About an hour and half to two."

"Right" Jack looked at his wrist watch, "I'll come back here in an hour and half or so to pick you up, OK?"

"OK, great, and thanks for the ride Jack."

"You're welcome Ace, hey, listen, I hope you're not neglecting your tennis for this body sculpting stuff."

"No way man," Ace enthused, "this is just part of my new training schedule – I tell you Jack, I'm going to be the fittest guy on the courts come the start of the summer."

"That's the ticket."

"Besides, you said that I need to bulk up a little."

"Fine, but don't go too crazy with those weights Ace, I've heard it said that all bodybuilding shrinks your vitals, besides we don't want you having the physique of Arnold Schwarzenegger. Looking like that and carrying fifteen odd stone of muscle it would be pretty difficult to speed around the tennis court. I think that you would look a bit silly anyway."

Ace made a mental picture of himself completely muscle bound limbering back towards the base line after being 'lobbed' by an opponent, and held it there for a second in his mind's eye, he chuckled to himself and quipped,

"Yeah, but imagine the kind of serve I would have though, Pow....one hundred and fifty m.p.h. plus!"

Ace pulled on the door handle, the inside of the car was illuminated instantly by the interior light, Jack looked into Arthur's' dark youthful eyes that sparkled with vitality, their whites shone like polished marble,

"You're looking in good shape Ace, that new diet plan must be working."

"Yeah, I'm really feeling the benefit, but unfortunately it has a bit of a side effect."

"Oh?"

Ace leaned his body to one side and released a very loud fart.

"Get out of here." was all Jack could say. Ace giggled like a schoolboy and endeavoured to lift his six foot odd frame out of the car. Jack smiled and shook his head while he watched his brother walk the short journey to the doorway of the gymnasium. He then pipped his horn and drove off.

Once inside the gym, Ace quickly changed into the appropriate attire, wasting little time in proceeding with his training schedule. He lay on the bench with his knees tucked up level with his waist and his legs crossed.

"Forty nine, just one more," Glynn, Ace's gym coach and proprietor of Bettabody's said, "One more and you can relax."

Ace pushed hard on the bar that had affixed round iron weights on each end, in the last five 'reps' gravity had proceeded to have its say in this particular exercise in the evening's programme. Glynn's expert eye recognised the fact and aided Ace, not physically but physiologically by placing the forefingers on each hand underneath the bar. Ace exhaled hard, his arms trembled under the strain as he transmitted every ounce of energy into his upper limbs. As soon as Ace's arms were straight up above his chest and his elbows locked in, Glynn snatched the bar from Ace's grateful hands and secured the weights onto the specially designed metal rods above Ace's head.

"Well done Ace, you're coming on now, rest there for a minute, we'll work on your 'abs' next, I've just got to go to the office and sort something out."

"Right, 'abs', .. yeah, .. 'abs' ..OK," was all Ace could manage to say. He lay there with his eyes closed and placed his hands over his chest and felt around the area of his anatomy he had just been working on, 'no pain, no gain' he thought to himself and sat up tugging at his T-shirt that was by now absorbed in perspiration and had begun to cling to his torso. He wiped his face with a towel, opened his eyes and looked towards the office, standing with his back to Ace was Glynn, whose enormous physique, due to years of bodybuilding seemed to take up the whole doorway. He appeared to be having a conversation with someone, although whoever it could have been was completely eclipsed. Glynn half turned himself around and gestured in Ace's direction and Ace caught a brief glimpse of a pretty young girl, approximately the same age as himself he guessed, with skin just a shade darker than his own, wearing a white tracksuit. Then Glynn turned and started walking towards the changing rooms and the young girl followed diminutively behind. On reaching the ladies changing room he knocked on the door, paused, then ushered her through and closed the door behind her. He then turned and walked back towards Ace, he pointed towards the next piece of apparatus on the agenda.

"Abdominals, come on," Glynn said, in a let's get back to business fashion.

"Right" Ace said and thought if he says 'it's Sunday, it's Sunday.'

Ace had never had much trouble with sit-ups and thought that this must be a good vascular exercise. He only started to feel the 'burn' after around the two hundred mark and at two-fifty Glynn said, "OK, take a rest, we'll be doing that exercise with a medicine ball next time. How are you feeling Ace?"

"Good... never better" Ace said between breaths and getting himself back onto his feet.

"Well, you'll be pleased to know that you've got just forty minutes of tonight's set to do" Glynn said with a very wry smile and looking at his stopwatch.

"Right."

"Thighs and calves now, let's get to it," the big trainer said clapping his hands together.

They made the short journey to the necessary equipment and Glynn said,

"By the way Ace, did you notice that young girl that I was talking to earlier?"

"Yeah, ... you mean?"

"The girl in the white tracksuit?"

"Yeah."

"Like you, she happens to be into tennis also."

"Oh?"

"Yes sir, in a big way, in fact she played in the junior Wimbledon championships last summer, it was in all the papers, didn't you see it? She was even on the TV"

"Yeah, .. I mean .. wow, is that her?" Ace said, and was genuinely impressed, "Was that Lorna Davies?"

"The little lady herself."

"What's she doing hanging out around here?"

"She's taking time out for a month visiting her favourite aunt and uncle, her uncle's an old bodybuilding pal of mine. He recommended to her that if she wanted to stay in shape then she'd better come and see me, so here she is."

"Cool," was all Ace could think to say.

"Thighs and calves," Glynn said assertively.

Ace obeyed enthusiastically and went about the business of complying with the big man's instructions.

"No pain, no gain," Ace told himself once more.

The red Ford turned into Argyle Street and made its way down the centre due to a variety of vehicles parked up on either side. The driver recalled the days when it was only the Gregson family that had the privilege of owning an automobile on the whole of the street and several streets beyond.

Two tiny figures caught Jack's eye fleetingly as they dashed for cover after rapping on the front door of one of the row of terraced houses. 'Knock and run' he said with a smile to himself, bringing the car to a stop outside his parents' house, then shook his head disapprovingly, reflecting that the two boys could hardly be more than six years old. He turned off the ignition and climbed out of the car.

"I'll give you knock and bloody run you little sods....I'll knock your bloody heads off." An irate man was shouting from his doorway after the two kids. Who, by now were at a good safe distance looking back at the angry adult from the street corner.

"Get stuffed mister," one of the boys blurted back at the man, who stepped forward as if to give chase. The two boys stuck up a finger in unison and disappeared around the corner. With that, the man cursed and made his way back through the doorway slamming the door shut, so hard, Jack thought that the doorknocker might fall off. After which, apart from the commonplace hum of suburbia, the only sounds left in the street was that of several varieties of the canine family yelping and barking.

He looked up towards the heavens and shivered slightly, not only at the thought of the decline of his home town's stature and communal disposition, over the last ten years or so, but, that the heavy clouds had finally given way to a gusty northerly wind that presented the night with a much cooler presence.

With his thumb, Jack pressed repeatedly on the small buttoned device that was attached to his keyring in an effort to engage the car alarm to act as a deterrent to would-be thieves. *'Needs a new battery'* he thought. Again and again he pressed hard down on the button until finally the pip-pip-pip simultaneously accompanied by flashing car headlights told him that finally the alarm was set. Satisfied, he made his way to the front door of number forty-six, as if by telepathy Jacks mother appeared at the doorway.

"Hello Jack lad," she said warmly.

"Hi ma."

"Have you set the alarm thing on your motor?" his mother said in a stage whisper.

"Yes,... mind you, car thieves these days are so crafty, that if they wanted the car they'd have it anyway."

"Happen you're right, but you can never be too careful."

"In any case, they've got so used to alarms going off around here, that no-one even seems to bother investigating the trouble anymore," Jack commented crossing the threshold of the old abode. His mother repeated the ritual of scanning the street before closing the door.

Jack contemplated on people's adaptability to the subtle changes that occur within the structure of the inner city's everyday existence and reflected that, once upon a time his mother would tap lightly on the door of any of the nearby houses and open and unlocked door, then enter with, *"hello.. it's only me... Mrs. Sharpe, have you got a cup of sugar that I could borrow 'til Friday love?"* And the request granted with a friendly smile and, "*will you have a cup of tea while you're here?, the kettle's just boiled."*

He recalled the week of the arrival of baby Ace, and his father saying "*There must be a sugar embargo at Salford Docks."* Considering that every man, woman and his dog within the neighbourhood had needed to 'pop-in' to number forty-six for a cup.

The mode of existence now, was to the contrary. Each house in Trafford North had chains, locks and double locks, ... and that's only around the sugar bowls, Jack smiled to himself at the mental image. He walked past the 'Best Room' and along the brightly lit narrow hallway to the base of the stairway, to the right of which was the living room. He opened the door and entered. The decor within had changed very little over the years. The cream and brown flecked wallpaper that Jack had assisted his father in hanging still decorated the walls, albeit in a tired fashion. Floral curtains hung dolefully down covering the window that in daylight gave sufficient light to afford to read a book or a newspaper, however, on a dull overcast day, that pleasure would be denied without the aid of a lamp or the overhead light. Below the window stood the gate-leg table, covering its surface was a hand woven table cloth that Jack had purchased whilst on holiday in Portugal some three years before. Helen, his wife, and his mother had agreed that it would go nicely over the old worn, although valued piece of furniture. The TV in the corner of the room was transmitting a Party Political Broadcast on behalf of the Conservative Party. A well groomed young man in a pinstriped suit whom Jack did not recognise, was pontificating about the positive action that his party had to offer the nation, whilst at the same time maligning the Labour Party policies and calling the SDP's the Socialist Deserters Party. 'Usual crap' Jack thought to himself. In the opposite corner was a display cabinet full of trophies and hanging proudly above it was a large framed, black and white photograph of Ace in full flight during a match in a Cheshire Tennis Championships. The one big change in the living room was the introduction two years ago of a gas fire, replacing the homely warmth of an open range. On the mantle behind the clock was the letter to Mr. Arthur Sharp and, standing in a military fashion on both sides of the timepiece was a collection of colourful birthday cards.

"Hey up Jack, how are you?" his father said from his favourite chair and turning his focus from the TV.

"I'm good dad, thanks,.... how are you?"

"Coping lad, aye."

Jack was not totally convinced surveying his father's pallid complexion. The face was drawn, his grey hair looked somehow whiter than ever before and the eyes in his head looked sad and weary. This once proud man had undergone an appraisement by the new management at the Blackthorn Engineering Works six months ago and they had decided to offer him an 'early retirement package', or as Jack's father had put it at the time, "I've worked there for some twenty odd years, never a day off, and some bloody whiz kid takes over and tells me that my back legs have gone."

"We'll go and have a pint sometime dad," Jack offered.

"When he gets his redundancy money from Blackthorns we'll all have a pint and celebrate" Jack's mother said, crossing the room. His father said nothing.

"I'll put the kettle on," she offered.

"Not for me" Jack said "I can't stop long, I'm going over to Greenbrow Park to join Helen and the kids for the lighting of the bonfire," he made his way over to the fireplace and plucked the buff envelope with Ace's name inscribed on it from behind the clock.

"Ace wanted me to pick this up for him, he wants me to go over it with him, do you know what it's about ma?"

"No idea Jack. It came with a couple of the Birthday Cards this morning, he was ever so secretive about it and said he wouldn't discuss anything about it until he had spoken to you, in fact, he resealed the envelope, not that me or your dad would...."

"No, we know that ma, anyway don't fret yourself, I'm sure it's just something and nothing," Jack assured her.

"Fancy," his mother said "Our Ace, eighteen tomorrow," and she looked over at the photograph on the wall, on her face she wore a broad smile.

Jack kissed her on the cheek and said his goodbyes to her and his father, then made his way to the park just in time to witness the ritual lighting of the large bonfire. When he joined Helen at a safe distance from the would-be inferno, she was busy assuring their four year old daughter, Annie, that the fully clothed figure that the 'grown ups' had thrown on the top of the wood pile was only a dummy called 'Guy Fawkes' and not a real man. Their son, Dan, the seven year old stood with wide eyed anticipation observing the bright flames licking their way expeditiously through the assembled timber.

"Quite a good turn out this year," Jack said, looking at the encircled gathering.

"Yes, but not enough adults," Helen prompted, and pointed over in the direction of a cluster of rumpled kids standing some thirty metres or so away from the main area lit up by the bright green emission from a firework.

"They're having their own display over there."

"Where do kids of that age get fireworks from?" Jack snapped "There isn't a one over the age of ten I'll bet amongst them."

Helen shook her head and added ironically, "If you was to go over there and ask them where their negligent parents were, they would tell you to sod off."

"Or worse," Jack concluded, and felt that he recognised two of the gang as the two 'knock and run' rascals from earlier.

The official fireworks display eventually got under way and Jack and his family enjoyed the spectacle immensely, roaring their approval with 'ooohs' and 'aaahs' in the appropriate places. The whole extravaganza of rockets, spinning wheels, etc. was all over within fifteen minutes.

"Is that it?" little Dan asked.

"That's it," Helen said.

"Till next year," Jack added glimpsing at his wristwatch, "I'll walk you and the kids over to the mini, I'm parked just behind you."

Chapter Seven

The Letter

The handle turned with a squeak and the shower head stuttered then burst into life. Ace held out a hand to test the temperature, satisfied, he then stepped in under the steady torrent and gave out a grateful moan enjoying with relish the warm water washing over his ebony body.

Ace had regarded her to a greater extent during the 'wind-down' section of his evening's programme. Lorna had disposed of the white tracksuit and modelled an alluring multi-coloured leotard which unveiled a shapely girlish outline. His feet had pounded rhythmically over the surface of the thick rubber fan belt track that was part of the running machine. She appeared oblivious to his observations of her as she went about her work around the gymnasium with an appetite that left Ace brimming with admiration for the petite, although perfectly proportioned young female, since what the girl lacked in height and strength, she more than made up for in guts, determination and zest. Along with these qualities Ace had been pleased to witness a sense of humour that sparkled through her dark brown eyes as, between each set of disciplines she bantered convivially with the big trainer.

Jack entered and scanned the interior of the gymnasium, on seeing the proprietor's burly figure, both men acknowledged each other, then Jack made his way over to where Glynn was putting an attractive black girl through her paces. Besides those two there was only two other people in attendance in the rather large hall. One, a middle-aged man wearing a yellow vest, black shorts and a black and yellow striped bobble hat and the other a man in his late twenties with long hair tied in a pony tail, who was totally engrossed in his reflection from the mirror pumping his lower arms up and down whilst holding a dumbbell in each hand. Jack turned his gaze back towards Glynn.

"How goes it?" he said approaching the trainer and his enthusiastic student.

"Fine Jack thanks, could be busier I guess, but, we're ticking over ... and you?"

"Ticking over."

"Ace has gone to shower down, he'll be back out in a minute,... OK take a break there." The big man advised Lorna. She blew out a gasp of air and stepped off the metal appliance.

"Hey Jack, you're a bit of a tennis freak, yes?"

"Yes ... well you could say that Glynn."

"Then allow me to introduce you to Miss Lorna Davies, the future Queen of Wimbledon and W.T.A. circuit," Glynn said proudly.

"W.T.A?" Jack enquired awkwardly.

"The Women's Tennis Association," Glynn prompted.

"Oh, I'm sorry" Jack said turning to Lorna and feeling rather embarrassed by his ineptitude. She smiled broadly and politely offered her hand. Jack responded acknowledging her invitation and shook her hand warmly, while Glynn introduced the pair, and he continued.

"Lorna turned professional last year, done pretty well for herself so far."

"Until last month, that is," Lorna said.

"Oh?" Jack prompted.

Lorna smiled up at the big man then turned to Jack,

"It was in the Brighton Indoor International."

"How did you get on?" Jack asked enthusiastically.

"I crashed out in my first match I'm afraid."

"Just nerves," Glynn assured her.

"I wish that was the case, but the simple truth is that I got blasted off the court by my opponent's power play ... a real heavy weight hitter."

"When is your next tournament?" Jack probed.

"Well you see after that dismal display, my coach and I have decided to go back to the drawing board."

"And it starts in here," Glynn added.

"It's crucial for me to get good sponsorship, so in order to get that, I have to be able to compete against powerful ladies and after my coach witnessed the pounding I took in Brighton we agreed that ... to build up my reputation then ... "

"You have got to build up your body!?" Jack cut in.

"Exactly that Jack," Lorna responded.

"Not too much I hope" he contested admiring her feminine outline, and continued.

"So where is your coach based?"

"In Hertfordshire, he's training a couple of other girls for the British Championships this month and I should have been competing also, but I'm determined to get myself in the best possible shape for next year. I'm just hoping that I have done the right thing, you see, I told my coach that I was injured and needed a month off."

"But surely competing is the best way to improve your game ... I'm sorry I'm being presumptuous."

"No worry, I'm doing this for my head, and there's another thing that I want to build up, my confidence."

"So tell me, who have you been practicing your game with while you are here in the area?"

"Well .. that's been a bit of a problem really."

"Actually, my wife, Helen, is a very good player she'd ... hey, wait a minute ... have you met my brother?"

"He means Ace, the guy I pointed out to you earlier," Glynn reminded her.

"He's your brother?" Lorna said with a bemused smile.

"It's a long story, listen, this could pay dividends for both of you."

"Oh?"

"He's the best player in the North," Jack exalted.

"At tennis?"

"Absolutely," Jack said emphatically. Lorna turned her focus on Glynn, who nodded his head approvingly and urged,

"I've never seen the lad play, but you can be damned sure of one thing, if it comes down to stamina ... well he's as fit as a fiddle."

"He's a natural" Jack continued, "Anyway, you've seen him haven't you? he's six foot two, got fantastic co-ordination and he's great at all ballgames, even at golf. He's got a swing like Cory Pavin."

"More like crazy pavin," Ace quipped from over Jack's shoulder.

"Oh, Hi Ace, ... I was just in the middle of arranging a spot of court practice with Lorna here."

"I'm sorry bro ... but I doubt that you would be able to give her much of a game, let alone help her with her proficiency," Ace said without malice. Jack laughed and retaliated, "No, not with me Ace, with you."

"Oh, sorry I thought ..."

"What about Monday at the new racket centre, say, nine o'clock?" Jack offered turning to Lorna.

"In the morning?"

"Best time ... you've got the pick of the courts."

"Ok, yes, great nine o'clock Monday, see you there then Ace, Oh by the way, I'm Lorna ..."

"Davies, yes I know," Ace cut in. The two shook hands with warm regard.

"Jack tells me that you're a good player."

"I'm better than that," Ace assured her with a huge smile that told Lorna that he wasn't kidding, and he turned to leave. *'We'll see'* she contemplated studying the two men making their way to the double doors with the younger man towering above his companion.

"They seem very close," Lorna said to Glynn after they disappeared through the doors.

"They'd kill for one another those two," Glynn replied in earnest.

After leaving the gymnasium Ace and Jack made their way to a local pub. Jack placed his pint of Best Bitter on the small round table, handed Ace a large glass of fresh orange juice and sat down opposite his brother. He put his hand into the inside of his coat and pulled out the buff coloured envelope. He then offered it across the table to Ace. Ace raised a hand and prompted Jack to open it. He took a small swig of beer and proceeded to open the envelope as requested and removed the single piece of foolscap paper, he opened it up and read,

PO Box 52
London W1

Mr. Arthur Sharpe
46 Argyle Street
Trafford North
Manchester GM18

Dear Mr. Sharpe

I have been instructed to arrange a rendezvous with yourself by a certain party whom, for now, without prejudice, I will simply call a mutual acquaintance, regarding a matter that is somewhat too delicate to include within this letter. However, I can assure you that it would be in your upmost interest to correspond at your earliest convenience to the Box number above. If your response for an opportunity to meet is a positive one, then you will receive further details and instruction within five working days.

Yours sincerely

A Friend

"What do you reckon bro?" Ace said, after Jack had concluded his examination and placed the letter back into the envelope. Jack shrugged his shoulders, although underneath the dismissive veneer that he displayed at this moment, he had a suspicion that the day he and his parents had anticipated had finally arrived, though happily somewhat late, (eighteen years late,) he mused, and too overdue now to alter the fact that they were brothers, maybe not by blood but in spirit they were established and inseparable, besides Ace was old enough now to choose his own destiny.

"Perhaps someone's won the lottery and wants to give you half" he said jovially.

"Come on bro, get serious."

"There's only one way to find out."

"Yeah." Ace enthused. "I'll send an answer first thing tomorrow."

"Well there you go then, what did you need me to read it for?"

Ace looked Jack in the eye and his expression became earnest.

"I know it's not written on official government paper or anything like that but, ..."

"But what, Ace?"

"You don't think it's ... about ... you know, my real parents do you?"

Jack felt suddenly ill at ease, an irregular quirk when in Ace's company.

"What do you think Ace?"

"I don't know ... I don't know if I want it to be or not."

"I don't think you've got anything to lose in replying, as I said, but in the meantime, don't worry ... it could be real good news."

"Yeah ... right." Ace said breaking into a broad smile.

Chapter Eight

Lorna returned his forehand with a double handed backhand and Ace was at the net to calmly volley the ball home for a point against her serve. Previous to this practice match which, Ace had insisted upon taking place, the two players went through an accustomed warm up procedure. Lorna arrived on court adorning a fashionable red tracksuit emblazoned with emblems illustrating her deserved accomplishments. She looked absolutely fantastic Ace thought examining her form as she strolled confidently across the court towards the base line at one end of the court. Ace himself, in contrast, felt uncomfortable in the kit that he was wearing and cursed the fact that his mother's washing machine had let him down, but convinced himself that it wasn't what you wear it's what you do. The match had got underway and Lorna had swiftly taken a five games to love lead in the third set with the first set going in her favour, 6-1 and Ace pulling back in the second by scraping through 6-4. Now, Lorna was beginning to doubt that practicing her tennis with Ace was going to assist her progress in her chosen profession. She did not want to hurt his pride or his feelings but she was a professional now. She needed to be stretched to the limit if she was going to improve. Lorna reckoned that she would supersede this little arrangement come the end of the session, it had to be done.

"You won't win this game," Ace hollered from the opposite end of the court. Lorna smiled pleasantly back towards him and responded,

"Come on Ace ... I haven't even broken sweat yet!"

"Don't worry, you will babe!" Ace assured her. Jack's voice boomed from the umpires chair, interrupting their banter.

"OK, four love .. fifteen all."

One aspect of Lorna's game today was that she had been able at least to practice her serve and it had been going exceptionally well and had gradually quickened in pace as the match had progressed. She tossed the ball up and connected with it perfectly, aided by the strings on the upper part of her racket, firing the ball over the net into the service area at the other end of the court. Ace hit the ball with a top spin backhand shot in return, which took Lorna completely by surprise, simply because she had not been aware that Ace had that shot in his arsenal. The ball landed on the baseline at such a speed that she had no time to react, let alone contemplate pursuing its flight.

"Fluke." Lorna muttered to herself.

"Fifteen thirty," Jack proclaimed from the umpire's chair wearing what Lorna thought looked like a priggish smile.

A thought broke through her concentration, *'that's the first time he's smiled in this match.'* She allowed the notion to leave her as swiftly as it had entered her mind. She bounced the ball in a well regulated fashion in readiness to deliver another serve. This time her delivery struck the centre line. *'That's an Ace'* she contemplated surveying the ball swerving away from her opponent's forehand. Yet, he was there to hit the return, albeit at full stretch. The ball came back over to her side of the court comparatively tamely this time, although Lorna was forced to race briskly towards the line, where she hit a full blooded forehand shot diagonally across court. Ace had read her answer and effortlessly replied with a winning strike down the line.

"Fifteen forty," Jack announced bearing the same pedantic grin.

Lorna assessed that this time she would serve to Ace's backhand, for surely he would not be capable of returning a shot likened to the one he had mustered up a few minutes ago. *'No, that was a fluke!?'* she told herself again. She bounced the ball and took in a gulp of air and hit the serve with every ounce of power and know-how that she possessed, and using the momentum of her service action raced towards the net in anticipation of killing the point with a volley. Ace's return was hammered back once again with top spin accompanied with formidable force. The ball was just a blur to Lorna, who was powerless to do anything but watch it fizz off the surface and inside the line.

"Game Sharpe, Miss Davies leads by four games to one, third set." Jack informed them, this time mimicking an umpire with a plum in his mouth. Ace donned a broad grin in response to his brother's foolery. Whilst, at the opposite end of the court Lorna's expression was to the contrary, she remained concentrated on the task in hand, namely, to end Ace and his brother's misapprehensions in light of what she regarded as Ace's unimpressive attributes as far as tennis was concerned. Sure, he's an excellent athlete and the guys were fun to be with but .... she rubbed the palm of her right hand on her tracksuit bottoms then gripped the racket and teased.

"Come on Ace ... you haven't won one of your service games yet in this set!"

Ace looked over the net towards his petite opponent, the grin that he had retained from Jack's whimsical escapade aggravated her slightly.

"Give me the best that you've got," she challenged.

"Do you mean that?"

"Sure, I'm ready!" She confirmed in a forthright tone.

Ace looked up towards Jack in the chair and gave him a wink. To Lorna's bewilderment, Ace deposited the racket from his right hand into his left and employed an entirely new stance. He bounced the ball competently in preparation for his first serve, he pitched the ball up higher this time than he had done previously with his other hand, then launched into the shot. Before Lorna could respond, Jack called the ball out, although she believed that it was very close to being on the line. The fact was, that the velocity at which the ball came over and landed, made it difficult for her to judge precisely because her eyes were not acclimatized, for until now, Ace had been serving at a standard club level pace. *'That one was supersonic in comparison,'* she mulled.

"Unlucky" she managed to mutter. Ace shrugged his broad shoulders indifferently.

"It just needs to warm up," he informed her whilst at the time swinging his left arm around in a huge circle in an effort to loosen the muscles.

"Are you ambidextrous?" she asked.

"Kind of," was all he said. Her aggravation by this time turned to anger. She would now channel that anger into her game and teach him a lesson that he would not forget, she told herself, *'how dare he take the piss like that'*.

Ace stroked the ball with the racket head, coming through at an angle succeeding in giving the ball an elliptical shape, similar to a gliding lemon, as it sped through the air over the net, landing in the service area and spinning dramatically. Lorna reacted well to its flight and returned a forehand shot over the net, though in endeavouring to make it she had left her court wide open for Ace to volley the ball away at the net for the point.

"Fifteen love," Jack retorted. Lorna angled herself in anticipation for the next of Ace's first serves. Ace wound himself into the service and the sound of the racket striking the ball was all Lorna knew about it. She lifted herself up from the squatted position to re-establish her deportment, but her mouth was agape.

By the time that Lorna had got her 'eye in' and established a modicum of rhythm against his left arm which was unmistakably Ace's natural one, for his game had improved immeasurably, they were tied at five games each and in the short time that it had taken him to draw level, her point of view had changed irrevocably, she was now convinced that his natural talent was outstanding, despite being a little rough around the edges, but nothing that could not be smoothed out.

She had by now taken off her tracksuit top, the perspiration caused her shirt to embrace her womanly curves. She did not notice Ace's admiring eyes touring the shape of her upper body when they crossed to change ends. She was totally focused, she knew now that she could not walk off court with the match, but she was determined to walk off court with her dignity.

Ace and Lorna had arranged to meet Jack in the cafe after they had gone to their respective changing rooms and showered. Ace was the first to go through and join his brother.

"What'll it be Ace?" Jack said.

"Fresh orange, please bro."

Before Jack could get up from the table to purchase the drinks, Ace handed over to him an identical buff envelope to the one that he had received before. He opened it up and pulled out the letter from within and proceeded to read its contents.

43 Frith Street
London W1

Dear Mr. Sharpe

My clients and I are delighted that you have undertaken to respond to our invitation to meet. I would ask you please to bring along with your good self a copy of your birth certificate and verification of your blood group, and also a trusted member of your family, to the above address. We will be pleased to accommodate any expenses accrued on your passage from your home to the above address and your return. So, until the 11th day of this month at 11.30 am I wait in anticipation.

Yours sincerely
Don Lawrence (a friend)

ps. Please find enclosed, train timetable and underground route to the office.

On finishing reading the communication, Jack folded the paper over and placed it neatly back into the envelope, he looked over at Ace.

"So, who do you plan to take with you?"

"I was hoping that you would come and hold my hand," Ace said with a smirk, he held out a hand on which Jack responded by 'giving him five'.

Presently, Lorna joined the brothers at the table sporting yet another tracksuit, this time in peach, Ace decided that the colour suited her perfectly and duly informed her of the fact. Jack stood up from his chair and asked Lorna if she would like a drink.

"Thanks, a mineral water please, Jack."

"So that's a fresh orange and a mineral water." With that he turned and made his way towards the cafe counter, leaving Ace and Lorna at the table.

"Here, take the weight off your feet." Ace offered, pulling out the chair next to his.

"Thanks ... you know Ace, you're a pretty good tennis player!"

"Thanks Lorna, you're not so bad yourself."

She smiled appreciatively, though the smile was short lived.

"I'll tell you though, I'm really annoyed with you."

"Oh, why?"

"Why? .. because you tried to take the piss out of me, that's why, if I didn't like you, I would have called you a big headed B......" She refrained from cursing this time, but Ace recognised by the expression on her comely features that she was indeed displeased with him. Ace found her demonstration endearing, to the extent that it caused him to go into a fit of the giggles.

"Sure," she continued, "You had me fooled all right; I thought for two sets and more that you were a waste of space."

He suppressed his sniggering to explain.

"It was an experiment."

"Experiment ... you tried an experiment on me?"

"Honestly, I've been practicing playing right handed for a while now."

"Do yourself a favour Ace, ... forget it."

"Right you are ... sorry!"

"I'll forgive you under one condition."

"And what's that?"

"That we continue with the arrangements and train together for the rest of my stay here."

"Wild horses couldn't stop me," Ace assured her.

Jack returned and placed the drinks on the table.

"So tell me Ace ... how long have you been playing tennis?"

"Ever since I cut down the handle of one of my rackets when he was about five years old," Jack intervened.

"You've created a monster," Lorna quipped.

"I didn't create one, he's always been a monster, he didn't need my help on that score." Jack retorted and sat down in the chair opposite to where Lorna was sitting then resumed.

"When he was five, he used to follow me around like a chick to its mother hen, and whenever I was going to Greenbrow Park to play tennis he would pester me to take him along with me, pwease, pwease Jack I wanna pway tennis he used to beg."

"Leave it out bro," Ace said in return to his embellished impersonation. Jack just smiled and continued.

"You see, when I said that he was a monster, I mean he was hyper-active, you know? Our ma used to say that we would have to find something for him to put all that excess energy into."

"And tennis did the trick?" Lorna responded.

"Almost ... when I say almost, I mean, once he got that cut down Donnay racket in his hand and started hitting balls with it, that was it. He used to practice every spare minute or hour of every day, he even used to take the bloody thing to bed with him," he teased, "I can see him now, his racket in one hand and under his other arm was Bjorn."

"Bjorn?" Lorna enquired.

"Yes, he had a teddy bear called Bjorn."

Lorna laughed warmly, while Ace portrayed a smile to cover his slight embarrassment. When the laughter subsided Lorna said,

"Seriously now, have you ever had any coaching Ace?"

"No, why, am I doing something wrong?"

"No, not at all, it's just ... I haven't asked you have I, what do you do for a living?"

"Well, when I left school I went to work as a Storeman at Blackthorn Engineering, but, I got fired."

"Why?" she asked. It was Jack who answered.

"Because our old man was made redundant there and Ace told them in no uncertain terms what they could do with their stores!"

"And now?" Lorna queried, trying not to push too hard, "What are you doing now Ace?"

"Not a lot ... there's not a lot of work to be had around here, I've tried."

"Good." Lorna interrupted, "I mean, good that you wouldn't be passing off a career or anything like that to endeavour into what I'm going to suggest."

"And what's that?" he responded with a confused expression imprinted on his puerile face. Jack leaned forward and placed his glass of juice on the table top. She concentrated her gaze firstly on Jack and then towards Ace and said,

"I would like to introduce you to my coach, I think he should see you play."

"Yeah?" Ace responded enthusiastically.

"What I saw out there today was quite impressive, you have ability, of that there's no question, especially when you use your best arm ..." she teased. He smiled and responded,

"Right."

"No left," she countered, they laughed and she went on.

"Your groundstrokes on both forehand and backhand are good, you time the ball well, you have brilliant reflexes and to top it all you're incredibly quick around the court, and before I go on anymore and cause your head to swell, this is only my opinion Ace."

"You think I've got a future in tennis?"

"Yes ... but like I say, it's only my opinion, there are one or two weaknesses that no doubt a seasoned male pro would be able to take advantage of, but I'm sure that with some first class coaching could be put right."

"Way to go," Ace said eagerly.

"My coach may think I'm crazy, I don't know, but I reckon you're good enough to make it."

"Do you? ... Wow, thanks Lorna, I won't let you down with your coach, you just watch me." Ace said. He was genuinely flattered. Jack looked over in his direction retaining a contented smile. He contemplated how good fortune had played its part in Ace's lucky encounter with this enchanting young girl. His heart filled with pride, for he had believed more than anyone, that maybe one day Ace would realise his aspirations.

"Have you ever had your serves timed?" Lorna was asking.

"No ... why?"

"Well, thanks to your height, there's natural elevation, anyway, I'm sure my coach will be impressed, some of your first serves in that last set, were ..."

"Were what?"

"Hot."

"Did you say hot?" He grinned.

"I said hot."

"Listen Lorna, you keep on giving me compliments like this and, as you said, I'll end up with a head big enough to fill the Albert Hall."

"Confidence is half the battle Ace."

"Speaking of battles, when are we going to get down to it again?"

"Tomorrow OK?"

"Yeah."

"And the day after and the next day and the next."

"What are you doing tonight?" Ace said, and the voice seemed to come from somewhere else. *'Had he just asked her for a date?'* Although girls found him very attractive, this was one aspect of his personality that did not exude conviction. He was basically shy in the company of the opposite sex.

"Are you asking me out?"

"Er ... yeah, I mean if ...?"

"I'd like that."

"Right ... good ... oh, but what about the gym?"

"Take a night off Ace." Jack butted in.

"Yes ... yeah, it'll do no harm, I will."

"Good, that's settled then, do you drive Ace?"

"No, I haven't got a car ... yet."

"Or a license," Jack added with a grin.

"OK, I'll come and pick you up at your place then, what time should I call?"

"Seven thirty OK?"

"Seven thirty it is then."

While the young attractive pair confirmed their arrangements, Jack wrote down the address for Lorna on a piece of scrap paper. Lorna looked at her wristwatch and stood up from the table.

"I promised my aunt that I would join her on an expedition to Manchester this afternoon and I'm a little behind on schedule already, so .."

"There's the address," Jack advised.

"Good job someone's got their head screwed on, thanks Jack. I'd have gone away and not known where to find you."

Chapter Nine

Jean Paul

Floss opened the door and entered the compact, though proficiently equipped gymnasium on the ground floor of the King household.

"Mr. King sir, Jean Paul has arrived home from his travels." she announced.

King was going through the final stages of his daily programme of disciplined exercises. His face was fixed with a grimace and the expression did not alter on learning of the advent of his son's visit.

"He said that he will be waiting on the terrace Mr. King, sir," Floss added.

Before responding, he finished off the last phase of the routine that he was engaged in.

"Right ... tell ... tell him .... I'll be there in ... a few minutes," King said between breaths.

"Yes, Mr. King, sir ... he looks very well." With that she left the sweaty stench of the room and shut the door behind her. King climbed off the apparatus and stood in front of the full length mirror, where he admired himself. He loved the image that his reflection gave and proceeded to tell himself just that. A sudden recollection abruptly stained his train of thought.

"Bitch," he roared, recalling the day some months ago by the swimming pool. King had been flaunting his prowess before an apathetic audience, namely, Danielle Marie.

"This is what women want," King boasted and gyrating into a variety of poses.

"Women like this," he bragged tensing and flexing.

"Tell me" she had responded coolly, "Do they like small dicks also?"

"Bitch", he blasted once more, throwing a towel around his shoulders and making his way through the door into the hallway, past the large fat black cat sculpture in the area's centre that King had commissioned Fernando Botero to construct. He climbed the staircase, not affording time to browse at the array of colourful paintings by artists like, Henri Goetz, Christine Boumeester and Jean George Inca, among other fine painters that graced the walls.

He arrived at the entrance to the terrace. Jean Paul stood with his back to King looking out over the balcony at the magnificent blue of the Mediterranean, without turning he said,

"Anywhere I go in the world, there's nowhere that compares with this."

King walked over towards where Jean Paul was standing. As he approached, Jean Paul turned around to face his father. Beneath his white baseball cap which he wore back to front his young tanned face allowed a brief smile and the two men shook hands. As far back as Jean Paul could remember this was as tactile as his father ever was, in respect to their relationship, and he himself in return had never felt an impulse to contribute towards any change in this constrained and unformulated pact.

"How was the journey?"

"Fine."

King walked over to the table where he had taken breakfast earlier and lifted the broadsheet up and tossed it over to Jean Paul who caught it and proceeded to read the article beneath his picture.

"So you've finally decided to take the bull by the horns?"

"Yes."

"I seem to recall that you were going to make your debut on the Senior Tour last year?" King baited.

"You know well that I was not fully prepared then, I had a few problems."

"Self inflicted problems."

"No."

"Yes, because of your lack of discipline, your coach decided to wash his hands of you."

"I dropped him and the academy, the place was like Alcatraz by the sea."

"I was informed by the academy that your behaviour on court made John McKenroe look like a choir boy." King pressed and Jean Paul recognised the familiar build up of tension between them and told himself to keep his composure and said calmly.

"I have seen the error of my ways and my new coach and me see eye to eye. I am not a little boy anymore so I do not want to be treated like one. Brad Holding understands that, unlike the coach at the academy."

"One hundred and two thousand Dollars!"

"What?"

"One hundred and two thousand Dollars, that's how much it has cost me since I first sent you there to the academy in Florida when you were fourteen years old." King announced, scathingly. Jean Paul bit his lip and said in a level tone.

"Welcome home Jean Paul."

"Nineteen thousand five hundred Dollars from September to May each year, in addition six thousand for academic lessons, tell me, have I wasted my money?"

"You will get your money back plus interest, trust me."

King was oblivious to his offer and continued his taunting conduct towards his son.

"It's a pity ... it was your mother's idea to send you to a tennis academy, I always hoped that I would one day see you wearing the green and gold Springbok shirt."

"I think father, that had I chosen to pursue a career in rugby, then it would be the blue of France that I would sport, besides, how many times must we ..."

"South Africa are the number one nation," King cut in, "Did we not prove that by winning the bloody World Cup first time of asking after so many years in the wilderness?" King pressed, raising his voice somewhat, to which Jean Paul reciprocated.

“Do we always have to have the same arguments every time we come together?”

For the past two years whenever they were alone in one another’s company, their tenacious temperaments had been clashing consistently and with added malevolence each time that they had converged. It would be true to say that in Jean Paul’s younger years, although he saw little of his father he held him high in his estimations, indeed he believed his Papa to be a true protagonist and was heedful to his every word and notion. Since reaching puberty however, and discovering his own mind he had gradually become not nearly as acquiescent to King’s points of view. Actually he was now sure that the appearance of the first fissures in King’s framework were beginning to open up.

Jean Paul only hoped that this homecoming would not dissolve into a squabble as it had done last time.

He reminded himself that that little altercation had taken place on this very same spot, that day King was looking over the balcony and down at the sloping private grounds below. He had been watching Maurice, one of the half dozen heavily built guards going about the daily task of checking the wire fencing that encompassed the property. Jean Paul concluded to himself that it would be futile for any prospective burglar to attempt to scale the fence without being incinerated to a percolated pulp from the fortified electric field. Besides, each of the Stallone look-a-like guards were armed to the teeth.

“It is as if you are afraid of your own shadow,” Jean Paul had mentioned, joining his father’s surveillance.

“I’m afraid of no-one,” King snapped.

“Then why the muscle-bound guards twenty four hours a day?”

“Because you can never be too sure.”

“Of what?”

“That’s my business.”

“And what is your business father?” Jean Paul had probed credulously. For until that moment, he was genuinely impartial to King’s ‘professional’ interests, for as far as he was concerned, the man played with stocks and shares and bought and sold extravagant works of art, and one thing was for certain, Jean Paul had no intentions of following in his father’s footsteps. Though, as a youngster, he would furnish his imagination with fanciful notions that when his Papa went away on his travels, he was on secret missions like James Bond or something. He surely must have been, he would tell himself, because he never spoke of his exploits to him, or as far as he knew to his Mama. He could not be sure but this was perhaps the reason he asked King that particular question that day.

“Were you ever ... some kind of crook?”

“What?” King rasped with surprise.

“I am merely curious to know how you triggered the ascent to your wealth, after all, you have this house here, and other homes dotted around the globe ..”

“Are you questioning my credibility?”

“No, I thought ..?”

“You thought!, listen, money is like horse shit, if you stack it up it stinks but if you spread it about things grow ... so think about that, besides, one day it will all be yours, and just be thankful of that.”

“Merci Papa, but I intend to make my own fortune by my own hard work and aptitude.”

“You mean in playing tennis?”

“Yes.”

“Well don’t tell me that my money didn’t help you in assisting you on your progress on that score.”

“Yes, I admit that ... but ..”

“Well then” King said loudly, cutting him short.

“Well then,” Jean Paul continued, “I am just saying that I want to make my own way independently without your money.”

“I’ll tell you something man, do you know if I had been so impudent with my old man he would have taken a belt to me.” King stormed, feeling his blood coming to the boil with rage at his son’s sudden self assurance and effrontery. Fully unaware at that moment in time that these attributes were a reflection of his own characteristics some twenty or so years before.

“So what was so fine about your father?” Jean Paul ploughed on unperturbed by King’s agitation.

“He was your grandfather ... don’t forget that.”

“Maybe so, but don’t forget I never met him.”

“Admittedly, that’s the case ...”

“Do you not feel bitterness towards him?” Jean Paul added coolly.

“For what?”

“For leaving on his death, the farm and all its acres in your beloved South Africa, along with the vast majority of his money to your brother?”

“He left enough for me.”

“Chicken feed.”

“What?”

“I remember you telling me that your father only left you a pittance, enough to maybe establish a small business.”

“Yes, but I took that money and I used this man,” he tapped his forefinger against a veiny temple that was throbbing somewhat quicker than normal and he went on.

“I left my beloved homeland, as you put it, because at the time the bloody blacks had a vendetta against whites, especially wealthy whites ...”

“Well that left you out then.”

“Don’t be so bloody flippant.” King griped bitterly, “I will remind you man, that your grandmother was mercilessly tortured by a group of rough-neck black radicals, while my father was away on business.”

“Radicals yes, ... but not all black people were ...”

“They were not people they were fucking animals man.” King spat ferociously. *‘How many times did he have to explain the perception he had towards his mothers’ enemy?’* King brooded to himself.

“Where were you when ... when this thing happened?” Jean Paul enquired awkwardly.

“At the time these things happened to my mother, I wasn’t born, thank God.”

“Tell me father, is your God white?”

King turned to Jean Paul, the familiar twitch superceded the arrogant gesture, which Jean Paul had reflected over the years, gave the impression, that the collar of his father’s shirt might be on fire. He mused now, that it was his father’s eyes that were ablaze.

Chapter Ten

A Status Quo

Last night had been without doubt one of the best nights of Arthur Sharpe's young life. Indeed, the whole day had been a pure delight and it had been shared with as much enthusiasm by his female companion. He and Lorna had began the day together at the racket centre exploiting every minute of the four hours spent on court, exercising and refining their all-round play. By the end of the session the two of them agreed that they were pleased to forego the gym in favour of dining out. Jack had recommended to them that they should check out Mr. Changs in Manchester's China Town. They were gratified by his advice on entering the restaurant. Although it was only eight o'clock in the evening the place was already over half full and the atmosphere within the establishment was extremely pleasant. In one corner was a party of approximately sixteen Chinese people taking nourishment at a large round table, dexterously manipulating chop sticks to feed their mouths.

"That's a good sign," Lorna said discreetly.

"What?"

"Of all the Chinese restaurants around here, those Chinese people over there have chosen to eat here."

A cheerful waiter showed them to their table and made sure that they were both comfortable before offering them a menu each. He then bowed and left them to browse its contents.

"I love Chinese food, don't you Ace?"

"Er ... yeah."

"You don't sound too sure."

"No, no, honestly I do ... it's just that I've been on this special diet, you know?"

"Come on spoil yourself."

"Truth is," Ace said fingering at the knot in his tie, "I've never been in a Chinese restaurant before, I've had Chinese takeaways ... but this isn't the same ... oh, there was a restaurant I went to once for Jack and Helen's Anniversary."

"Chinese?"

"No."

"Good, then you're in for a treat." Lorna enthused. He smiled back at her warmly. She was thrilled that he had made the effort to wear his one suit and tie for their date and had told him on picking him up from his parent's house how fine and handsome he looked. She was observing him now, his eyes widened more and more as they explored the price of the dishes on offer on the bill of fare, recognising his discomfort Lorna said,

"I'll stand the bill tonight."

Ace had already employed some mental arithmetic and he deduced that if he was to pay for the meal then he would have scarcely enough left to carry him through for the next week.

"No ... no ... I can ..." he managed to splutter.

"I insist Ace!"

"We'll split it .. we can go Dutch."

"No, consider it a birthday gift from me to you."

"Are you sure?"

"As eggs are eggs."

"Thanks .. I mean thank you." he said slightly embarrassed, though he was rather relieved by her gracious offer. "But listen up, I'll get you back for this."

"You better had," she chuckled, "Now what do you fancy?"

"You," he said with a huge grin.

"To eat!"

"You?"

The waiter returned to their table maintaining his friendly smile, he stood with pen poised in readiness to take their order.

"As you're paying, then I think that you should order the food."

"OK ... do you like fish?"

"Anything .. I like everything."

"Good ... then we will have prawns to start with," Lorna told the waiter, indicating with her finger the particular prawn dish that she desired on the menu.

"Then ... something naughty but nice, the aromatic duck with pancakes, followed by something sensible, boiled rice please ... Chinese vegetables and chicken, oh, and a bottle of house white."

"Wine?" Ace enquired with surprise.

"I'll only have one glass as I'm driving, but tonight we have got a double celebration and I think that some wine will fit the moment perfectly."

"A double celebration?" Ace asked, once again he played with the knot in his tie.

"Ace."

"Yeah."

"Relax, take it off."

"Hmm?"

"Your tie ... when the wine arrives we will drink to your Birthday, then we will raise our glasses to the good news that I have for you."

Ace folded his tie up and pushed it into the inside pocket of his jacket and speculated on what the good news might be.

When the first course arrived he looked down at his dish with a perplexed expression. They were the biggest prawns that he had ever seen. Noticing his slight apprehension she asked.

"You do like prawns?"

"Yes .. yes .. great."

"Bon appétit."

"Yeah," He agreed, if there was one thing that he was certain about, it was that he definitely had a good appetite and tonight he was simply ravenous. He motioned to pick up his knife and fork.

"Just use your fingers Ace."

"Right." he said, then without looking up, he picked up a prawn and bit into it heartily then proceeded to chew firmly into it. Lorna looked across the table in horror to begin with, then endeavoured to curtail her laughter by covering her mouth with her hand.

"They're a bit crunchy." Ace declared finally looking up from his plate at Lorna who was by now giggling uncontrollably. Her shoulders jerked up and down in quick short spasms. He refrained from munching on the crustaceous foodstuff and said innocently.

"Did I do something wrong?"

She choked back her laughter long enough to enable herself to say.

"You're meant to peel the shell before eating them." What started out as a grin turned into unfeigned laughter at his own naivety.

"I'm not very sophisticated I'm afraid," he chirped.

"Don't worry about it" Lorna said, frankly finding his innocence somewhat enchanting.

The duck course went down famously with them both and when they embarked on the rice, chicken and vegetables Lorna was impressed at Ace's almost integrated handling of chop sticks, considering the fact that he had never before attempted to use them. Throughout the three courses they delighted in light hearted conversation. The waiter returned to their table duplicating his routine by taking the bottle of wine from the ice bucket and offering to fill Lorna's glass for her. She had declined the first time round, but declared now that she would join her companion in a celebration drink. When the waiter had replenished Ace's glass and moved away from the table, Lorna said.

"I spoke about you to my coach today."

"Oh?"

"He wants to see you."

"He does?"

"I told him that you're a brilliant player and that as far as I was concerned you had a great future in tennis, if someone out there should take an interest in you."

"Do you really think that Lorna?" he asked modestly.

"I believe it, do you? That's more important."

"You bet."

"Good, because my coach has no time for scepticism, he will want to establish how hungry you really are for success."

"I'm famished."

"That's what I like to hear, now here's to you Ace and to success." And they toasted to the future. Ace swallowed down some wine before announcing excitedly.

"I've just thought of something, my brother, Jack and me are going to London on the 11th, I think it might be a good idea to combine the appointments if you can arrange a time with your coach. The first engagement is at 11.30 in the morning, what do you think?"

"Fine, I'll let you know what he says."

"Fabulous ... but promise me one thing Lorna."

"Yes, what?"

"That you won't tell him about the prawns," Ace joked and they laughed once again at the expense of his little misdemeanour. When the jocularity abated Ace was first to speak.

"I've enjoyed this evening."

"Me too Ace."

"I'd like ... if you would like ..."

"To do this again sometime?"

"Yeah?"

"Yeah!"

Chapter Eleven

The Love of Glory

Birds navigating their way in and away from the grounds on the afternoon breeze, chirped and whistled joyfully, oblivious of the somewhat acrimonious atmosphere between Jean Paul and his father, who now between them employed an atonement of silence that they had sustained for the last five minutes.

"This is so infantile, I think that I will go and cool off in the pool," Jean Paul declared severing the reticence.

"Do that." was all King said, and Jean Paul left his father to his conjectures, collected a towel and a gown. After changing into his swimwear he made his way to the pool, where he wasted little time in disrobing and diving immediately into the invigorating water. With smooth easy strokes he glided, practically without effort through the swimming pool as if assisted by a steady current from one end to the other of its twenty odd metre length. With every flourishing surge of his vigorous arms, his long hair sleekly animated itself in compatible time with his body. Danielle Marie, his indulgent mother, on her arrival back to the house following her meeting with Hickman and Lawrence, observed him from half way down the stairway that led to the poolside, momentarily halting before making her way down the remaining steps to welcome him back to the roost. On reaching the tiled water's edge she called out his name twice before disrupting his uniformed flow.

"Mama." he hailed zealously before completing the last few strokes of his front crawl, using his propulsion to commission a smooth departure from the pool, allowing his hands to spring him onto the poolside in one complete athletic movement.

"Jean Paul, comment ca va?"

"Tres bien, merci." He wiped himself down briskly with the towel before stepping forward and into her welcoming arms.

"You look fantastic." Danielle said with wholehearted prevalent pride.

"Merci."

"And what about your hair, I don't believe how long it has grown."

"Peut-etre une peu feminine?"

"No, no my son." She said and gestured her hands out to him.

"Le sense artistique tres developpe."

"Merci Mama, but what about you ... how are you?"

"I'm fine thank you, Jean Paul."

He eyed her closely for a moment, concerned and rather unaccustomed to his mother looking somewhat jaded.

"You look a little tired, Mama."

"No, no," she assured him rendering some energy to enliven herself.

"I had a fitful night's sleep last night, excitement you know, awaiting your return is all ... I'm fine."

"Yeah." he said, not completely convinced.

"Yes really, and tomorrow we celebrate your birthday, I have made special preparations, this year will be a very special year for you."

"You think so?" he said, pleased with her keenness, as it brought back the familiar twinkle in her eye.

"Believe me Jean Paul, I sense that you will engage in great accomplishments that most people can only dream of."

"Alright, I can live with that." he said, breaking into a broad smile.

"Now you carry on with your swimming and I will get busy finding out the progress for your reception tomorrow evening."

"Mama, you didn't have to go to any trouble on my behalf, I have already celebrated my birthday once, after winning my latest tournament in the States."

"It is a pity, mon cheri, but you will just have to endure another party. This time with your dear Mama," she said drolly.

"Do we have to dress up?" Jean Paul enquired lightly. He was hoping not to hurt her feelings in any way, as on the rare occasions that the house was made open for festivities, Danielle Marie insisted that it was infinitely more entertaining when a theme was initiated. The most recent merrymaking that had taken place was on Jean Paul's farewell extravaganza, six months ago before he returned to the United States to work and focus on his game with the aid of his new American coach, Brad Holding. That particular evening, the subject matter was 'American dignitaries'. The guests arrived in various guises, there were two George Washington's, a couple of Marilyn Monroe's, Theodor Roosevelt was present, Abraham Lincoln was a popular participant, as was Clint Eastwood and May West. One particular contributor got it completely wrong by turning up as Charlie Chaplin, but Jean Paul had to confess that everybody looked resplendent in their assorted costumes and that his mother's theme evenings always made for a splendid time.

"It is compulsory, as you well know." Danielle pressed with an air of humour in her voice. "And tomorrow, thanks to your new found golden brown locks, you will fit the bill to perfection."

"Oh, why is that?"

"Because, mon cheri, the theme is to be French fashion and celebrated French people, to welcome you back to France, you can come as Louis XIV."

"Magnifique!"

"Oui .. but tell me Jean Paul, is your coach, Monsieur Holding, still flying out to join us?"

"Yes, tomorrow morning he will be arriving."

"Good, I have his measurements, I can supply him with a suitably lavish attire."

"He will not be coming alone." Jean Paul informed her.

"Oh?"

"I have invited a young lady along also ... she will be accompanying him, though she will be with me, you understand."

“Do you know her ... measurements?” she said with an astute grin.

Jean Paul spent the following afternoon preceding the eagerly anticipated social gathering practicing on court with his coach, Brad Holding, who although feeling a little tired after the flight insisted that his young scholar should polish up his serve and volley shots before a video camera. The two later viewed the recordings, discussing and analysing the three hour session, which was comparatively brief to Brad’s normal drilling. Holding concluded the afternoon’s guidance with his thesis for Jean Paul.

“Eighteen days from today, you have got the big ATP Satellite Tournament that will determine your computer points, and give us your World Ranking.” Holding instructed.

“In preparation for the Australian Open, no?”

“Yeah ... but let me tell ya, if you don’t kick ass in this one, you won’t be playing in Australia. The opposition is gonna be a damn sight tougher than you’ve been used to up to date, there’ll be quite a few players out there that are already in the World Rankings playing for a qualifying place in the Open ... so it’s gonna want your best shot ... do you feel up for it?”

“Never more so.” Jean Paul said confidently.

“Good ... now I can’t let you ease off the gas for one moment, so I want us on a silver bird and back in the US the day after tomorrow, so after tonight, no more parties, lots of rest and practise, practise, practise, savvy?”

“Oui ... I mean , yes.”

“I want you fully prepared for this one and I want you to be completely focused, so be absolutely ready for a ball breaking schedule leading up to the showdown.”

“OK.”

“No shortcuts.”

“No, but can we not take a day off tomorrow?”

“OK, I guess so but remember, second best ain’t good enough for me Jean Paul, I only coach winners.”

“There is only one part of my game that I will not accept, Brad.”

“And what’s that?”

“Losing.”

“Way to go,” Holding confirmed.

An hour prior to the arrival of the guests, Danielle Marie had made her way to Jean Paul’s room, where she knocked on the door and awaited a response from inside.

“Oui.” His voice called from within.

“It is me Jean Paul, I have come to see how you are coping with your costume.”

“Oui, entree Mama.” He summoned. Jean Paul was carefully arranging the silk woven cravat that was the final embellishment to his magnificent robes, satisfied, he then turned away from the large wall mirror and over towards his mother. She took satisfaction in her choice of apparel for him, which indeed toned in with his long hair.

“Tres bien, Jean Paul, magnifique.” she said with pride.

"Merci Mama."

"You are the Sun King re-incarnated."

"Louis XIV certainly had flamboyant flair Mama," he said and bowed courteously, on retaining an upright stance he gestured towards his mother and said,

"Look at you ... you look glorious Mama."

"I am glad that you think so, rather adventurous wouldn't you say?" she said with a beaming smile and rotating herself so as to exhibit the dress's full splendour, he grinned and said,

"I think, Mama that you may cause one or two seizures amongst the male guests tonight." He was pleased to see that the weariness in her eyes that caused him concern earlier had dwindled and been replaced by her usual lustre.

"I must agree ... it is rather provocative." She said, walking towards the mirror and eyeing the Marie Antoinette fashioned garment. The front of which was audaciously low cut, boldly exposing most of her well rounded bosom. She was pleased with her reflection and told herself that tonight she was going to put her anxieties to the back of her mind, this was Jean Paul's Birthday celebration and she was not going to let anything blight the evening's proceedings. She turned and smiled at Jean Paul, he in return smiled momentarily, then it was replaced almost as swiftly by a perturbed expression that Danielle responded to.

"Is there something on your mind Jean Paul?"

"No ... no it just ..."

"Just what?"

There was a short silence between them before Jean Paul looked at his mother in the eye and said.

"I am not a little boy anymore you know, as I have grown older, so too has my perception."

Danielle speculated momentarily that he might have discovered her problem with the bottle, although she thought that she had skillfully disguised her quandary whenever Jean Paul had been home. *'One day at a time'* her mind prompted.

"Jean Paul, today is your Birthday and I mean to make it a day to remember for all the right reasons, so take that frown off your face and smile, no?" She walked towards her son and stretched herself up to enable herself to kiss him on both cheeks. He smiled and said,

"Maybe the perceptive part of my nature is working a little overtime."

"You're quite right." She agreed. Although he was not assured. He had been rather concerned about his parent's relationship for some time, but convinced himself that this was not the right moment to challenge his mother for answers. He was able to analyse one of the reasons for the improvements in her spirits, through her closing disclosure on leaving the room.

"I'm afraid ... your father will be unable to attend your celebration .. he .. he's been called away on business. I'm sorry Jean Paul."

Once again Danielle Marie's theme night was an undisputed success amongst the many participants who, without inhibition graced the avant-garde gathering with appropriate colourful costumes. Half way through the evening

Jean Paul made a speech that was very well received. He thanked everyone for coming along to his celebration and could not resist informing the gathering of his progress in his chosen profession after one of the guests, hideously dressed and made up as Quasimodo prodded for an up to date report.

“As I am attired in the style of Louis XIV, then I should quote him.” He said. “The love of glory assuredly takes precedence over all others in my soul.” The guests clapped and cheered his riposte and Jean Paul rounded off his eloquent oration on a positive note.

“Believe me when I tell you, one day, not too far away, I will be the tennis world’s number one, trust me, I know it.”

The eight musicians employed for the evening expediently played an arrangement of Queen’s ‘We Are The Champions’ as the large double doors opened up to make way for Jean Paul’s Birthday present. Two men wheeled the magnificent machine into the centre of the marble floor. Jean Paul walked over and mounted it, then fired up the splendid Harley Davidson engine. He smiled gleefully, although his outfit did not synchronise with the motorcycle he looked at ease on it, his inborn dynamic charisma saw to that. Sonya, the girl who accompanied Jean Paul’s coach on the journey from the States climbed onto the pillion seat fully clad in Joan of Arc chainmail. He flicked the enormous bike into gear and eased it around the fat black cat sculpture, then out through the doors into the Monaco night for a test drive, the guests cheered the handsome couple on their way. He steered their ride along Boulevard Rainier III then down towards the port, out along the Avenue Princess Grace to the sporting club and back via the Casino. En route he pointed out several points of interest to Sonya, who was enjoying the sensation of the powerful engine vibrating between her lengthy legs as it cruised along the road. Jean Paul was delighted with his new toy to go with his collection. For a young man of eighteen years, he had an admirable assortment of play things, including a Porsche sports car and a powerful boat. Later this evening after the conclusion of the conviviality, he would be indulging, he hoped, in another favourite pastime. The bedding of the sexy young female accommodating the back seat of his Harley.

Floss ushered Sonya and Jean Paul up to the terrace on their return to the house, where the merrymaking was in full flow. Superbly presented food, which had been prepared by an eminent chef was on offer, along with an abundance of Don Perignon champagne.

“Jean Paul!” Danielle called out making her way towards him and Sonya. Walking alongside his mother was Jean Paul’s Grandfather who, appeared to have aged by twenty years. It was as if gravity had finally got its own way with his once robustly sound body. His cheeks were hollow and newly formed wrinkles were etched around vacant and lacklustre eyes.

“Grandfather ... you were late for the party!?” Jean Paul said lightly, camouflaging his dismay.

“Ask your Grandmother why this was, she took a week and a day to dress for tonight.”

“Well at least you are here, where is grandmother anyway?”

“I do not know, last time I saw her she was doing what she does best.”

"Talking?"

"Talking!"

"Have you two been having words Papa?" Danielle asked.

"No ... well I mean .."

"I will go and find Mama, it is not like you two to be away from each other's company, especially ..."

"Do not fuss Danielle!" The old man hissed, taking the small gathering by surprise. Danielle then excused herself and went in search of her mother. She finally found her at the farthest end of the terrace, sitting on her own, gazing out over the sea. Danielle pulled up a chair and sat down next to her.

"He ... your Papa, he never discusses anything with me anymore." Her mother began, her eyes remaining focused on the water glistening under the moonlight.

"I blame those new shipping contracts, whatever they are, or whoever they are with, ... and him, going back to sea at his age!?"

Danielle put a reassuring arm around her mother, who reciprocated by leaning a weary head on her daughter's shoulder, then continued to vent her dismay through a flood of tears.

Danielle wanted to tell her mother what she had learned only recently, but she knew that for now at least, she would have to bite her tongue. At this moment, a shot or two of vodka might ease her plight. *'One day at a time'* the voice within her prompted. She held her mother closer to her and it was the first time that the older woman had ever heard her daughter curse.

After disrobing from her costume, Sonya prepared herself for a soaking inside the sizeable tub in anticipation of a night of restful slumber. She angled her tall shapely body in an effort to test the temperature of the water. Satisfied, she turned off the flow at the tap, then turned towards the mirror above the sink where she tied her hair up with a band.

"What the hell are you doing here?" She asked her reflection. *'What did I expect to find out?'* her mind probed. A knock on the bedroom door paid to add to her exasperation.

"Yes?" She called out towards the locked door.

"Sonya, it's me, Jean Paul, open the door."

She quickly threw on a robe and made her way to the door, where she turned the key and pulled it ajar.

"I was about to take a soak." She said as politely as she could muster.

"May I come in?"

"Well I ..."

"I would like to talk."

"Talk?"

"Yes, talk." He pressed, employing his beguiling attributes to full advantage. She smiled and stood aside to grant his request.

"Shouldn't sports people like you be tucked up in bed at this time?"

"Is that an invitation?"

"No."

"Too bad."

“Because I accepted your kind invitation to join you here for a few days doesn’t ...”

“Do not take me so seriously!” He cut in wearing a wry smile, while adjusting his costume. “Did I not cut a dashing figure this evening?”

“Sure.”

“Well then!?”

“Jean Paul, it’s true that I would be the envy of thousands of young women right now, having the opportunity of spending time with the handsomest young man to hit the pro tennis circuit in decades!”

“Merci Mademoiselle, and so?”

“So ... I don’t want to be one of your conquests!”

“What are you telling me?”

“Jean Paul, I want to make one thing very clear here, I’m not looking for romance, I have got neither the time or the need for that sort of thing right now, and, I might add am by no means promiscuous.”

“But I have known you now for ...”

“Around about a year sure, so you think that gives you the right to flirt with me once more?”

“When did I last come on to you?”

“Jean Paul, you have been trying to get me in the sack ever since I met you!”

“This is true mon amour.” He said smoothly and manoeuvred towards her, then delicately untied her headband and her hair fell loosely down to her shoulders. She wanted to fight this, this was not what she came all this way for, and dear God she had her reasons to discourage his overtures. A flurry of excitement caused the base of her hair follicles to stand on end as he swept his fingers through her mane. She closed her eyes delighting in the sensation that his tactility carried. It was her animal attraction that was now taking control, her reasoning had by now already deserted her. If nothing else, she needed to vent her frustrations, to rid her, if only for a short time, of the guilt that she had stored on herself over the past four years. Their lips adjoined and although there was no affection transmitting from either party in this love match, sexual magnetism transmitted between them with an invigorating charge. Her fingers unfastened his ceremonious clothing with comparative calm, disguising their feverish urgency to explore. They were naked now, with bodies needing. Her hand navigated around his abdomen, going slowly down towards his rigid structure, her fingers teasing around his male, he groaned at her touch, her hand encased it now and she was staggered instantly at its proportions. Her final rational thought was that she sincerely hoped that she was not going to regret this night.

Chapter Twelve

The Appraisal

It was a crisp winter's morning, the sun shone down from a cloudless blue sky, adding to the excitement that Ace felt at the prospects that the day might have install for him. The two brothers had caught the 7 30 am train from Manchester Piccadilly Station. Once on board they headed directly to the restaurant car so as to enjoy the luxury of a full English breakfast, along with which afforded them first class accommodation for the two hours fourteen minutes journey. They were equipped with their schedules and instructions for the trip along with tennis clothing and rackets packed in a bag that would be put to use in the afternoon when Ace was to make contact with Lorna's full time professional coach. The thought caused his stomach to flutter to some degree. That was a healthy sign he assured himself. The train pulled into Euston Station, London four minutes later than scheduled at 10 15 am, allowing them an hour and fifteen minutes to travel the relatively short journey across the city using the Underground. As instructed, they took the Piccadilly line to South Kensington and from there it was a five minute walk to the first destination at 43 Frith Street,W1, arriving at the address with three quarters of an hour to spare. On the opposite side of the street from the office building, stood the famous Christie's Auctioneers, Jack joked that he might go over and take a look inside and see what he could afford to buy.

"How much money have you got on you Ace?" He quipped.

"Ten pounds."

"In that case, we'll leave Christie's for another day, we'll go and have a coffee instead, come on." He advised Ace and they entered the tiny Cafe Nero that was conveniently situated next door to the tall brick building which was to house their appointment. Jack sipped his hot coffee then placed the cup back in its saucer and looked at his brother who, since their arrival in South Kensington had become somewhat disconsolate.

"You OK bro?"

"Yeah ... yeah." Ace answered without conviction.

"You were miles away then."

"Was I? ... I'm just ... you know ...?"

"Apprehensive?"

"Yeah ... I guess, a little."

"Don't worry yourself Ace, like the letter said, it's in your best interests."

"Is it?"

"What do you mean?"

"I don't know ... it's just that, if this meeting is about my real parents ... well, I don't really think I want to know."

"Are you getting cold feet?"

"I guess so, can you understand that Jack?"

"Sure ... sure."

"You see, ... you, mum and dad ... you've been my whole life up to now, I've never known anything else."

"It doesn't mean that all that has to change Ace."

"No, I know that Jack, but if this is about my legitimate family ... well it just feels like an intrusion, because until now as far as I was concerned they didn't exist."

Jack observed Ace's troubled young face and wished that he could erase his anxiety.

"I can understand that." Was all he could think to say, though he remained mindful of the turmoil a possible reunion might hold, if it were not a positive one, accompanied by benevolence and understanding.

"After all's said and done." Ace continued, "They abandoned me outside a hospital, with nothing more than a note telling whoever found me my date of birth and very little else."

"We don't know what their circumstances were though Ace." Jack stressed in an attempt to be productive. There was a short silence between them, while Ace considered what his brother had pointed out.

"If the meeting this morning is about those people that left me in a doorway, then stuff them I say." He declared ardently.

"It's something that can never be put right, but ...I think we should look on the bright side of this."

"All I want to say" Ace said, "And don't think me soppy now ... whatever happens Jack ... you and my mum and dad ... well, I love you."

"We love you too, Ace."

Having made his assertion known to Jack, Ace allowed his frame of mind to alleviate and mellow, the two of them spent the remainder of the time in the cafe making conversation on a lighter context until the time came to leave and walk next door to the green painted door, where Jack pressed the button to number seven.

"Yes." A distorted voice said through the intercom speaker on the wall.

"Arthur Sharpe, I have an appointment for eleven thirty."

"Up the stairs, third floor." The stifled voice instructed, followed by a buzz, giving Jack the cue to push the door open. They walked through towards the staircase and started their ascent while the green door clicked shut behind them. At the turn for the final flight of steps, Ace and Jack stood to one side in an effort to make enough room on the narrow stairway for a youth to make his way down past them.

"You going to the third floor man?" The youth said to Ace.

"Yeah."

"Good luck man, they got more chance of finding Lord Lucan." The youth said and chortled loudly to himself.

The two brothers watched his descent before giving each other an inquisitive look, and continuing the rest of the way up. On reaching the third floor Jack knocked on the door that had a metal plaque with D. Lawrence engraved upon its surface. A voice from within the office bid them to enter.

"Good morning, so glad you could make it." The tall bespectacled man said, greeting them with a polished English inflection.

"Don Lawrence, how do you do, you must be ... Arthur Sharpe." He said looking down at some notes on the desk, before offering a hand along with his eye contact to Ace, who shook hands with the man. Jack noticed that his brother's face displayed none of the apprehensiveness that his features had given way to earlier on in the cafe and was relieved to bear witness to the fact.

"I'm Arthur's brother, Jack." He announced offering his hand.

Once the formalities were out of the way, the three men inside the modestly furnished office sat down in their respective chairs around the black ash desk.

"Now have you brought along with you the necessary documentation that I asked for in my letter?" Lawrence said from behind his desk. Ace returned his questions with a puzzled look.

"The verification of your blood group etc, Mr. Sharpe." Lawrence appended to his request.

"Oh, yeah, it's here." Ace said, bending down in his chair and unzipping a small pocket located on the side of his sports bag. He took out the certificate and handed it over the table to Lawrence, who scanned its text. His expression showed no emotion at the information it held. He thanked Ace then passed the endorsed papers back to the young man across the table from him.

"How old are you Mr. Sharpe?"

"Eighteen."

"And your birthdate is ...?"

"Sixth November."

"So are you Sagittarius then?"

"Scorpio."

"How tall are you?"

"Six foot two ... three, I ..."

"Have you ever been in any trouble?"

"What?"

"Broken the law?"

"No."

"Been arrested for any crimes?"

"Shit no, what is all this?" Ace said with an air of agitation. "Mr. Sharpe ... or may I call you Arthur?"

"Ace."

"Ace?"

"Yeah, Ace, everyone at home calls me Ace."

"Very well then ... Ace, it is necessary that you understand that I ascertain your identity for my clients."

"Oh ... and who are your clients?"

"I'm afraid that I am not at liberty to reveal that information at this time."

"OK .. then, what's this all about?"

"I am merely aiming to establish where your origins are."

"In Trafford North, Manchester along with my mother, father and brother here!" He said shifting in his chair.

"I take it then, that you do not wish to establish who your biological mother is?"

"No!" Ace said vehemently and he felt his blood beginning to boil, a part of him that had lay dormant for the most part of his life was now being activated, a panic set in and he was not sure that he could address himself to cope. He bent down, snatched up his sports bag and in one flourishing move, he was on his feet.

"Come on Jack, I've had it here." He said turning to his brother. Jack was tempted to combat his brother's imprudent behaviour but rejected the thought. He stood up and instead he said calmly.

"Look Bro ... has it occurred to you that ... maybe you are not the fellow that they are looking for?"

Ace deliberated to himself for a brief moment, then smiled and came to a conclusion. *'I will sit down, chill out and let this Lawrence dude do his stuff. Can't hurt me, won't let it.'* He persuaded himself and said lightly.

"Nothing ventured."

"Nothing gained." Jack agreed and they both returned to their seats and Lawrence summoned them both to order.

"Now gentlemen, can we get on?"

"Shoot." Ace corresponded, then added, "I'm sorry about my little outburst Mr. Lawrence, you will have to forgive me, but I don't think you know what all this is doing to my head."

"No Mr. Sharpe ... Ace, on the contrary, it's me that should make an apology. I'm afraid that I was rather undemonstrative in my questioning. You see, I have encountered a string of young claimants in the past few days and you are my penultimate candidate, and well ... quite frankly, I am rather fearful of not finding a successful conclusion for my clients." Lawrence said, and Ace was beginning to wonder if this guy with the Eton College accent was for real.

"I will attempt to be somewhat more discreet with my questioning." Lawrence went on.

"OK." Ace said simply and mused *'can't hurt me, won't let it.'*

"Now let me see ... Do you have any distinguishing marks?"

"Hmm?"

"Scars .. birthmarks?"

"I have this small scar here." Ace pointed at a small faded mark a quarter of an inch long just above his right eyebrow.

"And birthmarks?"

Ace smiled bashfully and said.

"Well, I've got a birthmark on my right cheek."

Lawrence squinted over his spectacles in an effort to discover a blemish on Ace's face that he was sure that he had not detected. Ace noticing the man's perplexed expression advised him.

"Not on my face ... on my backside."

"Oh, I see, right."

"Do you want to see it?"

"Er ... no, I don't think that will be necessary, I will take your word for it." Lawrence yielded, then leaned forward placing his elbows on the desk top and entwined the fingers on both hands before continuing.

"I have one or two questions more, some fairly personal, so I beg of you not to ..."

"It's OK Mr. Lawrence, I won't walk out, but do me a favour, make it brief." Ace said, although feeling reluctant, he had decided to succumb to any confidential queries that Lawrence might have, if only to get this irksome interview over with as swiftly as possible.

"Can't hurt."Ace assured Lawrence *'won't hurt'* his mind prompted.

"Very well ... who is the person that you trust most in your life Ace?"

"Jack ..." He said without hesitation, "My brother Jack."

"Good ... then it's good that he's here with you."

"You bet."

"Are you presently employed?"

"No."

"Do you have any savings?"

"No."

"Do you gamble?"

"Only on myself."

"Have you ever used drugs?"

"Never."

"Do you have any educational qualifications, GCSE's?"

"None – I didn't take any."

"Do you have an open relationship with your foster parents?"

"I don't regard my mother and father as foster parents, they are my parents, full stop."

"Quite ... but do you have? ..."

"Yes, we do have an open relationship."

"Then you will know where it was that you were .. abandoned, for want of a better word?"

"Withington ... shit ... Withington Hospital."

"And is this hospital in Manchester?"

"Yes."

"Do you have any hobbies, Ace?"

"Yeah, I play tennis and work out every day."

"And how good are you at tennis?"

"He's brilliant." Jack said with pride.

"Do you think that you are ... brilliant Ace?"

"Bet your Arse!"

"And what distinctions do you have in regard to this sport?"

"Well, ... I only joined a proper club last summer ,,, see I couldn't really afford ..."

"He became the club's champion, first time of asking." Jack endorsed with a flourish and continued, "Not only that, but he won the Cheshire Championship at the end of the season and to cap it all, he only lost one set in the whole tournament ... no-one could live with Ace, he was just too good. In fact, this afternoon, my brother is due to strut his stuff for a top professional tennis coach with a view to giving him a chance to turn pro ..." He enthused, and wanted to go on, but was confounded by Lawrence's words that interrupted his flow.

"Would financial backing aid your progress, if that is, you were good enough to become a professional tennis player?"

"Is rain wet?" Jack said avidly. Ace, on the other hand, sat silently eyeing the man opposite him with a little suspicion.

"Well, I think that that concludes our meeting for today, I will be in touch in due course." Lawrence said, standing up and offering out his right hand to the brothers, who each took turns shaking his hand with a stunned expression on their faces.

"Is that it?" Ace said.

"For now, yes."

As they were about to leave the office and close the door behind them Lawrence halted their progress by calling after them.

"Ace."

"Yeah."

"Don't forget your sports bag." He said. Ace smiled at his own stupidity and walked back to retrieve it.

Lawrence took out an envelope from the inside pocket of his jacket and offered it to Ace.

"You will be wanting this."

"What is it?"

"Your expenses, I'm sure you will find more than enough to cover your excursion."

He accepted the envelope from Lawrence and thanked him.

"Oh, one more question Ace."

"Yes?"

"If one of my clients happened to be your biological mother ..?"

"Yeah?"

"Would you agree to meet with her?"

"No, Mr. Lawrence, I wouldn't."

In the time it had taken them to reach the bottom of the stairs and open the green door, Don Lawrence had got through on the telephone.

"Mr. Hickman?"

"Yeah."

"Lawrence."

"Well?"

"I am fairly confident that we have our twin."

"Fairly confident?"

"He shares the same date of birth ... he is six foot two, three, he wasn't quite sure which."

"That doesn't ..."

"He was abandoned outside the Withington Hospital in Manchester, England."

"Go on."

"He shares the same rare blood group."

"Good ... but it's still not enough."

"He also has a birthmark, which with verification from Solly or his sister should confirm my assumption."

"And where is this distinguishing mark?"

"On his right buttock."

"That's enough to go on for now."

"Of course, a DNA examination would confirm my theory beyond doubt."

"OK, so far so good."

"There was one negative thing that our exploratory interview uncovered."

"Oh?"

"He was rather adamant that he did not wish to meet his biological mother."

"I see."

"Oh ... just one more thing, I would like a further installment to my fee, preferably in US Dollars, the Dollar looks rather strong at the moment."

"Sure, but don't forget I want to know more about this guy ... by the way, what does he call himself?"

"Arthur, Arthur Sharpe ... but known to his friends as Ace."

"OK, I want you to let me know what this ... Ace is about."

"Right you are."

"Your Dollars will be with you by tomorrow, lunchtime at the latest." Hickman placed the receiver back in its cradle, satisfied with the progress to date. Although Lawrence had not come cheap, he thought him proficient enough for the task. The money that he would receive in payment for his employment as an investigator would come from a small proportion of Hickman's illegitimate funds compiled from the years in trafficking narcotics for King and the Boss, whoever he was? Now, he was contented to be out of the slimy grip of those loathsome men. He reassured himself that he had paid his dues and was now gladly reformed. Sure, the money that he had hidden away had paid for his modest villa in Los Pinos, along the coast from Calla Millor on the beautiful holiday island of Mallorca, from where he resided now, and he had plenty left over for his plans, but he refused to allow any feelings of guilt.

Hickman had left Monaco immediately following the meeting at the Hotel de Paris, fearful that King might discover his new found liberty by way of somebody, somewhere in the Principality recognising him and informing his adversary. To contest this probability, he had taken no chances by wearing two contrasting disguises on entering and leaving the hotel on both rendezvous with King's wife.

He looked out now through the window of the small villa, surveying the concentration of sturdy pine trees that serve to augment the deep forest carpet and contemplated how Madame Danielle might take the news that they had a very possible candidate, who wanted without reservation to remain alienated from her. *'You're jumping the gun'* he told himself, *'this guy Ace, might be a goddamn phoney'* either way, he would find out very soon.

Chapter Thirteen

Marbella, Southern Spain

Whenever the 'Bella Christina' arrived at the Puerto Banus she berthed in her customary mooring alongside an assemblage of other impressive vessels that illustrated their owners' abundant wealth. Magnificent though the rest of the yachts were, only one other craft at the quayside was comparable in dimensions to Agnazzio Bennetti's Bella Christina, and that apparently belonged to a multi-millionaire arms dealer. Bennetti had not skimped on extras when he had acquired the yacht. On the top deck, a helicopter pad accommodated a small two seater chopper. The interior of the vessel was designed and furnished by a leading Italian designer, and the Captain and adequately manned crew were handpicked by Bennetti himself. The only parts of the yacht out of bounds to all crew members, including the Captain, were the Overlord's bedroom (except by special engendered circumstances ordered by himself) and Bennetti's own personal galley, where his sister prepared and cooked food exclusively for him. Apart from his four highly paid special personal bodyguards, Bennetti was the only person on board that was armed with a gun, which he kept strategically placed by his bed. Everybody without exception coming aboard 'Bella Christina' was frisked thoroughly by the bodyguards before embarkation. Basically Bennetti left nothing to chance. He sat on the aft deck now and drained the remains of a glass of fresh orange juice and looked out over the array of chic restaurants and shops that stretched adjacent to the roadway along the quayside, several of the businesses presently making preparations for another day's trading beneath a clear blue sky.

Bennetti confirmed the time by his watch. Irwin King would be embarking within the hour. The Overlord's face gave way to a twisted smile at the conception of their first contrived encounter. How apprehensive the tall South African was at Bennetti's terms for an official offer to an emplacement into an eminent post within the organisation, and the way in which the sweat broke out on his upper lip at the Overlord's final proposition, which would be an initiation exercise that would grant the greedy son of a bitch such an expedient position. 'A man will do anything, and I mean anything for money' he had persuaded King, and his words were justified, for King had relinquished to the Overlord's desires, allowing himself to be physically touched and excavated, authorising his heterosexual mind, body and soul to be devalued, though be it only on that one day in Beleze. Bennetti never again propositioned him, nor was the event ever mentioned. He was under no delusions about King, indeed he despised the man, but what was rather more off-putting for Agnazzio Bennetti was that apart from their sexual preferences, King reminded him of someone whom he regarded greatly; himself. His sister fragmented his thoughts momentarily.

"Excusi Agnazzio," she said.

"Si, Margarita?"

"For lunch I prepare for you and Signor King fresh pasta calamari .. si?"

"Si ... bene, good."

"Then I bring to the table Scalopina, to your liking."

"Si, Margarita Gracie."

"Vino? Would you like me to bring wine to the table?"

"Si, Barolo ... yes, Barolo will do."

"Gracie, Agnazzio."

"Gracie, ciao bella," he said, and watched her making her way purposefully towards the galley. He called her 'bella' despite the fact that Margarita was always looked upon as somewhat dour and unfortunately for her, rather plain looking in comparison to the rest of the Bennetti family.

Regardless that his ugly duckling sister was often taunted by their father, two brothers and two other sisters relating to her unattractive bearing, Agnazzio had always been close to Margarita, his senior by two years. Within the family group it was always her that he would confide in during his formative years about his problems, worries and incredible aspirations, always satisfied that no matter what, he could depend on her confidentiality and loyalty, in addition to this even as a young boy, she never mocked his fantastic notions of one day being a millionaire. He would often act out this fantasy by giving out his orders to an imaginary army of protagonists before his approving sister, who on identifying his unmistakable megalomania, did nothing to discourage it. Although she was somewhat concerned at the young Agnazzio's cruelty towards dumb animals. She once disciplined the then nine year old, when, by chance she witnessed the delight he showed in his cherubic face while at the same time employing a garden spade to bludgeon a small dog into a state of unconsciousness. His reason for such a merciless act was that the animal merely barked at him and, when it did not stop, as he had commanded, he took what was in his mind to be the appropriate action. When Agnazzio was in his fifteenth year it was his sister to whom he turned for guidance, for since the advent of puberty he had surrendered slowly to the reality of his homosexual inclinations, but his tortured mind had not allowed him until then to utter a word to anyone, fearful that any person attaining this knowledge might consider Agnazzio Bennetti to be a weakling. Margarita had been extremely supportive and had assured him that 'this little setback would by no means stand in the way of his ambitions, indeed it might well serve to make him a stronger person.' His father's reaction to this revelation a year later was to say the very least rather to the contrary.

"You bring shame to this house." He had stormed, "You evil, weak, no good."

"But Papa." The sixteen year old Agnazzio pleaded.

"I want never for you to again call me Papa. How can I walk with my head high when a son of Bennetti wants to be a woman?"

"I did not choose to be the way I am."

"No ... you did not choose ... the devil chooses you for his son, so you go to him now." His father blasted, while Agnazzio's mother, Christina endeavoured, without success to alleviate her husband's anger. Margarita amplified her contentions from a corner of the kitchen where the squabble was taking place.

"Papa, your discrimination is disgraceful."

"You too .. you too can go, leave this house now and never darken my door again."

"Nooo!" Agnazzio's mother screamed as she walked towards her raging husband, who pushed her indelicately aside and declared.

"Anyone who advocates filth like him."

"But for God's sake, he is your son." Agnazzio's mother shrieked.

"No, no longer is that thing there anything more than an animal!"

Agnazzio's mother's anguished face looked over towards her son, woeful tears shed down her cheeks, she was powerless against her husband's intolerance and from that moment on she would grieve the loss of two of her children from the family home. The last thing that Agnazzio Bennetti remembered from that fateful day as he and Margarita walked out through the back door for the last time, was the smell of his mother's cooking on the stove.

Before leaving Malaga Airport for Marbella, King made a call from a payphone, cursing the fact that the batteries inside his mobile were flat. He would not normally dream of making a 'business call' in such an impractical place, but it was necessary to do so. His two personal minders stood vigilantly a few metres away with their backs turned to their employer, near enough to him to create a small cordon to avert the prospect of any unwelcome eavesdropping while at the same time they scrutinised the large busy terminal building. To the two men King's words were indistinct beneath the hubbub surrounding them.

"Was the delivery good?" King was saying into the handset.

"Best canned fish that I've ever come across." The voice said at the other end of the line.

"Good ... now I want you to put the money, in stacks of fifty pounds sterling, along with the measure of ice as agreed, in a holdall in the safe deposit box at Euston Station .. you have the necessary details!?"

"Yes, as agreed."

"Good, then that's all that needs to be said for now, so I'll bid you goodbye.."

"Just one thing before you go ..."

"Yeah?"

"Who was the old sea dog?"

"Sea dog?"

"Yes ... the Captain on the cargo vessel?"

"Why?"

"He seemed a little out of his depth, you know?"

"Did he make delivery on time as agreed?"

"Yes ... but.."

"Then there's no more to be said." King cut in. "It's been a pleasure doing business with you." He placed the receiver back into its cradle. His face showed no emotion as he turned around and ordered the two men accompanying him to escort him to their taxi. Inside King's ego had been fed to bursting point, he was euphoric, for unbeknown by the Overlord, he had managed to sneak the deal through without a hitch. His money was safe and it was all due to his own canny planning. The surplus of white and brown powders that he had accumulated over the past five years, due to shrewd appropriation had just embellished him with a fortune of his own, devoid from Bennetti and his empire. On the taxi journey he decided what he was going to do with his windfall, with that concept his face gave way to a broad smile. The cab pulled up at the entrance to the port and King paid the fare. The harbour's moorings were systematically regulated into several categories of status. The most eminent crafts were secured to the right. King and his two strong-armed aides did not turn left, they strolled along the walkway and admired the lavish assortment of impressive ocean going yachts, until they drew up alongside the 'Bella Christina'. He smiled up at its ostentatious presence, then gestured to an armed guard on deck to lower the gang plank.

"I'm expected." King announced. The guard spoke into a walky-talky and was almost immediately joined by another equally thickset sentry who looked over the rail towards King and his assistants before approving for the narrow bridge to be lowered onto the quayside.

"Climb aboard." One of the guards instructed, then added. "On your own."

The instant that King stepped on board the boat, the two uniformed men went about their routine procedure, running their hands over the reluctant recipient. They were extremely thorough and once they were satisfied that King was unarmed one of the guards asked him to follow him, while the other sentry walked behind King and they made their way up towards the aft deck. On King's entrance the Overlord remained in his seat.

"Ciao, Irwin, come sta?"

"Bene Gracie, Signor Bennetti."

"Bene ... good, I am happy for you." Bennetti said in his usual comradely tone, though as ever underneath the bronzed face, it was impossible to know what he was thinking. He was garbed in a light baggy suit, designed to be worn by a younger man, though the Italian carried the contemporary accoutrements admirably. He gestured a hand towards the comfortable seat opposite him. He then picked up and rang one of the two bells that were appointed on the table top, a few moments later Bennetti's sister approached the two men seated on the aft deck.

"Si Agnazzio?"

"Signor King will be wanting a drink after his journey, I will have a Martini Dry." He instructed.

"Si ... and for you Signor King?"

"Martini sounds just fine."

"I am happy Irwin that you were able to join me aboard."

"I'm happy to be here Signor Bennetti." King lied.

"Bene ... good, then you will not mind that I have had your two strong-arm boys sent away, no? They will be no use to you on board Bella Christina."

"I see." King said, though not entirely sure that he approved, his facial expression hid his displeasure.

“We have much to talk about.” Bennetti informed him and reached for the other of the two bells which he had used to summon his sister’s service. This bell peeled out a different pitch. A silence between the two followed momentarily. Bennetti smiled benignly, while through the large glass sliding doors from the luxuriant lounge area appeared a young Asian boy, *‘no older than fifteen’* King speculated. Bennetti stood up from his chair and held out an immaculately manicured hand towards the approaching young male. Revulsion gripped King’s insides as in turn the boy placed his adolescent hand in the Overlord’s.

“This is Shambu ... Shambu, say hello to Mr. King.”

“Hello Mr. King.”

Bennetti then kissed Shambu on the forehead and turned to King.

“Shambu here is a perquisite ... a little bonus that Agnazzio Bennetti allows himself to steal from his merchandise .. capiche?”

King’s guts felt as if they had been suddenly twisted inside out. *‘Could Bennetti have found out somehow about his own little deception?’* he brooded, though his facial muscles held well to camouflage his thoughts that panicked, in preparation for any investigative misgivings that the Overlord may extend. The Italian’s eyes continued their hold on his, then the man’s lips curled upwards into a thin smile.

“Just a little reminder for you, of the rules.” He said, then the grin departed swiftly from his face, replaced by a scowl. “If you ever try to fuck Agnazzio Bennetti about Irwin!, you know the consequences, no?” He rasped and drove a fist hard down on the table top.

“I know the rules Signor Bennetti.” King answered evenly, though his heart was pounding inside his ribcage.

“Bene ... good, I am happy for you.”

“I have nothing to hide from you.”

“For your sake I hope not.”

“I should try to trick you Signor Bennetti, ... come on, what do you take me for, a bloody fool?” He said drolly.

The Overlord sat across the table and said nothing in response, which unnerved King, his palms were beginning to moisten. *‘He knows nothing’* his mind reasoned, and the few moments prior to the Italian re-establishing conversation felt like an eternity to him.

“After we have eaten, we leave for Morocco.” Bennetti announced finally.

“Morocco?” King said, concealing his disenchantment at having to make the trip, throughout the duration of which, he knew that he would have to be on his toes, remaining at all times aware of the Italian’s shrewd and inquisitive nature. Soon though, he assured himself, he would be free from the Overlord’s clutches forever.

Chapter Fourteen

The Talisman

Jean Paul polished off the remains of a substantial breakfast on the terrace in the company of Sonya and Brad Holding. He had satisfied a ravenous appetite, devouring the varied flavours of fresh bread, cheese, cold meats and fresh fruit. He then displayed his satisfaction with an ear-piercing belch, which did not exactly cohere with the beautiful morning that had greeted the Port de Fontville Harbour. Under a blue heaven, the sea danced a sparkling rhythm beneath the radiant sunshine. Jean Paul adjusted his sunglasses with an index finger.

"I think that later on I will take the boat out, the weather is warm for the time of year, is anyone in the mood for water-skiing?" He enquired.

"Sounds like fun." Holding responded, "But I'll take a rain check on that one, I've got some phone calls to make, guess I'll just laze by the pool and make them from there." He winked an eye in Sonya's direction, she smiled and said enthusiastically.

"Count me in, I need the exercise."

Jean Paul looked towards her with a surprised expression. *'After last night?'* He reflected, but said nothing. She sipped her coffee in a refined manner. Her shoulder length hair was slicked back after her early morning swim. He viewed her somewhat differently following their night of tireless passion, he was confident that the young woman that his beholden eyes studied now was more beguiling than any man could perceive. His mouth watered in delicious recollection of the ripened texture and flavour of her pert nipples now poking out provocatively through the cream silk robe. She was aware of his observations, and turned her head slowly to face him, they exchanged a smile. She then climbed out of her chair and ambled gracefully towards the edge of the balcony. He scrutinised the curvature of her buttocks through the luminous garment. Yes, he had made up his mind. She was just three years his senior, possessing a mature mentality, she was elegant and simply fantastic in the sack. Yes, he had decided that once he was back in the States, he would terminate any likelihood of consolidating a relationship with her. *'No doubt about it, it would be a good career move to breach the affair, sooner rather than later, we still have today though'* he mused and with that rather fickle notion, he became aware of his member swelling under his robe.

Danielle Marie had risen early following the soiree the night before. While she ate a light breakfast of croissants and coffee on the terrace, she played spectator to her son's American friend, Sonya, who swam industriously up and down the pool unaware of Danielle's gaze. *'There was no wonder that the*

American girl was reputedly in such demand on the International Catwalks', Danielle acknowledged to herself, while observing her admirable outline coast silkily through the water. *'Although beautiful the young woman maybe, she is not nearly good enough for Jean Paul'* Danielle shuddered slightly, rebuking her thoughts. *'Was she envious of Sonya's youth? or somewhat more disquieting, jealous of the girl's relationship with her son?'* She rebelled against these notions and cast her eyes away from the pool, allowing them to accommodate the horizon for a moment. *'I will have to learn to let go.'* she reflected *'just as you did eighteen years ago''* a dark voice inside her head taunted. She licked her lips and closed her eyes, *'one day at a time.'*

Before leaving the house she asked Floss to inform her son to make arrangements for himself and his guests today and that she would see him sometime this afternoon. On reaching Avenue Des Beaux-arts, she backed her Mercedes sports car into a parking spot outside the Piaget Jewellers Shop. Today was the day that she would be talking to Hickman by telephone. She looked at her wristwatch, which informed her that she had half an hour to kill, she would appreciate that time to collect her thoughts and prepare herself for whatever news the American had gathered. She opened the door and climbed out of the car walking the few steps on the narrow pavement towards the Jewellers Shop. Some of the cheapest trinkets behind the glass would give a person very little change from a thousand dollars. It was the Gemini Twins beautifully engraved on a platinum disc that first caught her eye. Next to it was a similar item with a scorpion etched into it in a cluster of small diamonds.

The Harley sprang into life the instant the start button was pressed. The engine produced a low vibrant sound that belied the powerful ferocity concentrated within the metal framework, secured by the safety stand and with the gears engaged in neutral, Jean Paul revved back the throttle and tilted his head to one side, like a dog being told that there was a treat coming its way. He then turned to Sonya, who was standing a few metres away observing the young man's furore over his new plaything.

"She makes beautiful sound this machine, no?" He said zealously.

"Purrs like a big contented cat." She conceded with a smile.

"Come, get on the back, we will go now to my boat."

"No."

"What?"

"Let me have a go." She summoned.

"What do you mean?"

"I mean, let me ride the beast."

"Am I hearing you right ... you want to ride this?"

"Sure, why not?"

"But ..."

"But what?"

"But you are a girl and .."

"Don't give me that continental, sexist, macho crap, take some time out why don't you." She said firmly and loudly though without malice and in addition so that this time she could be heard clearly above the noise of the throbbing engine. He looked back at her with a slightly bewildered expression.

"Can you drive a motorcycle?"

"Sure, what is this .. the middle ages?"

"I mean, can you drive a bike like this?"

"Hell, I used to ride my brother's all the time back in Florida."

"Very well then, it is your arse." He said climbing off the enormous motorcycle then gesturing towards the front seat and the bike's controls. *'Serve her right if she breaks her pretty neck'* he mused and looked on disdainfully. Sonya's long shapely legs straddled the bike and with her feet firmly in place, she dexterously pushed the machine forward off its stand then held it in place with its centre of gravity. Revving the engine twice she now looked over towards the owner and smiled.

"OK, let's go!" She said.

"No .. no, merci, you go ahead, come back after your joyride, no?"

"Don't be so half assed, climb on for Pete's sake."

He walked forward and reluctantly climbed onto the pillion, instantly regretting the references his mind had made regarding her pretty neck.

"If we fall off this thing, it could be the end of my career, I hope that you are aware of this?!" He said over her shoulder, unable to disguise his nervousness.

"Don't worry, we ain't gonna fall off, and anyway I got a career also, do you think I'm gonna risk that, come on relax." Sonya assured him, with that she put the Harley into gear and they moved off slowly along the drive, allowing time for the guard to open one of the large gates and stand aside to give them access to the Boulevard du Jardin, whereupon she turned her head to ensure that she could be heard clearly.

"Have you got a spare pair of pants on board the boat?" She enquired. Before he could analyse what she had implied, Sonya opened up the gas, accelerating to what struck her travelling companion to be break-neck speed, once again he repressed his earlier notion. The short space of time that it took them to reach the Port de Monaco, which was under two and half minutes, felt like an eternity to the pillion rider, for if there was one thing that he certainly had an aversion to, it was not being in control and although Sonya was obviously a proficient rider, on coming to a halt at the quayside Jean Paul was nothing short of livid. He propelled himself off the seat as if it was ablaze and proceeded to launch into a string of explicit text in his native language before reverting back to English.

"You stupid bitch." He screamed out venomously. "What do you try to do ... Jesus, you are a crazy woman."

Sonya laughed openly at his petulance, and took the keys out of the ignition, then dismounted the machine.

"Calm yourself .. here!" She said then tossed the keys over to him. He caught them and ignoring her advice, persisted.

"If your face was ugly, then I would break it." He chided.

"Hey, take it easy you'll bust a gut!"

"You know what it is I'm saying, you take such a risk driving like .. like.."

"A crazy woman?" She offered.

"You! You fool, your face, your body is your living, you could have ended up looking like a piece of raw meat, and me, I am a professional sportsman and a ..."

"A bad tempered son of a bitch." She cut in.

"You take that back, my mother is not a bitch." He screamed.

"No .. but I am eh?" Sonya countered, Jean Paul stamped his foot hard on the ground.

"Never again, I tell you, that was the last time you ride my bike."

"Gonna take your ball home?" She taunted, maintaining a grin that matched the size of his temper.

Sonya had also been quite amused the first time that she had witnessed this personal shortcoming in his make-up. That was during a satellite tournament in the USA some six months before. There, he had been warned twice for his 'unsportsman-like behaviour' by the umpire, whom it was obvious to the crowd of spectators was losing his authority over the impetuous young Frenchman. Then, finally after breaking another racket for the second time in the match and yet another tantrum following a line call, the official called for the tournament referee, who, after being verbally abused, did no more than disqualify him from the competition, provoking a mixed reaction from the assembly of onlookers, the younger section amongst which, Sonya was incorporated, chortled at Jean Paul's outburst, while in stark contrast, the more senior observers frowned and hissed their disapproval. As a result of this episode of high drama, Sonya was later informed at a party for celebrities and VIPs at the event, that Jean Paul's coach had *'washed his hands of him'*. Many of the sports pundits and ex-professionals present at the function, unreservedly had denounced his behaviour. Others, that is, the minority, including Brad Holding, concluded that it was merely his adolescence to blame. Brad Holding was, and still is, a man that does not allow grass to grow under his feet, and on learning of the young Frenchman's coach's apparent abandonment of the would-be star, had not hesitated in scheming a way of attracting Jean Paul to his nest.

Danielle entered the phone booth and with a forefinger punched out the digits that she had committed to memory, then held the receiver tight to her ear awaiting an answer at the other end of the line. Her eyes wandered over the picturesque Port de Monaco, digesting little of its characteristics, for her concentration at that moment was being guided by one contrite conclusion, *'what can I possibly offer this boy if he were to be found? A woebegone offspring, purportedly my own, what could I nominate in return for the unprecedented neglect that I have no doubt in his eyes shown towards him?'*

"Yeah?" The voice peeled through the receiver into her ear, producing a slight jolt from the caller, she instantly summoned up her composure.

"Monsieur Hickman?"

"Who's asking?" The voice said evenly.

"Danielle Marie King."

"Ah .. Madame Danielle." He said with a much more affable bearing, "How are you?"

"I am well, thank you."

"I am pleased to hear that."

"Do you have any news Monsieur?"

"Well, not ten minutes ago our man in London called me on the phone to say he thinks we might have a guy that resembles our requirements."

"Requirements?"

"Sure, there's a lot to be done yet before we can be sure, let's put it this way, out of the sizeable group of orphans and beached assed kids born around the date and year in question, there was one guy that for a laying of the foundations fits the bill."

"And what are these foundations?"

"Like I say, it's a shot in the dark at the moment, but this guy has the self-same rare blood group as your son, and husband running through his veins."

A B Negative?"

A B Negative!"

"You understand Monsieur Hickman, that this is not nearly enough."

"I know, but it's a start."

"Monsieur, I need consummate proof."

"Rest assured Madame Danielle, we ain't just finished there. Why, as we speak, Lawrence is digging for verification on several other factors, and in the meantime, I want you Madame, to verify a few naked truths."

"Oh?"

"I think, that the time has come now for you to ... for want of a better word ... question your housekeeper about one or two things."

"I see, I am glad at last that I once again can resume a genuine standing with Floss."

"She might well be the component that we need for success, yeah?"

"Yes."

"OK .. here are some questions that I think you should ask to be going on with, all right? .. first, did the baby .. she'll know this because she'll have changed a few diapers on the journey .. did the kid have a birth mark, if so, where?"

"Yes .. so where?"

"As I say, that's for you to find out."

"Very well."

"We need to ascertain where exactly the boy was abandoned."

"Monsieur Hickman ... how optimistic are you?"

"We've got a way to go yet as I'm sure you understand."

"About sixty-forty against?" She enquired, while being conscious that she dearly hoped that Hickman would cut those odds, and he did.

"More like fifty-fifty, but those odds are changing all the time. We are obviously dependant on circumstantial evidence, and of course if things tally with Floss's account of events then we will be getting closer to completing the daisy chain. I guess the final link needed then to finish the job for sure would be a DNA examination, although at the moment this young fellow is playing hard to get."

"What do you mean .. hard to get?"

“Well, he made it positively clear to our Mr. Lawrence that he in no way wanted to be re-united with his legitimate guardians.” Hickman affirmed, and there was a brief lull in the conversation. *‘What did I expect? That I would be organising a welcome home party?’* Danielle mulled to herself.

“Hello ... are you still there Madame?”

“Yes, yes I am sorry Monsieur.”

“I guess from all accounts that the young guy’s happy with his lot, yeah?”

“Yes .. I can understand.”

“Now, here’s something that you might find interesting, this kid’s an ambitious sportsman ... must be something in the genes, wouldn’t you say?”

“Let us hope that you are right.”

“Then again it could simply be pure coincidence.”

“What?”

“He wants to be a tennis pro.” He said with a hint of scepticism in his tone.

“A tennis pro ... and is he good enough?”

“Hell I don’t know, but I’m pretty sure that in time we’ll find out.”

“If .. if he is talented enough then .. well, then no doubt I can help him along that way no?”

“Sure, I guess ..”

“Financially, I mean.” Danielle enthused.

“Yeah sure.” Hickman advocated with a laugh, “But don’t let’s run before we can walk here’s all I’m saying. Like I say, we got a way to go, seems to me you really want this?”

“It must be my maternal instincts, call it what you will, that is driving me now ... but yes Monsieur I do hope that your assumptions are correct.”

“Good, I’m sure glad that’s the case, it kinda makes the whole darn thing worthwhile.”

“In the meantime Monsieur, I have procured a small talisman that ... I would like for you to give to ..”

“Arthur.”

“Pardon Monsieur?”

“Arthur ... that’s the guy’s name, or Ace for short, that’s the nickname his stepbrother gave him.”

“Ace?” She grinned, “This is an excellent name for a tennis pro, no?”

“Right on the line.” He endorsed with a laugh, “I take it that you want Lawrence to deliver this talisman, even though at this time we don’t as you put it .. have consummate proof of Ace’s true origin?”

“I know that it is rather impulsive of me, but yes ... I would like for this boy, Ace to have it, I hope that it will bring him good fortune, I have acquired one also for Jean Paul with much sentiment in mind.”

“I sure hope the kid appreciates such a generous gesture.”

“I would like to look upon it as a pledge of optimism or should I say gesture of goodwill, no?”

“I’ll go along with that.” Hickman concurred.

Danielle turned herself around in the small booth; her eyes scanned across the harbour and came to rest on two familiar figures climbing aboard the sunseeker mystique speed boat. Although the couple were some fifty metres or so away from where Danielle was standing, she could see from Jean Paul's animated gestures that he was rather displeased about something. Sonya, his American friend appeared to be somewhat amused at her son's frivolous conduct.

"Hello .. hello Madame Danielle?"

"Yes .. I am sorry Monsieur, I have just caught sight of my son .. Jean Paul. Call me paranoid if you will, but for one horrible moment I thought that I had been followed here."

"Has he seen you?"

"No .. but if he had, then I think that he would find it rather strange to say the least, discovering his mother making a phone call from a public telephone in the middle of the Port de Monaco, when he knows very well that I have a mobile that I carry everywhere with me, not to mention a car phone and eight fully functioning handsets in my home."

"I guess you'd have to tell him you had a lover in tow." Hickman chuckled.

"As if things are not complicated enough Monsieur."

"We will resume seven days from today, till then, take care Madame." He confirmed.

"Same time?"

"Yeah."

"Goodbye." She said and placed the handset in its cradle keeping herself hidden long enough to hear the boat start up.

The powerful twin 550 hp caterpillar engines pulsated with a low steady drone as the sleekly designed craft cruised slowly away from the marina and out into the bay. Once out of the speed restriction zone, Jean Paul opened the engines up, taking them to a speed of thirty knots. At a mile or so out at sea he slowed the boat right down to a steady rate, climbed out of the seat at the cockpit and gestured Sonya to follow him down the stairwell towards the aft of the boat and through a wide sliding door to the accommodation below, where he took up a position at the interior helm on the starboard side of the forward end. Sonya demonstrated her approval of the small, though luxurious quarters. The modification were superbly finished in American cherry joinery, the plush seating was in sumptuous leather.

"You like my boat?" Jean Paul said turning around in the large chair at the helm.

"Beats sailing on a raft I guess." She smiled. Jean Paul opened a cupboard at the side of the console and pulled out a small container, he looked up at her and grinned while he opened it up and took out a package from within the receptacle. He then poured out some of its contents, making a thin powdery white line on the galley top to his left.

"What are you doing?" Sonya frowned.

"Today, we are going to have fun." He declared while rolling up a banknote in his fingers.

"What is that stuff?"

"Trust me, this stuff as you call it, is the best that money can buy."

"Speed ... is that speed you got there?"

“Trust me.” He said and pressed a forefinger against one side of his nose, he then leaned down over the white powder and snorted hard through the rolled up banknote, using it like a straw to inhale the substance into his open nostril. He repeated the procedure with the other nostril before looking back up at Sonya.

“Want some?” He said, blinking in an effort to quell his tear ducts from spilling over.

“Are you crazy?”

“Trust me, today we will have fun.”

Chapter Fifteen

The Big City

Ace and Jack walked down the London street at a comparative snails' pace to that of its citizens, each and every individual singly making a statement with their mode of dress and body language. Every facial expression a mask, shrouding in a network of intricate personal thoughts, all hastily making their way hot-foot to who knows where and each accustomed to the incessant vibrations of petrol and diesel engines that pervade the air. Underneath this bustle and clamour that is the heartbeat of the capital there was a positive magic. This was Ace's first visit to the big city and he caressed the wave of euphoria that it lavished upon him, until that is, the brothers reached the entrance to the tube station, where Ace came to a halt alongside a man sitting on the cold stone floor holding a placard between two soiled hands. Scrawled in black ink, it shouted noiselessly out to the apathetic commuters; "Jobless, penniless and homeless." The man's face was unshaven and sullied, the bags beneath his wretched eyes were testimony to many nights without decent sleep. A thought passed momentarily through Ace's mind, *'I wonder what he dreams about, and in those dreams, when he sleeps, is there room for hope?'* He looked into the man's despairing eyes and he fought to hold contact with them, as an unnerving feeling of guilt stabbed into his conscience for the injustice that befalls some unfortunates in modern society. The tramp's body jerked in accord with a thick raucous cough that echoed around the passageway. Ace guessed that the man was probably in his mid-forties or maybe even older considering the wisps of grey wiry hair that fell down onto his shoulders beneath his woolen hat.

"What are you doing bro?" Jack said, tugging at Ace's jacket.

"Wait."

"What?"

"Hang on a second." Ace said and pulled out of his pocket the screwed up ten pound note and pressed it into one of the man's grubby hands. The tramp looked down and blinked in disbelief at the gift that the tall good looking black kid had given him. His voice was hoarse when he finally spoke through cracked lips.

"Thank you kindly young sir, may God go with you."

"I think you need that ten quid and God a lot more than I do mate." Ace told him.

"Do yourself a favour, use it wisely, get some good grub inside you." Jack added.

"How old are you?" Ace asked the tramp.

"Who wants to know?"

Ace shrugged his shoulders and turned to walk away. The tramp's voice resounded around the tile walls.

"Twenty seven." His gravely words informed Ace, "And good luck to you my friend."

Ace turned and waved farewell to the man, who, no doubt, he would never happen on again. *'Twenty seven, did he say?'* he reflected, not quite believing his own ears.

"That was a rather benevolent act bro." Jack declared and shook his head, "He'll probably go out now and piss the lot up the wall."

"It's his money now to do what he thinks best. Besides, we've got this." Ace responded, waving in the air the envelope that Lawrence had given him, not fifteen minutes earlier.

"Two crisp fifty pound notes, that makes this a cheap day out." Ace added with a grin. Jack smiled back at Ace and in his heart he felt proud of his brother's compassionate nature, but still posed the question.

"What made you do that though?"

"I just thought, you know ... I've got family, friends, that guy could have been me ... could have been any one of us Jack ... I mean, who the hell's he got?"

"Point taken Ace, and I'm sure he meant it."

"What?"

"The tramp, when he said good luck my friend."

As Lorna had instructed them both yesterday evening, Ace and Jack set out on the tube train that would take them to Baker Street, from there they embarked upon another train that took them north of London to a place called Rickmansworth in Hertfordshire. From this station it was a short taxi ride to their destination.

"Where to Guv?" The taxi driver enquired.

"Moor Park." Jack informed him.

"What, the Golf Club?"

"Er ... tennis club?!"

"Well yeah, they have got tennis as well and anyway, believe me, there's only one Moor Park round here mate." The driver assured them.

Within a few minutes they were entering through two large iron gates and the car rolled slowly along a narrow roadway with the golf course running along either side of them, an avenue of mature oak trees complemented the lush fairways. They eventually pulled up outside a mansion encased in Portland Stone with a magnificent portico supported by Corinthian columns. The building was enriched by a superbly cultivated Italian garden, augmented by stone statues and fountains that spread out from one side of the manor house and around to the rear. At the front of the property was the car park that lodged a collection of the club member's expensive motor vehicles. Ace sat in the taxi, open mouthed at the mansion's imposing beauty, his stomach fluttered with a flurry. *'Had he come here expecting to meet Lorna's coach in a wooden hut?'* he pondered. Detecting Ace's uneasiness in these somewhat alien surroundings, for a rag arse kid from the back streets of Manchester, Jack smiled and said.

"Not exactly Greenbrow Park is it?"

"No ... no, it's not."

"How are you feeling?"

"Bit nervous, I guess."

"Don't be awe-struck by all this; there ain't nothing that can buy the natural talent that you've been given ... nothing." Jack assured him, Ace smiled broadly and said.

"Bet your arse bro."

"Way to go Ace ... come on, we've got time to spare, so what say we take a look at the tennis facilities."

They strolled over towards the farthest end of the manor house following the sound of the thwack, thwack, thwack of tennis balls. When they reached the courts Ace granted his eyes to feast upon the impeccable assortment of surfaces, grass, clay, all weather and concrete. The whole area encircled by a vast array of elegant cedar trees.

"Nice ... very nice." Jack commented looking up at his lofty brother, whose ecstatic expression put Jack at ease. Any tension regarding their meeting earlier in the day, or when they had first arrived at this impressive location had taken a back seat in Ace's thoughts. When it came down to playing ball, everything took a back seat.

"How long before we meet the coach?" Ace asked, "I'm straining at the leash."

"Easy Ace ... easy, come on we'll do as instructed and have him paged from the main reception."

They walked through the doors to the entrance hall where they had been informed that the reception desk was.

"Wow." Jack gasped.

"Wow again." Ace whispered surveying the illustrious interior. Prodigious paintings by Italian artist, Amiconi, gave prominence to the high walls. Five solid marble doorways crowned with sculptured figures positioned around the great hall added to its grandeur. Above these, a gallery surrounded by gilt railings ran its entire length and breadth. The ceiling was painted and gilded, depicting the dome of St Peter's, Rome. Despite its exuberance, the hall had a magnanimous atmosphere to it and it helped in putting Ace at his ease, though at this point in time, he did not quite understand why. Jack turned to Ace,

"I bet there's more money in this room alone, than the whole of bloody Trafford North."

"You're probably right Jack, but it's bloody fabulous. Look at the furniture, it's like going back a hundred years or more, it's out of this world."

They walked over to the highly polished oak reception desk and spoke to a well-to-do looking middle aged woman. Ace made his enquiries.

"We are ... that is, I have an appointment with Mr. Fenton."

"Mr. Fenton?" The woman said looking over her half moon glasses.

"Yes ... Greg Fenton, the tennis coach?" Ace said, and for one sickly moment wondered if they had come to the right place. The woman behind reception looked the two of them up and down and Jack was pleased at that moment, that they had taken Lorna's advice and worn smart casual clothing.

"Ah yes, Greg Fenton, do you have your card?" She said.

"Card?" They both said.

"Your business card to pass on to Mr. Fenton."

"Er ... no ... we…" Ace stuttered.

"Very well, write your names down on this piece of paper and I will have him paged." She said in a matter-of-fact way. Ace duly obliged her request and passed the paper back to her, whereupon she handed the message to an elderly attendant who nodded his head and walked away towards the dining room at the farthest end of the room from the reception desk. A few minutes later Greg Fenton appeared through the large doorway following the page, who said something and motioned a hand in the brothers' direction. Fenton acknowledged and approached them with an assured stride that could have been termed as something of a swagger, had it not been for his distinguished posture, which certainly helped him make the best of his stocky six foot frame. Another couple of details that Ace was not quite prepared for raced through his mind, for Fenton was neatly dressed in colourful golfing attire as opposed to a tracksuit and something that Lorna had not mentioned was that the coach's weathered face sported a patch over the right eye. Fenton's leathery features creased when he smiled and held out his hand while introducing himself.

"Greg Fenton."

"Arthur Sharp, and this is my brother, Jack."

If Fenton was wondering how the two men did not resemble each other, his face did not register the fact.

"Glad to meet you, I trust your journey was a good one?" Fenton said in a rugged Australian inflection.

"You're Australian?" Ace asked, this was something else that Lorna had not mentioned.

"Blacktown, Sydney originally, but I've lived over here for the past ten years, ever since I had my little accident." He said with an intonation in his voice that made his statement sound like a question.

"Oh." Ace said, and was curious to know how he could coach tennis with only one good eye.

"But that's another story." Fenton continued.

"Ace has been looking forward to today Mr. Fenton and ..." Jack began before Fenton cut in.

"Ace?"

"Sorry ... that's Arthur's nickname, Ace."

"Ace, I like it."

"Yeah ... as I was saying, Ace can't wait to get out there and give you a sample of his talent." Jack enthused.

"Good, then we can talk about it on the course."

"Course?" Ace said somewhat bemused.

"Yeah mate, golf is my weekly recreation."

"Golf, but what about...?"

"One thing at a time mate ... now I hope you don't think me presumptuous if I ask you two fellows to caddie for me and my good mate, Jerry?"

"Caddie?" Ace said confounded by the Australian's nerve.

“Yeah, Jerry will be waiting at the caddy shack for us and we’re due on the first in five minutes, have you got a pair of trainers in that bag?”

“Er ... yeah, but ..”

“Right, put them on in the dressing room and we’ll get under way.” Fenton suggested then turned and beckoned Jack and Ace to follow. Ace was furious and felt that he had wasted his time coming to meet Mr. Greg bloody Fenton, the one eyed wallaby with an arrogant demeanour. He looked at Jack, who winked an eye and simply said.

“Come on, we’re here now, might as well get on with it.”

“OK.” Ace said reluctantly, he had certainly not envisaged himself and Jack spending the afternoon trudging round a golf course carrying the tennis coach’s golf clubs and could not help transporting his disenchantment around with them for the first few holes at least. By the time that they had reached the seventh hole his disappointment had subsided to a degree but his heart felt as heavy as the bag that he was carrying. Ace concluded that the only positive factor to the afternoon so far was the wonderful scenery that the old course had to offer.

“Give me a seven iron, mate.” Fenton said. Ace obediently passed him the club he had requested. Fenton wasted little time initiating his attempt. The shot pitched up short of the green and came to a halt on the perimeter.

“I should have taken a six iron.” The Australian said with a frown and Ace agreed before making their way towards the ball and Fenton’s next shot. Jerry, his opponent, played his second shot and succeeded in finding the heart of the green, much to the one-eyed coach’s displeasure.

“Good shot.” He said, though he concealed his competitive characteristics. Ace hoisted up the bag and they continued on towards the green.

“So young fella, you want to be a tennis player eh?” Fenton said.

“More than anything, it’s my dream, my goal.”

“Well, young Lorna tells me you play a mean game, mate.”

“Lorna’s right.”

“I think I’ll be the judge of that.”

“Oh, when?”

“When I’ve seen you play the bloody game.”

The last statement served to put a smile on Ace’s youthful face for the first time since the round of golf had started. On reaching the green’s periphery and Fenton’s ball, the coach took out his pitching wedge along with a tin of boiled sweets from his bag. He offered his caddie one of the sugary treats. Ace declined his offer, while Fenton placed one into his own mouth and commenced sucking noisily on it while embarking on sizing up his next shot.

“I would take a putter from there!” Ace declared. Fenton looked at his caddie ambiguously, ignored his advice and proceeded to play the chip, albeit a little too strongly, the ball, after taking to the air for a moment rolled fast down the slope and past the flag by five feet.

“Here.” Fenton said, turning his gaze to his caddie and dropping another ball down in approximately the same place that his was before he hit his chip.

“What?” Ace said, slightly puzzled.

“Take out the putter, see if you can get it any closer.”

Ace shrugged his shoulders and did as the tennis coach had instructed. He studied the line to the target before delicately stroking the ball along the superlatively groomed surface, where it came to a halt pin high and just three inches to the left of the hole. Without a word Fenton picked up the ball and tossed it back to Ace. Jerry made his birdie with his put winning him the hole. The two players and their caddies walked the short distance to the next tee.

"So as far as tennis goes Ace, how ambitious are you, mate?" Fenton enquired.

"Very."

"Oh, and what's very?"

"One day I aim to be Wimbledon champion." Ace declared confidently. The tennis coach hawked stifling a laugh and in struggling to do so, almost spat out the sugary bonbon from his mouth. On overhearing Ace's proclamation Jerry, Fenton's friend and golfing companion displayed an equally condescending expression.

"Did I say something to amuse you?" Ace asked, endeavouring to control his displeasure at their derogatory manner.

"No mate, ... you see, I've seen more hopefuls come and go than ..."

"But my brother's different." Jack cut in.

"Sure, look mate if there was a young tennis player on the horizon with a modicum of the tenacity needed to maybe ... just maybe lift lawn tennis's most coveted prize, don't you think that I would, or my colleagues would know about this would-be Borg, McKenroe, Connors, Becker, Sampras or Andre bloody Agassi?"

"Let's just say, till now I've kept myself a low profile." Ace prompted.

"Low profile? Listen, I don't want to hurt your feelings son, but I've got a list of names from clubs up and down the country who are possible candidates to make it to becoming pro's. One out of a hundred of them might ... I say might make the Senior Tour, but the chances of one of them winning one of the big tournaments is like chances of a seventy year old granny hitting this golf ball three hundred yards."

"With a nine iron." Jerry quipped, in return Fenton's laughter aggravated Ace and the coach continued. "Besides which, your name isn't on the list, your name came to me via a young novice that I have under my wing, who to be honest with you, will be, if I see no improvement in her performances, another also ran." Fenton concluded and turned his attention to Jerry who was poised to tee off. Fenton's opponent hit his drive with no deviation, down the middle of the fairway.

"Looks to me Jerry, like you mean business today." Fenton informed his friend, who simply smiled complacently. The one-eyed coach placed his ball onto a tee peg and without a practice swing thumped the ball with a degree of venom, sending his shot down the fairway some ten yards past Jerry's. Fenton then turned to Ace and handed his driver over to him.

"Do you play this game?"

"Not very often ... why?"

"I'd like to check out your eye-hand co-ordination, that's all ... come on Ace, I want to see you hit a golf ball OK?"

He wanted to tell the tennis coach that he normally played with left handed clubs, but thought better of it, beside Fenton was challenging his athletic prowess and Ace liked nothing more than someone winding up his competitive temperament. He placed the ball on top of a peg, then took three smooth practice swings before stepping forward and launching into the drive. The clubhead connected exquisitely, dispatching the ball through the air with a fizz, the shape of the shot had a touch of draw sufficient enough to give it additional forward momentum directing his drive some twenty metres past Fenton's effort.

"Shit." Was all Fenton said, though he had meant to say shot.

"He normally hits longer than that." Jack chirped.

"Longer?"

"Yeah!"

"See Mr. Fenton, I'm left handed." Ace informed him. Fenton turned to his opponent who no longer displayed a smug smile.

"Jerry, do you mind?" Fenton asked his golfing friend. "I wanna see him do that again, OK?"

"OK by me ... in fact I'd like to see him do that again."

"One time for me." The Australian urged.

"Just one question before I do Mr. Fenton."

"Sure, go ahead."

"In your mind, I think I'm right in saying ... you've formulated an opinion of my tennis abilities without even seeing me play."

"No, I just .."

"Let me finish please, rather than me being out here caddying for you, I should be out on those courts back there proving my future worth."

"And that's to be a future Wimbledon champion is it?" The coach said with an air of sarcasm.

"Bet your arse."

"Now I have a question, how old are you son?"

"Eighteen ... just."

"Eighteen eh?"

"Yeah."

"That's a little old in tennis terms to be looking for a career, bad habits would be hard to break, besides I've got a kid holding number three in the British rankings, he's just seventeen and looking good for moving up to bigger things."

"Does he have what it takes to be a champion?"

"That's for us to find out, I've known him since he was thirteen and obviously he's got better and stronger every year, his performances in the past twelve months have been pretty special, by next year he should be mature enough for the Davies Cup Team.

"Has he got what it takes to be a champion?" Ace pressed once more.

"He needs a little hardening up when it comes to his mental application, but he's confident and technically he's good, real good."

"Is he the best you've got?"

"You said you only had one question."

“I want to play against the best you’ve got.” Ace requisitioned the coach boldly, maintaining direct eye contact with Fenton, who found himself warming to the young black kid with the preposterous aspirations and an abundance of self-assurance.

“OK ...OK, request granted, I’ll organise a challenge match.” He conceded, allowing himself to smile back at the would be prodigy, then shook his head at the thought that British tennis had been in despairing exploration of a new Fred Perry ever since the great man’s Wimbledon wins all those years ago. He looked on while Ace took a practice swing and shook his head again, not at Ace’s quite admirable golf technique but the thought of vanquishing at last the sceptical character that is British Tennis suited and booted. *‘Too much to even contemplate let alone dream of.’* He brooded and banished the foolish notion from his mind. Ace propelled himself into his second drive from the tee. Fenton studied the improbable tennis champion’s timing on contact with the ball and recognised that the young man had natural eye-hand co-ordination, coupled with natural brawn. This time the ball skipped on beyond his initial assault by another ten feet. Jack and Jerry applauded their approval. Fenton’s face registered little emotion, though he did venture.

“And that’s your weak side, mate?”

The proprietor of the mini-market cast a discriminating eye over at his most recent customer who was filling one of the shop’s metal baskets with merchandise from the Beer, Wines and Spirits shelf. He told himself to be ready to hold his breath as best he could when the time came to tot-up the sum total for the goods purchased by the foul smelling consumer. The ill-groomed man, once satisfied with his alcoholic investment shuffled along the white tiled floor towards the till behind which the proprietor stood in wait. He placed the basket on top of the counter.

“One large bottle of cider, three Special Brew, I take it you can pay for these?” The shopkeeper said scornfully.

“And some tobacco and papers.” The unkempt man said ignoring the question.

“That’ll be nine pounds and six pence.”

“In that case, I can afford one of those.” The tramp added pushing the ten pounds across the counter with a grubby hand, while pointing with the finger of his other hand at a gregarious poster advertising National Lottery scratch cards. The shopkeeper opened a draw and passed a card to the tramp. Then, in an effort to ward off the latest acrimonious stench that drifted towards him from across the counter he wafted a hand under his nose.

“That’s another six pence.” He wheezed.

“Oh dear, I’ve only got four.”

“Take it ... never mind, just sod off out of my shop.” The proprietor said in desperation, and watched the tramp drag his feet along out through the door and back onto the street. *‘I hope that’s the last I see of him, dirty old bastard,’ he affirmed under his breath.*

Chapter Sixteen

Unsavory Deeds

The Bella Christina dropped her anchor a quarter of a mile from land. King had been a fairly frequent visitor to the shores of Morocco over the years since his appointment to the Bennetti federation. In the first twelve months his function had been to inspect the quality of the goods. In those days the consignments composed mainly of cannabis, an additional responsibility bestowed on King was to keep a vigilant eye on the Overlord's appointed employees. It was on one of these trips that King first took advantage of the latter entrustment. He incurred his revenge on the South American who, along with his accomplice, Carlton Watt the West Indian, had instigated the beating that King endured prior to his introduction to the Overlord in Beleze. In advance of the voyage King had discretely informed Bennetti that he had his suspicions that the Hispanic hand had sticky fingers and should not be trusted. Initially the Overlord's response to his supposition robbed King momentarily of the faith in his strategy.

"Let me remind you, the guy has worked for me for five years .... four years longer than you if I'm not mistaken!?" Bennetti had retorted.

"Yes, but Signor Bennetti you have given me a job to do and ..."

"Five years." The Overlord went on regardless, "I have never had reason to suspect the guy before, so why now?"

"Well ..."

"You have proof?"

"No, but ..."

"Then don't waste my time, get the fuck out of here!"

"You're right Signor Bennetti ... forget I said anything, the crazy thing is that I have recently become his friend, he respects me now and I think ..."

Friend?!" Bennetti chided, "There is no room for friendship in Agnazzio Bennetti's organisation, capiche?"

"Yeah .. yes, I understand." King said in conclusion, satisfied that the bait had been set. Thereafter, off the shores of North Africa he took his opportunity following the routine inspection of the produce and the disembarkation of Arabic traders, King told the Captain to prepare the men to set sail. As soon as the hold had been vacated and he was alone, King purloined a slab of the compact black illegal substance measuring approximately the size of one of his hands. He then proceeded hastily to wrap it crudely in a towel that he had seized from the Hispanic's quarters a couple of days earlier. Satisfied now that the men would be going about their duties, securing ropes and battening down the hatches, he made his way up on deck, where, under the moonless sky he made his way to return the towel to its owner.

It was not until the vessel reached the coast of Sicily, that the package was unearthed following a direct order from King for the administration of random examination of the ship's crew quarters. Ensuing this spuriously staged operation King had ordered that the culprit be brought directly to the aft deck for interrogation. The Hispanic arrived flanked on both sides by two fellow smugglers, their grip on him was firm, though he did not appear to be struggling to escape, it would have been futile anyway, his face showed little apprehension to begin with. *'What was he to fear, he had done nothing wrong'* he reasoned. Then he came face to face with King and panic gripped his guts.

"This was found hidden in the wall at the head of your bunk." King declared holding up the towel covered package.

"What!?"

"You look surprised man."

"Si."

"Is this your towel?"

"No."

"No?"

"No ... si .. I mean, yes the towel, it belong to me but ..."

"Yes, this is your towel!" King agreed unwrapping it. The Hispanic's brow broke out into a sweat under the warm afternoon sun.

"The shit it is no mine." He said through dry quivering lips.

"Right you are it's not yours, you have been taking the piss out of the Boss man, I wonder what he will have to say about this?"

"No, the shit it no mine I tell you."

"Do me a favour man, who have you been dealing with?"

"No, I don't steal the shit, I don't deal, it's no my sheeeeet ...." He squealed on impact as King's foot met head on with the man's testicles.

"Let this be a lesson to any one of you, it doesn't pay to lie to me, and let me tell you, it would be a bloody fool thing for any one of you bastards to try and steal from the Boss, for that reason this son of a Spanish bitch will be going for a little swim." King promulgated to the assemblance of hardened traffickers, who momentarily seemed to quake somewhat at King's domineering temperament. The South African's aura became blemished almost at this juncture by a dissident voice in the crowd.

"How do we know that the shit wasn't planted?" The American voice had emitted, and King turned to face the man who had questioned him.

"What's your name boy?"

"Hickman." Came the answer, "Larry Hickman."

"Well, Larry Hickman did you plant the shit?"

"No, I'm just advocating that maybe somebody on board could have done, that's all." Hickman had reasoned.

"OK ... what's your name?" King then said pointing indiscriminately at one of the cluster of men.

"Jones."

"Tell me Jones, did you plant this on our Latin friend?" King asked holding up the slab.

"No chance."

"Right then ... will the man that did, show his hand so he can join the greasy bastard in the drink." King then proclaimed, and the sound of raucous laughter served to quash Hickman's contention on the matter.

Still in a kneeling position on the deck succeeding the heavy blow to his groin, the Hispanic's eyes reeled anxiously in their sockets around towards his shipmates.

"I no take the shit!" He screamed as loudly as he could muster in an effort to be heard above the hilarity. One individual aimed and spat at the accused man, the thick slimy fluid landed squarely on his anguished forehead. This act was followed by a deluge of frothy mucus from the mouths of the majority of the gathering. King looked on with a smug expression, while the same thug that had instigated the bout of spitting threw the first of a barrage of kicks and punches that came next from three other crazed males, succeeding in rendering the accused semi-conscious before King finally called a halt to their brutal assault. The Mexican fell prostrate onto the wooden deck. Blood poured freely from his nose and mouth, forming a slowly expanding pool beneath his battered face. The gathering fell silent under King's command and again the dissenting spokesman in the crowd uttered his displeasure.

"This is goddamn barbaric." A black American had declared ardently. King turned slowly around, his face masked none of his annoyance.

"You again boy?"

"Hickman, my name's Larry Hickman."

"Listen boy, anymore crap from you, and you will be joining this robbing greaseball bastard for a swim with the fucking sharks, do I make myself clear?" King declared acrimoniously.

"Perfectly clear." Hickman submitted.

"Good." King said then turned his attention back to the proceedings, "Right, I want this deck clearing of unwelcome debris, then scrubbing clean, I will be back later to inspect your handiwork, do I make myself clear!?"

King's thoughts relating to the past were temporarily encroached by the sound of a winch being commissioned and the yacht's anchor being lowered into the sea. The woman's voice came from behind where he stood on the starboard side of the 'Bella Christina'. He turned around taking his gaze off the coastline to face the Overlord's sister.

"Signor Bennetti tell me to let you know he needs to speak with you."

"He wants to speak with me now?"

"No, he is presently making preparations for our guests, he says he want to see you in ten minutes."

"Very well."

"My brother ... he is no in a very good mood."

"Oh, is there a problem?" King enquired. She responded by pouting her thin lips and shrugging her shoulders before turning to make her way to the galley. He lit a cigarette and looked on at some members of the Overlord's crew, who were actively preparing to set afloat the motorised tender, which would be employed to ferry the 'guests' from the Moroccan coast back to the yacht. Only on three occasions had King accompanied the Overlord on what he described as his 'little sideline expeditions'. The 'guests' whom Bennetti would insist that they should be called, would be of various ages (none over twenty), of both sexes and of assorted nationalities, corresponding to the requirements or needs of Bennetti's wealthy recipients. The hostages would board the yacht in a thoroughly confused state, though with the application of a sedative drug were generally subordinate towards their kidnappers.

The last time that King had looked on these shores had been on his first of these 'little sideline expeditions', that was over four years ago, King recalled Bennetti's boastful claims, that for each virgin under the age of sixteen he could command up to $100,000 from one of his petrobillionnaire associates.

"Even more for that one." The Overlord had bragged, pointing down from his private deck towards one of three teenage girls. She was tall, King recalled, and although sedated, moved in an elegant fashion.

"American!" Bennetti had continued.

"In Morocco?" King then queried.

"She was on vacation, so my little taxi driver friend tells me ... went ashore from a cruise ship, she was accompanying her sister, well ... we presume that the other girl was her sister." Bennetti said and smiled sardonically then went on. "You know, people never learn, people all over the world go missing without trace, never to be seen again, no? .... and there they were, two young beautiful girls without a chaperone in the middle of Tangier."

"I take it then, that the other girl did not come up to standards?"

"No, at least not the specifications required by my associate, she was too old."

"Too old?"

"Well, chances are she would not have been a virgin."

"How could you possibly ..."

"I take no chances with these things." Bennetti cut in.

"So what will become of this girl?"

"She is now a guest on board the Bella Christina, all her wants and needs ... to a certain extent you understand?! ... they will be met, this way she will become accustomed to affluent surroundings, no?"

"Yes, I see but ..."

"Let me tell you, I leave home at a very young age, I can tell you, like me this girl is young enough to forget her past life, like the rest of these people they all adjust!" The Overlord explained with a pompous air.

"And when we reach the other end?"

"She will become an additional concubine at my friend's harem." Came the answer, and the Italian's features gave way to an odious grin when he intimated to King,

"For this girl I will get top dollar, she is below sixteen years old, white and American."

"So Signor Bennetti ... what may I ask is my role in all this?"

"Your function ... I'm sure you will agree, will be a pleasant one, you simply have to look after the merchandise for me, same as you always do."

"You mean you want me to babysit for you?"

“Si ... yes, very good joke .. ha, a babysitter.” Bennetti had chortled. Then abruptly his amusement was replaced by a scowl. “Like I say, just take good care of the merchandise, only difference is ... this time you don’t taste the goods!” Bennetti cautioned him, and although King had several unpalatable characteristics, foolhardiness certainly was not one of them, despite that fact he reflected now on how alluring it was, to have maybe, just sampled that girl’s essence, his face broke into a crooked smile at the concept of such a deed. *‘That American kid would have been nineteen years old now.’* King calculated while gazing out over the calm surf towards the tender making its course towards the shore. Then he imagined that the billionaire recipient had probably tired of her by now, along with a host of other unfortunate young girls following his self-centered trespass on their vestal bodies. *‘Then again, what the fuck do I care!’* Was his callous aftermost thought on the subject, as he turned to make his way to the aft deck and the appointment with the Overlord.

Chapter Seventeen

The Brown House

The weekend following their appointments with Don Lawrence and Greg Fenton, Jack had acquired some cinema tickets for his wife Helen, Ace, Lorna and himself. They had all agreed enthusiastically to an evening out down town. Jack and his wife had called for Ace at Argyle Street, then to Lorna's uncle's house from there.

On their arrival Lorna was standing outside readily awaiting their calling. Jack pulled the red Ford up alongside where she was standing, Ace opened the rear door nearest to her and beckoned her to climb in.

"Hello." Lorna said with a broad smile and joined Ace in the back seat. Jack turned around in the driver's seat as best he could to afford himself to face the new passenger. Helen also turned and smiled warmly while Jack introduced the two respectively.

"It's nice to meet you finally, Helen." Lorna enthused.

"Likewise Lorna .. now perhaps these two reprobates might hold their promise of a doubles match between us?"

"How about tomorrow?" Ace prompted.

"Perfect."

"Right ... tomorrow it is then." Jack endorsed, while shifting the car into gear and accelerated away smoothly, then said.

"How's the training and practice going Lorna?"

"Just fine Jack, thanks to Ace here and of course Glynn, at Bettabodies."

"So you'll be ready to face your coach again soon?"

"Eye to eye as it were." Ace jested, the other three groaned playfully in response.

"Well ... he is a bit weird." Ace retaliated.

"How so?" Lorna inquired.

"For a start he looks like something out of Treasure Island."

"True enough Ace .. and in a way he is like a pirate."

"How do you mean?"

"He's out there looking for gold."

"So he can fill his chest with honour and pride." Jack piped up and it was his turn to receive the chorus of groans.

"Another thing is, he's Australian." Ace went on.

"Well?" Lorna said, slightly bemused.

"What's he doing over here? The way he goes on, he figures that 'Poms' are crap at tennis ... funny that."

"What?"

"I told him that one day ..."

"One day what?"

"I feel a bit stupid now, saying what I did." Ace said with an air of reticence, then proceeded.

"It was just that at the time I was a bit wound up."

"What did you say to him?"

"I said .. that one day I would win Wimbledon."

Lorna was unable to suppress herself from hooting at Ace's recapitulated boast. Although she was brisk to apologise, taking notice that his expression barely cracked into a smile.

"How did he react to that?" She managed to ask evenly.

"He did exactly what you just did."

"What?"

"He fell about laughing."

"You can't really blame him for that, but one thing's for sure, Greg Fenton will like you for that, to coin one of his stock of phrases, *'there ain't many spunky poms'*, yeah, you will have impressed him all right."

"Let's all hope then Lorna, that he will be equally impressed with Ace when he plays that challenge match." Helen suggested.

"I'm sure he will."

"Have you any doubts?" Jack queried.

"No none ... though ..."

"Though what?" Ace frowned.

"Did Greg mention to you who he might put you up against?"

"No .. but I stressed that I wanted to play against the best he's got, like I say, I was kinda wound up when I laid down the gauntlet."

"So he didn't mention any names?"

"No ... no names but he did waffle on about a seventeen year old protégé he had under his wing."

"Drummond ... Paul Drummond."

"Tell me more." Ace said eagerly.

"He's good .. almost won junior Wimbledon last year but for his only weakness, as I see it he might well have done it."

"Weakness?"

"Don't get me wrong, he's got all the attributes to be a really good player, he's very polished, agile and elegant with his stroke play and a pretty big serve to go with his pretty big head."

"How do you think I would do against him?"

She looked candidly into his eyes before answering and wanted to tell him that he had nothing to worry about but logic convinced her otherwise.

"It would be foolish of me to speculate on your chances Ace." Was all she could muster.

"You think he will beat me!?"

"I didn't say that ... it's just that, hell ... he's been playing and competing at a high level for quite a long time and .. well to be honest with you, out there on court it will show." She concluded. Jack looked up briefly into his rear mirror at Lorna.

“So what’s Paul Drummond’s Achilles heel, prey tell?”

“I don’t know, I suppose it would be his temperament.”

“Ah, the spoilt brat syndrome.” Helen endorsed with a wry smile.

“Exactly, that’s where in the past his weakness has unquestionably been, however, more recently it seems that Greg Fenton has managed to bully him out of his tantrums.”

“So you’re saying that he doesn’t handle pressure very well?” Jack probed.

“Like I say, it looks like he’s grown up a lot recently, under Fenton’s guidance and coaching.”

“A leopard never changes its spots.” Helen sprightly commented.

Jack flicked the indicator lever, taking a left turn off the main road.

“Why have you done that?” Helen frowned.

“I know a short cut.”

“But .... that’ll take us through ..”

“I know, it will take us through a bad part of the city.”

“Not a good idea Jack, going through those back streets at this time of night!?”

“It’s OK ... we’ll drive through on the crest of a slump!” He grinned.

The two young passengers in the back of the car continued their conversation regardless.

“What’s important is that you give this opportunity your best shot, that way even in defeat you may turn out to be a winner in Fenton’s eyes.”

“I have no intentions of losing Lorna!”

“Anyway, we’ll be there to cheer you on.” Helen enthused and Jack proceeded to mimic a BBC commentator’s summary.

“And you join us as Arthur the Ace man Sharpe, prepares once again to deliver another blockbuster serve against the now down and disgruntled Drummond, who since coming out to face Sharpe on court has had simply no answer to Sharpe’s phenomenal prowess. Ace serves down the line to the backhand, Drummond returns to Ace’s forehand and Ace goes to the net and pins Drummond to the baseline, Drummond tries to lob him ... but Ace smashes it away for another winner, game, set and match to Arthur the Ace man Sharpe, six love, six love.”

The car’s occupants cheered their approval.

“Look out” Helen cried out.

Impulsively, Jack slammed on the brakes and swerved the car to avert a collision with the skin headed youth who had heedlessly run out into the road from the shadows of the dimly lit road. The youth slapped his open hand down hard onto the roof of the Ford as it skidded by him.

“Jesus, did I hit him?” Jack shrieked unable to hide his dismay.

“No, he was just playing silly buggers.” Helen affirmed. All the same Jack manoeuvred the car to a halt and habitually turned off the engine then lifted his gaze into the rear-view mirror, whereupon he saw another similarly attired male join his friend in the middle of the road, both of whom were now making animated gestures towards the car and its occupants. Ace was first to open his door and climb out.

“Are you trying to kill yourselves?” He called over to the two coarsely dressed young males, whose faces looked menacingly back at him under the crude yellowy glow of the street lamp.

“Come into the light where we can see you, you black bastard.” One of them shouted back.

Ace could have quite easily thrown Jack aside and made his way towards the reprehensible duo, indeed for a moment he almost did just that.

“They’re probably tooled up Ace, leave it be, get back into the car.” Jack urged, holding on to his brother’s arm while the skinheads continued taunting and hollering obscenities. Ace, reluctantly climbed into the back seat and Jack closed the door after him. He himself then got back behind the wheel. He shut the driver’s door and hurriedly pressed down the central locking system to secure the doors, fortunately just in time for evidently assuming that Ace and Jack had ‘chickened out’ of a confrontation with them, the two hoodlums had summoned up the audacity to run the twenty metres to the side of the car and then attempted in vain to open its doors. In his frustration one of them crashed his fist hard against the driver’s side window.

“Give us your fucking money!” The shaven headed ruffian that Jack had avoided ploughing down screamed through the glass. His accomplice meanwhile was vigorously kicking at the door and window behind which Ace was sitting. The engine fired into life the second time of asking and Jack scolded himself for having turned it off in the first place. He rammed the gearshift into first and sped away at precisely the moment that Ace’s window gave way to the size ten boot. The car’s sudden momentum dispatched the Kung Fu impersonator through the air, spinning him ultimately down onto the unyielding tarmac.

“Are you OK in the back?” Jack asked.

“Smashing.” Ace japed calmly while attempting to pluck some of the minute pieces of the shattered glass from his hair.

“Lorna?”

“Yes ... I’m fine ... I think ... hell, what was all that about?”

“They were drugged up to the eyeballs, they’ll do anything to get money to pay for their craving.” Helen contended.

“I think Jack, that we might have broken that guy’s leg back there when we drove off.” Ace commented.

“I don’t think we’ll turn back and see how he’s feeling Ace.”

“Now that’s not very humane of you bro.” Ace responded dryly, sparking the four of them to laugh albeit nervously, reflecting on the absurdity of the circumstances that had been presented to them only moments ago, encouraging Jack, Helen and Lorna to rally together their viewpoints on the problems within the inner cities and advocating their individual thoughts on what might or should be done to improve their social structure. Ace fell silent and closed his eyes, content to let them vent their views. The draught from the car’s gaping window buffeted against his cheeks and he reminded himself of the object lesson that Jack had given to him years ago when Ace was just twelve years old. At that time his brother was a man of twenty five years, more a father figure than a brother and indeed if that was the case, then Jack played the role rather fittingly. It was a day that neither of them would ever forget.

Jack had taken Ace through into the 'Best Room' at their parent's house and sat him down on the sofa.

"Me and my old school chum, Davy Simpson have just come from the hospital." Jack had begun.

"The hospital?" Ace said with a puzzled expression on his then pubescent face.

"Yes, the hospital."

"Oh?"

"Today has been a bad day." He went on and tender in years though Ace was, he recognised that beneath Jack's brave front he was deeply distressed.

"My old mate Gary Witney lost his battle against addiction and with it his life ... Gary's dead Ace."

It was the first time that anyone close to Ace or his family had passed away and the young boy was at a loss for words.

"What a waste, just twenty six years old, he was a smashing bloke as you know ... that is, till he got involved with bloody heroin!" Jack declared in a broken voice mixed with sorrow and sheer anger.

"Ace."

"Yes?"

"I want you to read this." He said and handed over to his younger brother a shabby hardback book

"Gary's mam gave it to me at the hospital."

"What is it?"

"It's Gary's diary Ace."

"Oh!?"

"Before you open it up, let me try to explain something, OK?"

"OK"

"Gary was a sensible well-educated lad, he thought that he was too smart to become a junkie. But drugs are nasty and horrid, they don't only just screw you up, they kill. Now I want you to read and learn, if there's anything in there that you maybe don't understand, ask OK?"

"Yes, OK." Ace agreed, then he got up from the sofa and was about to leave the room. Jack said nothing but the youngster sensed his brother's disapproval.

"What ... you want me to read it now?"

"There's no better time bro."

Ace returned to the sofa and sat down, he opened up the dog-eared journal and while Jack looked on intently he set about his examination of its contents.

January 22:

Dropped out of college today, need a break I guess
looking forward to my new job in concert promotions,
hell I need the money! Maybe I'll go back to college
next summer?

Ace read attentively and found that the horror story worsened with the turn of every page. His young mind toiling with the chronicle's unbearable reality and he had become by now aware of its author's agony. Jack assisted in answering several queries along the way.

One of Ace's questions brought a smile to Jack's face for the first time that day.

"Won't Gary get into trouble keeping a record like this?"

The then twelve year old turned the page that displayed the final days of October and the first days of the following month. Ace was beginning to have a problem deciphering the handwriting which by November had deteriorated to scrawl. Jack sat down next to him on the sofa and aided his progress.

Thursday:

When this was my heroin day we used to get a tenner bag to last the weekend and not do any for the rest of the week. Now I'm up to £120 worth a week!

Friday:

The television's still on and I can't remember sleeping. When you take heroin you kind of doze. It's an effort to move, I can't be bothered I'll stay here and watch my video's. Got a litre of cola to keep me company. I'll sign off for now.
My mate Alf called round to see if I want anything delivering. Told him what the hell, let's do some and make a night of it. Alf calls this the Brown House because all the dudes that live here do smack, we only smoke the stuff though – injecting the stuff it's the beginning of the end.

Saturday:

The place is still buzzing, the guys are still here, going to have a toot. Haven't eaten again today. Think I'll go and get me a bowl of cereal or something before I write anymore.
The cornflakes made me want to puke. I have to go and see my mam and our Doreen today, I'll maybe give my body a break and stay over there for a few days. I'll only take a bit of smack with me.

Sunday:

Feel crap today, really lethargic, though I actually slept last night. Mam made me eat my dinner. I've eaten more than I have in ages. I didn't know how ravenous I was. I guess when you take heroin the meal time routine goes out of the window.

Monday:

Taken no heroin now for two days, well nearly two days! I don't feel too bad! Fingers and toes crossed I don't get those serious withdrawals I had a couple of months ago. I got real bad cramps and the sweat just oozed off me, drenching my clothes through, worse, I couldn't stop bloody shaking. Before all that happened I met this girl who said that her mates are into E and cannabis. I said can they get me some smack and her chin nearly hit the friggin floor.

Tuesday:

Back home now, our Doreen was giving me a hard time, had to split, called at the dealer's on the way back, thought I'd better make sure I got some in case my mates are having a little toot and I fancy having one when I got home.
Saw my old mate Jack and his little bro, Ace today. They must have been going playing tennis somewhere, I knew that because they had their tennis rackets with them, bloody hell, Ace has grown since I last saw him, he's going to be a big guy when he grows up. I can't stand tennis, it's a girl's game anyway. I was going to call after them but thought better of it, I wasn't feeling too good anyway. Maybe I'll pay them a visit another time when I don't feel so crappy. I miss Jack and my old chum Davy Simpson, they were my bestest mates at one time. I did the right thing calling in on my supplier, it's party time again at the Brown House, Alf and the guys are toot-toot-tooting and I'm going to join them! In for a penny as they say!

Wednesday:

Woke this morning, I had got really heavy hunger pangs. Got my mam to thank for that. I think she got me into regular meals again. Can't remember much about last night, I remember though I kept dozing and coming round again, can't remember going to sleep. I'm glad I'm keeping an account of things in this diary. It was nice to see Jack again (I thought I'd dreamt it) hadn't seen him since I left my mam's to live in the Brown House. Just been sick, nothing much came up though, just bile. Going to have to get some cash from somewhere, I won't worry about that just now. Think I'll have a little toot, make me feel better. Heroin is something I'm experimenting with, I'm not hooked, no way! It's just something I want to do right now. I really enjoy the buzz. I can kick it any time I like.

Ace lifted his gaze up from the journal and looked forlornly at Jack.

"Why did he do these things to himself?"

"I wish I had the answer to that question, until today, Davy and me had no idea that he was involved in drugs."

"Could you have helped him if you had known?"

The proposition stirred Jack's conscience, and ignited a flame of anger in his guts.

"I don't know if I could have helped him Ace, but I dearly would have liked to have tried, maybe .... there's a lot of maybes, but perhaps if he had called over to us that day he said in his diary that he'd seen us then maybe ..." Jack explained, then gave way to a lengthy sigh before continuing.

"I don't really know to be honest with you, if I could have helped Gary, you see when a person is in the grip of evil, and that evil happens to be drugs, there's really only one person who can actually help them and that's themselves. I suppose it's a bit like being in a wilderness and unwittingly stepping into quick-sand, if there's nobody around to give you a hand to pull you out and you don't holler for help, you're gonna sink without a trace."

"What about Alf and his other friends at the Brown House, couldn't they have helped Gary?"

"I doubt it ... you see, they're in a wilderness of their own also."

"One thing's for sure Jack."

"Yes?"

"You won't find me experimenting with drugs."

"That's what I wanted to hear you say bro." Jack said fervently and with his hand, ruffled the twelve year old's curly hair playfully. Jack took the journal from Ace and turned the pages to its final entry. He then read the last words that Gary had untidily scribbled down on the sullied page.

Monday:

Tried to eat some toast, couldn't keep it down, puked it up. Think I'll get back to college soon, getting a bit pissed with the Brown House. No-one here, don't know where Alf's gone. Might have a snooze, I feel crappy. I found a needle earlier, it was hidden in one of the guy's drawers, haven't got a lot of smack left so might try pricking my arm just one time. Feel real tired, no energy, can't remember going to sleep.

Chapter Eighteen

Home Truth

The Mercedes came to a halt at the end of the driveway, Danielle turned off the engine. She remained there in her seat and collected her thoughts while observing the hunched figure of Solly studiously tending to the garden. He looked up from his work momentarily to acknowledge his mistress's return with the wave of a hand, his face conveyed a brief flickering smile that did little to mask his torment before returning to his handiwork. Subsequent to the interview at the Hotel de Paris with the American and the Englishman Solly had retreated into his shell somewhat and had made every effort to avoid any further confrontation with regard to the meeting and its conclusions. Indeed, he had gone to great lengths to evade bumping into Madame Danielle since then, for fear that more questions might be asked and he would be unable to cope. To add to his embarrassment, he had been discovered cowering in the broom cupboard within the confines of the kitchen, on a rare visit to that part of the house by the Mistress. She had gone in there to see how the preparations were coming along for Jean Paul's birthday party and had gone into the broom cupboard in order to obtain a brush and shovel to assist in cleaning up the mess caused by a young commis chef accidentally dropping a serving dish onto the floor. Although he was certain that she had seen him hiding within the spacious cupboard she protected his dignity by saying nothing.

Danielle opened the car door and made a mental note as she climbed out of the open top sports car to speak to Solly and put him at his ease. But in the interim she had a more pressing undertaking, namely, an audience with his sister, Floss. Danielle let herself into the house and made her way immediately to her bedroom, where she expeditiously changed from her Yves Saint Laurent two piece outfit into a pair of blue jeans and a white silk blouse. She then stepped into a pair of comfortable flat shoes, satisfied, she picked up the internal phone and pressed the appropriate digit, it rang three times before it was answered and the familiar voice came on the line.

"Bonjour Madame Danielle?"

"Bonjour Floss, I would like coffee in the drawing room please."

"Oui Madame."

"And cake, we will have cake also."

"You have a guest Madame Danielle?"

"No Floss ... in the drawing room in five minutes."

"Oui, five minutes, merci Madame."

"Merci Floss."

Floss put down the receiver and promptly prepared the provisions for her mistress.

'Had she misunderstood Madame Danielle's request ... had she said coffee for one or two people?' Floss puzzled over, then decided on a pair of matching china cups, saucers and plates, placing them alongside the coffee pot and a selection of delicate cakes on a silver tray, which now fully laden she picked up and carefully made her way to the drawing room. Once outside the room she placed the tray on a table strategically appointed to one side of the sizeable double doors at which she knocked and awaited direction.

"Oui, entree Floss." Danielle prompted and Floss turned the handles and opened the doors then entered the resplendently furnished chamber. Danielle sat alone looking almost diminutive in one of the capacious armchairs.

"Oh ... you are alone Madame?" Floss stuttered, slightly embarrassed at her miscalculation, "I have brought coffee and cake for two Madame Danielle."

"Good .. please Floss, bring it through."

"Yes Madame." Floss said and accommodated her request.

"Sit down Floss." Danielle rendered lightly and gestured towards the armchair directly facing her.

"Madame Danielle?" Floss responded while nervously fidgeting with the stringed belt of her immaculate white pinafore.

"I will pour the coffee for a change, no?"

"But Madame?"

"Make yourself comfortable Floss, as we are alone in the house we will not be disturbed."

"Madame?"

For the first few minutes the two women made light conversation and Floss was enjoying the rare privilege of taking coffee in the drawing room with the Mistress. Danielle decided it was time to dispense with the informal chatter and make a move towards their tete-a-tete.

"The time has come Floss, for you and I to have a serious conversation that is rather overdue." Danielle said in a moderate tone.

"Madame Danielle .. I ... I am confused, ... a serious conversation, about what?"

"Before we begin would you like some more coffee? .. Oh, how wretched of me, I have known you all these years Floss and I do not know whether you take sugar."

"No .. no sugar thank you Madame, just a little milk."

Danielle poured the hot drink to her housekeeper's liking along with her own then sat down in the chair facing Floss. The only sound within the room for some seconds was that of the Grandfather clock ticking a precise cadence. Danielle sipped her drink and swallowed before conveying her thoughts.

"Floss, you have been a servitor in this house and all who live here for a long time now, and during this time I have become very attached to you ... you are indeed like a member of my family, no?"

"Merci Madame Danielle, I feel honoured."

"No ... it is I that should be honoured."

"Madame?"

"You have fortitude and loyalty beyond that of most people that I have ever known Floss, something that my husband does not seem capable of recognising."

"But Madame Danielle, I have known Mr. King Sir for all of his life ... since being a small boy he ..."

"I despise the way he treats you and your brother."

"But this is only his way, he's ..."

"Why," Danielle cut in, "Why, do you protect him Floss?"

"Protect him?"

"Yes."

"Well .. because I .. I have been a servant to his family since being a child, to Mr. King senior and Mrs. King Madame."

Danielle took another sip of her hot coffee and placed the cup back into its saucer before continuing.

"Do you not think it odd Floss, that I never met my husband's father before his death, nor his mother, come to that."

"Yes Madame, I can understand ..."

"Nor have I met my husband's brother, who by all accounts was left the lion's share of the family estate when their father died. Please do not get me wrong Floss, I am not being mercenary, I merely would like to know." She sighed before proceeding, "What I am saying is that I want some home truths, no?"

Floss shifted uneasily in the comfortable chair and placed her cup and saucer down onto the small round table by her side. She had been utterly unprepared for this reconciliation with the past.

"Bruce was the older of the two brothers, you understand Madame." She explained.

"Yes ... yes, I do understand, but to deny his younger son a part of his inheritance well ... his father must have disliked my husband greatly, no?"

"I believe that his father loved him Madame."

"Then why?" Danielle challenged without malice and although the room was warm, Floss felt a sudden chill embrace her, she drained the rest of the beverage from her cup in an effort to quell the thirst that emanated inside her mouth, the coffee only seemed to add to its dryness.

"Well Floss?" Danielle pressed.

"It was his mother's wish that he should be disinherited."

"Why would she do such a thing?"

Floss wanted to excuse herself and get back to her daily chores, indeed there were many things that she would prefer to brave at this moment. *'To endure someone pulling her teeth one by one would be a preferred alternative.'* She mused.

"So, my husband's mother ruled the roost?" Danielle continued.

"Well .. no .. I."

"You see, I do not understand why he should have given way to his wife's bidding, I sense intimidation, no?"

"Intimidation?"

"What did Irwin's mother have on her husband Floss?"

Floss's stomach somersaulted inside her as if she had suddenly plummeted a hundred metres. Her thoughts wrestled desperately in search of an equivocation to somehow side-step the issue. Her mouth was agape though mute and the clock had become the prevalent sound within the room, tick, tick, ticking the seconds out for round one of what was to become a sombre hour of verbal exchange. Floss' aged countenance displayed her anxiety and Danielle frowned slightly.

"Did I hit a nerve Floss?"

"Yes ... you could say that Madame." Floss managed to say in a whispered tone.

"Oh?"

"Really Madame Danielle, this would be better ... far better for everyone if it were left well alone." She urged. Danielle forced a smile.

"Please ... calm yourself Floss, anything said today between you and I will go no further than these four walls, I promise you." She assured her. Floss shook her head negatively.

"Floss .. I simply would not be asking these questions but for the fact that my life has changed recently and is changing moreover day by day."

"Yes Madame."

"Now where were we? .. ah yes, so you think that my husband's mother had a squeeze on her husband?"

"I will try to explain the best I can Madame Danielle."

"Good, please take your time Floss, would you like some more coffee?"

"Yes ... yes please."

Danielle poured the coffee then sat down and awaited her housekeeper's expose. Floss looked over towards the double doors and sighed. Her daily chores would have to wait. The day that she had feared for so many years had finally arrived. She turned her head back towards Danielle and contemplated the Mistress' benevolent eyes.

"I was thirteen when I started my calling for the King household. When I first arrived, I had a lot to be thankful for. At the time I was half-starved and there I received sustenance to build my strength back up and I had a roof over my head."

"What about your parents Floss?"

"They were very poor Madame Danielle, they could not afford to tend to my needs, besides they had four other children all younger than myself to feed and nurture as best they could, you see, in my village at thirteen a girl was considered to be an adult."

"An adult at thirteen years of age?"

"Yes, I know it might seem strange to you but, my parents were delighted when Mr. King Sir's father made a bid for me."

"A bid ... you mean that he bought you?"

"With enough money to feed my family of six for a whole month and more."

"My God."

"No Madame, you must understand that this was a good thing that happened, as there was a terrible shortage of good food that year, and there was a drought the like of which had not been experienced by my parent's generation." Floss explained and awaited a response that never came and continued.

"At first I was very happy .. very content."

"Did my husband's father pay you a living wage?"

"I was given gifts."

"Gifts Floss?"

"Yes, clothes, shoes ... perhaps every now and again I would be treated to have my hair done."

"And who usually would bestow these gifts?"

"Mr. King Sir's father."

"And did you have any contact with any other people apart from the King's?"

"There was a boy .. I say a boy, he was eighteen at the time and worked the land for the Kings. He and I became very close, but one day the young man disappeared without trace.

"This boy you say, vanished and nobody knew where or why?"

"It was said that Mr. King Sir's mother held the young farm worker responsible for my ... falling pregnant, Madame, and that it was she who had him banished."

"You were with child at such a tender age?"

"Yes Madame."

"How awful for you Floss, and were you punished for this misadventure?"

"No Madame, I was not."

"I see ... I mean, I think I see .."

"Mr. King Sir's father had to be seen to be doing what was right in the eyes of the community; he had his position to consider."

"What as, a farmer ... a landowner?"

"A man of God, a Preacher Madame."

"Pardon me?" Danielle gasped.

"Madame Danielle, you mean you didn't know?"

"No Floss, it appears that there are many things that I do not know, it seems that for all these years I have been married to a stranger."

"The reverend King, or to give him his favourite title, Doctor William Irwin King, this was what most white African people called him." She said with a narrow air of disdain.

"What made the Kings go to such lengths ... to look after you and the child that you were expecting?"

"To save face I would think Madame, ... to be seen to be doing the right thing."

"The right thing?"

Floss fell silent again for a moment.

"My dear Floss, I regret you having to weather all this, I know that it is painful for you and by comparison I have lived a rather sheltered existence, but believe me I am on your side ... and if I sound a little careless it's because ..."

"Do not fret Madame, I appreciate that like most people you have your troubles."

"I am thankful for your wisdom Floss."

"And I am thankful for your concern for me also Madame, please continue, we have come this far." She pressed and with a sniff of her nose, she sat up and regained her composure. Danielle eyed her attentively before saying.

"Are you sure, can I get you anything?"

"No, I'm fine Madame, please ..."

"Dear Floss, may I compliment you once again on your fortitude."

"Thank you ... though it appears that my loyalty is not going to survive intact."

"In that case Floss, if you do not wish to continue then please, you are free to go with my blessing, I will not hold it against you." She said gesticulating a hand towards the chamber's double doors. Floss looked over towards where the Mistress' hand had indicated, *'it would be so easy to simply get up from the chair, lift up the tray of used china, pay her respects and leave, but why .. why did Madame Danielle need the answers to these questions?'* As painful though the memories were, she decided to reconcile with her past, she had been living the lies for too long and perhaps, just perhaps by talking about it she may be liberated at last and when death finally came to her door she might be forgiven and go to heaven, or at least be able to rest in peace. She toyed with the small silver cross that was hinged on a chain around her neck.

"No Madame ... we will talk, we will finish our discussion." She said in a slightly stifled tone. She closed her eyes and the brief wordless instant between the two women added to the ambiguous atmosphere which had been generated within the room, somewhat in contrast with the steady unbroken rhythm from the grandfather clock, beating out a measured tempo decidedly more conservative to that of the heart that ached inside Floss' chest. Her mind mustered up a short prayer *'Oh dear Lord be with me this day, I want once more to join your glorious house, to praise your goodness and fight against evil, give me strength O Lord to help you in your work, Amen!'* Slowly she opened her eyes and looked across at her Mistress who gave her a brief reassuring smile reflecting a temporary breach in her apprehension.

"Did Mr. King Sir ... has he ever spoken to you about the reverend King's wife's ordeal at the hands of a gang of men Madame?"

"Yes ... he spoke of a day before he was born when, as he put it, a posse of black natives broke into the house while his father was away and raped his mother."

"Well it ..." Was all Floss had chance to utter before Danielle interrupted her.

"That's it, that is it .. the connection." She enthused. It was all abundantly clear now. Her lost twin boy, as Hickman had insisted that she had brought into the world was a genetic throwback, the adrenaline rushed through her veins. The time had come now to confront her housekeeper with the question, *'Where did you and my husband take my child?'* But before she was able to speak, Floss' next statement confounded her.

"Nobody was raped by a gang of black African men at the house, or for that matter, within an inch of the acres that surrounded the property Madame Danielle."

"Are you saying then that the story was a fabrication ... a lie?"
"Yes Madame, that is what I am saying."
"I do not understand, why?"
"To protect the reverend."
"Protect the reverend .. from what Floss?"
"From people finding out the truth." She said and her eyes welled with tears, she cleared her throat before continuing.
"I was the victim ... he told me that he would cleanse me with his hands, that his hands were the hands of God and with those hands he raped me."
Floss' revelation rendered Danielle momentarily speechless. A stunned expression prevailed on her face, while her mind deliberated and grappled with her housekeeper's disclosures, another haunting thought invaded now, '*one day at a time*' her inner voice shrieked.
"What are you saying Floss, that ..."
"That Mr. King, Sir ... is ..."
"Your son, is that what you are telling me?"
"Yes Madame."
Suddenly, the irony of the entire scenario caused Danielle to laugh out loud. Floss raised her eyebrows in surprise.
"I am sorry Floss ... or should I say, ... I am sorry mother-in-law." Danielle declared and Floss sat silently across from her mistress, though her face displayed some apprehension.
"Your secret is safe with me Floss ... if that is what you wish?"
"Thank you Madame."
"Though, I need to know more ... would that cause you further consternation?"
"Simply to talk about this has, I believe, lightened my wretched heart."
"My dear Floss, I do not consider you wretched in any way, I believe that for a son, a mother will do anything no?" Danielle reasoned and beneath the smile she had managed in return, Floss knew that from this day, nothing would ever be the same.
"Was the Reverend's wife ... was she aware of her husband's adultery?" Danielle enquired.
"As far as I know ... Mrs. King accepted that the farm worker was to blame for my dilemma."
"I see ... but did she know about her husband's involvement with you?"
"Involvement, Madame? There was no involvement with him, I ... I was raped!"
"Yes ... yes, I'm sorry Floss, forgive me for my indiscretion." Danielle said, scolding herself once again for her cumbersome delivery of the question.
"Yes ... Mrs. King knew, you see, Mrs. King was not able to have any more children after her only son, Bruce, was born."
"Even knowing that her husband had been an adulterer, Mrs. King still agreed to take responsibility for your baby ... why?"
"I do not know Madame, I did not ask such questions. But to remain an upstanding member of the community was of the upmost importance to her. I think when they learned that the child was almost as white in appearance as they

themselves, Mrs. King decided that rather than the scandal of her husband's discreditable behaviour being discovered, a better alternative would be to adopt the child."

"But what did the King's offer you in exchange for your part in playing the surrogate mother, Floss?"

"Security ... a roof."

"If you had refused to hand your child over to them, what do you think would have happened?"

"Had they dismissed me from their home, how long do you imagine a mother of fifteen, with a baby, would have survived in those days Madame Danielle?" Floss evaluated honestly, and the large clock ticked the seconds away for the following ten minutes, during which time, she continued to comply with little hesitation to Danielle's interrogation into the King dynasty, until that was, there was a sudden switch in the questioning halting the flow. Confounding her, the eight simple words that Danielle tendered sapped her, entering her ears like an unwelcome octet of miserable flat musical notes.

"Did my other twin boy have a birthmark?"

Inside the study, three doors along the corridor, from the room that the two women were deliberating, the fax machine activated with a click and whirred out its communication.

For Miss Sonya Kennedy
Foto shoot has been arranged at a European location
to commence the day after tomorrow.
Please contact Cat Walk International for further
details and flight information a.s.a.p.
Kind regards
Cas

Chapter Nineteen

Karen

Larry Hickman sat back in his leather chair within the private confines of his small office. He closed his eyes allowing his thoughts to go back to the final six years of his prison sentence. He had used the time prudently by taking a University course and had achieved academic accomplishments for his efforts, one of which, was the publication of a strong, hard hitting book relating to modern day slavery throughout the world and so-called civilisation. He named the work *'Cause Against Slavery'*, and within its pages it spoke of the flourishing slave trade that exists in our time, the estimated 200 or so million men, women and children who can be categorised as slaves. The victims of back-breaking manual labour, peddlers of drugs and pornography, satanic rituals and among many other abominable things, sex objects to opulent perverts and paedophiles. He had received many letters in response to his disclosure and in the concluding six months before his cell door was closed and locked behind him for the last time, he had a several visitors, ranging from Politicians and Clergy to inquisitive well wishers, one of whom he had, at first sight, mistakenly thought to be one of the latter, but turned out to be an intriguing young woman with a strong will and unquestionably brave heart. His mind pondered now at her first visitation. Her beautiful face had studied him through the glass that separated them, and using a telephone they made their initial conversation.

"I read your book Mr. Hickman, it made harrowing reading!" Had been Sonya's initial remark.

"Thank you ... then in a small way I guess it may have done some good." He said honestly, then added in an almost mocking tone. "Have you travelled from the States, all the way here to a French prison to tell me that?"

In return her beguiling features hardened momentarily.

"I'm a member of the oldest of all human rights organisations."

"The Anti-Slavery Society?"

"Yes."

"Don't mind me saying ... but young folks with your kinda looks are usually more concerned with fashionable pastimes, like ..."

"Don't be mislead by my appearance Mr. Hickman, I am extremely serious." She cut in sternly.

"I'm sorry ... I guess I was a rather flippant." He said with an expression that seemed telepathically to welcome her.

"You're forgiven." She said and smiled.

"So ... was there something in the book that you wanted specifically to talk about?"

"Yeah, but I would like for you to hear me out first."

"You got a story for me?"

"If you've got the time."

"Shoot!"

"OK ... I'll be as brief as I can."

"Take your time, I'm listening."

"Well ... four years ago, when I was eighteen years old, my mom and dad decided to take me and my kid sister, who was at that time just fifteen, on a vacation around Europe, and what better way than to take a cruise around the Mediterranean. One of the locations that we visited was Tangier, Morocco. Now the night before we anchored there, the weather had been particularly bad, and my mom had suffered badly from sea sickness throughout the night and had decided not to go ashore. My dad had been awake all night tending to mom's needs and was obviously exhausted, so Karen ..."

"Karen?"

"Oh sorry, Karen's my kid sister."

"I see, please go on."

"So, Karen and me decided to go ashore and take a cab to the Kazbar, the cab driver assured us that he would double as a guide, that was our first mistake."

"Mistake?"

"Trusting that Arabic son of a bitch!"

"Oh?"

"He took us on a tour of the many different quarters, you know ... like the French, British, American and Arabic parts of Tangier. I guess he must have done this to gain our confidence in him. Then he asked us if we wanted to go do some shopping and bartering, you know?" She explained and fell silent for a moment and sighed before continuing.

"Mr. Hickman, have you ever been to Morocco?"

"Yes ... yes Ma'm, I sure have." He said and was unable to stifle a snigger at what he thought at first to be her naivety, though he was quick to apologise and explained.

"That was when I pursued a certain vocation."

"And what was your work there?"

"If I get to know you a little better, then maybe I'll tell you, but for the time being all I will say is, in those days I was what you might call a low life!"

"And prison ... has prison reformed you?"

"I reformed myself with the help of the Lord ... hey just a minute I thought you wanted me to hear you out, not the other way round, besides, visiting time's almost through, so I suggest little lady that you get on with your story before they come to drag me back to my cell!"

"I'm sorry again Mr. Hickman, I ... I didn't come here to pry, I just ..."

"You were saying you were haggling with some guy?" He cut in lightly and she looked him in the eye and continued.

"Morocco was something of a culture shock for my sister and me you know?"

"Sure, I can understand."

"The driver ... he took us down these narrow streets and into several stores that sold leather goods and earthenware among a variety of other things, Karen wanted in particular to purchase a pair of leather shoes at a good price. I must admit that we were both becoming kinda enthusiastic, bartering with the locals. I guess that that's when we let our shields down and left ourselves vulnerable."

"Vulnerable?" Hickman enquired, and through the glass partition he recognised pain transmitting through her dark honest eyes.

"We ended up walking down through a tiny alley that had small shops on both sides of the walkway. A guy came up to me ... he was selling jewellery, among his trinkets there was a ring that I examined closely, not that I'm an expert you understand? ... but compared to the rest of the stuff he had, the ring was ... I would say, of excellent standard ... really cool, I remember thinking to myself, hell, this guy doesn't know what he's got, so I began to haggle a price with him. While I was busy putting all my efforts into knocking him down to an affordable sum, the taxi driver had beckoned Karen towards a shop that was situated directly behind me. My sister walked over towards the window, in her excitement she hollered over to me that she had seen a pair of shoes that she wanted, I glanced over my shoulder and called after her to wait, I'd just be a minute ... but by the time I had got the words out she and the driver had entered the shop. Suddenly the ring was no longer important and I tried to escape the guy's sales pitch. I told him that I didn't want his goddamn ring but he continued to pester me and by the time I got him off my back, I'd say a good two minutes had rolled by." She shut her eyes tightly for a moment, as if in an endeavour to blot out the scene in her mind. Her bottom lip quivered slightly while her words echoed around the cold grey walls.

"I walked into the shop ... and ... there was no sign of my kid sister ... she ... she and the driver had disappeared, ... through the back of the shop I guess, I don't know!?" She choked and dried her eyes with a handkerchief.

"I haven't seen her since that day!" She announced finally.

The fax machine inside his small office stuttering out its confirmation of the transmission to Sonya served to convey his thoughts back to the present.

Chapter Twenty

The Challenge Match

For the third time in as many hours Ace opened up the small elaborate container and studied the ornately detailed scorpion, he turned the piece of precious metal over, the simple inscription read, (blood group) AB Negative. He chewed on his lip for a moment, then placed the talisman and its chain back into its receptacle and pressed it shut. He then dropped it indelicately into his sports bag. The parcel had been delivered on his doorstep that morning together with another letter with the London postmark, which remained unopened and had unceremoniously been stuffed into a compartment of his overnight case.

A horn sounded in the street outside number forty six and he bounced up from his springy mattress on which he had been sitting waiting in anticipation for Jack's return from collecting his small party of supporters from several points of call. He looked through his bedroom window down onto the rented mini-bus which was to be their means of transport to Hertfordshire for what promised to be the most thrilling day in his life. He snatched up his sports bag from off the bed and threw it over his shoulder, in his excitement, he was half way down the stairs before realising that he had neglected to pick up his overnight case from the bedroom floor. He hastily made his way back up the stairs to retrieve it. By the time he got to the bottom of the staircase, Jack and his mother and father were outside standing by the open driver's door of the mini-bus, which was occupied by Ace's small legion of supporters.

"Are you sure you don't want to come Ma? ... it'll take you five minutes to pack a bag, that's all!" Jack was saying.

"No Jack lad, no ... you younger ones get off and enjoy yourselves, you don't want a couple of old fuddy duddies like me and your dad slowing you down."

"Don't be silly you won't slow us down," Helen said, leaning across the front passenger seat towards them.

"It's too far to go for just a day and a half, thanks all the same Helen ... besides, Jack will tell you that his dad's not a very good traveller, don't you remember those day trips to Southport?" She said turning to Jack, "He'd be sick three or four times before we even got there and that's only down the road in comparison to where you're going."

"She's right, I even get green around the gills watching the travel programme on TV," the old man quipped.

"Well .. maybe another time when Ace is playing nearer home dad?" Jack said, and as Ace approached the vehicle its occupant's attention was side-tracked momentarily while they allowed their vocal chords to open up and cheer clamorously for the young hopeful. He smiled coyly in return to their enthusiastic welcome. When the noisy approval finally subsided, Ace turned to his guardians and smiled. He shook his father's hand first.

"You go out there and give them hell lad." His father advised.

"You can bet on that dad." Ace assured him before turning to his mother, who was by now making use of her handkerchief to wipe away her tears of hope and joy for the boy who had furnished her family with so much happiness over the years, added to which she was proud that he had developed into an honourable young man.

"Now ... have you got everything you will be needing?"

"We're only going for an overnight stay Ma."

"I know ... it's just .."

"The only thing I need on this trip is my tennis racket."! He grinned and bent down to kiss her on the cheek.

"Don't forget lad, give them bloody hell." His father said again, this time he made an enthusiastic motion with a gnarled fist.

"We'll be thinking of you tomorrow Arthur." His mother added.

"Thanks Ma .. so long." Ace said with a wave of his free hand and he climbed aboard the bus. Jack started the engine and the vehicle pulled away smoothly. Ace sat down in the seat next to Lorna and wasted little time in thanking everyone for taking time out to accompany him and support him. Mike, the proprietor from the local fish and chip shop had left the weekend trading in the capable hands of his wife, who, through her husband had sent her best wishes. Jack's old school chum, Davy Simpson, accepted his invitation with keenness. Glynn and his wife Susan from Bettabodies were thrilled to join the throng.

Arrangements had been made at the other end by Lorna's father appertaining to their accommodation. Jack, Helen, Davy and Mike had been booked into a small Inn that stands on the top of a steep incline above a Hertfordshire village. Lorna's parents would be playing hosts to Glynn, Susan and Ace at their home which was conveniently situated ten minutes walk away from the Inn. The journey took a little under three hours and on arrival at their respective lodgings, they agreed to meet and dine at the Inn that evening.

The group including Lorna's mother and father assembled at seven o'clock. By two rounds of drinks and thirty five minutes later the Innkeeper had given the Manchester party a chronicle of the Olde Worlde Inn. They had appreciated his enthusiastic account, especially the tale that associated Langley Hill to the Grand Old Duke of York and his ten thousand marching men. He was about to launch into another story when Glynn, who by now was becoming not only bored but also in need of sustenance to fuel his substantial appetite, held two enormous hands in the air indicating a surrender.

"Stop, enough, sorry mate, you spin a good yarn, but might we order some eats now?"

The Innkeeper looked up at the man towering over him from the other side of the bar and immediately reached for a pad and pen, and for the first time that evening fell silent, much to the amusement of the happy gathering.

"Don't worry Landlord, his bark's worse than his bite." Susan assured the Innkeeper.

"All the same, if there's any trouble on the cards this weekend, I for one am happy that you and your wife will be on our side Glynn." Jack retorted and the body beautiful couple returned a grin as broad as their individual shoulders.

Although the Inn was small and did not have an appropriate dining area, the food was of a good standard and appreciated by everyone, as was the ale and wine, though Ace, Lorna and Susan did not join in with the consumption of alcohol, Glynn, and Lorna's father had decided to sample a few alcoholic beverages, with Glynn explaining that 'This was a once a year day'. The group made conversation about a manner of subjects, however, the main topic employed was primarily aimed at Ace and his hopes and fears for the following day. Ace answered any questions fervently and appreciated their evident interest in his future, above all he felt honoured that these people had taken the time to come and support him. All the same, on catching a glimpse of the time on the clock above the bar informing him that it was ten o'clock, he excused himself from their company in order to get a good night's rest. Although Lorna's father had noticed his daughter's apparent fondness for the tall handsome Mancunian, he did not anticipate what happened next. Lorna stood up and bid everyone goodnight and with a beaming smile on her young face walked hand in hand out into the night with Ace. Lorna's father was half way out of his chair in pursuit of his daughter, before being blocked by his wife's reasoning words.

"Lorna has her own life to lead now, she doesn't need a chaperone, so just sit down and relax." She said in a steady tone. The big man looked back almost sheepishly and returned to his seat, where he smiled to some degree before countering.

"All the same ... she'll always be a baby to me."

Jack on the other hand, had something else on his mind, *'Don't athletes keep away from sex the night before a competition?'* He kept his thought quiet and reassured himself that his brother was sensible enough not to cavort with the opportunity that had been extended to him by Greg Fenton, along with the prospects that a good demonstration of his skills might present for his future.

"Jack .."

"Yeah?"

"You were miles away then." Helen grinned.

"Oh .. sorry."

"Ace will be fine, they've both got their heads screwed on the right way." She confirmed and for the remainder of the evening he allocated these considerations to the back of his mind, which, with the help of several more pints of beer subsequently consumed, became rather intoxicated. To everyone's amusement, by the evening's end, Jack had to be guided bodily up the stairs by Helen and the moment that his head hit the soft pillow he fell into a deep slumber.

The coming of the morning after what had been for Jack a rare binge had arrived, it seemed swiftly, he obviously had slept well, and had recuperated sufficiently enough to exchange banter with Helen, Davy and Mike, who teased him while they ate breakfast, over his rubber-legged exit, along with his incoherent speech as Helen aided his progress.

After collecting the rest of the party from Lorna's parents, the bus transported with its passengers a convivial atmosphere along the route to the tennis club.

Scaffolding supported the wooden bench seats tiered six high and ran the length of one side of the tennis court, in front of which the presently unoccupied umpire's chair loomed above the net. Jack was surprised at the amount of interest that the challenge match had evidently created, he estimated that there were at least one hundred people in attendance, and underneath the hazy sky and tepid sunlight of the afternoon they eagerly awaited the gladiatorial spectacle to proceed. Jack felt a surge of pride fill his heart, his eyes busily searched in the hope of catching sight of Greg Fenton, but the Australian coach was nowhere to be seen. A smartly dressed man climbed up on to the umpire's chair and the small crowd's anticipation amplified on observing a number of other officials taking up their various positions. There were even four volunteer ball-boys on hand.

A few minutes later enthusiastic applause welcomed the two players on their entrance onto the court's concrete surface. Paul Drummond was impeccably clothed in a dazzling white tracksuit which ornamented his confident stride, his Sponsor's name was emblazoned on the chest part of the jacket. He waved a hand towards the gathering who in return cheered their approval. Ace, although a good inch or two taller than the young professional appeared almost uninspiring in his grey sweatshirt walking alongside his opponent. *'It isn't a fashion show'* Jack mused, while trying to catch his brother's attention for a moment to give him the thumbs up. Jack guessed that Ace's mind was focused on the game and little else, for on his walk towards his chair placed next to the umpire's, he did not look up towards the audience at any time and once he had organised his equipment he carried out a routine of basic stretching exercises with his back to the small crowd in preparation for the warm up and what was to date the biggest match of his life.

Once the warm up and the formalities were out of the way, Drummond having won the toss, had chosen to serve first. As the young professional collected two balls in readiness to proceed with the first game and the official's instruction to 'play'. Jack genuinely hoped that his brother's stomach did not resemble his own abdominal anxiety, he spat out the small piece of fingernail that he had just chewed off.

Throughout the opening set, Ace had struggled to stamp any authority on the match, due he believed, to the fact that his serves had been singularly inadequate against his artful opposition and his all-round game had suffered because of it. To underline his frustration, at set point on Drummond's second service he had completely misread the spin applied and had involuntarily played an air shot. To rub salt into the wound, the adjudicator's voice announced the score and Ace had to admit to himself that it clearly reflected the contest so far.

"Game Drummond, and first set Drummond by six games to one." The voice from the chair proclaimed and Ace looked briefly for the first time over towards where his brother and friends were sitting, Jack gesticulated with a fist and mouthed a "Come on Bro," and as he made his way towards his appointed seat, weary from embarrassment, Ace caught sight of the Australian coach, who was sitting with his arms folded in front of him, his face displayed no emotion. *'I want to play the best you've got'* he had told Fenton *'What must he be thinking now'* Ace's thoughts taunted. He sat down heavily into his chair, then buried his head in a towel and considered momentarily their conversation prior to the challenge match.

"Are you feeling confident mate?" Fenton had asked.

"I guess so." Ace responded.

"He wasn't keen when I made the proposition."

"Who?"

"The boy Drummond."

"Why, Mr. Fenton?"

"Well, I can see his point of view ... what the hell was I doing accepting a challenge match against a rank amateur that he's never even heard of?"

Reflecting on Fenton's imprudent pre-match words, Ace cursed and was instantly rather grateful that the towel had muffled his expletive. *'Could it be that the coach was testing his character?'* Ace mused and he castigated himself again for his negative thoughts. He took the towel away from his troubled face and draped it over his knees then listened to his inner voice instructing him to *'Come on Ace, this is make or break ... come on!'*

"Time." The umpire's voice declared from above where the players were seated, Ace lifted himself from the chair and, with a purposeful stride made his way towards the baseline in preparation for the start of a new set and a chance to redeem himself for what was, so far in his mind, a dismal performance.

"Second set, Sharp to serve." The voice from the chair announced. Ace wasted little time in launching into his serve which he delivered with as much potency as he could muster. His racket connected with the ball with a loud thwack, though the serve was not as deep into the service area at the other end as he would have liked. He followed behind its flight and ran towards the net, but was confounded by Drummond's reflex backhand and was able, only to watch the return fly by him, out of reach and inside the line. The cheers and applause from the small grandstand extended their approval, Ace swallowed hard and chewed on his lip, he felt impotent. The match continued in a similar vein, that was, until at three love and forty love in the fourth game, Drummond commenced throwing a new complexion on the contest. He was by now beginning to toy with Ace, playing shots that a professional might show off in an exhibition match. He even had the audacity to play one of his shots during the game through his legs. Then much to the amusement of the throng of Drummond supporters and to add to Ace's humiliation, the young professional delivered one of his serves over the net at such a slow speed that in his attempt to get to the ball before it bounced a second time, Ace lost his footing and crashed to the floor, losing yet another game to his opponent. Livid at the opposition's gamesmanship, Ace was determined not to allow such contemptuous behaviour to get him down, on the contrary, he would channel his wrath into his game.

"It's never over till the fat lady sings!" He heard Jack's voice call from the stand, when the hubbub of merriment had receded from the Drummond quarter.

"Thank you ladies and gentlemen." The umpire said and appended, "Drummond leads by four games to love and by one set to love, Sharpe to serve."

Ace summoned himself in readiness and looked over the net towards the opposition, who was by now wearing a smug expression on his features, though it was replaced a couple of seconds later by a frown after Ace's service was dispatched at such a speed that the only reaction he could find to marshal, was a glare, towards the linesman. Ace punched the air in exhilaration in response to his first ace of the match, coupled with the fact that he had finally established the problem in his service action and had put right the defect. There was now light at the end of the tunnel.

Four games and twenty minutes thereafter Drummond's 'showboating' had terminated, being replaced with a determined effort, using a huge variety of shots to thwart his challenger's speed and doggedness, indeed the match had, by now, been turned on its head, with Ace improving with every shot, rally and every bead of sweat that oozed from his unflinching brow.

To pull this match from the jaws of adversity, Ace was aware that he had now only to hold his serves, then squeeze Drummond in the following game in which the added pressure of serving for the match, might unnerve the young professional. Ace was confident, that if the match went into a tie-break, then with his superior power, he should win this second set. Indeed, at 40-30 his convictions looked to be indomitable, but serving for the game to bring the set to 5-5 saw a rally of eighteen shots between the two sportsmen, with Drummond using a string of textbook strokes and techniques against Ace's speed and brawn. The point was finally won by an exquisite drop shot that flummoxed Ace completely. Thereafter, the score fluctuated between the players and following the fifth deuce called by the umpire, Ace had miscalculated a bounce of the ball and hit his shot low into the net, to hand advantage to Drummond. The audience were by now euphoric and yelling out their preferences, making the small gathering sound infinitely louder than anything that Ace had ever experienced before at any of his previous encounters on court. The adrenaline was now pumping through him, he took a deep breath and composed himself, while the official in the tall chair made his request for the crowd to be silent. He was not going to take his foot off the gas now, he would continue with his game plan and 'attack the net at every opportunity'. He tossed the ball up into the air and hammered the serve deep into Drummond's service area. The return was a good one, almost wrong footing Ace on his chase towards the net. He was forced at full stretch to volley on his forehand side, catching the rim of the racket, consequently taking the pace off the ball. Drummond got to the ball with four expeditious strides then with an assured stroke lobbed the ball over his challenger's six foot two head, Ace turned in pursuit of the flight of the small yellow ball. Normally his turn of speed would have seen him through to return the ball into his foe's court, but today providence was not on his side of the court, for the second time today he lost his footing. Squatting on one knee he was powerless, able only to watch the ball land on the baseline. His serve had been broken, along with his heart.

The paper thin walls that separated the two small changing rooms did little to avert Ace's dissatisfaction, although, putting into consideration the fact that Drummond had believed that the challenge match had been an insult to his status, he, along with a cluster of his friends, were loudly sounding off their jubilation of his victory, and his buddies were commending their man's professional effort. Ace sat alone with his head in his hands listening to their boisterous impressions of the match.

"Brilliant ... just brilliant!" One exultant faceless voice said.

"You ran the guy ragged." Another explained.

"Class won out there, sheer class."

"Yeah, when it comes to hey lads hey, you were the pro, and it stood out like a sore thumb!"

"Six one, seven five."

"Another day it might have been six love, six love."

Amidst the clamour in the adjacent room, Ace heard a rapping on Paul Drummond's door and someone had entered. Another voice could be heard now, it was Greg Fenton.

"Well played young fella!"

"Thanks coach."

"You held it all together well ..." Fenton was saying. It was a knock on his own door this time that caused Ace to sit up.

"Yeah?" Ace responded.

"It's me ... Jack!"

"Come on in bro." He invited and Jack entered, closing the door behind him.

"Well played Ace, you did yourself ... you did us all proud today!" Jack enthused, Ace managed a brief smile before shaking his head in a negative fashion.

"I didn't start competing till it was all too late."

"I know bro ... but I'm proud of you, we all are!"

"Thanks Jack."

There was another rap on the wooden door, before Ace could reciprocate, Greg Fenton had entered.

"How are you feeling Ace?" The Australian enquired.

"Crap."

"Why ... because you lost?"

"Bet your ass!"

"Don't be sore mate ... you gave a damn good account of yourself out there today."

"I did?"

"Sure ... listen, I took a big gamble on my reputation as a tennis coach to grant you this match, I didn't know how you were going to shape up against one of my best players ... but."

"But I lost."

"To be honest with you mate, I didn't expect anything else, but my instincts were right!"

"Your instincts?"

"Yeah, you've got guts, balls, call it what you like. I think that, had the match today been played on grass, it would have been a lot closer." Fenton emphasised and Ace speculated whether Drummond and his confidants would be listening to these words through the plasterboard partition.

"Why do you think it would have made a difference if we had played the match on grass?"

"Because the boy Drummond performs like a donkey on grass ... he would be better off eating the stuff than playing tennis on it!" Fenton said and guffawed heartily at his own sarcastic assessment. Ace and Jack laughed along, albeit with an air of bewilderment. When his laughter had abated Fenton looked Ace in the eye and cleared his throat.

"What would you say Ace to a chance of receiving some tough tuition from a tenacious one-eyed son of a bitch Aussie coach that thinks maybe you've got a future?"

Chapter Twenty One

Late for Dinner

The telephone rang out twice before Danielle picked up the receiver, instantly her conscience was filled with guilt on hearing the caller's voice at the other end of the line. They chatted in their native tongue and, as usual, when they spoke by telephone their conversation was very animated.

"Danielle Marie?"

"Mama!"

"You did not call me yesterday, so I thought that I would call you to ...."

"I am sorry Mama, I ... "

"How long has it been now?"

"Pardon?"

"How long has it has been since Jean Paul's birthday party?"

"I know I said that I would call you, but I have been rather busy."

"Busy with what?"

"Nothing Mama ... nothing that would concern you." Danielle lied. "So don't worry."

"Worry? ... that is all I seem to do lately ..."

"Mama?"

"Anyway has Jean Paul returned to America now?"

"Yes, he left at first light."

"And his girlfriend?"

"Sonya? ... she has been gone just over an hour, she had to fly to Spain, she has some work to do there it seems."

"Spain you say?"

"Yes, there was a fax sent here for her"

"I see, that explains it then."

"Explains what?" Danielle asked, slightly perplexed.

"She did not mention anything about going to Spain yesterday."

"Are you saying that you met with Sonya at your house?"

"Yes, with Jean Paul, he brought her to Villefranche in his boat ... he did not tell you?"

"No."

"I was right then!"

"What were you right about Mama?" Danielle frowned.

"I think ... I think that Jean Paul had been drinking."

"Jean Paul drinking?" Danielle gasped.

"He did not stop talking all the time that he was here, and much of the time he spoke gibberish, your Papa and me have had words over it."

"You and Papa have fallen out?"

"Well, your Papa said that Jean Paul was so spaced out that ... " The line fell silent.

"Mama, are you still there?"

"Yes."

"So spaced out that what?"

"I told him not to be so ridiculous, Jean Paul would not take drugs, I told him."

"What!? Is Papa there now?" Danielle shrieked in exasperation and continued, "How dare Papa be so presumptuous!"

"This is exactly what I said to him and ..."

"I am on my way over there." She cut in. "What is Papa thinking of .. Jean Paul is a sportsman." She reminded her mother and herself. She glanced at her wristwatch, then sighed in an effort to quell her anger.

"I will be there by three o'clock, will Papa be home?"

"Yes ... I mean I don't know, he is very unpredictable lately." Her mother explained. Danielle bid her goodbye and without wasting any time, made her way to the car.

During the drive to Villefranche her mind was actively fighting to comprehend the numerous revelations that in the past few weeks had almost bombarded her into submission. She licked her lips and recited her daily ritual aloud. The temptation to pour herself a long drink had been at its most compelling twenty four hours earlier, after her heart to heart with Floss, which along with other disturbing disclosures, confirmed conclusively her twin son's existence, then hearing how King had imposed his callous scheme onto Floss, she was gratified that her spouse was away presently, for she was sure that, harebrained though the notion was, she would surely have murdered the man. In fact, under the stress that she felt herself under, she had for the first time in her life almost discarded her pacifist beliefs that very morning, when discovering the sleek black cat roaming her bedroom, between its vice-like jaws was a petrified bird, in a desperate bid to escape the feline's blood-thirsty intentions, one of the small bird's wings flapped frantically from the side of the cat's bloody mouth. If she had been able to reach for a gun, she told herself, she would have blown the feline away. *'What in heaven's name is happening to me?!'* Danielle brooded, *'Am I looking for someone or something to blame for my own stupidity and heedlessness over these past years?'*

She stopped the Mercedes outside her parent's house, applied the handbrake then switched off the engine. Before getting out of the vehicle she reminded herself not to take her frustration out on her mother, nor indeed her Papa for his outrageous indictment with regard to Jean Paul's apparent behaviour. Danielle made her way to the back door, where she felt sure her mother would no doubt be presently preparing the early evening meal. She opened the unlocked wooden door to the kitchen, the smell of burnt food invaded her nostrils on entering and the whole area was beclouded by smoke emanating from the stove, causing her eyes to sting and water profusely. She hastened her way to the old range and switched it off, then opened a window.

“Mama?” She called between coughing. “Mama where are you? Papa!?”

She made her way through to the sitting room where she found her mother sleeping in her armchair. Danielle stood in the doorway then shook her head and smiled.

“Ma ma!” She said again, then, her mother stirred and mumbled something that Danielle did not comprehend, her face twitched and her eyes flickered open.

“Mama.”

“Hmmm ... Danielle Marie?”

“Yes.”

“The oven!” Her mother said bolting herself upright in the chair.

“The food is ruined I’m afraid.” Danielle advised her.

“Oh dear, I will have to cook your father a stew instead.”

“Come, I will help you with your preparations.”

“Thank you.” And with that mother and daughter walked into the kitchen and put things quickly in order. While Danielle prepared the vegetables she turned to her mother.

“You must be tired Mama, it is most unusual for you to leave the oven unattended, no?”

“I only sat down for a moment, I ... oh dear.”

“Have you not been sleeping well at night?”

“No Danielle, what with your Papa and well, one thing and another.”

“You told me at Jean Paul’s party Papa had been behaving oddly recently, and frankly, after what you told me earlier on the telephone what he had said about Jean Paul, I must agree reflects his wayward judgement at present, no?”

“Did you see Jean Paul yesterday when he returned home?”

“I saw him this morning, and he was fine, really, how could Papa besmirch his grandson so readily!?”

“You know your father, he always says what he thinks!”

“Where is Papa anyway?”

“I really do not know Danielle Marie, lately he has been walking around like a zombie, I caught him the other day talking to himself, and .... using bad language also, this is not like him as you know!?”

“Will he be at the boat?” Danielle asked.

“That boat!” She answered acrimoniously, Danielle frowned as she contemplated her mother cutting into a piece of meat more vigorously with the knife than necessary.

“That boat!” She repeated, louder this time and continued, “Ever since that husband of yours assigned that boat to your Papa, our lives have never been the same, he will not be at the boat, like me, I think he hates the thing.”

“Where will he be then?”

“God knows? ... just lately he has gone missing for hours on end, then when I ask him where he has been, he simply says, out, out where?, I say to him ... just out! ... he tells me.”

“Mama, I am going out to look for him, would he have gone to the factory?”

“The factory has been locked up and out of use for some time now, there is nothing there for him.”

The colour drained from Danielle's face. She scolded herself once again for her negligence regarding her parents' recent plight.

"So it is true that the factory is no longer in production?"

"Your father did not want you to know about this Danielle Marie, he ..."

"I must speak with him, we can find a way around this Mama ... now please, do not worry anymore, I promise we will sort all this mess out!"

"He will probably be spilling out his problems on some stranger somewhere, God knows, he won't speak to me about them!" Her mother's anguished voice confirmed. Once again a flood of guiltiness washed over Danielle's conscience.

"Try Julian's cafe in the harbour, maybe he will be there drowning his sorrows."

"I will Mama ... and when I find him I will bring him directly home and give him a good talking to, no?" Danielle forced a smile and walked the few paces towards where her mother was standing, then bent down slightly and kissed her on the cheek in the hope that perhaps, this small deed might somehow hearten her ageing parent.

"I will be back soon, there is much to talk about Mama."

"Try Julian's cafe."

"Yes Mama, I will."

"Will you be staying for dinner?"

"Yes, as I say there is much to discuss."

"Good ... good, it will be like old times Danielle Marie, no?"

"Yes, it will Mama." She agreed, though in her heart she knew that the debate that she and her parents would be having this evening would undoubtedly be more distressing than any deliberation that they had had at any time at the dinner table over the years. She closed the old wooden door behind her, the afternoon was warm and bright so she decided to look for her father on foot. As she meandered towards the waterfront through the intricate streets she asked a number of familiar locals if they had caught sight of her father during their day's activities, each of them to varying degrees dawdling her progress by instigating friendly conversation and only when Danielle explained politely that she was in rather a hurry did they come around to answering her initial question. *'Not today'* one said, *'Is your Papa unwell?'* another asked, *'Not the man he was'* was another comment. Danielle was by now beginning to wish that she had opted to make her exploration by car. An hour later, subsequent to her drawing a blank at Julian's cafe along with several other establishments, Danielle decided to make her way towards the old canning factory, and if he was not there then she would return to her parent's house on the Rue de Poilu, by which time she told herself, her Papa would doubtlessly be there amusing himself at his daughter's rash behaviour and turning this disappearing act into a light-hearted joke. On reflection, that was exactly how the old man would have viewed the whole situation, but how much had her father changed? All the same, Danielle was not going to let him off lightly, why was he being so reticent? Furthermore, how dare he accuse Jean Paul of being 'spaced out', as he apparently put it, on drugs? Yes, she would reprimand him the moment she next set eyes on him.

The old man rubbed his heavily creased brow with a gnarled hand and sighed. The chair on which he had been sitting for most of the day creaked under the weight of his jaded body.

"I will see you in Hell, Irwin King!" He said aloud and his crestfallen words echoed around the cool vacant factory walls. The chair groaned once more as he leaned forward in the darkness to prepare for his final undertaking.

The sight of the old building saddened Danielle, she stood motionless reluctantly sanctioning her eyes to tour its run down exterior. A number of cracks had appeared on the hapless walls since last Danielle had paid the factory a visit. In the fading sunlight, the once brilliantly white paint work was now diminished to a lustreless grey, to add to the structure's ominous aura all the windows had been boarded up. She made a mental note that she would forward the money needed to re-establish his old business, as proud as her Papa was, she would insist on this, she stepped forward to make her way towards the main doors.

The explosion knocked her clean off her feet, her head was the first thing to meet the hard surface of the roadway. The whole thing happened in an instant, though to Danielle, that instant occurred in slow motion before the flash of bright light ignited behind her eyes. The last thought that she had, was that she was eight years old again, and Charles D'Anjou, the Count of Provence had come to her village on a white charger to sweep her away to his castle in the air. Then there was only darkness.

Chapter Twenty Two

Larry Hickman was at the wheel of the Renault, he and his passenger had chatted lightly over various everyday subjects for the first half of the journey from Palma Airport. It was not until they reached Manacor, situated towards the centre of Mallorca that their conversation took on a more significant nature.

"So tell me, did you meet our villainous friend on your little errand to Monte Carlo?"

"Unfortunately not." Sonya replied with a frown, "It was a mistake, what did I think I was going to learn about Karen's disappearance by going there!?"

"I'm sorry Sonya, but didn't I say ..."

"I know, I know." She cut in "I just kinda thought that I ..."

"You kinda thought that Irwin King was going to maybe turn around to you and say, hold on a moment while I check out the abduction file, under Kennedy!"

"You're mocking me."

"No, I'm just telling you, it was a damn fool thing to go nosying in the enemy's backyard. Besides, it's a shot in the dark, a thousand to one, that King and the rest of the organisation ever came near your kid sister."

"I know, anyway, he'd been gone from the place a couple of hours before I got there."

"Well, take this anyway you care, but, I'm sure glad about that."

"Well, I'm sure glad you care." She confirmed with a smile.

"And how are you getting along with the young King of the courts?"

"That's another reason why I shouldn't have gone there."

"Oh?"

"I sure made a damn fool of myself in that department."

"What ... did you challenge the guy to a tennis match or something?" He said lightly, Sonya ignored the jocular effort and, for the first time on the journey their conversation was stifled, though the atmosphere between them was not strained in any way. Hickman hoped that his next question was not going to be too clumsy.

"Are you sweet on him?"

"No!"

"No?"

"Jean Paul King is rich, intelligent and infuriatingly sexy but ..."

"But?"

"But on the other hand he's insular, he's obtuse, immature and darn-right conceited ... and to top it all off, I've known the guy on and off now for fully twelve months, and learned nothing from him about his father."

"Yeah, but does Jean Paul know what a low life his father is?"

"The first time that I had approached the subject with Jean Paul was when we went out on his boat. He informed me that he had had his suspicions that his old man might be involved in some kind of underworld activity."

"And that's all he knew?"

"Yeah."

"Do you believe him?"

"Sure, I don't see any reason why not. I reckon from what I could gather, he don't like his Papa anymore than he likes losing a tennis match."

"Did you tell Jean Paul about your sister?"

"I didn't see the point, besides by the time I had got that far, the guy was out of his head on the rich boy's drug."

"Speed ... Coke!?"

"Yeah."

"What's the kid trying to do?" Hickman gasped.

On arriving at his modest though cheerful villa at Los Pinos, Hickman showed Sonya to the guest room.

"Not very palatial I'm afraid Sonya, but I'm sure you'll be comfortable."

"This is just fine Larry thanks." She said testing the single bed's mattress with a hand.

"Good, than make yourself at home." He smiled and turned to leave.

"Oh Larry ... thanks again for arranging this, I guess I needed a vacation, even though it'll only be for a few days."

"Stay as long as you like, I will enjoy the company, when did you say your next modelling assignment was?"

"Six days from today in London for Vivienne Westwood."

"Did you have somewhere else to go before then?"

"Not really."

"That settles it then, ... say, how would you like to make an old guy like me jump up and click his heels?"

"What do you mean?"

"I know a real nice little restaurant, would you give me the pleasure of your company for dinner?"

"I would be delighted to!" She agreed gleefully. Hickman responded with a tiny leap accompanied with a swift clicking of his heels as he left the room.

Sonya used the only mode of transport that she had employed throughout her mini vacation on the island of Mallorca, to arrive at the cliff top. She perched the old fashioned looking bicycle up against a large boulder then glanced at her wristwatch, the timepiece informed her that it was 8 am and the penultimate day prior to her departure to London. Her hair shimmered in the light breeze, she inhaled deeply, filling her lungs with the invigorating morning air and treated her eyes to the view of the rich blue of the Mediterranean. The smile on her face was testament to her thoughts relating to her stay in the company of the Larry Hickman, who by now she regarded as her soul mate. During their evenings together, they had made conversation covering a multitude of subjects, some of which caused them to laugh wholeheartedly and others that brought rather more sombre moments. Sonya discovered Hickman to be a humorous, genial and intelligent man, the book that he had written, 'Cause Against Slavery', was a credit to his humanitarianism she believed. Her mind went back to their chat the previous evening.

"For an ex-con you're a hell of a nice guy." She had declared.

"Thank you, I sincerely hope that I'm worthy of such a compliment, from a hell of a nice gal." He reciprocated, with what by now she regarded as his familiar smile. Sonya had almost wished at that moment that he had been a younger man, and with the aid of a few glasses of Rioja she had related her consideration verbally.

"No ... no, when I was a younger man I was a degenerate asshole, I don't think you would have liked me then, but two compliments in one evening from such a beautiful young lady warms my tired old heart no end." He replied.

A subtle change in the air temperature dislocated her from her thoughts. The sun had been eclipsed by a band of dark cloud, suggesting an imminent storm. She turned and hastily climbed onto the bicycle then, carefully manoeuvred her way over the rugged terrain towards the road that, with a little luck would take her back to the villa in advance of the fast approaching deluge. Once there, she would keep her promise to prepare breakfast, after all, it was her turn. In fact, it would be her first attempt at doing anything in the kitchen. She had been thoroughly spoilt by the chap ever since she had arrived there. Sonya hoped earnestly that he had received a phone call from Jean Paul's mother while she had been out, the poor fellow was very concerned yesterday when she had not called as had been arranged. Sonya considered now, that when she had met Danielle King on the eve of her son's birthday, she had thought her to be a very elegant, gracious woman who displayed a self-assured disposition. Since then however Sonya had discovered from Hickman, that beneath this gallant veneer was a rather troubled soul. Learning of the treacherous abduction of one of Danielle's twin sons had appalled Sonya, and Hickman's disclosures relating to Irwin King's reasons for such a shameful deed, sickened her to the stomach. He had rounded off his account of these discoveries to date, by giving her a detailed description of the young man that he honestly considered to be Jean Paul King's absent twin brother. Hickman had then produced a photograph which had been taken at the entrance to a tube station in West London. The snapshot displayed a tall dark young man exchanging words with what looked to be a vagrant, standing to one side of this powerfully built would-be twin, was a shorter man somewhat older.

Sonya felt the first splashes of rain, interrupting her thoughts and she contemplated now taking shelter at the beach bar, which she knew lay back off the road approximately one hundred metres ahead, but by the time that she had covered only half that distance the downpour had intensified and she was drenched through to the skin. *'No point in taking cover now'* she judged, with that in mind she lifted her bottom off the saddle to allow herself more leverage on the pedals. Her lengthy legs pumped vigorously to gain speed.

Fifteen minutes later, her aching limbs pushed her towards the final rise, where at its summit, she would be able to free-wheel down the other side all the way to the villa, she comforted herself with that fact and rallied all her strength to make the final climb.

It was thanks to her skill on two wheels, coupled with good reflexes that she avoided meeting the speeding car head-on at the apex of the hill. In making the evasive manoeuvre Sonya and the bicycle had finished up begrimed in red mud, emanating from the ditch where she now turned and hollered her displeasure.

"How much of the goddamn road do you need asshole!" She chided towards the offending car which was by now barely visible, it was cocooned in a cloud of spray in the distance.

"What are you in such a frigging hurry about anyway!" She yelled, but her words were drowned by the rain pummelling over the road's surface. In frustration she slapped an open hand against the handle bars and cursed at the futility of her anger against the elements and the son of a bitch driver who had just almost wiped her out. She pulled herself and the bicycle out of the ditch. Apart from a grazed elbow, she was relatively unharmed in the ordeal, and besides being covered in grime, the bike appeared to have survived intact.

She used the rear entrance at the villa when she arrived there, opened the door then kicked off her trainers before crossing the threshold, she bent down and picked up the sodden footwear then entered. The delightful aroma of fresh coffee greeted her in the narrow passageway that ran adjacent to the kitchen.

"Larry!?" She called. Her wet feet offered her little confidence as she walked tentatively over the sleek tiled surface. At the kitchen doorway she came to a halt, the door was ajar, with her free hand she pushed it open wide to find the area unoccupied. The radio was on, albeit turned down low, broadcasting a flamenco rendition. She was almost tempted to pour herself a hot coffee from the percolator but, looking down at her mud ridden blue jeans she decided that that delectation would have to wait.

"Larry! ... if you can hear me, I'm gonna take a shower, OK ... listen, don't you dare go start making breakfast, it's my turn remember?! She said loudly and cocked her head to one side, in an effort somehow to pick up a verbal response. Sonya assumed that Hickman was probably in his study at the farthest part of the building from where she stood. *'On the phone I'll bet'* she mused *'Never know, he could be talking to Danielle King'* she concluded optimistically, then made her way over the short distance from there to the guest room, where she went directly into the small en suite bathroom and turned on the shower, she placed her shoes on the floor to one side of the tub, then with a hand tested the temperature of the water, satisfied, she then turned to undress and espied her reflection in the fairly sizeable mirror on the wall, the saturated blouse she wore was translucent and exposed the full firmness of her breasts, causing her to smile in recollection of a Miss wet t-shirt competition that she had taken part in at a party back in fifth grade. The sensation of unbuttoning the garment and taking it away from her skin made her shiver. She peeled off the remainder of her clothing and climbed into the warm torrent and groaned with pleasure, wishing for it to melt away, for the time being at least, her thoughts of what could have been only ten minutes earlier a premature meeting with her maker. She would acquaint the episode with Hickman over breakfast and doubtlessly between them they would discover the funny side of her plight.

Over the time since her first visitation in prison, she had learned to trust Hickman. As far as Sonya was concerned credence was the most important component in the relationship between them, especially now that Hickman had pledged that he would join her in a concerted effort, regardless of the risks to investigate and gather as much knowledge as they possibly could to establish her sister's whereabouts. Her mind floated back to the evening before last and the latter part of their conversation.

"Listen Sonya ... I don't want to crush your hopes of ever seeing your kid sister again, but you've got to realise that ..."

"Larry." She had cut in. "I need to know one way or the other, I need to know!"

"I understand, but this is going to be dangerous, I mean fucking dangerous, do you understand!?"

"So when ... when do we start Larry?"

"What say, when you've finished your business in London?"

Yes, she confirmed to herself, now, between them they would find the truth about Karen's disappearance and with a favouring wind and good fortune on their side they may find her kid sister alive, "Please God." Sonya said aloud, while at the same time pushing the lever to halt the lavish flow of water. She then reached for a towel and hastily dried herself off before donning a long towelling robe, picked up a brush from the shelf and glided it through her hair, then made her way back towards the kitchen, whereupon she fully expected to discover Hickman making provisions, having ignored her insistence on the breakfast arrangements. She frowned slightly, walked over to the radio and turned it off.

"Larry ... you still on the phone?" She hollered, then filled a cup of the aromatic black liquid from the percolator and sampled it, relishing its flavour and warmth. She called out his name twice more between sips and reckoned that, before commencing with the cooking, she would amble over to the study and find out if he was ready to eat.

She knocked on the door and entered, declaring as she did so.

"Larry, I'm famished after all ..." She stopped mid-sentence, shaken by the disorderly state of the compact room. His papers were strewn over the whole area.

"Jees ... did someone leave a window open?" She said to herself, it was her first visit to this part of the building and reflected that some intellectual people actually thrive in such organised chaos. She turned and shut the door.

"Larry ... where the hell are you?" She said with a hint of frustration in her tone this time. Sonya walked through the sitting room, toward the dining area and opened up the sliding doors. The sound of the torrential rain pelting against the patio doors was the only reception that she received there. She drained off the remainder of her coffee and placed the cup on top of the Spanish designed table and wandered over to peer out through the windows towards the pine woods. His car was on the drive when she returned, *'he must have gone for a stroll and like me got caught in the downpour, I guess he must have taken cover somewhere'* her thinking reasoned. She looked at her wristwatch and considered that consequently it would be brunch that they would be sharing now. She decided that another cup of coffee would have to help service her appetite for the time being and retrieved her cup from the table. On her way back towards the kitchen she stopped outside Hickman's bedroom door, that was another part of the villa that she had not visited before. A wave of anticipation swept over her *'why?'* she asked herself then reprehended her uneasiness and tapped lightly on the dark wooden panel.

"Larry, are you in there?" She summoned and smiled at her contemplation that there might be something foreboding on the other side of the door. *'After all Sonya, you ain't no psychic'* she reminded herself, with that in mind, she turned the handle, pushed the door open and entered the bedroom.

The cup fell from her hand and smashed into pieces at her feet on the hard floor. His feet were the first things that her eyes registered, as they were just below her eyelevel. She raised her startled gaze slowly from the man's feet that swayed slightly like a pendulum. A strong stench of human excrement assaulted her nostrils, wrenching her gut, she covered her gaping mouth with a tremulous hand. The normally benign facial features were twisted in a grotesque grimace, his tongue hung out from one side of his mouth in a hideous fashion and two bloodshot sightless eyes stared down at her. The obnoxiously pitched scream, that seemed to come from her toes, echoed around the four walls and against the dark wooden beams. From one of these beams Larry Hickman dangled from the end of a noosed rope.

She stepped back a pace, her eyes transfixed to the heinous spectacle before her, so numbed were her nerves that she did not feel the fragment of porcelain pierce her foot, she turned and fled, an intermittent trail of blood followed her to the kitchen. From there she would telephone the police and inform them of her friend's suicide, she picked up the handset and with the index finger of her trembling hand pressed the first digit, then placed the receiver back in its cradle. *'Larry Hickman would not have killed himself'* her mind reasoned. She needed to compose herself and deal with the situation rationally.

"Think, goddam it Sonya ... think!" She told herself. Her foot by now was beginning to throb in time with the beat of her heart. She reached into the cupboard where she knew that Hickman kept a first-aid kit, plucking out the small casket she hopped on her good foot and sat down at the small table. Then, as carefully as she could summon her unsteady fingers, she extracted the small remnant of earthenware from her heel, then hastily dressed the wound which would probably need stitching, but presently that was the last thing on her mind. Employing a mop and bucket she cleaned up the trail of blood from the kitchen floor that led back to the dark wooden door. She took several deep breaths and gritted her teeth before re-entering the chamber then swiftly soaked up the bloody mess, while at the same time trying desperately not to look up into the corpse's hideous gaze, with the aid of a brush and shovel she hurriedly scooped up the broken coffee cup. The noise startled her, resulting in her almost dropping the shovel, once again Sonya found herself staring at the two bulging eyes. *'Merely the poor guy's internal gastric system having its final say'* she surmised. Quickly she turned and left the ghastly scene closing the door behind her. By now she was aware that she had broken out in a cold sweat, she had to get out of the place now, hobbling to the guest room she expeditiously dressed herself and packed her bag. Within six minutes Sonya was behind the wheel of Hickman's Renault. *'The ring, as Larry had referred to them, had paid a visit'* she had by now convinced herself. She reached the location where, an hour or so earlier in the day, she had virtually collided head on with a car. '*That car ... and that crazy driver'* her brainwork shrilled '*Could they have been making good their escape from Larry Hickman's villa, after murdering him, then disguising their evil actions to look like suicide?'* Another disturbing thought confounded her now '*Do these faceless hoods see me as a threat to them somehow, if so, did that crazy son of a bitch driver deliberately try to put my lights out?'*

"You're being paranoid!" She remonstrated with herself. All the same, she wanted no more to do with this scenario, even if it meant neglecting any further aspirations in pursuit of her sister's whereabouts. Today's appalling events had cracked her veneer leaving her feeling utterly vulnerable. She turned the windscreen wipers off, the rain had finally abated and the sky ahead appeared to be clearing. It would doubtlessly be a fine afternoon on the island of Mallorca though Sonya had no intention of staying to determine the outcome of her meteorological observations.

Chapter Twenty Three

Mind Games

This was only the second time that Jean Paul had returned to Monaco since the accident that had claimed his Grandfather, and very nearly taken his mother's life. That unfortunate episode four months ago, had halted his bid in his first major tournament, effectively almost destroying his confidence and titanic aspirations overnight. He had flown from Melbourne to be at her bedside, and stayed there for several days, while she remained unconscious. With each hour that passed, Jean Paul became progressively more ambiguous, for the first time in his life, his thoughts engaged in a negative dimension. Until that is, on the fifth day of his vigil, he had fallen into a fretful slumber, after a while his dreams mollified. The dark illusory vista inside his head, gently gave way to an enlivening dawn, Jean Paul drifted into its warmth. *He was looking out over Le Jardine Antoinette, towards the azure of the sea, a clipping sound caused him slowly to about face. There, at the foot of the house, by an archway, his mother with her back towards him was busily tending to the beautiful bougainvillaea plant which embraced and climbed the white walls that had served as a backdrop for the flourishing purple blossom. She turned around and smiled.*

"I am really glad you came." Danielle said.

"Mama!" He replied, then stepped forward and clenched her to his chest. After a moment he stepped back and cast his eyes over her.

"I have been looking through some old photographs and video recordings." She grinned, "There was one particular video that I played over many times. Would you believe it, I am giving you some tennis coaching, ... before that is, the rain came along and drenched us both to the skin."

"Yes, I know the one, I was I think just six years old." They both laughed heartily, before Jean Paul spoke again.

"It is a long time ago Mama but, ... I remember that day, you told me ... Jean Paul, you said, one day I believe that you will be the best tennis player in all the world!"

"Yes, Jean Paul, and I meant it." She smiled then continued. "This means that you should follow your dream, do not let me encumber your hopes." Danielle's tone then became serious when she suggested to him.

"To worry about me will only serve to destroy all of that ... promise me, that until I am back to normal, you will not fret about my well-being."

"What do you mean .. back to normal?"

"Promise me Jean Paul."

"I promise Mama ... but ..."

"Promise meeee!"

Jean Paul's eyes had snapped open, he stood up from the chair in which he had been sleeping, then stepped the couple of paces forward towards the bed, where his mother lay. Her face was motionless, the only signs to reassure the onlooker that she was still alive was the monitor, that regulated the measurement of her heart beat. This was the first and only time since learning of the accident that Jean Paul had cried, he looked down over his mother's unstirring body, and thanked her, for he had been convinced that his mother's spirit had somehow paid him a visit.

Now, Jean Paul was back in that part of the world on business, competing in the Monte Carlo Open. (The first major of the season on clay). He had trained hard with Brad Holding that morning, after which, he had promised the coach that he would return after lunch, to go through a session of light routines in preparation for his quarter finals match, which was scheduled on court for the early evening.

He had done his uppermost to decline the invitation, though his father was rather insistent, demonstrating that it was very important that they meet.

Presently, Jean Paul sat on the terrace at the Vista Palace Hotel, at the summit of the Grande Corniche, a great vaulting wall of grey rock, off which, as he spectated, several hang-gliders under the guidance of enthusiasts, every once in a while, were launched then piloted, swooping and spiralling on the warm breeze, to who knows where. He looked at his wrist watch, if his father did not arrive in the next few minutes, then he was leaving, *'damn it'* he was ten minutes late as it was. His stomach felt taut, he was not sure if that was due to his impending encounter on court this evening or ....

"Got held up." The South African accent announced, now Jean Paul knew the reason for his slight anxiety. The waiter pulled out a chair for King, and he sat down opposite his son.

"I will have a scotch on the rocks waiter ... what about you?" He asked Jean Paul.

"Orange juice."

"Got that? .. oh, and fetch me the menu!" King commanded, and the waiter scurried away, as if being chased by a poisonous reptile.

"I see you are through to the quarters eh!? .. make it a good'n, I've got a lot of money riding on it!"

"So ... hello Jean Paul, how are you? Very well thank you Papa! Tell me won't you, how are you!?" Jean Paul said sarcastically. King ignored his son's satirical attempts, choosing instead, to light a cigarette. He proceeded then to exhale the smoke into the waiter's face, as the man leaned forward to present the bill of fare. Another waiter placed the guest's drinks, proficiently upon the table. Then, while inspecting the menu King announced almost in a matter of fact way;

"I'm afraid that your mother's condition has worsened."

"But .. this should not be so, she is after all out of her coma." Jean Paul frowned, "Has been now for over two months, surely .."

"Probably the bump on the head." King interposed, "It's made her ... how shall I say this, a little unbalanced!?"

“How can you say such a thing, you have not even been there for her.” Jean Paul declared managing barely to keep himself from shouting.

“Nor, ... I do believe have you!?”

“I intended to call in and see her, once the tournament here was over ...” His pulse was racing now, “I need to channel all my thoughts and efforts into my game!”

“Yeah ... now while you have been nurturing your tennis game, you will be pleased to know, that I called in on her yesterday.”

“That ... I believe I am right in saying, is the first and only time you have called on her!”

“You don’t seem to understand boy, I’m a very busy man!”

“What are her chances of a full recovery?”

“Not good I’m afraid.”

“What do you mean ... not good?” Jean Paul’s troubled voice exclaimed, while another voice inside him beckoned. *‘Promise me Jean Paul ... promise meeee!’* Though he did not disregard this inner reflection he continued. “I was informed that she was improving steadily!”

“Who gave you this information?”

“Floss did.”

“Floss!?” King responded with a pompous air.

“Yes, she should know, do you not think, after all, she is in attendance day and night!”

“But what does Floss know, eh?”

“That is it .. I am going to see for myself!” Jean Paul affirmed, standing up from the table.

“It’ll do no good.”

“What do you mean?”

“Your mother will not be there.”

“Pardon me?”

“I have sent her away on a vacation.”

“A vacation ... where?”

“She needs to rest, she is in good hands, trust me ..”

“I would trust Lucifer, before I would you!”

“Sit down and relax, you will need to conserve your energy.”

“Where have you sent her to?” Jean Paul demanded in a stifled tone, in an effort to quell his growing anger at what he regarded as his father’s callousness. He felt the inquisitive eyes of the gathering of diners on him. So, to avert treating them to a scene, he relocated himself in the chair opposite his father.

“She needed to convalesce.” King continued.

“How long for?”

“As long as it takes.”

The two men sat in silence, while the waiter placed a bowl of olives on the table.

“Are you ready to order Monsieur?” The waiter asked. King dismissed the man with a wave of his hand.

“Believe me ... it will not help you or your mother to visit her at this time.” King then remarked.

“What makes you think this?”

“Since she came out of the coma, she has not been able to recall anything of her past, she has started having bouts of ... what I am told is severe depression ... black moods, call them what you like. I believe Jean Paul, that your mother has suffered a nervous breakdown.”

“Who made this diagnosis?”

“The Doctors at the ... convalescence place that I had her admitted to.”

Jean Paul became mindful once more of his dream. *‘Promise me, that until I am back to normal, you will not fret about my well-being,’* Danielle’s words echoed, *‘promise me Jean Paul.’*

“I promise Mama.” He said aloud. King looked across the table with a puzzled expression.

“What?” He asked.

“Oh ... nothing, I was just reminiscing.” Jean Paul declared, and as if King had read into his thoughts relating to the dream he announced.

“It would be best for both of you, that you concentrate on your tennis!”

“Yes ... you are probably right.” Jean Paul agreed, and tried to recall the last time the two men had been in agreement about anything.

“Good ... now what shall we have to eat?” King said.

“I seem to have lost my appetite.” With that, Jean Paul stood up from the table and left. The news that King had bestowed upon him, undoubtedly provided his opposition early that evening, with a comparatively painless passage through to the semi-finals. Irwin King collected his windfall from his wager the following morning.

PART II

Chapter Twenty Four

The Ascent From Base Camp

Over the past sixteen months, following the Australian's promise of *'tenacious coaching',* the tactical part of the new young professional's tennis skills had advanced immeasurably. Ace, had over this time also impressed Greg Fenton, who recognized his student's unequivocal need to learn and develop throughout the countless hours of arduous drills and exercises during their daily practice sessions. Now, all that hard work was finally beginning to pay off where it matters most, on court and in competition. For Ace, these formative months had been a period of financial struggle although, fortunately for him he had not been disillusioned by this, after all he was quite accustomed to such difficulties. In addition on a more positive note, when he was not travelling to various locations to compete, he had set up a temporary home in Hertfordshire, above commercial premises, where a friend of Greg Fenton's had given Ace a job working as a Salesperson in his sports shop, underneath his small apartment, albeit on a part time basis to subsidise his poor earnings thus far in his chosen profession. As luck would have it the proprietor turned out to be a benevolent advocate to Ace's aspirations, and was currently the only sponsor willing to invest in the player's talent. He had been supplied with a range of rackets, tennis shoes and other first class accessories needed to perform at a professional level, and Ace would be eternally grateful for the man's support.

Today had seen him win a place in the British Satellite Trophy final and, an opportunity to collect a much needed cheque to the value of one and a half thousand pounds as runner up or, three and a half thousand if he was to actually go on to win the trophy.

Ace had quickly showered and dressed into his fashionable tracksuit and trainers.

"Well played." The voice in broken English broadcasted from behind, where he was seated busily tying his laces. He turned to face the person who had offered the congratulatory words.

"Tony Wang." The thickset Hong Kong Chinese and former world ranking number seven said offering his hand.

"Yes ... yes, I know." Ace replied with instant recognition. Wang smiled as Ace out of respect unwittingly rubbed his hand on his tracksuit, before grasping the other man's hand firmly.

"I'm a big fan." Ace managed to say in a slightly nervous tone.

"I watch you play today, now I am a fan of yours, you are good!" Wang grinned.

"Thanks."
"I will see you in the final."
"Yeah ... yes."
"I think I will have a lot to think about between now and then, I believe it will be a good final."
"Yeah ... bet your arse!" Ace confirmed, with that Tony Wang turned and left the room.
Ace puckered his lips and released a whistle. He, Arthur Sharp, was set now to do battle against one of the world's top established players. It was true that Tony Wang was not presently even in the top one hundred, due to his sustaining a bad knee injury twelve months or so ago, which required the former world number seven to undergo surgery. Ace was mindful also that Wang was simply using this tournament as a stepping stone in order to regain match fitness. Despite this, none of Wang's opposition had managed to win a single set against him up to now. Ace's thoughts were interrupted when Greg Fenton bounded through the same door that his opponent for the final had made his exit. Jack followed the coach in, poking a thumb over his shoulder.
"Guess who I've just passed in the corridor bro?!" Jack enthused.
"Tony Wang." Ace grinned.
"How did you ...?"
"He came to say hello."
"I reckon you've got the guy worried." Fenton said in an incidental tone.
"Who ... Tony Wang?"
"The very fellow, on what I witnessed today Ace, he won't be relishing mixing it with you."
"Do you really reckon?"
"I reckon, anyway we'll discuss all that later, are you ready to leave?"
"Yeah, just about Greg, why?"
"Got some good news for you, come on mate, let's go!"
"Slow down a minute coach, don't keep me in the dark, tell me what's this good news?"
"I've just been chatting to the British Davis Cup Captain."
"Oh?"
"He watched your match today."
"And?"
"He was pretty impressed, he asked me if you might consider working and developing a liking for team tennis."
"Hell, the Davis Cup Team, that would be fantastic!"
Ace displayed those immaculate white teeth of his with a broad grin. At last he felt that the fruits of his ambitions were starting to develop in this, the early springtime of his life and career.

Ace had never before encountered opposition with such an assortment of ground strokes. Tony Wang was a very compact figure, a strong and skilful player with a dextrous touch and despite his knee operation he exhibited extraordinary mobility. Until now, with the match at three games all in the opening set, it had been Ace's simple brawn that had kept him in the first set, he knew by now that that alone would not influence the outcome of the match. *'Time for a change in tactics'* he considered, while crouching low, vigilantly awaiting the delivery of Wang's first service in the seventh game.

Although he had to date never won when he had competed in major top ATP tournaments, Wang had actively achieved his high ranking, (along with much respect from the world's top professionals) due to his tenacious performances throughout the sport's foremost championships over an impressive twelve month period, until that is, the inopportune injury that served to blight his progress. Ace remembered in particular watching his present opponent with admiration on TV, losing narrowly on the famous number one court at Wimbledon to the then number two seed, Carl Emerson in the quarter finals. The American, Emerson, went on to take the Wimbledon title, in a final that was not nearly as closely contested. Yes indeed, Tony Wang was a man that deserved respect for his achievements *'but not too much'* Ace prompted himself before employing a sliced backhand in reply to the serve and in doing so, taking the pace off the ball. From now on Ace was determined to dictate the tempo, to do that he knew that he would have to outfox his more experienced foe.

It was evident at the conclusion of the first set that with a mixture of mental effort and natural racket skills, Ace's strategy had worked indisputably well, rewarding him with a 6-4 triumph and first blood.

The wheels came off in the second set. His seasoned rival had moved up a gear and enrolled into the battle of wits. Consequently the match had been turned on its head. Although obviously very talented, in the opening set Ace had regarded Wang as somewhat orthodox, in truth he had been, but in this new set Wang had become showmanlike, using every shot in the book, what was more disconcerting for the younger man was that some of Wang's endeavours were certainly not text book material. As the two men made their way towards their respective chairs at the completion of the said second set, Ace believed that Tony Wang had gained a few inches in height.

"Second set to Wang by six games to one." The man seated in the highchair broadcasted to the gathering while Ace slumped into his chair, then covered his head with a towel in an effort to cocoon himself from the setting and collect his thoughts. He was mindful now that to beat Tony Wang tactically was improbable, but what was more frustrating was that if he was to attempt to manipulate the match by utilising one of his biggest assets, that being his natural power would be foolhardy. By doing that, it was possible that he would lose accuracy by overhitting on the slow playing indoor carpet. Besides, he reminded himself, Wang had faced the best services from some of the finest players in the world, on the quickest surface of all, the grass of Wimbledon. He slowly lifted the towel from around his head and placed it on his lap, then picked up a small container of spring water and sipped in a mouthful of the clear refreshing liquid, allowing it to wash around his tongue before swallowing it gratefully down. On the opposite side of the court to where he was sitting, Ace espied the one-eyed coach amidst the crowd. The distinguished features displayed no emotion, though Ace knew what Greg Fenton's thoughts were conveying, reflectively Ace asked himself.

"How much do you want this?"

The umpire called 'time' and Ace took in two long deep breaths before climbing out of the chair.

If at the outset of this match, the audience watching had been impartial to the final result, it was certainly not the case now, as the final set progressed towards its normal completion, they clapped and cheered their approval of the talent and determination of the two competitors. By the time that the set had got to a stalemate situation at 5-5, a good proportion of the onlookers, aware that in the final set there would be no tie-break, wondered if they might still be viewing this gladiatorial encounter deep into the night. These suppositions were not too far wrong, for at nine games all, it appeared that neither player was going to concede under pressure, indeed, they both appeared to delight in the situation.

Each game in this extended set had gone with serve, appropriately the ensuing action continued in that vein, when at 40-30, Ace followed in on his first serve to volley away Wang's reply for the winner to advance the score to 10-9.

Now it was Wang's turn to answer on his serves. Incongruous to the scenario so far, his serves had lost a degree of potency and his groundstrokes had also become comparatively defective. *'Was the Oriental Warrior succumbing under pressure at last?... surely not'* Ace wondered to himself, while stooping in readiness to receive another service. Another languid serve was punished with a wicked top spin backhand to give Ace match point. Ace whooped with glee and was suddenly mindful of the spectators seated around the court. Their applause had become disproportionate, quite a number did not clap or show approval at all, he was curious to know why this was, *'had they wanted this to go on all night?'* Ace brooded. A rally of seven shots between the two players followed Wang's service to stay in the match. Ace knew now what he had obviously failed to notice, having been so engrossed in the battle, and why the crowd's sympathy was now perhaps biased towards the other side of the net. What would have been Ace's finest hour, as it came to its climax, had turned sour. He waited at the net and looked on while the Oriental Warrior walked lamely towards him to shake hands with the victor. *'Winner by default'* Ace reflected. Wang's handshake was as firm as it had been before the initiation between the two.

"Is it your knee?" Ace enquired.

"Just a twinge, I'm sure it will be fine."

"I hope so ... thanks Tony by the way, I learned a lot out there today."

"Like I say, you are a good player Arthur."

"Ace ... call me Ace."

"I will see you at Wimbledon!"

"Wimbledon?"

The two athletes shook hands with the umpire in his tall chair, Ace's features gave way to an enormous smile.

Under the torrent of warm water, Ace busily washed his well-knit body, halting the process momentarily, and not for the first time today, allowing his thumb and forefinger to examine the talisman which hung on the chain around his neck. '*Strange*' he mused *' that guy Lawrence ... yes, Lawrence, that was his name, strange ... he never got back in touch, the guy must have been barking up the wrong tree, I must not have been the bloke he had been looking for'* Ace concluded, though one thing was for sure, since the day he started wearing the fancy piece of jewellery, (rather than chance it being lost or stolen from his bag), he had not to date lost a match. He laughed aloud to himself at such a superstitious notion.

Chapter Twenty Five

A Dark Imprisonment

The Roman crowd continued to display their adulation towards the young Frenchman, they related this with his zealous personality, his animated body language, they were one with him inside the white marble stadium, set amid a natural grove of pines.

A year ago to this day in May, saw Jean Paul's first appearance in an ATP final and, although he had lost the match that day, the Il Foro Italico tennis crowd had taken him to their hearts. They had liked him then, now they loved him, especially the female contingent gathered inside the vibrant sporting arena. As the temperature of the day increased, so too did the anticipation around the blood-red clay court. The crowd screeched, screamed and gesticulated during and, even between every point. Now, with the match drawing closer to its conclusion, the fans were almost oblivious to the Italian umpire who repeatedly called for *'silenzio per favore!'* Jean Paul's opponent in this final, Carl Emerson, the present world ranked number one, no less, appeared unable to hide his agitation towards the local's one-sided support, which only served to feed the Latin frenzy that came to a crescendo when Jean Paul King volleyed away the match winner, and raised his arms aloft in victory.

After the obligatory handshake at the net, Jean Paul peeled off his drenched shirt, then tossed the used garment high into the crowded stands. It landed in the middle of a group of young female fans who wrestled frantically amongst themselves for possession of their handsome hero's souvenir offering. He reached down into his large bag, adorned with his sponsor's name, then pulled out a new identical top, before pulling the pristine white replacement over his head. Several teenage girls inside the stadium, whooped and unashamedly made known their approval of Jean Paul's finely tuned physique which, as strong and healthy as it appeared to be, hid within it a dilemma which in time to come would cause the young tennis star inevitable anguish. For, unbeknown to their host, the white corpuscles in Jean Paul King's bloodstream had only but a few moments ago, silently and without warning, waged their first offensive and declared war on their unsuspecting red neighbours.

With her thumb, Floss lightly brushed away a tear from her cheek. Jean Paul's triumphant features filled the TV screen, the commentator's excited voice expressed his praises and approval of the new champion. She glanced over towards Danielle, whose facial expression remained almost impervious. Her emotions impeded, lost somewhere inside her encumbered spirit.

"A very proud day for you Madame Danielle!?" Floss said.

“Yes ...” Danielle replied, forcing a smile. The two women looked back towards the screen. Jean Paul hoisted his Il Foro Italico trophy high, and the crowd yelled their acclaim. He then stepped towards the microphone, the spectators steadily succumbed and became hushed in anticipation. The silence within the stadium was almost eerie.

“Gracie Italia, I love you.” Jean Paul declared and abruptly, the marble bowl became a cauldron of steaming excitement. This was a TV Director’s dream come true, the cameras panned onto several pockets of ardent devotees. The frame lingered a little longer on two stunningly beautiful Italian girls who, it appeared, were unable to conceal their sentiments, openly, they shed tears of joy and repeatedly mouthed Jean Paul’s name. Although in the last few seconds of this sequence the cameraman contrived to take a close-up of their pert nipples.

“This crowd have really taken this champion to their bosom.” The television broadcaster’s voice announced. The picture then switched, and focused in on one man in the stands.

“There’s a man who can stand tall today.” The commentator continued. “Jean Paul King’s American coach, Brad Holding.”

Floss’ eyes danced to and fro from the TV screen and towards Danielle who remained lounging in her seat. The only move that she made, was to rub her fingertips over the scar above her left eyebrow, which fortunately for Danielle was the only visible damage that she had sustained from the explosion at her father’s factory. Jean Paul was speaking again now, his attempt at the Italian language was quite impressive. He thanked his coach and spoke graciously of his opponent’s quality as the world’s number one player, he promptly ended this part of his oration by officially circulating his ambitions to the foremost money winner, Signor Emerson.

“I want your crown.” He said. “I had a sticky start to the tour last year because of personal anguish ... but now I am in full flight, my pain it is my strength, I believe that I can win the French Open, and Wimbledon will be my chance to realise my goal, ... and it is you people of this wonderful city of Rome, that have helped to escalate my game, once more Gracie Italia and arrivedierci Roma, I love you.” With that, he turned and walked slowly towards the exit amidst the cheers. Obstructing his progress somewhat, was a cluster of cameramen who surrounded the new superstar, their cameras clicking and flashing as they jostled for position around the new Italian Open champion.

Danielle closed her eyes, her fingers continued to massage the blemish on her forehead. Behind the dimness of her eyelids, she allowed her mind to wander.

She had been very close to death. It was probably only her fortitude, that had pulled her through the eleven and a half days that she occupied in a deep coma. When Danielle finally regained consciousness, in their wisdom the doctors had deemed that, only when they believed that she was strong enough, would they allow her to receive the news.

Danielle had almost flinched when the woman went to take her hand in hers. Had she not felt so debilitated, Danielle would surely have rejected the woman’s flagrant tactility. She was somewhat confused, *'what did this woman at her bedside want from her?'*

"Danielle Marie ... how do you feel?"

"Fine ... I feel fine." Danielle had lied. The woman smiled unconvincingly back at her, the smile was then slowly replaced by a grimace.

"I ... do not know ... how to .." The woman began to say. Danielle frowned, *'who are you, what do you want?'* Danielle's thoughts taunted her. The woman began to cry.

"Your dear ..." She sobbed, her shoulders convulsing in spasms, she took a deep breath in an effort to calm herself, her lower lip trembled almost in compatible time with the quivering hand that gripped Danielle's

"Your dear Papa ... he is dead." The stranger said finally. Until that moment the woman at Danielle's bedside had put the patient's coolness towards her, down to her obviously feeling unwell. Now she knew by the reaction to this grave and painful disclosure, that her daughter was no longer in possession of her own history.

Presently, Danielle squeezed her eyelids together tighter, endeavouring as she had done on countless occasions, to recall the sound of her father's voice, to picture the way he walked, how he sounded when he laughed, his mannerisms, anything ... but there was nothing. Like her Papa, her memory was dead. Her eyes flicked open, focusing on the TV screen once more. Jean Paul waved a hand to his adoring audience, then stepped into the tunnel and disappeared into its darkness. *'Into a black hole, that was disturbingly akin to her oblivious past'* and that notion, assisted to add further to her depression.

Following his initial diagnosis, her doctor had informed Danielle, that it was no doubt related to her serious amnesia, that she was suffering from depression. After this conclusion, she had tried hard to fight her despondency, even with the aid of some anti-depressants like Prozac, she had actually even undergone a course of electro convulsive therapy but nothing was able enough to rid her of the cold unfeeling mist, that enveloped her, from the first waking moment of every day, reducing her to a listless lump of emptiness. That was in the beginning, by now, the condition had left its mark on her, her once radiant head of dark hair, hung lifelessly over her thin shoulders, she had lost a lot of weight, and looked drawn and grey, the depression had actually etched itself into her features, her outer appearance reflecting the bleak internal landscape within. *'Will I ever get well?'* Danielle mused to herself.

Invading her troubled mind now, was another thought. *'What on earth could her former self have seen in that man ... that rude obnoxious being, that she had been informed was her husband?'* She could be grateful of one thing, she assured herself though, that in the time succeeding her being struck down with her unwelcome amnesia, she had only met with him on two occasions. If their first confrontation had been an anxious affair, the one that followed, some two months later was positively ghastly. His tone had cut her like a knife.

"Do you know what I think!?" He had chided. "I think, this depression thing is just a pretence, the truth is, ... I reckon it's the menopause that is the real problem with you."

Danielle's attempt to slap his egotistical face had been thwarted, and the blow from his free hand sent her spinning across the room. With the taste of her own blood in her mouth, she looked across at this insufferable man, while he hollered out his incongruous words.

"I think you need to see a cranial osteopath or something, eh!? ... or better still ... yes, I have a more suitable solution!"

"Madame Danielle!?" Floss said again, this time managing to break into Danielle's thoughts.

"Yes?"

"Will you be needing anything else Madame?"

"A room with a view Floss ... a view of the gardens."

The two women were interrupted by a sturdy female who, without as much as a tap on the door, entered the room. She was garbed in an immaculate matron's uniform, a woman in her early thirties, though her bearing and overall manner rendered one the impression of a much older woman. Coupled with an overbearing, not to mention morose personality, this woman driven by an inner bitterness was, Danielle had mentioned to Floss during her last calling, *'simply wicked.'* Two tall men, dressed completely in white, followed her in and stood guard at the doorway.

"That's it, time's up!" The big woman said, her piggy eyes ignoring Danielle as she simply nodded her head, signaling Floss to leave. Floss wriggled her way out of the chair, then moved over to where the mistress was seated. She crouched over towards Danielle and kissed her on both cheeks.

"Get me out of this place Floss!" Danielle wheezed.

"Now, now, that's not very nice Mrs King, is it?" The matron responded to her plea, in a sanctimonious tone.

"I have to get out of here Floss!"

"How ungrateful of you Mrs King ... to think of all the money that your dear caring husband is spending on your well-being this past year and more." The big woman added. Danielle turned her head around to face her. The matron's hook nose only served to enhance her cold features.

"Do not patronise me ... I am not crazy!" Danielle snapped, using no effort to disguise the resentment in her voice.

"Do you hear me ... I am not insane!" Danielle screamed.

"That is what they all say in this place Mrs King." The matron said through a thin crooked smile and went on.

"Now ... you must calm yourself, you will be just fine after I have administered you with your daily medication."

Chapter Twenty Six

Sonya

Sonya could easily have taken the soft option. Indeed, that initially had been her plan, to forget the time that she had spent in Mallorca, to simply put everything, that Larry Hickman had acquainted her with that week firmly behind her, and yes, even give up on her quest to encounter her sister's whereabouts. After all said and done so far, Irwin King and the rest of the detestable mob, were very dangerous people, and evil to the core. Was not Hickman's appalling murder testimony enough? Subsequent to her swift departure from the Spanish island, she had spent her first week or so, at home in Florida, grappling with these thoughts, until finally making a decision. It would take time and careful preparation but, she told herself, it had to be done.

The gun club that she had joined was of the highest quality, and Sonya was pleasantly surprised at what her instructor described as a 'natural aptitude with a handgun', benefiting her progress swifter than normal. Her jujitsu lessons however, were not quite so successful to begin with, although twelve months following her first instruction, through hard work and avid application, she had proudly advanced herself to a respectable standard.

Presently, she was almost tempted to employ her newly acquired martial arts talents on the man sitting on the opposite side of the desk from her. His personality, Sonya reflected, was incongruous to the small dingy office in which they were seated. A lick of paint would probably not succeed in cheering up the atmosphere within the cream daubed walls. The only item of fixtures and fittings that was not somewhat soiled or stained, was a framed certificate hanging on the wall above his head, directly behind where he sat. Sonya had done some homework prior to this meeting, and to her amusement had discovered that the diploma displayed disdainfully, for all visitors to see, was in truth a facade. Don Lawrence, she had learned, had been thrown out of the British legal profession after being found guilty in a court of law, of corruption. Thereafter, having served a prison sentence, he had embarked on a new vocation, that of a most unlikely looking private detective. His condescending manner was beginning to irritate Sonya now.

"As I have explained." He was saying, "Even if this Mr ... er.."

"Hickman, Larry Hickman." She prompted.

"Ah yes, Mr Hickman ... if he is ..."

"Was!"

"Was?"

"Larry Hickman. as you know well, is dead, as dead as the squid I ate for lunch yesterday, so quit stalling."

"As I was saying, if Mr Hickman was my client, be he alive or deceased, then any information relating to him, or any investigative work done on my part, would be strictly confidential."

"Look Mister, cut the crap, do you like to be paid in cash?"

Lawrence studied her over the top of his half rimmed glasses before asking.

"What exactly do you have in mind, so that I might assist you?"

Sonya smiled wryly, *'that magic word, cash ... this guy would sell his own mother'* she mused, but said.

"Prior to my friend, Larry Hickman's sad demise, you were employed by him to do some research on a guy called Irwin King, am I right?"

On hearing King's name uttered, the investigator's facial expression changed visibly.

"Indeed ... though my explorations were done from afar, and with a great deal of caution, Irwin King is an extremely dangerous adversary." He warned, in a grave tone of voice. He plucked the spectacles from his nose and chewed on one of their supports, then went on.

"What in heaven's name would an attractive young woman like you be doing wanting to get involved with a detestable man like Irwin King?"

In the following one and a half hours, Sonya gave the investigator her designation of the circumstances that had driven her to take on such a precarious pursuit.

Two weeks following that first meeting, Sonya had had to admit, although as a gumshoe, Don Lawrence did not look the part, he had gathered together to date, some rather useful data regarding the target, along with something that would no doubt be useful, when the time came, namely, Irwin King's coitus preferences.

"How the hell did you find that out?" Sonya asked, failing to secrete a giggle.

"Oh ... let us just say that, our man tends to throw caution to the wind somewhat, when his pants are down."

"His Achilles' heel?" She implied lightly.

"Possibly." Lawrence said, then with a ruffled brow declared. "Whatever happens, do not, I repeat do not ever under-estimate Irwin King, not for one moment!"

"I got it." Sonya said in return, her smile was not so assured.

"Good ... good." Lawrence said sitting back in his chair, which creaked a little under his weight. He regarded her for a moment before speaking again.

"Apart from perhaps ... finding your sister, what do you hope to gain from all this?"

"I, like my friend, Larry Hickman, want to see Irwin King and the rest of the filthy mob put where they belong ... I intend to carry through what Larry started!"

"I must admit, I admire your indomitable ambitions but, clearly you must understand, this is merely a delusion on your part."

"Listen Mister .. if you're going belly up on me, then I'll go find someone else to do the ground work."

"Don't misunderstand me, I am simply conveying my concern for your safety. These people are .. and I don't think that I need remind you, they are utterly ruthless .."

"Are you with me?" Sonya pressed.

"My God ... you honestly think that you can infiltrate an organised drugs ring?"

"I never said I could."

"Well then!?"

"What we can do though, is maybe cause our Mr Irwin King to catch a cold!"

"So he might spread the virus!?..."

"And provoke an epidemic inside the organisation."

"My dear young lady .. I really do think that you should leave all this well alone."

"Are you with me or not?"

Lawrence remained silent for a long moment. He considered her exquisite face, and he knew that, if he agreed or not to her proposition, her crazy intentions were resolute. He believed that at this moment, for the first time in his life he felt protective towards another human being, almost paternal. He shook his head slowly in a negative fashion, both at his patronising notion, and the pure madness of her designs. He placed his spectacles on his head then leaned forward in his chair. His thoughts had not been evident in his facial expression, though he hoped that the sigh he released did not give too much away.

"May I ask how you intend to make your first move?"

"Pay Danielle Marie King a social call."

"That may be easier said than done ... I will explain why later, all the same, if you successfully acquire what you need there .. then what?"

"We go step by step, when I say we, Mr Lawrence ..."

"Please, call me Don."

"OK Don .. are you with me?"

"I must be out of my mind but .. yes!" Lawrence affirmed.

Sonya reflected that that was the first time that she had observed Don Lawrence abandon his stiff upper lip approach, and allowing his features to surrender a smile, albeit short lived before he succumbed to his usual constrained approach.

"Apart from calling on Mrs King, what are your plans for the next two months or so?"

"Well, I have several modelling assignments over the next few months, after all, I gotta find some ways of paying you, ain't that right?" She quipped.

"Are these assignments in London?" He enquired.

"Some."

"Splendid ... now, King will be visiting London late June, early July, he will probably spend a fortnight here, attending several art exhibitions, to coincide with his other interests."

"Namely?"

"Wimbledon."

"Of course, the tennis fortnight."

“Yes.”

“Doubtlessly, he’ll be taking an interest in Jean Paul’s progress ...”

“At the bookmakers perhaps.”

“Say again?”

“The Twain are at loggerheads, and have been for some time, my source informs me that ...”

“Source?” Sonya cut in.

“The King’s housekeeper.”

“Floss ... yes, that was her name, Floss!?”

“Yes ... now seemingly, Jean Paul has relinquished all ties with his father, as far as he is concerned, Irwin King does not exist.”

“I was aware that they weren’t close but ...”

“I believe that things came to a head when the young man learned of his mother’s institutionalisation to a ... for want of a kinder title, ... to a psychiatric retreat.”

“Danielle King is in a nut house?” Sonya gasped, genuinely shocked.

“Apparently so, following an accident which also claimed her father’s life.”

“What was it ... an automobile accident?”

“No ... I was informed, that the old chap detonated his factory, blowing himself along with the plant to pieces. Unfortunately, unbeknown to him, Mrs King happened to be in the vicinity at the very moment that the explosion occurred.”

“I take it then, that Danielle suffered head injuries.”

“Head injuries, yes ... though Floss believes that the damage that she has sustained, at least in her humble opinion that is, were not enough to warrant her commitment to a nut house, as you call it.”

“Then why should ...?” Sonya began, before becoming cognisant with the scenario.

“Irwin King!?” She declared. The investigator neither agreed, nor did he disagree with her evaluation, he simply conveyed another opinion.

“I believe that, King had a stranglehold on the old man, which pressed him to a point of no return.”

“My God, the guy leaves in his wake a trail of turmoil and goddamn misery wherever he goes.”

“Indeed ... One wonders why though, Jean Paul hasn’t applied himself to liberate his mother from the hospital.”

“The love of glory.”

“I beg your pardon?”

“Something I heard him say once .. it was at his birthday party some time ago ... you see, I guess, like his father, though not for one minute would I compare Jean Paul to his old man, you understand but, ...”

“But, naturally they would share one or two similar characteristics!?”

“Yeah, I guess that’s what I’m trying to say, now ... how did the speech go? ... I remember, he was quoting Louis XIV, it went something like ... the love of glory, surely takes precedence over all others, ... something like that anyway.”

“The two share an egotistical disposition obviously.”

"I guess that's so, but with one big difference, Jean Paul uses his ego to drive his talent." Sonya concluded. The investigator's face presently revealed a look of concern.

"Was Irwin King present, at that birthday party?"

"No."

"So as far as you know, he doesn't even know that you exist?"

"As far as I know, that's the case."

"Good." Lawrence said, then picked up a folder from the desk and handed it over to Sonya.

"I have put together a dossier for you to peruse."

"Right." Sonya replied, opening the document. On the first page was a photograph. Irwin King's face stared out at her, provoking a dreadful aberrant sensation in the pit of her stomach.

"He usually reserves a suite at the Royal Lancaster Hotel when he's in town, although from what I can gather, he has used other top class accommodation at times."

"Very nice." Sonya retorted with an air of sarcasm.

"He also commissions an agency to be the premier organisation in the capital, both for their client's discretional purposes and, I am informed, they have the most appealing pool of young ladies likely to be found anywhere and, I must say, for the price that they charge their clients, then so they jolly well should be."

"Excuse me saying Don, but sometimes you talk in riddles, an agency you say?"

"An escort agency."

"I see."

"From what I can gather, clients can satisfy their libido by offering a supplemental fee."

"So these girls ... these escorts, are kinda high class prostitutes?"

"Some."

"Some?"

"I think that a number of these young ladies draw the line when it comes to having sexual relations with the customer."

"So sex is not obligatory?"

"I think not."

Sonya fell silent for a moment, then on impulse said,

"Get me an appointment, for an interview!"

"What ... with the agency?"

"Sure, I could play escort."

"Don't you think that would be rather imprudent?"

"Hell no, don't you see this could be my chance to cast the bait."

"Are you sure about this?"

"Don't worry, I can look after myself."

"Very well." Lawrence said in conclusion, earnestly anticipating that her confident boast was not merely a facade.

"Just one question before I go, Larry told me that you had found Jean Paul's long lost twin."

"I'm afraid that my explorations as far as that is concerned, came to rather an abrupt halt."

"Why was that?"

"The reasons are three fold, without wanting to sound too mercenary, my interests receded when Mr Hickman breathed his last breath, then to arrest any further investigations, Danielle King's memory had been severely impaired following her accident, and well .... she did not remember anything appertaining to any agreement that she had made with Mr Hickman to compensate my professional expertise."

"No pay, no play, you say?" Sonya said with a knowing grin.

"Exactly."

"But was the guy you found Jean Paul's brother?"

"Yes, ... I believe he was."

"It's a pity, to have got so near and yet so far."

"Yes, perhaps when she has recovered from her plight then ..."

"You probably think I'm nuts, but I still want to pay a call on Danielle Marie King, organise that for me will you."

Chapter Twenty Seven

Team Ace

Since his triumph in the British Satellite Tournament over the highly respected Tony Wang, Ace had grown in confidence, giving his inborn talent a new edge and was subsequently beginning to enjoy some of the benefits gained by his sheer determination. Another challenger victory in Hong Kong had prompted one journalist to proclaim in his column, '*This new kid on the block is endowed with a physique, more liken to a cruiserweight boxer than that of a tennis player, though he possesses the speed and grace of a panther on court.*'

During their flight back to the UK, Greg Fenton had been rather restless, which was uncharacteristic of the pragmatic Australian. Ace on noticing this, put a stop to his musical solace by pulling off his headphones then saying.

"Are you OK coach?"

"Sure mate ...why?"

"I don't know, you seem a bit sort of edgy."

"No, not edgy Ace, deep in thought that's all."

"About what?"

"Your future Ace ... your future."

"Oh?"

"OK, I'll tell you what I've got in mind. The time's come now, to formulate a team of people, professional people .. to safeguard your financial future. A team of people you can trust, don't you agree?"

"Sure."

"Your brother Jack ..."

"What about him?"

"You trust him don't you?"

"If you don't mind me saying, that's kind of a daft question."

"He's good with figures, monetary things?"

"A qualified accountant no less."

"That's it then, soon as we get back, we'll offer him the job of personally looking after your accounts et cetera."

"You mean, like a personal manager?"

"Yes."

"Excellent!"

"He can join me in negotiating with the interested parties and help strike some good deals."

"Are you talking about sponsorship?"

"I know it has seemed to you a long time in coming, but I've been holding back the reins, waiting for the right time. Now that time has arrived and the iron's hot."

"You mean there's been people ... companies knocking on the door and you've been turning them away?"

"Sure thing."

"And I was beginning to think it was me."

"The way I see it, if these companies want to invest in your future now, they're going to have to dig down deep into their pockets!"

"I reckon you, Jack and me are going to make a great team!" Ace grinned.

"You bet!" His coach agreed.

Ace, along with the aid of his team, had struck a modest deal with a high street bank. A newly established little known soft drinks firm eagerly advanced money his way, in the hope that, they might gain prominence by taking a piggy back ride, to where they believed that Ace was hastening (global eminence), was how they had put it. The sportswear company were to be the main sponsors. Jack, Fenton and Ace had negotiated with each of the assembled benefactors, at their respective boardrooms. The last port of call that week had been at the sportswear company's head office. The Board of Directors had initially suggested an advance of one hundred and fifty thousand pounds, spread over three years. Ace, had almost fallen through his chair at the offer, then was astounded further when his coach had rejected the offer point blank. He had gathered that, *'coach and brother, had obviously drawn up their own plans before going to this table.'*

"Don't get me wrong." Fenton had said, "We think that your offer is a generous one ... but ..."

"We have a proposal to put to you." Jack then linked in, "That will be of benefit to both parties."

"What do you have in mind?" Was the Chairman's response.

"A contract regulated by the player's performance." Fenton declared.

"Over four years!" Jack added.

"Four years?"

"Yes." Jack and Fenton said in unity. Fenton continued.

"We propose, that we start at fifty thousand for the first year." It was Jack's turn again now.

"Thereafter, determined on the player's achievements, the money should increase or reduce depending on Ace's success or ..."

"Let's call it an incentive plan!" Fenton came in, by now Ace was beginning to wonder if his brother and coach had rehearsed this presentation.

"We are looking at say a 100% increase for each time our man wins a tournament." Jack rendered.

"The contract, should also be re-negotiable at the end of the first two years." Fenton proposed. Jack then said,

"And for a Grand Slam win ...."

"Grand Slam?" The Chairman scoffed, "Aren't we being rather presumptuous!?"

"Believe me when I tell you, that Ace here, is made of the kinda stuff that it takes to win at the very highest level!" Fenton responded in an assured tone, then winked an eye in Ace's direction. The Chairman turned to his co-directors. To Ace, the break in talks between the two parties, while the board mumbled at the other end of the table, was almost unbearable. Finally, the Chairman cleared his throat before saying.

"Hypothetically speaking, if Ace ... do you mind if I call you Ace?" The Chairman had enquired.

"Not at all." Ace had replied modestly.

"Thank you ... as I was saying, if Ace was to ... let's say win the Wimbledon title two years from now ..."

"It would cost you a small fortune, but imagine the publicity that your clobber would get!?" Fenton said lightly, fracturing the Chairman's flow, and almost causing Ace to cringe. To his relief though, the Chairman saw the funny side of his coach's somewhat abrasive wit. The Chairman then turned towards Ace and asked.

"Do you believe, that you will ever be good enough to win a Grand Slam event like Wimbledon?"

"Bet your arse." Was all that Ace could honestly think to say, so overwhelmed was he by the scenario, which was to be magnified further by the Chairman's ensuing proposition.

"If you win Wimbledon, within the first two years, under contract with us young man, then our company will endorse that effort to the tune of one million pounds!"

The meeting lasted a further forty minutes or so. It was not so much the agreements that had been lodged that day, that had thrilled the young hopeful, it was the fact that, by complying not only with Jack and Fenton's audacious terms, in Ace's mind it simply meant that his primary sponsors, had considered Ace a sound investment, even though, on paper at least up until then, his pro record was on balance rather superficial.

On the train journey back to Hertfordshire, the three had chatted excitedly about the afternoon's successful outcome. Jack and Fenton informed Ace that, prior to the engagement with the sportswear people, they had been confident that a good deal would be struck, because, Fenton told Ace, *'the Chairman is a tennis fanatic'*, and had, apparently, been out in Hong Kong on business. While he was there he had found time to attend the Challenger Final. It had got back to Greg Fenton apparently, that the said Chairman had been overheard to say, that he believed that the winner of the tournament was, in his eyes, probably the second best young prospect in the world presently.

"Did he mention, who he thought was the best young prospect?" Ace had asked.

"I believe so."

"Well ... who?"

"Let's just say, we've got a bit of catching up to do."

"Who was he speaking of Greg?"

"The guy he was referring to, is the former junior number one."

"Number one in Britain?"

“No Ace ... number one in the world, and after a shaky start on the ATP Tour last year, has recently taken some eminent scalps, he’s ...”

“Who?” Ace inquired once more.

“Jean Paul King.”

After winning two rounds of the qualifying events for entry for the Il Foro Italico Tournament, Ace’s first attempt at a major ATP Tour event had been terminated in the third, when he was narrowly beaten. Ace had made no excuses for his defeat that day at the hands of a more experienced clay court opponent. He had, he thought, hidden his disappointment well, but Fenton knew only too well that defeat, was something that his prodigy found very hard to swallow. Player and coach had returned home that week, to prepare for their next endeavour, which again would be played on clay. A surface that, in contrast to others, Ace was comparatively uncomfortable on. In an attempt to augment the player’s technique on the slower playing surface, they effectively practised, hour upon hour, day-in, day-out, intensively striving to build up his confidence and approach to the unfavourable red clay coloured courts.

A week prior to his arrival for qualification for the next tour event in St Polten, Austria, Ace and Fenton had sat and watched the Il Foro Italico final between Carl Emerson and Jean Paul King on Sky Television. Throughout the live transmission, Ace had been particularly agitated, which for Ace, his coach considered was quite uncharacteristic.

“You’re playing into King’s hands Emerson!” Ace yelled at the TV screen.

“What’s eating you?” Fenton frowned.

“Nothing, it’s just ...”

“Just what?”

“Well, that guy King, he’s milking the crowd.”

“That’s just part of the pro game mate!”

“Gamesmanship, that’s what it is!”

“Call it what you will ... the guy’s beating the world number one, just keep watching Ace, you might learn something.” Fenton had responded innocently. Although this comment had only added fuel to the fire within Ace’s belly, he was unable to submit himself to viewing the spectacle a moment longer. He got up from his chair and bounded out of the room, cursing as he shut the door noisily behind him. Ace had been utterly confused by his own behaviour that day. He had been filled with an emotion that was rather alien within his make-up, jealousy ... yes, that was it pure jealousy, *‘but why?’* he had asked himself over many times, for all the world he could not find an answer to that question and, with a degree of effort, had recently put as best he could, the absurdity to the back of his mind.

Chapter Twenty Eight

Sonya and Floss stood in the reception area of the institution. It's cold, clinical walls had sent a chill down Sonya's spine on her arrival there. Now, fifteen minutes on, she wondered what the hell she was doing getting herself involved with Danielle Marie King's personal circumstances, let alone planning her abduction from a nut-house, after all, she only had Floss' word for it that the woman that had been committed to this funny farm, was not as mad as a March hare by now anyway. She looked over at the large matron presently, whose frosty gaze added to Sonya's uneasiness.

"Please understand .... I have travelled half-way round the world to see my aunt." Sonya said, and contemplated whether it was the second or the third time that she had made that same plea.

"Then you have had a wasted journey, as I have already told you, I am under strict instructions." The big woman said, her lips resembled a gash somewhat more than a mouth.

"But surely .." Sonya began.

"Look ... I'm sorry." The matron interposed, holding aloft a fleshy palm, "Mr King has made it totally clear that his wife should receive no visitors, apart from that is, his housekeeper here ... and of course Mr King himself!"

"With respect matron ... having made such an extensive trip to see my favourite aunt, surely should merit me a five minute consultation."

"And ... with respect Miss ... Miss?"

"King ... Miss King, Uncle Irwin is my father's brother." Sonya lied with an assured skill, that almost took Sonya herself by surprise.

"Then, you will not mind if I take a look at your passport !?"

"My passport?"

"Yes."

With her heart in her mouth, Sonya produced the document from a small compartment in her shoulder bag. She handed it over to the woman with a confident smile that belied her thoughts. *'Goddamn it Don Lawrence, you'd better have made a good job of it!'* The matron eyed Sonya suspiciously for a moment, before studying the contents. Every aspect of the sizeable matron exhibited a potent stubbornness; her powerful build amplifying the fact, except *'Thank God'* Sonya reflected, *'except for her eyesight!'* Recognising her struggle to some degree to focus in on the small photograph along with its accompanying information, Sonya seized the moment.

"It's all in order! I really don't know why ..."

"Yes ..yes, I can see that."

"Well?"

"Well ... don't you think then that as you and Mr King are so closely related, that it would have perhaps been in your interest to have phoned him to inform him of your intentions before embarking on such a fruitless pilgrimage?"

"I didn't think ..."

"No, obviously not!"

"You're so right matron, it's the story of my life, like my daddy always says, babe, he says ... you was blessed with good looks .. but when it came to dishing out the brains, they musta gone to lunch." Sonya said, rounding off the sentence with an almost juvenile giggle, and hoped sincerely that she had not gone over the top. The big woman's expression remained aloof, and the next statement she made caused Sonya's stomach to flutter.

"Mr King gave me a phone number to call if ever we had a problem here."

"Great ... perfect, go ahead matron, call him." Sonya responded brightly, masking her escalating anxiety.

"Very well." The matron replied, then made her way around the reception desk where she thumbed through a directory. On the front of the ledger, in black ink was written 'Patient's Next of Kin'.

"Ah, here we are." She said finally. Then lifted up the handset, her lips silently mouthed the number, at the same time employing a stubby index finger, she pressed the appropriate digits. Satisfied, she rested her free hand on one of her sizeable hips and stared across at Sonya, who hoped by now that her manufactured composure was not beginning to show cracks by way of her facial expression. The matron let out a sigh, before placing the receiver momentarily in its cradle, then mumbled something about an incompetent service. *'The International Operator must have answered my prayers'* Sonya mused, although her relief was rather short lived, as she surveyed the matron frowning down at the number and with the same chubby finger, began the digit punching motion once more. Sonya turned to Floss and forced a smile. If the King's housekeeper was nervous, then she was doing a sterling job in disguising the fact. Holding the phone to her ear, the matron used the fingers on her other hand to manipulate the small round timepiece pinned to her uniform. She squinted at the watch's dial for a second or two, before allowing it to fall back in position, resting on her ample breast. Sonya had prepared herself mentally, to turn on her heels and make good her escape through the door the minute that Irwin King exposed her fraudulent escapade. The matron clicked her tongue before again replacing the handset. With another glance at her watch and in a reluctant tone suggested to Sonya.

"Five minutes ... that is all I can allow, I really should not permit you this prerogative, but as you have travelled so far .."

"Thanks ... jeeze, it would have been so awful to have been denied the chance to see my aunt."

"Never mind all that, just be glad that today you found me in such a good mood."

Sonya and Floss followed the matron down two long corridors, every fifteen metres or so, on either side of the narrow walkway robust looking doors were tightly closed. The sound of crazed muted voices filled the air. The atmosphere was positively eerie. An acrid smell of urine assaulted Sonya's nostrils, to the point that she honestly believed that she could actually taste the pale yellow fluid. The matron came to a halt outside one of the doors, then unhitched a large ring of keys from her belt. Her fingers toyed noisily with the collection of metal instruments, before selecting the appropriate key and inserting it into the lock, with a swift flick of her wrist the restraining bolt gave way with a loud clunking sound. Somewhere, from within the despondent walls of the asylum, an ear-piercing shriek echoed around the passage, so wretched was the voice's miserable essence, that Sonya likened its vocal quality to a badly injured hound. She sincerely hoped that the hideous scream had not emanated from behind the door through which she was about to enter.

"You have visitors, isn't that nice." The matron announced, entering the dimly lit chamber. The woman seated in the far corner of the room hardly acknowledged their entrance. It took a few moments for Sonya's eyes to acclimatise, and when they did adjust finally, she was shocked at what they perceived. The matron turned to Sonya from the doorway, where she used the bright light from the corridor to focus in on the timepiece on her uniform.

"As we agreed, five minutes! .. now there are things that require my attention, when I return it will be Mrs King's time for her daily medication." She declared.

"OK matron, and thanks."

"Oh ... and in the meantime, I will try once again to get through to Mr King." The matron intimated with a twisted grin. She then closed the door, and to Sonya's astonishment, bolted it behind her.

Sonya cursed under her breath and asked herself again, what the hell she was doing getting herself involved here. She walked over towards the corner where Floss was now attempting to evoke conversation with the listless inmate. There was no time for small talk, *'five minutes'* Sonya speculated *'would that be enough time to convey my plan of action!'* Before she had chance to utter a word, the room was suddenly illuminated, causing the occupants to grimace and shield their eyes from the unexpected brilliant light. The low whirring sound of a surveillance camera, activating and focusing in on the three women was presently the only noise within the four grey walls.

"Hey, what is this?" Sonya protested, squinting towards the camera lens.

"A general procedure .. merely protecting our patient's best interests." The matron's voice responded through two small speakers situated on the same wall as the camera.

"The patient's best interest?" Sonya frowned.

"Yes ... you can never be too careful, besides ... you too could be at risk, after all this is an institution for the mentally ill, many of our patients are extremely dangerous!"

"Are you suggesting that ..."

"I am suggesting Miss," The faceless voice punctuated, "That you get on with what you came all this way to do."

Sonya asked herself if the matron had any inclination as to what she had really come here to do. She turned away from the camera, back towards Danielle and the housekeeper, noticing that panic was beginning to register in Floss' eyes, she hoped that on the screen which the matron was viewing, her own consternation had not betrayed her. She looked directly at the 'patient' now, *'Goddamn it Danielle Marie, don't let me down, I've come to get you out of here!'* her thoughts screamed.

"So aunt, how are you?" She asked. Danielle returned a puzzled expression and said nothing.

"Don't you remember me?" Sonya pressed lightly. Promptly wishing that she had turned the automobile around when they had arrived at the perimeter gates. The armed guard stationed there was moreover, another reason against the success of this somewhat rash undertaking. The gun that she had primed to deter anyone from foiling their escape, was cleverly concealed beneath her baggy shirtlike garment. On reflection, she wondered if she would have the courage to fire the weapon at any would-be assailant. *'Hell, come on Sonya positive thoughts, think positive!'* Her mind brooded. Under the circumstances, trivial conversation was all that Sonya could partake in, while her imagination engaged furiously in a new plan of action.

"So ... tell me, how are they all treating you?" She inquired, while her mind wrestled frantically, *'where were the two sturdy male attendants earlier, the two guys that Floss had warned her about?'*

"Is the food good?"

'Come to think of it ... where were the nurses and the rest of the people employed at this goddamn hell hole? 'til now, the only staff I have seen was the guy guarding the outside gate and the overweight matron.'

"You look like you could do with a little exercise." Sonya continued, to an apathetic Danielle.

'On the matron's return' her reasoning persisted, *'I'll pull the gun on her ... she'll be our insurance .. our shield for a safe passage out of here.'*

"Not much daylight gets in here, do you ever get to take a walk?" Sonya asked glancing towards the only small window in the chamber. *'Even without the metal bars, there'd barely be enough room for a small child to squeeze through'* she mused, *'no means of escape through there that's for sure!'*

"Has Jean Paul been over to visit?"

'What if the big woman tries to make a break for it, when she sees the gun?'

"He's doing real well on the tour." She went on, *'I'll fire a shot at the camera lens ... that'll be a kinda warning .. then tell the pig-eyed bitch to goddamn freeze!, then ..'*

"You know aunt, I can't tell ya how proud we all are of Jean Paul's achievements this far .."

Sonya looked hard into the two glazed, bloodshot eyes that were once so alive and intelligent, anticipating some sort of reaction, anything! *'Shit!'* her mind brooded, *'Her lights are out.'*

"Would you like me to brush your hair or something?"

"No!" Danielle snapped.

'Eureka!' Sonya's thoughts declared triumphantly, *'I finally got through.'*

King tapped his foot impatiently on the rubber matted floor of the London taxi, he held the mobile phone to his ear in anticipation, allowing his thoughts to mull over the information that the matron had just enlightened him with. The silence at the other end of the line was suddenly breached.

"Hello, Doctor Benamou speaking, what can I do for you Mr King?"

"Who is this young woman matron informs me that you have there?"

"All I know ... or should I say, all I have been told is that she is your niece."

"Can't be."

"Oh?"

"I haven't got a bloody niece!"

"I see."

"This is a hell of a fucking inconvenience to me, I can tell you man!" King chided.

"Yes, Mr King .. I can understand ....."

"Then understand this ... they tell me that it's a very fine line we tread between sanity and gaga land, would you agree Doctor?"

"Without doubt."

"In that case, I think then that it would be perfectly reasonable to assume, that this girl ... this impostor has a mental disorder, a split personality ... she's probably a psychopath, ... very dangerous to underestimate such people, wouldn't you say so Doctor?"

"Yes Mr King." The consultant agreed, foreseeing another fat pay day on its way to him, similar to the one he had received on the day he advised the institutionalisation of the wife of the man he was conversing with presently.

"I'm glad that you can see my point of view Doctor. So, I trust that, until I can find the time to pay you another little visit, you will put together the necessary paperwork for this impostor's internment!?"

"Yes, Mr King, without delay."

"I er ... also suspect a conspiracy here Doctor, so I believe it may be an idea to offer accommodation to my housekeeper, see to that will you!"

"Of course Mr King."

"Oh ... I almost forgot, give my wife my good wishes." King concluded.

Sonya glanced at her wristwatch, and to her bewilderment the allocated five minutes had passed, she had by now been inside these oppressive four walls for fully twelve minutes. *'Be calm ... just stay cool!'* she told herself.

"I will ask the matron, if maybe I can take you for a walk around the grounds, would you like that?" Sonya asked.

Danielle's solemn demeanour alleviated for a short moment before she frowned and said.

"They will not allow me to go outside."

Sonya angled herself closer, immediately sensing Danielle's slouched body stiffen.

"I'm gonna get you out of here." Sonya whispered into her ear. The voice through the speakers caused Sonya to jerk upright once more.

"That's enough." The voice intervened. "I have just had a very interesting telephone conversation." The buxom woman declared. Sonya said nothing in return. Beneath the baggy garment covering her torso, her armpits suddenly felt disagreeably damp.

The taxi came to a halt outside a Harley Street building. It was with a Doctor of a different kind, that King had a face-to-face appointment with in London today. He had taken the initial precaution of booking his appointment under the assumed name of William Bruce. In his initial visitation to the specialist's rooms, he and the surgeon had discussed the implications involved in undergoing the treatment that King himself, had deemed to be necessary as an insurance for his future well-being.

"I have all manner of people coming to me for various problems." Mister Halpen, the Harley Street specialist had begun by saying that day, "Many of them are high profile subjects ... film or television celebrities and the like, they invariably will go under the knife in a bid to re-capture their youth. I won't name any of these people, they respect me you see, because they can rely on me and my treatment for their problems ... and, with me they enjoy total confidentiality."

"Glad to hear it Doc." King had then declared.

"Which brings me to my first question." The surgeon went on.

"No questions Doc!" King had then cut in, "Just do the job when the time comes, that's what I'm paying you for!"

Halpen had initially been taken aback somewhat by his would-be client's approach, and had been furthermore bewildered by the man's next set of demands.

"For total confidentiality ... and I mean total .." King had continued, "I will be willing to treble your fee ... how does that sound?"

"I'm listening Mr Bruce."

"Good." King had said with a smile, for he had done his homework on Halpen, and had ascertained that, as prominent the man was in his skilled profession, he was nonetheless only a man. A man King had considered not unlike himself, a man with a notorious human weakness, namely an avaricious appetite for money.

"These are my requirements." King went on, "Any photographs or any material relating to my good self will be left in my safekeeping, you will even delete my appointment with you today from you secretary's diary, clear so far?"

"But ..."

"No buts Mister Halpen ... clear so far?"

"Yes." Halpen answered hesitantly.

"You ... and you alone will conduct the necessary surgery!"

"Without the help of an anaesthetist?"

"Am I right in saying that, prior to you turning your hand to cosmetic surgery, you were an anaesthetist?"

"How ..."

"Look man ... if I am wasting my time and a great deal of money here, just tell me!" King had asserted, rising from his seat.

"No ... please, Mr Bruce, sit down please, we will talk about this." The surgeon then said. King smiled once again, by now he had known his preconditions would no doubt be met.

Irwin King, had made up his mind to alter his facial appearance and form himself an entirely new identity long before Bennetti had chosen to go into isolation and consign King to supervise the Overlord's crumbling empire. He was aware even before the Italian that, the Cuban drug barons allied with other underworld contemporaries, including the Mafia, were making preparations to wield their mighty sword, and cut off any of Bennetti's future illegitimate transactions along with his balls, if they bothered to discover his whereabouts. 'No matter how big a noise Bennetti was, there were guys out there with infinitely more decibels to their voices' King had considered, and wondered on whose toes the Italian had trampled. Well, he was not going to hang around to find out. To further fuel King's decision, a book that was brought to his attention some time ago by Bennetti, which was written by an ex-convict called Larry Hickman, stated in a footnote that his next publication would open a can of worms and, name some names involved in the clandestine world of modern day slavery and the shipping of hard drugs. At first, King did not put two and two together until, that is, Bennetti had reminded him of the man that King himself had set up, to take the rap for Doctor Pettett's murder. So on their yachting trip to Palma in Mallorca a year or more earlier, when the Overlord had ordered him to 'silence the son of a bitch', he had been more than happy to do just that, thanks to the help of one of the mob's strong armed hoodlums. They had searched the small villa for lists of names and manuscripts, but found nothing. King's next undertaking was going to be, a mission to seek out and snuff out a young woman that Hickman had befriended and learned had been privy to Hickman's objectives. Now though, thanks to his commitment and promise of a new identity, he did not feel the need or the inclination to go to such troubles. A curious thought crossed his mind now, 'who could this girl be, that had been so audacious as to impersonate an imaginary niece of his.' He would telephone the institution in the next few days and question the matron to a greater extent. He concluded, that he would put these thoughts to the back of his mind, for the time being at least, besides, he had his elaborate all-new looks to consider presently.

She heard the key enter the lock on the other side of the door. In an instant, with her left hand, Sonya ripped open the front of her loose blouse, with the thumb of her other hand she flicked the stud releasing the thin leather clasp on the holster and swung around. The door's bolt relinquished at the turn of the key with a 'clunk', prompting that appalling hound-like squeal, resembling the one heard earlier from somewhere within the godforsaken walls. Sonya's somewhat rebellious legs now carried her to the wall farthest away from her two female companions. *'What the hell were you thinking of, getting involved here?'* her mind screamed one more time. The whirring sound of the surveillance camera searched above her head.

"Wait!" The matron's voice yelled through the speakers, too late, the two sturdy men clothed in dazzling white had entered the chamber.

"Freeze!" Sonya advised them, as assertively as her voice could muster. Her clammy hands encased the weapon's cool metal handle, she cursed her trigger finger, poised for action for trembling so.

“Get your goddamn hands in the air.” She ordered, this time she cursed her larynx for yodelling, but she was gratified to see that the two sons of bitches had done as they were told. The slightly taller of the two displayed, what Sonya thought to be a mocking smile on his pockmarked face.

“Nice tits.” He said through gross sloppy lips.

The bra supporting her breasts clung to her flesh, she released her left hand from the gun and with fumbling fingers, endeavoured to re-fasten the gaping garment. On discovering that most of the buttons had been torn away, she abandoned the task, and now she cursed the bead of sweat that slowly trickled down between her cleavage, the sensation, coupled with the man’s lecherous stare ignited her indignation.

“Not another word from you asshole .... speak, and believe me you’ll just be a hole without an ass around it!” This time her vocal quality did not let her down. She took a deep breath and licked her dry lips, *‘gotta work fast’* she reflected, *‘keep calm.’*

“Okay ... this is what we’re gonna do!” She said without taking her eyes off the two male attendants. “Floss ... nice and easy, fetch Danielle over here and stand beside me! ... Matron?! .. I know you can hear me, get your big ass in here now!”

Once Danielle and Floss had joined her by the wall, Sonya gestured with the gun.

“You two ... over there and sit down on the cot ... do it!” She instructed, while her reasoning reiterated *‘gotta work fast .. if that piggy-eyed bitch don’t get here soon things could go pear-shaped’*

“Keys ... throw over your keys!” She said to the two men now seated on the bed, both with their hands firmly placed on their sizeable craniums.

“Just one of you ... you!” She decreed with a nod of her head towards the one with the blemished features, whose vile eyes indelicately toured Sonya’s breasts once again, causing her stomach to turn.

“Do as I say ... nice and slow!” Sonya said as the man went through the process of disengaging the large keyring from his belt. Sonya hastened to warn him.

“I sure hope you ain’t as dumb as you look mister, let me tell you, in case you was maybe thinking of chancing your muscle-bound arm, it’s a scientific fact that a bullet travels faster through the air than a bunch of keys.” She forced a smile that masked her inner growing nervousness. *‘Where’s that damn matron?’* she brooded. The keys were in his hands now.

“Okay ... place one hand on top of your ugly head.” She prompted “Now, nice and gently toss the keys along the floor towards Floss here!”

The man obediently followed her instructions, then linked his fingers together once more on top of his head.

“Good ... good, Floss pick the keys up off the floor ... matron? .. where the hell are you ?!” *‘You’re our goddamn ticket out of this hell hole.’*

“We’re going on a little excursion ... and you’re going to be our special guest.”

‘Shit, something wrong here, these two pompous male nurses are too compliant by far ... you’ve got the gun you fool, that’s why!’ she reasoned.

"Do you hear me?!"

"I hear you." The matron's voice cracked through the speaker system, finally.

"There will be no excursion today I'm afraid ... Doctor's orders." The voice said flatly.

"I'm the one giving the orders around here now, I've got the gun remember!"

"You are making a big mistake young miss." The matron said in that condescending tone, which irritated Sonya right down to the bone.

"Listen to me ... get in here now, or I'm coming looking for you!"

"Don't you think, that you are being rather impetuous?" The question was asked in that same disdainful way. Sonya released a short nervous chuckle at the irony of the enquiry.

"Tell me about it."

"Perhaps, if we could sit down somewhere and talk this over?" The voice from the speakers extenuated.

"All I want is to get out of this goddamned place in one piece with my ..." She almost said, with my aunt, "shit" she chided to herself.

"We just want out of here!"

In the compact observation room, the large matron viewed the monitor screen. Although the two men in white, seated on the bed were the only figures clearly visible within the chamber, every once in a while, the gun in Sonya's outstretched hands became clearly perceptible, flashing at the bottom of the black and white picture.

The matron had activated the video recorder just a moment prior to the two nurses' entrance through the door. She continued the negotiations presently with the supercilious emphasis in her voice, which by this time was beginning to ferment Sonya's anger.

"I think that I had better caution you, that Mrs King will be in need of her vital medication, and I warn you ..."

"Warn me?"

"Why yes, without her daily prescription, she will become a danger to herself and indeed, anyone around her."

Sonya gave Danielle a cursory glance, though she had not needed to, she had already sensed her agitation, *'she really was a shadow of the person she was,'* she thought on reflection *'they've turned the poor woman into a junky.'* But said,

"Alright ... don't let's waste anymore time matron, get your oversized butt in here now!"

"I will get my butt in there .. as soon as you hand your weapon over to the nurses."

"God damn you." Sonya chided.

"Now, now, it will do you no good getting yourself all worked up."

"Don't patronise me, with all that holier than thou shit, it won't wash I tell ya!"

"It is simply my job to care for the patients' welfare." The matron explained, behind a crooked smile *'the girl is digging a nice deep hole for herself'* she mused.

"Oh yeah, looking after the patients' welfare, pumping them full of dope .... sure, that helps!"

"Believe me it is absolutely necessary with our patients, that they receive regular medicine and the time will come shortly when you yourself will be receiving yours."

"Yeah? ... Well don't include me in that scenario!"

"Oh, but I do."

"We're on our way out of this place now ... with or without you." Sonya declared, she then moved towards the doorway. Her back was in full view of the camera now. The gun remained aimed at the two men in white.

"The police are waiting for you." The voice scoffed through the chamber.

"Good, good ... then I can explain to them what the hell goes on around here." Sonya countered. At that moment there was a knock on the observation room door. Doctor Benamou entered and was followed in by the Police Inspector. With the flick of a switch the matron closed off communication from the viewing room temporarily, and turned to greet the gangly policeman.

"Glad you could be here so promptly."

"Now ... what have we here?" He asked moving towards the small screen.

"As you can see Inspector, a rather precarious situation."

"A patient?"

"One of our most recent internee's Inspector." Doctor Benamou explained. Sonya's evident outline crouched menacingly on the screen, she now stridently rendered her intentions.

"Floss, bring Danielle over here and stand behind me ... you two sons of bitches, if I hear so much as a spring squeak on that cot .. so help me I'll shoot .. do you hear me?!"

The two male nurses nodded their agreement.

Inside the observation room, the Inspector rubbed his prominent chin in contemplation. The bushy eyebrows on his forehead almost joined together as one, in a frown.

"Her clothes ... the aggressor is not dressed in the customary institutional clothing, no?" He said. Matron and Doctor were silent for what seemed like a long moment, before the large woman submitted.

"A special concession ...believe me, when all this is over, that privilege will be withdrawn!" She scowled. All three would-be escapees were now in view on the monitor, grouped together at the door to the chamber.

"How did the inmate acquire the firearm?" The policeman summoned.

"This one." The matron said, pointing at the screen, Floss' fretful eyes stared into the camera at that moment, as if psychologically being aware of the accusing finger. The big woman's blood ran cold for a moment, though she continued, "She is a visitor ... I believe that she must have smuggled the gun in." She offered as a vindication, then pressed the switch to re-open communication from her end of the intercom system, bending her sizeable figure. She spoke condescendingly once again into the microphone.

"This is matron again." She began "Now, be a good girl for me and hand over the weapon ... give yourself up now .. I will personally see to it that you do not get punished too harshly for your silly behaviour, I promise you that."

"For Christ sake." Sonya bellowed in exasperation "Don't talk to me as if I'm one of your crackbrain detainee's. If anyone's crazy round here ... it's you, not me, I know what I'm doing, and why .. no ma'am I ain't crazy!"

The matron covered the microphone with a hand and turned to the Inspector, wearing a priggish smile.

"They all say that in here," she said.

Chapter Twenty Nine

The Internationaler Raiffeisen Grand Prix, Austria

Although regarded on the ATP tour as an important event, the Austrian tournament's organisers had been unable this year, to temp any of the world's top ten ranking players to take part. However, the competition could still boast a pool of worthy professional star names, all eagerly prepared to compete for the $425,000 cheque for first prize. Ace had earned himself a place in the thirty-two man event, after winning his three qualifying rounds and thereafter, to his and his coach's delight, had confounded everyone here by doggedly carving his way through to the semi-finals and taking with him one or two eminent scalps. Today though, it was generally believed that his match against Pedro De La Vega would be the newcomer's swan song. The players entered the sweltering heat of the arena, around which flags from around the world fluttered in the warm breeze.

The first set, mirrored the pre-match speculation, with the world ranked number twelve and number one seed, accomplishing a comfortable 6-2 win. The next set, saw Ace fight his way back into the match. His diligent efforts paying off and causing cracks to slowly appear in his opponent's make-up, De La Vega frequently bemoaned his grievances with the variable bounce that the court provided. Finally on dropping his service game and losing the set 3-6, the Mexican threw down his racket in frustration. The concluding set, produced some of the most compelling tennis witnessed at this Grand Prix to date. But again, towards the latter part of the set, Ace's Latin rival became flustered, frustrated this time apparently, by the swirling breeze that by now had, to some degree intensified. At 4-5 and with De La Vega's serving at 30-40, it was a lucky bounce from a service return that forced the Mexican to play from his baseline, inviting Ace to attack the net. The war of nerves along with the match was over, Pedro De La Vega cussed the wind and his opponent's mother for his misfortune.

An hour or so after the match, Ace was summoned to a press call. Flanked on either side of him at the table was Jack and Greg Fenton. Once the clicking and flashing of cameras had abated, the first of the journalists opened the proceedings.

"Graham Roberts, Daily Tribune ... firstly may I say congratulations Arthur..."

"Ace," Fenton declared.

"Beg your pardon?"

"Ace ... my friends call me Ace." The young conqueror explained.

"Then may I call you Ace?"

"Sure!"

"Thank you ... having just come into the big boy's league as it were, how does it feel to find yourself in the final of an ATP tournament?"

"What can I say ... it feels fantastic."

"Were you nervous out there at all today?"

"Strangely enough no, I felt good, stronger than ever."

"Once again, well done you did yourself and your country proud today Ace."

"Thank you Mr Roberts."

"Although, Pedro De La Vega has made it clear that he wishes to vindicate his below par performance on his part, due to him suffering from heat exhaustion, what are your thoughts on this?"

"Heat exhaustion did I hear you say?"

"Yes."

"Well there's no doubt about it, he did get hot under the collar once or twice, but when it came to playing tennis, I think that I was a lot hotter than he was this afternoon!"

A peel of laughter filled the room, while photographers momentarily peppered the area with an array of dazzling flashes.

"Malcolm Stringer, Morning Post ..... your quickest serve today was clocked at one hundred and twenty five mph .. that's pretty quick, is there room for you to improve on that speed?"

"No doubt ... but that's just part of the game that my coach here, along with my friend and practice partner, Tony Wang, have been working hard on."

"You must be rather disappointed that Mr Wang was knocked out of the competition so comprehensively, by the man you face in the final!?"

"Sure I .."

"Charles Winters." A voice in the gathering intruded. "I personally have witnessed your racket skills on two occasions, do you think that there might be room for a measure of finesse to be incorporated into your game?"

"I'll answer that question." Fenton said. "Perhaps Mr Winters you should be reporting on ladies' tennis!"

This comment caused a mixed reaction from the assembly, unbridled by this, Fenton continued.

"Let me tell you, Ace has all the finesse as you put it, that he needs, and is the most versatile player I've ever had the pleasure of coaching!"

"How much money have you earned so far?" Another probing journalist asked, again Fenton responded to the question.

"Come and ask that question the same time next year!"

An attractive female magazine columnist probed lightly.

"With such a hectic schedule Ace, do you find time to enjoy the company of the opposite sex?"

"Do you mean do I have a girlfriend?"

"Or three perhaps!?"

"This will be a pretty boring answer I know, but right now I live, eat, sleep and dream tennis, I'm afraid that I have very little time for anything else, that is, if I'm going to achieve my ambition, to be the best, to be number one!"

"Charles Winters again, speaking as a purist and .... I do not wish to pour scorn on your aspirations Ace ..."

"Mr Sharpe!" Fenton interjected, recognising another derogatory question impending.

"I'm sorry, I merely .."

"Only his friends call him Ace."

"I see ... I just simply wanted to point out, that to accomplish such a boastful claim, to as it were, one day be a world-beater ..."

"Get to the point why don't you Mr Winters!" Fenton said with an air of impatience. The room suddenly became noticeably uneasy and amidst the hubbub, Winters went on.

"I think Mr Sharpe .. you should look at some of your contemporaries ... who are already rightfully able to vaunt their standing ..."

Winters was by this time having to shout to make himself heard above the remonstrations from his fellow reporters.

"Look at Ove Olsen of Sweden." He continued, "Ranked seven .. and ..and of course the phenomenal talent of Jean Paul King!"

"Just exactly what are you trying to say Winters?" Greg Fenton chided.

"That with all due respect, to liken Mr Sharpe's proficiency on a tennis court with Jean Paul King ... would be like comparing a voyage on an oil tanker with a cruise on a luxury liner."

In conclusion to this rash statement, Winters succumbed to the sentiment of the majority and sat back down in his chair. In response, the smile on Ace's face, masked his anger as he said as evenly as he could muster.

"In answer to your theory Mr Winters, in the event of an inevitable collision on the high seas, between a tanker and a liner, I wonder which vessel would be the first to sink?"

"Who is the gentleman sitting on your left?" Another voice summoned. Ace turned to where the woman's hand gestured, and with a huge smile replied proudly.

"This ... ladies and gentlemen, is my big brother, his name's Jack."

As if (big brother) had been a verbal cue, an inundation of clicks and flashes from the photojournalist's cameras bathed the room.

The capacity crowd that had welcomed the two finalists onto court for the best of five final, were, by halfway through the third set, acclaiming their approval of the performance from the man, surely fated to lift the Internationaler Raiffeisen trophy. Mark Costello's performance today, had been as blistering as the heat inside the arena. The key to the supremacy that he had enjoyed in the opening two sets, had been his service returns, rewarding him with an impressive six games to one account in the first and to further highlight his domination a 6-2 win in the second. The Canadian, Costello, swiftly took a three games to love lead in the third.

It had been an experiment, Ace had told himself that he did not need to rely on it, not even in a big final and, not for the first time today his fingers searched in vain for the talisman around his neck. He shook his head as he slumped into his chair between games, then scolded himself for being so ridiculously superstitious, *'maybe though'* his mind reasoned *'it could be psychological'*.

For, the fact was, that since he had first donned the charm, his ambitions had without doubt advanced to date at least, beyond his wildest dreams. He bent over and plucked out a new racket from his bag and unwrapped its polythene covering, then proceeded to test the tautness of the strings, satisfied, he cast the one that he had been playing with previously to one side.

"Time." The man in the chair announced. Ace unfastened the zipped compartment at the front of the bag and pulled out the chained trinket, then quickly slipped it over his head, before making his way towards the baseline in readiness to continue. Incredibly, something of a comeback took place thereafter, with Ace holding three of his succeeding service games. By this time, although his endeavour was indeed admirable, it was clearly not enough, his opponent was on devastating form, eventually winning the match a clear three sets to love 6-1, 6-2, 6-4. Be it for psychological or even superstitious reasons, Ace vowed that he would never separate himself from the talisman again.

Chapter Thirty

The Halpen Rooms, Harley Street, West London

Irwin King stared and smiled conceitedly at his reflection. His fingertips explored the contours of his face, his eyes examined the specialist's handiwork assiduously, inch by inch. The operation to reduce the size of his nose, had been the most agonising, though by now, the heavy bruising around his eyes was on the mend. The scars across his eyebrows, where the delicate skin over his eyelids had been lifted, were healing nicely. He had considered growing a full beard to assist in the physical transformation, but thanks to the superbly administered surgery to his lower jaw and chin, he decided presently to shave away only some of the stubble and leave himself with a moustache. That would be sufficient, he told himself. His once regular routine, with the aid and application of a colorant to conceal the considerable expanse of grey in his hair had terminated. The collar-length style that he had sported for as long as he could remember would have to go, his thoughts advised. Yes, before visiting a barber, he had a number of pressing arrangements to embark on. Prior to departing from the decorous apartment appointed on the floor above the Halpen surgery, King surveyed the profile on both sides of his new face for a time. Satisfied, he ambled slowly into the adjoining sitting room, there, he selected a CD from the generous collection on the shelf and placed his chosen piece into the music centre, pressed the play button and sat down in one of the luxurious armchairs. Then, while Vivaldi's melodious rendition of the Four Seasons reverberated around the splendidly furnished room, King plotted the demise of the eminent plastic surgeon.

May 12, 19:35pm – St Johns Wood, London

It was a pleasure cruiser on the River Thames that discovered the gruesome remains. An article in the London Evening Standard, had stated that to determine the full identity of the deceased male had proved to be difficult, given that dental and fingerprint ID was unachievable because the corpse, had no hands and had been decapitated. It was thought though, that one or two personal means of identification had all but satisfied the investigative force, that the body was that of a white male in his mid forties by the name of Irwin King.

After reading the minor feature, he raised his glass of scotch aloft and proposed a toast to himself, to Irwin King's memory. It was a shame, he almost felt remorseful at having treated those hands that had performed such a superlative job in reshaping his facial features, with such irreverence. *'How liken to the smell of cooked bacon the flesh was, when it was incinerated'* he mused. It was a pity, he had quite liked the surgeon, but no matter how much the man had guaranteed confidentiality, a visit to his rooms perhaps by a couple of Bennetti's bully boys or another intimidating group of thugs, would doubtlessly have loosened the surgeon's tongue, and he really could not risk that. Now there was only one living soul, in the whole world that knew of the transfiguration and that was himself. A new start, a new life lay ahead. He appreciated the fact that, on paper he was nowhere near as wealthy as he was, but then again he assured himself over many occasions recently, that Bennetti and, his own wife had a strangle-hold on that capital. It would have been nice to make a few transactions regarding his valuable art collection, though that could have proved to have been a foolhardy mistake. It would have been like leaving a map, leading any would-be pursuing party to his door. Besides, he concluded he would survive very well indeed over a good period of time on the money that he had purloined and amassed from Bennetti. Two and a half million pounds Stirling invested in two accounts in Jersey and Switzerland would determine a comfortable lifestyle. Both accounts were in his new name, which was on his newly acquired passport.

He pushed his fingers through his now short grey locks, then toyed with his thick moustache, which was now a prominent feature, he was pleased at how distinguished it made him look. He smiled smugly to himself, things were going even better than he had hoped. This evening though, was going to be his first evaluation of the validity of his new identity. The first thing that he had done on his arrival at the Regents Park Hilton, after checking into his room was to telephone the escort agency that he had regularly used on trips to the UK capital in the past, employing an eloquent English accent, which he had actively worked at over a number of weeks with the help of a small tape recorder. He had requested the company of a certain young woman, he explained had been highly recommended to him by a lifelong friend. That lifelong friend of course was himself.

Indeed this evening was going to be a rather testing enterprise, considering the fact that he, Irwin King, as on other visitations to the city had been sexually intimate with this certain young woman on more than three occasions before, and in an effort to foil the escort girl's discovery of his identity, he had gone to some considerable lengths to meld in with his new face. He had shaved away his chest hair, had applied a generous splashing of Paco Robanne in preference to his usual brand of aftershave, tonight he told himself he would drink vodka instead of scotch whisky, as he had done before in her company, *'no'* his musing resigned himself to the future, *'tonight it would be champagne'*. It was all an elaborate game, set for his own amusement. He had been enamoured by this young escort *'Tanya was her name'* he mused, the image of her firm youthful body occupied his mind's eye, causing a stirring in his loins, something in addition grew in anticipation now, the smirk on his redesigned features.

May 12, 19:35pm – A Converted School House, Somewhere in South of France

The cramped windowless chamber's present occupant stooped over the washbasin, pressing her troubled brow up against the stark grey wall, the coolness transmitting from the inert concrete did little to alleviate her doleful frame of mind that co-existed with her gloomy surroundings. From above the narrow bed on the opposite wall, to further amplify her misery suddenly came the irksome sound of the surveillance camera clicking into action, followed by the lens winding and focusing, in short twitching spasms. Sonya squeezed her weary eyes tightly shut, and wheezed a long heavy sigh. She then slowly turned around and gave the lens an abrupt glare before, with leaden steps making her way across the small expanse to the bed, its springless mattress provided the inmate with somewhere to be seated. The only other piece of furniture was the commode. Rather than sitting on the bed, Sonya chose to lie down on its virtually unyielding surface. The camera hovered above her, inspecting her. She turned over onto her side and reflected that, she certainly understood a particular George Orwell novel infinitely better now, than she had some years past, when as a teenager she had read the story. Rather now though, it was not big brother watching, but the big woman and her inhospitable eyes, her thoughts continued, *'along with that half-assed Doctor, what's his shit ..?! and a number of other shameless voyeurs.'* Sonya stared contemptuously, over at the timeworn commode in the corner. For as long as she had been locked up in this stinking cell, those dreadful onlookers had been literally watching her every movement.

'How long had it been ... how long since she had been incarcerated inside this unholy place?' she brooded, but had to submit that, she honestly could not answer that question, indeed she did not even know if, outside the institution it was day or night. She felt a by now familiar melancholia swelling slowly inside her. She closed her eyes, endeavouring to use affirmative thoughts, to repress it's unwelcome invasion. *'You ain't beaten yet babe,'* she told herself, *'come on Sonya .. it's spring time .. the trees are budding, the whole world is enriched with the zest of new life ..'* her thoughts pressed. She toiled hard to etch these pleasant images into her mind, making every effort to shut out the reality of her pathetic circumstances which had, of late been nibbling at her resolve, gnawing into her spirit, like a vermin onslaught over a perishing animal.

Within an hour of falling asleep, and instigated by a lucid dream, Sonya's eyes twitched and flickered in a rapid fashion, her overwrought body began to twist and turn in frenzied movements. The dream recollected the ill-fated hour engaged during her aborted attempt to champion Danielle Marie to freedom. Sonya's face contorted, while her mouth actively mimed the words fitting the pictures inside her head.

"What?!" She cried out aloud through the parapet of her slumber. Floss' features portrayed a vivid depiction through her agitated imagination.

"I cannot go through with this." Floss said from the ingress of the reception area of the asylum.

"She's right ... your situation is hopeless." The matron advocated unexpectedly appearing from a doorway adjacent, alongside her stood a lofty untidily tailored man with a prominent chin, beneath thick bushy eyebrows he wore a scowling expression. Flanked on the matron's other shoulder was the spineless 'Doctor what's his shit', Sonya swivelled around pointing the gun threateningly at the trio.

"I warn you ... I'm not afraid to use this!" Sonya bellowed, and at that moment she sincerely believed her words. Her threat was instantly quelled by the frosty sensation from the narrow nuzzle of the gun pressing hard against the nape of her neck.

"Throw the gun to the floor!" The voice dictated behind her. Two armed uniformed policemen, as if being cued at that moment hurtled athletically through the main doors of the lobby. Sonya realising that her options were instantly zero, complied with the order. Her weapon glided over the floor's slick surface, one of the two armed officers that had just burst in on the scene, hastily moved over to the place where the gun came to rest. He promptly stooped and gathered it in his free hand.

"Hands behind your back!" The voice behind her commanded sternly. Again she obeyed, then, with the use of only one hand, while the other held the gun pointed firmly at Sonya's head, the officer at her back dextrously secured handcuffs to her wrists. Although reluctant, Sonya suppressed the temptation to voice her protestations. Instead, she asked the lofty man, who she guessed to be the Policeman in charge.

"Are you taking me down town?"

"Down town?" He said slightly bewildered by the question.

"She means ... I think Inspector." The matron offered, "Are you going to take her into custody."

"Oh, I see." He responded, then muttered some words in French, that Sonya was unable to quite interpret, in a deep bristling tonality that seemed to blend in with his prominent features, he then continued in English, bearing a broad French accent.

"Well ... your behaviour under normal circumstances would force me to take you away and charge you with a number of serious offences, but ... as there has been nobody hurt during your little escapade, and thanks to the matron's charitable endeavours on your behalf, I am only going to serve you with a caution." He announced. The big matron exhibited a crooked grin and augmented validity of his words, and in that familiar condescending tone amplified.

"The Inspector, along with Doctor Benamou and myself, have agreed that it would be in everyone's best interest, that you remain here where you belong."

"What?!" Sonya gasped, "I don't belong here ... please Inspector, these people are trying to kidnap me!"

The grip on her arm from the officer behind tightened. Her heart thumped heavily inside her ribcage, her eyes wide with fear and anticipation.

"Can't you see!?" She shrieked in exasperation, "Please sir, ... you've got to believe me, you are making one goddamn big mistake here!"

The Inspector's expression remained impervious to her noisy overtures. But, for one brief moment Sonya believed that the man's stony features revealed a modicum of conviction in return, she was mistaken. To increase her frustration, the double doors behind Sonya buffeted open, and the two male nurses announced their arrival and the attendant with the pockmarked face explained, that they would have been on the scene much quicker, had the skeleton key that they had employed to make good their escape from the room, not got a little jammed in the lock.

"No matter." The matron said, "You are in perfect time to escort our mischievous friend here, to the isolation unit to cool off."

"Nooooo!" Sonya wailed, as the two burly men in white advanced towards her flanking her, each taking a tight hold of her restrained arms. The officer behind stepped to one side, leaving a clear passage through towards the doors, that lead to the maze that lead to the rooms occupied by its maniacal inmates.

"I am a US citizen and I demand representation." She proclaimed struggling against the stalwart grip on her arms. She lashed out with her feet, she was beginning to panic now.

"You can't do this to me ... do you hear? I am a United States citizen .. I don't belong in here."

"Take her away," The matron ordered.

"As you can see Inspector, she is becoming delirious." Doctor Benamou said. The tall Inspector said nothing in return, his cool expression gave away nothing of his thoughts, while he watched the young crazed woman being dragged unceremoniously through the double swing doors, her screaming voice echoing her objections. *'She did,'* he thought, *'sound quite mad.'*

10:45pm – St Johns Wood

The game was over, it had been great while it had lasted, but now having relieved himself of his sexual frustrations on her, he regretted not only the act, but his utter stupidity at chancing her possible detection. It had all been an extravagant game before, before he had climaxed that is, in fact the whole facade had served to turn him on to such an extent that he could not call to mind, the last time his dick had remained so reliably solid for so long. He peered out presently, through the window of the sixth floor room that overlooked Lords Cricket Ground, to the right of the hotel was Regents Park, he was not actually taking in the scenery, nor for that matter, the hubbub of traffic and pedestrians below hastening around the streets and roads of St Johns Wood. He was immersed in thought, it was something in her eyes that had told him that the game was up, at the very moment that he had ejaculated, that was when he knew for sure. *'You're not being paranoid!'* he told himself, she had not mentioned anything but he knew that she knew his secret.

From the bathroom King could hear the jetting flow of water from the shower. He pictured her cleansing the curvaceous contours of her comely feminine body. Skin glistening sensuously beneath the electric light. The conspicuous red hair on her head and the exquisite tuft of ginger between the top of her shapely legs clinging to her under the torrent. Beneath his towelling gown, his erection made a stimulated return, motivating him to make a decision, he would screw the high class hooker one more time. *'Not here ... not in the hotel,'* he told himself, and considered an alternative, his senses were ablaze now with anticipation, of once again manoeuvring the fullness of her magnificently shaped breasts, kneading them in his hands.

Two hours thereafter, Tanya, the escort girl, became another victim to those malevolent hands. Her lifeless eyes stared up towards the coal black, moonless sky, her hair redder than ever, clinging to her head, above a pool of blood on a deserted tow path on the Camden Lock.

Some six hours or so into her turbulent slumber, Sonya's hair had become matted with perspiration, clinging to her feverish brow, the uniformed cotton top embraced her moistened skin. Now, her head pitched from side to side in nervous spasms. The vivid image within this new dream brandished her with unwelcome anxiety. The agitator was standing at her bedside, she could sense his wanton eyes exploring her body. *'My God!'* she could even hear him breathing. She squirmed and let out a pitiable whimper, when she felt his depraved hand touch her shoulder, she could even smell the acrid stench of sweat from his armpit, inducing her stomach to wretch. Irwin King was talking to her now, his voice echoing around inside her skull.

"You have a special treat coming your way." He said, "An extra large portion especially for you ... but first I want you to taste it, tell me what you think." His hand shook her shoulder, harder this time. Jolting her into consciousness, her eyes sprang open and stared anxiously up at his face, she then released an ear-piercing scream.

"Hey, take it easy." The nurse with the acne scarred face declared. Her breathing was heavy and she hitched her upper body up, taking the weight on her trembling elbows, her eyes danced around in their sockets, while her brain sluggishly tried to latch on to reality. *'No ... Irwin King had not caught her napping,'* her reasoning assured her. She took three long deep breaths manoeuvring herself to the edge of the bed, where she sat bolt upright allowing time for her mind to cleanse itself of the ghastly nightmare.

"Who was it that you were being intimate with in your dreams then?" The male nurse asked, while his associate standing by the door, giggled like a juvenile.

"What?" Sonya frowned.

"Well ... you were thrusting and wriggling those childbearing hips of yours like a rattle snake. I was almost tempted to climb on top and take a free ride."

"Is that so?" She asked rubbing her throbbing temples.

"Sure."

"Dream on ass hole." Sonya quipped, the smirk on his hard-favoured face, was replaced now by a frown while his colleague's laughter filled the room. The man's clumsy endeavours to somehow woo Sonya took a further set-back, when he lifted the cover off the paper dinner plate that he held in one hand and said.

"Here ... I have brought you some sustenance, like I say, an extra large portion."

"That's how I like 'em ... extra large, tell me, does yours fall into that category?"

From the doorway, the other male nurse held a hand aloft and gestured by way of wriggling his little finger, indicating that his workmate's manhood fell well short of her sardonic remark. The man at the brunt of the gibes was unable to hide his growing anger, with his jowls and cheeks glowing red, he mumbled an angry exchange in French towards his colleague, then turned to Sonya.

"And ... fuck you too!" He roared.

"Wouldn't you just love to!?" She teased, while her brainwork begged the question *'on what part of this ugly person does the son of a bitch keep the skeleton key?'*

"Are you going to eat this?" He said, thrusting the dinner plate accommodating the offering of grilled fish and vegetables.

"You know the rules." She remarked evenly.

"Rules? .. You do not make the rules around here."

"Come on ... it's the only procedure I can afford in this goddamn hole."

"Very well." The attendant conceded. He plucked the plastic fork up off the plate, and proceeded to cut off small segments from each item of food. He chewed and swallowed firstly the morsel of fish, then the potato and finally the green bean.

"Happy now?" He asked, Sonya shook her head.

"Uh .. uh ... no, open wide for mommy, just to make sure it all went down!" Sonya summoned. She always almost regretted this daily request, and today was no exception, *'the sight of his discoloured molars and grotesque tongue, could surpass any dieting programme'* she mused, then pushed the thought to the back of her mind, *'got to stay strong'* she told herself, and made a start on the meagre offering, without looking up, she bid farewell to the two attendants. As her mouth worked on the tasteless cuisine, her mind chewed over the procedures she would schedule for the rest of her waking hours on this day. Once she had made allowances for the food to have been suitably digested, it would be time then to commence her self-imposed strict routine of physical exercise which she had deemed from the outset of her incarceration, to be essential to maintain her health and yes, her sanity. It also served to keep her mind alert, and after all she told herself over and over again, that would be a crucial factor when the time came for her next attempt at escaping from this infernal place. Another thought presently descended upon her, causing a temporary halt to her chewing on her rations, she cursed aloud while she concluded, *'the only person who knows of my possible whereabouts is Don Lawrence ... goddamn it girl, why did you ever place your trust in that dumb-ass gumshoe?'*

Chapter Thirty One

A Breath of Fresh Air – May 13th, 09 38 am

On receiving their surprise visitation, the man whom, the matron had guessed correctly to be in charge, initiated their objectives through his assistant who acted as an interpreter. He was a younger man and, although shorter in height to his supervisor, displayed a much sturdier build that combined fully with his stern verbal approach with which he converted the English language into French with great proficiency. So impeccable was his diction in both tongues, that the matron was frankly, unable to pinpoint from which of the two extractions he could have been raised. The taller of the two introduced himself as Alan Dobson-Fraser from the ECLHR and extended his identity card before her. The matron examined the document as best she could, before concluding to herself that an eye test was long overdue. She felt a wave of panic flush through her body, their calling had caught her off guard. But, she told herself they were not going to hoodwink her ... *'No way!'*

"Wait ... wait just one moment." She said, holding aloft two fleshy palms, "I speak English perfectly well ... now let us start again from the top, you have been employed by the Government you say?"

"From the ECLHR, working on behalf of the Government." Dobson-Fraser affirmed.

"The EC ...?"

"ECLHR ... you saw my ID, now if you don't mind, we would appreciate your co-operation and allow us to go about our business." He declared, with growing impatience.

"But with respect Mr ...erm?"

"Dobson-Fraser!"

"I do not know what these initials represent, how do I know that you are not..."

"They represent matron, the European Commission's League for Human Rights."

"Yours is not the only hospital or institution under inspection." His assistant supplemented, delivering the overweight woman a reassuring smile.

"We have been sanctioned to inspect the sanitary conditions, and the health and safety of your patients here, that is all .... do you have a problem with these requirements matron?" Dobson-Fraser continued.

"No .. certainly not but ..."

"Jolly good ... now, we would be obliged matron if you would answer one or two elementary questions before we ask your good self to show my assistant and I around."

"Your collaboration in all aspects during our time here, would favour you in our final report no doubt, you understand." The younger man added smoothly.

"You have caught me on a bad day that is all." She responded, and indeed they had.

This morning had witnessed the confirmation of her monthly cycle, she cursed the fact that invariably, this predicament saturated her energy and caused to slow her down physically, although, what exasperated her rather more was that her power of concentration always suffered with the condition, *'you will simply have to diet ... lose some weight, as Doctor Benamou had advised!'* she brooded.

"Well?" Dobson-Fraser snapped.

"What..?"

"You haven't answered my question!"

"Your question?"

"Yes ... I asked you matron, how many staff do you have on duty today?"

"I apologise ... my mind was .."

"Look here .. we could save ourselves a good deal of valuable time, if you would contribute your full support into our enquiries, do I make myself clear matron!?" He said, and by now his tone had become somewhat austere, coinciding at that moment with a sharp excruciating throw assaulting her guts. She wanted to retaliate by screaming as loud as her lungs would allow, for the smart-arsed English bastard to go to hell, before she did something to him that she might possibly regret later. Instead she answered, manipulating her tone in return to conceal her irritation.

"Are you speaking of medical personnel sir?"

"That will do for starters."

"Our medical practitioner on duty today is Doctor Benamou."

"And nurses?"

"We employ four nurses."

"How many are on duty at any one time?"

"Two." She said, observing the younger man actively scribbling notes.

"Do you consider ... two nursing personnel adequate enough to cope with the every-day running of this establishment?"

"You must understand, our overheads here are substantial, we ..."

"A word of advice." The young assistant intervened, without looking up from his annotation, "You would do well to speak of ways of improvements towards the benefit of your patients."

"But we have had to cut back recently, at one time we had as many as eight full-time nursing staff here."

The two impeccably clothed men brought a brief halt to the proceedings, while they regarded one another. As if scrutinising her words by means of telepathy, their action served to augment her resentment towards these two pumped-up do-gooders. And hell, if she had not felt so much under the weather, she would have given these two shit kickers a piece of her mind. But, her reasoning however threadlike it happened to be presently, advised her to curb these irrational notions, which were motivated she speculated by the biological intrusion that her body had fallen victim to this day. Instead, she chose to take an alternative route, that way she could be rid of their meddling presence sooner rather than later, it was she who breached the narrow lapse in dialogue.

"I can assure you gentlemen, we manage extremely well under the circumstances."

"I think matron, I will be the judge of that." Dobson-Fraser affirmed, in a matter of fact manner and persisted, "Be so good now, to summon your Doctor Benamou and the two nurses presently on duty, ask them to assemble here would you!?"

Benamou was the first to arrive in the lobby, where he was formally introduced by the matron to the two men, the male attendants garbed in white, entered the reception area a few seconds later, they had obviously just shared a joke with each other, as their presence was accompanied through the double doors by a peel of laughter from them both. The grave expressions on the awaiting gathering severed their merriment instantly.

"Now ... as we are all here, my colleague and I would appreciate a tour of the building, along with a word or two with some of its patients ... matron, can I ask you to lead the way." Dobson-Fraser said authoritatively.

"Very well." She replied glancing down at the timepiece pinned to her uniform.

"How long might I ask do you imagine ..."

"As long as it takes." He put forth.

"I have many things to attend to you understand." She lied, for her intentions were she had decided, to abandon her post for the rest of the day and retire to her quarters, that is, as soon as these two interfering busybodies had completed their function here, and removed their obnoxious selves from the asylum and out of her sight. My God, how she loathed the English. Today she loathed just about everything and everyone. She turned and ushered the small troupe through the same doors, that some time past Sonya had disappeared, screaming her justifiable protests at her bizarre abduction. The matron lead the way, their footsteps echoed loudly around the bare walls of the narrow corridor. Dobson-Fraser came to a halt outside a door on which an imposing sign written in both French and English warned, 'Strictly Private, No Entry.'

"I'd like to take a look in here." His reverberating voice beckoned. The matron, whose body appeared almost to take up the width of the walkway, stopped and turned around, the indignant expression on her face Dobson-Fraser mused clearly seemed to say, can't you read? This caused to amuse him somewhat, though his demeanour remained thoroughly resolute. He made an attempt to enter by turning the door handle.

"I think you will find that the door is locked." The big woman said walking back the few steps towards the door, her chubby fingers vigorously meddled through the ring of keys she had snatched from her belt.

"What is in here that is so important that you feel the need to lock the door and advise people to keep out?" The young assistant asked, while the matron entered the latch key and turned it, releasing the catch.

"This is our observation room." She replied. Doctor Benamou turned to the two visitors as they entered the room.

"It's a necessary function to keep a vigilant eye on one or two of our more troublesome inmates." He explained, then added as an afterthought in an effort to impress the callers, "It is, I believe, in the interest of security and safety to themselves as well as others."

Dobson-Fraser's eyes perused the assemblance of monitors, he sniffed and turned to Benamou.

"If this is the case ... then why are the screens turned off right now?"

"We have to turn them off from time to time, they have a tendency to overheat otherwise."

"I see ... well let us have a look then!"

"What?"

"Turn the bloody things on!"

"Very well." Benamou agreed, then pressed a switch on the consul. The TV screens flickered on successively. All eyes in the room stared up now at the pictures, the monitor nearest to Dobson-Fraser's line of vision displayed, to him what was obviously a young woman, for though she had her back towards the camera, it was obvious that she was engaged presently in a strenuously animated work out. The male nurse standing at one side of him discharged a low-pitched wolf whistle. Dobson-Fraser turned and gave the attendant a cursory glance, carrying with it an air of disdain. The young woman that they were observing had brought about a temporary halt to her gymnastics and turned around to face the camera lens, which now focused closer, encompassing her features that glowed as a result of her physical exertions. Her eyes, devoid of cosmetics glared for an instant through the screen, before she resumed with her work-out.

"Is this, one of your more troublesome inmates, as you put it Benamou?" Dobson-Fraser scoffed.

"Do not be taken in by this woman's appearance."

"Oh ..? But I am, she's really quite stunning."

"That is as well be ... but the fact is that the woman is a certified psychopath."

"She is?"

"Yes indeed."

"And ... who might I ask attested her unfortunate condition?"

"I did." Benamou confirmed pompously.

"You did?"

"Yes."

"I see ... and who referred her to you?"

"If you want confirmation of her more recent unbalanced behaviour." The matron intervened, "Then you need only to speak to our local Police Inspector."

As if on cue, Benamou continued.

"The woman that you are looking at on the monitor, instigated a violent disturbance here not so long ago, which, thanks only to police intervention, would in my opinion without doubt have resulted in someone being hurt or, even killed!"

"Your opinion Benamou, to be candid does not exactly inspire me with confidence, although I will take heed of your words, and be on my guard when the time comes to meet the young lady in her quarters ... now tell me matron, could I take a look at your guest list?"

"Guest list?"

"Yes, along with the patient that we have been regarding, I wish to interview a number of, shall we say rather less violent internees."

On receiving a copy of the register, Dobson-Fraser picked out a number of names at random. (Danielle Marie's happened to be amongst them.)

Some thirty minutes later, the small entourage had finally made its way through the maze of corridors, calling in along the way on the chosen few, they were presently on the threshold to Sonya's chamber. Before unlocking the door, the matron tried to make her excuses to be released from the proceedings. This had been by now her third attempt, once again Dobson-Fraser insisted on her accompaniment.

"Your professional assessment is, I believe extremely important ... besides ... in five minutes from now we will be gone." He reasoned. *'And good riddance'* the big woman brooded to herself while noisily entering the appropriate key into the lock. Accompanying her boisterous action came the obnoxious howl from the madman in a neighbouring cell, startling Dobson-Fraser for an instant, though again, the expression on his face remained unruffled and businesslike. The metal door squeaked open and the matron entered.

"You have some visitors ... isn't that nice?!" She announced, and was followed into the tiny quarters by the two male nurses. The taller of the two visitants entered behind Benamou. Sonya was seated on one corner of the bed, her arms resting on her knees, hands clenched together, head bowed, giving her the bearing of a vanquished soul. She did not bother to lift her gaze to greet the gathering.

"Where are your manners?!" The pitted scar faced assistant bawled, stepping towards the cot and grabbing her roughly by the arm. As Sonya raised herself from the bed, she shrugged her arm away from his boisterous grip. Her eyes were ablaze, fixing the man dressed in white with a contemptuous stare.

"Keep your grubby hands to yourself asshole!" She advised, and at that moment had been a gnat's stride away from practising a number of drilled jujitsu manoeuvres on his lumpish being, one hundred and one moves in the art of self defence had saturated her thoughts in that split second, but, none of these would-be tactics had proved to be instrumental in causing her antagonist to yelp like a seal and drop to the floor as if praying to Mecca. The 'knee in the balls' had never occurred to her as being say, 'plan B', it was purely instinctive. A flash of near pandemonium superseded Sonya's rather petulant assault. The other male attendant on witnessing his colleague's embarrassing dilemma, wasted little time in seizing the opportunity to throw himself bodily at the young woman, sending her reeling backwards towards the small bed. Her efforts to resist his endeavour to revoke any further active undertaking on her part, had been quelled by his superior brawn. He held her presently face down over the surface of the cot, with one of her upper limbs twisted up her back in a tight arm lock. At the same time all this was happening, the matron had promptly plucked the walky-talky from her belt, her voice bellowing into the receiver requesting immediate assistance from security.

"And tell them to fetch a straight jacket!" Benamou advised, then declared through tightened lips, "I warned you gentlemen ... this woman is extremely dangerous, in my opinion you would be well advised to vacate the room at once!"

"Like I say Benamou, your opinion does not exactly inspire me with confidence." Dobson-Fraser affirmed, with a hint of sarcasm. In her constrained physical predicament, all that Sonya's eyes were currently able to focus on, was the stark grey wall. She tried without success to turn her head around to enable her to face the man who had just spoken.

"I think matron ... the time has come for our young female friend here to take in some fresh air." The voice from somewhere in the room was saying now. The grip on her arm eased slightly granting her a degree of relief. *'What took you so long, you limey two bit gumshoe!'* Sonya mused, motivating her features to break into a broad smile.

"I think you will find, that your security people are a little tied up right now." Don Lawrence's voice echoed around the small dismal room.

Chapter Thirty Two

Intuition – Allan House, Kensington – May 30

The three women of varying ages, sat around the sturdy oakwood table within the roomy kitchen of their accommodation; a smart cheerful apartment, off the main Kensington High Street. Their stay or, (their convalescence as he had put it) arranged by Don Lawrence himself. Sonya had had to admit that she had totally underestimated him, both as an investigator and indeed a man. She had almost caused him to blush when she told him so, on the day that they had arrived there. Sonya also asked him to pass on their thanks to the gentleman who had assisted him in delivering them from 'Lucifer's Lodgings', as she had put it. His collaborator, he had explained, was an ex-SAS Military man no less, adding that he had not come cheap, though terribly necessary. Now although it had only been two weeks and three days since making good their escape, Sonya and Floss had witnessed huge improvements in Danielle's physical health and overall general demeanour, her spirits improving with each passing day. Floss was delighted to see that the sparkle in Madame Danielle's eyes was beginning gradually to return. Unfortunately though, except for the occasional inconsequential recollection from her past, her memory remained stubbornly at odds with her. In the past few days, Sonya had been unsuccessful in trying to coax Danielle into taking a trip with her to Paris, to watch her son play in the French Open Championships, in the hope that perhaps being re-united with Jean Paul, might trigger something, somewhere deep inside her and catapult her back to her senses. Sonya poured herself a fresh cup of coffee, then re-joined Danielle and Floss at the table.

"It's a pity." She rendered, "Paris in Springtime would have been nice."

"As I have told you before Sonya, I will not return to France until I can be sure it is safe to go home."

"But Danielle ... the American Embassy has assured me that, that goddamn loonybin will soon be closed down, and the big ass matron along with Doctor what's his shit have been found out ..."

"I know ... but at the moment there is not enough evidence to ..."

"Look Danielle." Sonya intervened, "I don't think that the French Authorities or whoever, are poised for your return, ready to lock you up again the minute you step off the plane!"

"I appreciate what you are saying, but I still do not feel prepared to take any chances."

"The only bogey man out there that ever did you any harm, or could do you any more harm is your h..., is Irwin King!.... and he's,... well, he's dead .." Sonya declared rounding off the sentence awkwardly.

“Do not be embarrassed my dear.” Danielle assured, “From what I have learned of that man, I am gratified that I have no memory of my life with him .. Hell strikes me as being the perfect place for him.”

“I do not believe that Mr King Sir is dead.” Floss uttered nervously across the table, her words taking Sonya and Danielle completely by surprise.

“Not dead ..? what in heaven’s name are you trying to say Floss!?” Danielle summoned.

“I do not know ... call it intuition if you will, but ...” Floss broke off, slowly shaking her head. *‘Call it intuition’* Danielle mused and those words sparked something deep inside Danielle’s cloudy consciousness. The sudden sound of the telephone ringing at that moment served to dissolve her train of thought.

“I’ll get it.” Sonya said, getting up from the table. The telephone was situated directly behind where she had been sitting, she lifted up the handset and put it to her ear.

“Yeah!?”

“Sonya?”

“Who’s asking?”

“It’s Don Lawrence!”

“Hi Don.”

“Hello ... just a courtesy call really, how are you all getting along?”

“Fine ... just fine, thanks.”

“Jolly good, would you be so kind as to thank Mrs King for her cheque? Please tell her that it was more than sufficient for services rendered.”

“Sure!”

“Thank you ... so tell me Sonya, what are your plans?”

“Regarding what?”

“Just curious to know, if you are still contemplating the pursuit of your sister, considering our only lead is now deceased!?”

“I’ve had time since coming to London to think hard and long about it Don ... truth is, I don’t want to give up on her ...”

“I understand.”

“Trouble is ... my resources are running a little low ... missed out on a whole lot of good paying assignments, thanks to my unwelcome vacation in that French looney bin.”

“Hmmm.”

“No doubt about it ... the glamour world is a damn superficial one!”

“Did you explain your circumstances to your agent?”

“Sure.”

“And ..?”

“She wanted to sell the whole goddamn story to the tabloids, she got kinda belligerent when I told her that I’d like to take a rain check on that idea.”

“But I would have thought Sonya, that the publicity would have favoured you kindly, financially!?”

“That’s exactly what my agent said.”

“And would have perhaps assisted you in your devoted quest ...”

"Towards finding my kid sister ... hell I know!" She confirmed, then chewed lightly on her lower lip, *'call it intuition Floss had said.'* She turned around to face the wall, her tone was now just above a whisper.

"You may think this is dumb but ... I've got a hunch that King did not as you suggested, fall victim to his unsavoury friends in the underworld."

There was a moment's silence between the two before Lawrence spoke.

"Are you saying that you think Irwin King might have contrived his own death?"

"It's just a hunch like I say ... but it's sure enough to make me think twice about having my face splashed over newspapers and magazines with an accompanying article explaining, how we'd succeeded in liberating the guy's estranged wife from the crazy house that he'd had her committed."

"Point taken ... but if that was the case and King is still alive and kicking, he could be anywhere ... anywhere in the world."

"All the same Don, I want you to make me that appointment with the escort agency."

"But I implore you ..."

"Do it Don ... please ... besides, goddamn it, I need the money."

"Very well." Lawrence said, and Sonya recognised the reluctance in his voice.

"I'm a big girl Don as you know, and yes, I will be careful, OK?"

An awkward break in their conversation now, "Don .... Don, I'm sorry I .... hello, are you there?"

"Sonya, that young man I spoke to you about."

"What?"

"In my office." He declared unable to hide the excitement in his voice.

"There's someone in your office?"

"No ... I'm at my apartment, ... on the TV now, Sky Sports, that boy I interviewed, Ace .... he's on the TV, you have Sky where you are don't you?"

"Yeah."

"Tune in."

"OK."

"I will call you back."

She placed the receiver back in its cradle, while employing her other hand to busily press the buttons on the TV's remote control. She glanced for an instant over towards Danielle, who appeared to be pre-occupied, as if working on a conundrum.

"There ... Sky Sports." Sonya declared, immediately recognising the athletic prowess belonging to the man the television screen displayed. By means of employing slow motion the picture presented the famous talent of Francisco Satori, majestically advancing over the red clay surface and rhythmically sweeping his tennis racket and connecting with the small yellow ball.

"OK ... we pan out here." The commentator's voice was saying, "You were at the receiving end of this top spin forehand shot, from the world number five ... take us through it if you will."

"OK ... as you know this was the penultimate point for the match .. I honestly thought he'd hit long." Satori's opponent's words emitted.

"So you left it?"

"As you can see I didn't commit myself, I didn't play a shot."

Indeed, the image on the screen verified his claim, although it was difficult to determine, even in slow motion if the ball had landed on or outside the baseline. The commentator's voice continued.

"Though you did not make a big deal of it, you believed the ball should have been called out?"

"Sure ... but it's like my coach said, these things happen from time to time, it's part of the game I guess, but he was not very pleased that I didn't play the shot."

"All the same, it was a big point, let's have another look, this time from another angle."

The position of this camera had been strategically fixed along the length of the baseline, it then closed in on the moment that the ball made impact onto the ground, then the freeze frame was implemented. The piece of footage incited the commentator into a new excited tone of voice.

"The rules state that any part of the ball touching the line is deemed to be good ... on this evidence, no doubt about it, match point should have been yours Ace!"

"What's done cannot be undone." Ace smiled, the scene now conveyed him sitting inside a small studio. His dark, handsome, affable face transmitting through the small screen caused Sonya to wonder, *'could it be ... that this guy is ... that grainy photograph of the young man in Larry Hickman's villa but yes, the likeness was there.'*

"We are joined now by Ace's coach, Greg Fenton, welcome Greg." The commentator went on, "Quite an achievement, Ace's first major Grand Slam Tournament here in Paris, and only by a whisker in the fifth and deciding set, losing out to the world's number five?!"

"And let's not forget." Fenton enthused, "Ace had to compete also in the qualifying rounds, and to perform as he did today in a scorching five setter, against Satori's superior experience, simply underlines what I've said all along ... Ace is made of what it takes to become a champion."

"Will we be seeing you at Wimbledon this year Ace?"

"Bet your ... you bet." Ace grinned.

"Grass is my man's favourite surface, so beware Emerson .. Wang, King, whoever!" Fenton affirmed ebulliently.

"So there you have it." The commentator's voice droned.

"Is this just a flash in the pan? ... Or have we today witnessed the birth of a future champion .. a champion in the sport of tennis from the British Isles .."

"That boy ..." Danielle said from the table. Sonya turned and noticed that she looked rather flustered, her face had gone pale, eyes wide, mouth agape, her fingers fidgeted with the neckline of her blouse. The voice emanating from the TV was a mumble to Sonya now.

"What?"

"That boy ...Ace ... should I … do I know him?" Danielle asked.

On learning that the address that Don Lawrence had provided her with, could be reached comfortably on foot within thirty minutes, Sonya had taken advantage of the warm sunny morning, departing from the apartment at Allan House a good deal earlier than necessary to enable herself to make her way at a leisurely pace and arrive for her appointment, in a good clear frame of mind. She stopped several times along the way, window shopping here and there, along Kensington High Street. It was while browsing in the window of a certain fashionable clothes store that, on this warm morning she first had the chilling impression that she was being followed. *'Don't be so dumb'* she told herself *'who'd be following you?'* all the same, she contemplated hailing down a cab, instead, she turned and upped the tempo of her stride, glancing every so often over her shoulder along the busy street left behind in her wake. Some five minutes later, comforted that by now, she was clear of the hullabaloo of the high street she turned around, walking backwards for several metres, her eyes busily searching the horizon, until that is, colliding with an elderly woman and her poodle dog. By the time that she approached the Royal Albert Hall standing conspicuously across the road on her right she came to a halt, cursing her high heeled shoes for being *'so goddamn high'*. She swung around to face her would-be stalker. Using the iron railing perimeter to Hyde Park for support, she slipped off one of her shoes, sighing both with the relief that this basic course of action had bestowed upon her throbbing toes, and the fact that as far as she could see along the wide sidewalk, the only pedestrians visible was the old lady and her dog ambling slowly towards her in the distance, and a couple of joggers that had, only seconds ago passed by running towards Kensington. *'Just your imagination'* Sonya uttered under her breath, actively replacing the shoe onto her foot, then resuming her progress at a rather more relaxed tempo.

She reached her destination in Knightsbridge with fully fifteen minutes to spare. The exterior to the establishment was not quite what Sonya had expected. She checked the address again against the one she had written down on a piece of paper, indeed they did tally. Emblazoned boldly in gold leaf across the smoked glass window, was spelt the name Aphrodite, in the bottom left hand corner of the entrance door was a skilfully sign written list of services attained within. There was no mention of an escort facility. *'A beauty parlour'* Sonya reflected *'must serve well as a pretext for such an enterprising modern day business involving high class hookers.'* She pushed the door open and entered into a modestly sized reception area surrounded by a collection of blooming green potted plants. A young woman whom, Sonya guessed to be the beautician was sitting behind a stylish desk. She looked up towards Sonya with a smile that displayed an immaculate set of flawlessly straight teeth, so white were they, that Sonya surmised that they were probably capped, and instantly scolding herself for entertaining such puerile thoughts.

"Miss Crabtree?" The young woman said, turning her attention back to the computer on her desk, "Manicure and facial?"

"No ... I'm sorry I got here a little early, I have an appointment with Miss Peterson, mind you, the thought of a manicure and facial right now sounds to me like an agreeable alternative." Sonya joked, though it seemed her little quip had fallen on stony ground. Those perfect teeth were now concealed behind her equally superlatively formed lips, the beautician's expression almost instantly conveying a rather more sombre bearing. She lifted her gaze from the computer and swung around in the swivel chair, then got to her feet.

"Please take a seat won't you?" She said gesturing towards a comfortable looking leather upholstered couch. "I'll pop through and see if Ms Peterson is ready to see you." These words were delivered with a smile, though along with it, her tone of voice was not nearly as genuinely hospitable as was the case when Sonya had first entered the establishment. *'That greeting had been reserved exclusively for her own personal clientele, like Miss Crabtree,'* Sonya reflected, with an air of amusement. Although her feet were throbbing, Sonya resisted the invitation to sit down, what was rather more tempting presently, was to simply abandon the whole ludicrous idea which had been based on a whim, that, Irwin King just might still be alive, and not, as Don Lawrence had suggested fallen victim to his unsavoury friends in the underworld, she chewed lightly on her lower lip, another conflicting thought primed her to turn and make her way towards the door, through which only two minutes earlier she had entered, then make swift her exit and forget the whole crazy idea. Now she reached out for the door handle, the beautician's voice declared from behind.

"Ms Peterson will see you now."

From across the crowded street, the man kept a vigilant eye on Sonya's tall silhouette-like form through the smoke glass window. As she about faced at the doorway, then walked across the width of the room's interior and disappeared from view, Don Lawrence loosened his tie and unfastened the top button on his shirt. The day was growing warmer.

Sonya guessed that there must have been fifty or more video cassettes, stacked on the two shelves on the wall, each individual tape ran along from A to Z in alphabetical order. *'Ms Peterson'*, as she had insisted on being titled, when she had introduced herself on first meeting the potential employee, plucked one of the cartridges out at random then pushed the plastic receptacle into the video machine's appropriate cavity and pressed the play button. She stepped back a few paces and turned to Sonya, *'the woman wears more make-up than a circus clown,'* Sonya mused. She was a woman in her mid-forties, obviously attempting to bury the fact. Now she caught a blast of the Ms Paterson's excessive application of perfume, causing Sonya almost to choke. Like the scent and the cosmetics, Sonya had decided that there was a word that could best describe Ms Peterson, erroneous, and the woman's pretentious high hat utterances, served to irritate further.

"Best move I ever made enrolling my little enterprise with the internet." She said, and Sonya wondered when she was going to take the plum out of her mouth, though she concealed her thoughts with a wry smile.

Ms Peterson went on,

"This will give you some idea of the kind of promotion we will require you to undertake, for our clients that use the net."

"I see." Sonya uttered.

"All my girls are required to ..." Ms Peterson's voice broke off the moment that the screen displayed a young attractive woman with a shock of fiery red hair. She cussed herself at that moment for neglecting to dispose of the old recording.

"Hi, let me introduce myself." The red head began on the screen.

"My name is Tanya."

"Oh dear, this isn't a very good example I'm afraid." Ms Peterson declared above the words emanating from the TV.

"Oh, why?" Asked Sonya.

"Well ... because she no longer works for me."

"That's a pity, she's one swell looking girl!"

"Yes ... yes, I'll show you another tape I think."

"No Ms Peterson, this one is just fine." Sonya said, and wondered why the woman standing next to her had suddenly become rather flustered. She looked back towards the screen, the picture closed in on Tanya's comely features, her lips curled seductively into a smile, her intelligent blue eyes sparkled and displayed a hint of humour, as she began to recite a poem, which she explained she had written especially for her would-be internet date.

"If you feel an evening of solitude taking a grip." She began, "And you truly need some womanly companionship, encircle my name with a ring, and I will make you feel like a king. Whenever you might feel the need, I'll bring you satisfaction guaranteed."

The corny verse almost caused Sonya to burst into laughter, though with a degree of self control managed to suppress her amusement. From across the room the telephone rang out, Ms Peterson turned and answered it.

"Yes?"

"There's a Mr Latimer on the line." The voice said through the receiver.

"Latimer ... do I know him?" Ms Peterson asked.

"A potential client."

"Have him call me back would you."

"It's the third time he's called in the last ten minutes, he's rather insistent."

"Very well, put him on would you ... hello!?"

"Ah, Ms Peterson?"

"Speaking, can I help you?"

"I sincerely hope so, the name's Latimer and I am personal secretary to Lord Bucknall."

"I see." Ms Peterson said genuinely impressed.

"His Lordship requires a personable female escort for this evening and you, Ms Peterson, came highly recommended."

"May I ask who gave you this recommendation?"

"I'm afraid that that information, would breach his Lordship's rules of conduct."

"I understand, though I'm afraid that by and large our patron's call at least seven days prior to their arrangement with one of my girls."

"Had his Lordship known that then ..."

"You see, all my female escorts have schedules for this evening I'm afraid."

"That's a pity, Lord Bucknall is in town for one night only, can I just add however, money is not a problem!"

The latter proposition evoked an idea that would doubtlessly serve to satisfy both parties.

"Would you excuse me for just a moment Mr Latimer?"

"Very well."

Ms Peterson put a hand over the mouthpiece of the handset, clutching it close to her chest, she turned to Sonya.

"Would you like to be escort to a Lord Bucknall this evening?" She asked.

"Why not?" Was her response. though she hoped, that an evening with this Lord what'shisname would not end up being a wearisome one.

"His Lordship will have to pay double the fee Mr Latimer." Ms Peterson said into the phone, resuming her conversation. Two minutes later, the transaction, along with an agreed rendezvous location, had been agreed upon. Ms Peterson replaced the handset in its cradle, her face displayed a satisfied grin.

Sonya had agreed to meet with Don Lawrence an hour prior to her engagement with Lord Bucknall. The small pub, boasted only a handful of customers, and presently, Sonya was pleased to note that none of the early evening patrons were in earshot of their conversation.

"I'm sorry Sonya, but I really do not believe that this escorting job is a good idea." Lawrence was explaining.

"You don't approve?"

"Certainly not!"

"It pays well!" She responded. The investigator regarded her, peering over his half-rimmed spectacles.

"What .... if you don't mind me asking what does the job exactly require ... of you I mean?"

"It's quite simple Don, I just get to flaunt my attributes!" She said with an impudent grin, across the small table, she recognised his discomfort at her immoderate statement, then in an effort to eradicate her sportive jest, added,

"All I've got to do in other words is, keep some lonely millionaire company for an evening ... you know!? .. Accompanying the guy to the theatre or dinner, that sort of thing!"

"Yes I know but ..."

"That's all there is to it Don!"

"Did you stipulate to our Ms Paterson, that your relations with the agency's clients would be purely platonic?"

"Sure."

"And, what was our Ms Paterson's reaction to that?"

"She was kinda horrified that I even brought up the issue." Sonya explained, then proceeded to mimic the woman's pretentious English accent, and recited the lecture given to her earlier in the day, "This is a respectable business, if I learned that any of my girls had behaved like a harlot with our clientele, it would cause me considerable distress."

"But you know Sonya, as well as I do that some of these young ladies, sell rather more than simply their looks and personalities."

"Sure, and so does Ms Peterson know, she's just covering her own ass that's all, anyway, believe me Don, screwing with some old sugar daddy sure as hell ain't on my bill of fare!" She said adamantly. Lawrence smiled and nodded his head in approval. The rare smile was somewhat short lived, replaced now by a look of concern.

"Hypothetically speaking Sonya, what do you honestly imagine that your chances are of meeting up with Irwin King on one of these nocturnal escapades?" He asked, lifting his small glass of Guinness to his lips, Sonya smiled wryly back across at him.

"You think I'm crazy don't you?"

"No, I don't think you are, I know you are!"

"OK, truth is, it's a shot in the dark, but the only way I'm ever gonna get to see my sister again, is probably through that evil son of a bitch!"

Lawrence placed his drink down, leaned forward resting his elbows on the table top, he then pressed his long fingers together to form a steeple.

"I have done a little homework on this escort agency."

"Yeah!?"

"Yes, it appears that, some weeks ago one of Ms Peterson's young girls was murdered."

"My God!?"

"A particularly nasty homicide by all accounts."

"Have they found the culprit?"

"Afraid not, apparently the police suspected the man to whom the young lady had played escort, amongst other things, on the night of her appalling demise, unfortunately the suspect has simply vanished without trace, so now I'm sure that you will understand my rather paternal concern if you like, on your behalf."

"Yeah, thanks Don, I truly appreciate that!" She replied sincerely.

"Even so, I don't suppose I can perhaps persuade you to abandon these foolhardy aspirations and using the escort calling as a vehicle?"

"I'm afraid not."

"I must say, your stubbornness is a quality in you that I admire."

"Why thanks Don." She smiled, then drained the remainder of orange juice from her glass, "So, tell me, what was the girls name?"

"Georgina Thompson."

"Georgina?" Sonya enquired, and the gumshoe's next statement made her wish that she had not asked the question.

"That was her real name, at the agency they knew her as Tanya." He said, and noticing Sonya's mouth was agape added, "You look like you've seen a ghost my dear."

"I did ... I have today, at the agency on video, jeeze, what a goddamn waste."

A moment of silence fell between the two, Sonya quietly contemplating the image in her mind's eye, of Tanya's long flowing red hair and her intelligent blue eyes. Lawrence had leant down and picked up his attaché case, it came to rest on his knee, then he opened it up and plucked out a small square shaped colourfully wrapped parcel, he passed it across the table.

“For me?” She asked.

“Yes, for you, but please don’t open it here, best you use a ladies powder room prior to your rendezvous later on, unwrap it in the cubicle, thus avoiding prying eyes.” The package felt quite weighty in her hands.

“I sincerely hope that you do not find a need to use it, let’s just say that it will offer you some insurance.” Sonya’s astute smile made Lawrence conversant with the fact that she knew exactly what the elaborate wrapping contained within.

“A word of warning Sonya.”

“Oh, yes?”

“If you intend taking a long trek, in future wear yourself a pair of sensible shoes!”

“So it was you shadowing me this morning!?”

“Merely a precautionary undertaking.”

“Against what ..... who?” Sonya demanded, feeling a wave of annoyance invade her.

“Look, if King is alive or dead, you know at first hand he has had associations with some extremely dangerous people!”

“I’m sorry, but I really can do without someone stalking me, goddamn it Don, it gives me the creeps!” Sonya chided in a stifled tone. Lawrence held a hand aloft in an effort to appease her obvious anger.

“I apologise profusely, that I have clearly provoked you Sonya..” He affirmed candidly, an awkward breach descended upon them for what seemed like a long moment.

“No ... no, it’s me that should apologise.” She said, looking her self appointed protector in the eye, “I’m a little on edge about tonight I guess.” Her voice calmer now, she looked at her wristwatch, took in a deep breath of the pub’s stale air, then let out a sigh.

“I’d better shape up.” She advised herself, slipping her handbag onto a shoulder and clutching the parcel in her left hand, she got to her feet. Lawrence was also standing now.

“What do you reckon to that kid Ace, Don?”

“If he is who we think he is, then his mother can be very proud. Have you tried to coax her memory regarding the young man?”

“Maybe in time, but right now I don’t think she’s quite ready to cope with it, she’s got enough on her plate as it is.”

“I see, I understand.”

“Anyway, I’d best be on my way.” Sonya held up the package in her hand and said. “Thanks again Don.”

“Once again, I sincerely hope my dear, that you don’t have occasion to need it!” Lawrence rendered.

Outside the old Inn, the air was still warm, to the west, the sun was low in the sky, reflecting its crimson hue upon the odd light fluffy cloud. In contrast to the east however, the heavens displayed a rather dismal perspective of charcoal grey.

“Looks like we’re in for a storm.” Sonya declared.

Chapter Thirty Three

Jacques Bistro – Paris, May 30th at 21:27

The decor inside the small restaurant was unpretentious, it resembled, Ace had thought initially, nothing more than a corner street cafe. Although he and his companions this evening, all agreed that the food and the atmosphere within was first-rate, and more than compensated for the establishment's lack of grandiose furniture and decoration. In addition to the bistro's charming qualities, Ace was surrounded by people that he considered to be his most intimate friends. His brother Jack had been joined earlier in the day by his wife, Helen. The two had been spectators this afternoon at Roland Garros, and despite witnessing Ace's unlucky departure from such a prestigious championship, as the French Open, felt deeply proud of the young Arthur Sharp. Along with his coach, Greg Fenton, and Ace's fellow professional and practice partner, Tony Wang, they all toasted.

"To good friends and future endeavours."

"Speaking of future endeavours Tony!?" Fenton said, placing his glass down on the table, "As Ace and me have decided to forego our trip home in favour of lending our support for you in your match the day after tomorrow."

"Oh yeah!?" Wang rendered with a knowing grin.

"I just thought, we might have a little wager, that's all mate!" Fenton volunteered. A moment of friendly banter then followed between the five diners. Fenton slapped an open hand down on the table, temporarily subsiding the jocular display of bravado.

"OK ... hands up, who's going for Wang?"

Ace's hand was first to go up, followed then tentatively by Helen's.

"Hey, come on Tony." Ace piped up, "How about you give yourself a vote of confidence!?"

Tony Wang smiled across the table at his friends.

"Come on, the guy's good, but not that bloody good!" Ace pressed, then Wang raised a hand slowly above his head.

"Way to go!"

"Are we betting in Francs, Dollars or Pounds?" Jack enquired.

"Pounds!" Ace suggested.

"Hang on, how are we going to do this?" Jack prompted.

"You and me will give these three, two to one odds." Fenton offered.

"No way!"

"Tony's opponent will have a partisan crowd on his side ... he'll be playing on home soil, plus the fact that he is joint favourite with the bookies to win the championship!" Helen affirmed.

"Point taken." Fenton said, raising both hands before him as if to parry the vigorous verbal bombardment. "OK, how does three to one sound?"

"What's the stake?" Jack enquired.

"A pound!" Fenton bid.

"One pound?" Helen giggled.

"Ooooh, big money!" Ace quipped.

"Come on Greg." Helen added.

"Hardly a bet at all." Jack scoffed. The banter continued for a further minute or more, before they all agreed to agree, that the gamble was simply a bit of good wholesome fun, despite this, even taking into account such a laughably meagre monetary stake. Ace silently wondered why suddenly his conscience was in such turmoil. He certainly was not envious of his friend, Tony Wang, on the contrary, he simply wished that it was himself that was going out to do battle in the next round with Jean Paul King.

21:27 – Allan House, Kensington, London

The crack of thunder over Allan House, seemed to shudder through the building, right down to its very foundations. Such was the thunderclap's ferocity, it incited a moment of sheer terror for Danielle Marie King, her eyelids flickered in spasms, Papa's old factory disintegrated before her. Then, within the twelve seconds that followed, prior to the grey-black sky's ensuing outburst, Danielle was reunited with the recollection of a number of events and experiences, from earlier periods in her life.

21:27 – Euston Road, London

A concierge outside the Landmark Hotel held a large black umbrella aloft, in an effort to protect Sonya from the heavy downpour while she hurriedly paid the taxi driver. Once inside the splendid reception area, she thanked the smartly dressed man, garbed in top hat and tail coat.

"Oh ... could you tell me please where the nearest ladies room is?" She inquired. He gestured a hand towards the far end of the reception.

"There's a ladies room on the left, before you get to the short flight of steps that lead into the Winter Gardens. If you need to know anything else, please ask, our staff are here to help Madam."

"Thanks again." Sonya said, and with a smile, the concierge wished her a pleasant evening. Sonya certainly hoped that that would be the case.

Once inside the lavatory, she locked herself in one of the cubicles, then as briskly and quietly as her fingers would allow, unwrapped the package that Don Lawrence had given to her earlier. Sonya then opened up the cardboard container, inside which, she found a small handgun stowed inside a bed of straw. She plucked out the weapon then checked the barrel for ammunition. Satisfied, she clicked the cylindrical container back into place and wedged the metal firearm inside her shoulder bag and dispensed with the unwanted debris in the sanitary disposal bin, *'OK Sonya .... stay cool!!!'* she told herself, *'you're in control"*. She flicked back the bolt and opened the door, glanced round the tiled enclosure then, with a determined step vacated the lavatory. Outside the door, she turned and made her way up the broad flight of marble steps, that led into the Hotel's so called Winter Gardens. At the top of the steps, she came to a halt allowing herself a moment to take in its splendour, eight floors of the Victorian building facia towered all around this extensive area. A glass domed roof had been erected in recent times, cocooning the area from the outside elements. Tropical foliage thrived in precise sections, and eight tall palm trees flourished within the elaborate domain. Beneath a balcony on the far side, a large grand piano was being played, softly penetrating and assisting the ambience. There were several groups of people dotted about in variable numbers enjoying conversation, some dining and others simply favouring a glass of their favourite tipple.

Sonya was aware of several of the male hotel clientele surveying her form, as she made her way over to a table close to the piano. A waiter expediently pulled out a chair for her to be seated, she thanked him and sat down.

"Would Madam care to see the menu?"

"No thanks, I'd like just a drink for the time being."

"Certainly Madam, would you like to see the bar tariff?"

"No need, I'd like the special house cocktail."

"Very well Madam." He said, with that he walked smartly away, and while the pianist's dextrous fingers performed a rendition of Clare de Lune by Debussy, she mentally reiterated the short list of instructions that Ms Peterson had acquainted her with. *'Be at the table by 9 30 pm, near the pianoforte'* she had told her, Sonya smiled to herself at the woman's pretentious use of vocabulary *'pianoforte indeed ... order yourself the special house cocktail, this will assist our client to identify you, then wait patiently,'* she reflected, while allowing her eyes to scan each tables' occupants with a view to hazarding a guess as to which one of the men might be his Lordship. Then her gaze lifted towards the expanse of large windows, she wondered if this Lord Bucknall might be looking down upon her from somewhere up there, from one of the rooms?

"The house special cocktail, Madam." The waiter declared, breaking through her thoughts.

"Thanks." She said, looking down at the glass of lavishly assembled fluid. She had no idea what variety of alcohol might be contained within the brightly coloured mixture, all the same, she decided to sample it. Despite the fact that the concoction tasted delicious, she decided that another sip or two would be more than sufficient. Tonight, she told herself, she would require herself to hold on to all her faculties. Another thought crossed her mind at this instance, *'did the man sitting a couple of tables away to her right just make a pass at me?'* she asked herself, '*did he, only a moment ago wink an eye in my direction?... or did the guy have a nervous tic, maybe?'*

The man with the short cut head of grey hair and sporting a rather prominent moustache, lifted his tall stature from the chair at which he had been seated, then proceeded to walk the short distance towards Sonya's table. Their eyes met once again, albeit briefly this time, Sonya was primed to ask if he might be Lord Bucknall, although before she had had the opportunity to utter the question, he had sauntered by her, she watched his impressive bearing ebb away towards the farthest end of the palatial milieu and speculated that, '*the guy might be some kind of English Nobleman, or a well-to-do Baron even,* but concluded that '*he was probably just a cock-sure son of a bitch!'*

After having a brief word with a concierge in the lobby, King took the elevator to the first floor, whereupon he went directly to his suite. He closed the door behind him, then made his way to the large glass doors, through which his inquisitive eyes studied the Winter Gardens and its patrons. He picked up the telephone and pressed the appropriate digits.

"Hello, Head Waiter Paul speaking, how may I help you?"

"Ah yes, I'm speaking from the Dalton Suite and I noticed from my window, someone I know sitting near the piano, I would like to speak to her, would you ask her to come to the phone?"

"I can do better than that sir, I will take the phone to her, is it the young lady with the dark hair?"

"And legs that don't quit, yeah that's her Paul!"

"Yes sir, I know exactly who you mean!" Paul grinned.

The waiter returned to Sonya's table, in his hand he held a mobile telephone.

"There's a call for you Madam."

"For me?"

"Yes."

"Did they say who was calling?"

"It's one of our hotel guests."

"Thanks." Sonya said accepting the phone and holding it to her ear, "Yeah?!"

"How's the cocktail?"

"I would have preferred martini ... who am I speaking to?"

"You have come from the agency?"

"The agency?"

"You are to play escort for Lord Bucknall tonight, am I right?"

"Well ... yeah, and you are?"

"Let's just say, I'm one of his Lordship's associates."

"I see, so tell me where is ... his Lordship?"

"The agreement with Ms Peterson was that, engagements with young ladies like yourself should be treated with the upmost discretion!"

"Yeah!?" Sonya rendered, rather taken back by the man's tone and the statement.

"If you agree, then why do you think it necessary to hire a bodyguard to chaperon you?"

"A what?"

"Are you telling me that you don't know you were followed here?"

"Yeah, I can ..."

"Business this evening is closed." He interrupted tersely, and the line went dead. Sonya was livid, her eyes searched frantically for Lawrence's face, which at this moment she felt she could gladly slap. *'You've gone too far this time Don ... too goddamn far!'* she brooded. She got up from the table and plucked a bank note out from her purse then placed it alongside the telephone on the table top. With a sigh, she hoisted her bag onto her shoulder and cussed under her breath.

After swiftly making her way to the reception area, she found the concierge, whom had greeted her on her arrival and asked him to hail a cab for her. Within less than a minute, her request had been answered. Outside, although the storm was by now beginning to subside, the friendly concierge insisted on once again employing the large umbrella to shield her on the short walk from the doorway to the vehicle. Above the rattly drone of the black cab's diesel engine, Sonya summoned her destination to the driver through his half-opened window, then climbed into the back and made herself comfortable on the seat, the man with the top hat closed the door, and she was gone.

King picked up the phone, before it had chance to ring out a second time.

"Yeah?"

"I have the information you required sir." The concierge announced.

"I'm listening."

"Kensington, Allan House, Kensington."

"Thanks." King said, then placed the receiver back in its cradle. He gathered the small collection of photographs from the top of the coffee table, they had been sent to him some time ago, along with an accompanying letter by the matron in France to a PO Box Number, before that was, the stupid overweight bitch had let him down. Once again he examined the snaps, one by one, taking in the girl's attractive features and contemplating what should be done about her. '*What could she possibly be up to?*' he mused. He considered perhaps paying a visit to this Allan House in Kensington and finding out for sure. He wondered if his wife, Danielle, might be residing there also, for he knew that she had not returned to Monaco following her escape from the asylum. King weighed up the pros and cons of venturing on such an errand, then concluded that to embark on that idea, had one or two unfavourable implications, one of which he was most certainly not going to risk, his redesigned identity had to be protected at all costs. Tonight had been no exception to that rule his thoughts reasoned. Could it be, that this girl staring back at him from the snapshot, had turned up as scheduled as an escort, and by some extraordinary coincidence, unknowingly been employed to play his companion for the evening. This surely had to be the case, '*but who was the guy that the concierge had informed him had entered the hotel behind her?*'

"How do you know that he was tailing her?" King had asked.

"Simple." The concierge had replied, "The man on his arrival, asked me where the young lady that I had ushered from the taxi moments before had gone, she's gone to powder her nose I told him, but, what made me suspicious, that he must be following her, was when the girl left the ladies room, he didn't call after her or anything like that, instead he turned and pretended to leaf through some brochures."

King had then thanked his informant and handed him some money for his troubles, adding that he would appreciate learning of the young woman's lodgings or residence.

Now, King opened the letter from the matron and began to read the last few paragraphs.

'I have enclosed some photographs of the young woman, whom we have detained here at the institution, as you have ordered. If, as you have insisted, she is not your niece, then she has gone to great lengths in an effort to mislead us.'

Underneath her scrawled signature the matron had added a postscript, it read : *this young woman is extremely obstinate, although I can assure you that under my charge, she will soon reform her ways.* He folded the communication back into four, once again he chose to study the tormented expression on her exquisite face, '*what would this bit of skirt be doing risking so much ... to go to such trouble, to free his wife from an asylum?'* he pondered '*what was she to Danielle? .... where's the connection?'*

He slipped the prints along with the letter into the envelope, he would mull these questions over another time, for right now, or at least before the night was over, he would need to satisfy his libido on some hooker, this would no doubt, he told himself, help to clear his thoughts.

The taxi came to a halt outside the Allan House apartment building, the driver turned on the lights inside the car to assist his passenger in counting out the money to pay her fare. Sonya glanced at her wristwatch, then on a whim, instructed the driver to drop her off at the welcoming lit Inn that stood approximately one hundred metres away on the other side of the street. From there she decided that she would order herself a long cool martini then, telephone 'his lordshitface or his aid-de-camp whoever', and give him a piece of her mind. After all, she stood to lose all credibility with the escort agency, along with that a sundry of much needed pay days, and however preposterous the odds might have been, a chance of coming face to face with her sister's probable abductor.

Inside the pub, the atmosphere by this hour was boisterous, the clamour of fuddled voices filled the stale smoky air. A table of brash young men, whom Sonya guessed to be off-duty sailors from a nearby naval base, let out a chorus of wolf whistles, adjoined by the odd verbal obscenity as she weaved her way through towards the bar. Normally Sonya would have accommodated this show of bravado with some amusement, tonight though, she responded to this unwanted attention by gesticulating a finger and announcing that they 'go swivel'. She now regretted her decision to call there for a nightcap, rather that is, than go back to the apartment with its somewhat despondent atmosphere, motivated by Danielle's unfortunate predicament with amnesia. When finally she had purchased her drink, Sonya asked the barman where the telephone was situated, he pointed to a small booth in the far corner, she thanked him then took a few sips of the cool drink, and was grateful for the stimulating effect as she swallowed it down.

Inside the booth, Sonya placed the glass of Martini on the top of a small shelf, then thumbed her way through the phone directory that hung from a chain on the wall. On finding the number, she pressed the appropriate coinage into the slot and proceeded to dial, then awaited an answer from the other end of the line.

“Good evening Landmark Hotel, how may we help you?” A starchy voice inquired.

“Hi, could you put me through to Lord Bucknall please!?”

“I’m sorry could you repeat the name again?”

“Bucknall ... Lord Bucknall!” Sonya pronounced, aware that her voice conveyed an air of impatience.

“One moment please.” The faceless voice replied. Sonya sampled another taste from her drink, then placed it back down again on the tiny shelf.

“Is the gentleman a guest or merely dining here at the Landmark?”

“He’s a guest, I was there earlier and I spoke to him by phone, he was speaking to me from his room, or suite, whatever!”

“Lord Bucknall you say?”

“Yeah.”

“I’m sorry Madam, but there is nobody registered here by that name.”

“What?... But I ..”

“There is a Lord and Lady Beresford staying here but ...”

“You are the Landmark Hotel on Euston Road?”

“There is no other Landmark Hotel in London.”

“Shit!” Was all Sonya could think to say, before hanging up.

Chapter Thirty Four

Roland Garros, Paris – June 1st

Such was the fervour that the young charismatic Frenchman had generated in the hearts of his fellow countrymen and women, Jean Paul King now enjoyed the kind of worship reserved for heroes. Adjoining this adulation, most fashionable magazines displayed his majestic looks on the cover, or within the pages of their world-wide distributions. Eminent clothing and accessory corporations such as Yves Saint Laurent, Gucci and many other big names had offered him huge amounts of money to model their apparel. Cosmopolitan had invited him to pose in his birthday suit for their centre pages. Brad Holding, his trainer, had been delighted that his young star had turned all these offers down flat, in order to concentrate all his energy into his tennis, and thus, achieve his insatiable ambition of becoming the undisputed world's number one player, inevitably though, pressures beyond his control had infiltrated into his everyday life, as his success on the ATP tour flourished. Everywhere he went, especially since arriving in France, the man was surrounded by hordes of newsmen and photographers, although in recent days, it was his fanatical female following that had forced him to plead for protection from the Parisian police, following a succession of worrying moments involving groups of besotted teenage girls intent on getting a piece of him, literally. But without doubt by far, the heaviest pressure that Jean Paul King had had to contend with during his ascent to world-wide fame, had been his mother's disappearance. Although he had channelled this anguish in a positive manner throughout so many months, the phone call from his mother, twenty four hours earlier, had lifted his spirits immeasurably and alleviated much of this worry.

Today, beneath the warm midday sunshine, an air of anticipation prevailed amongst the Roland Garros crowd surrounding the bright red clay court, and although the match between Jean Paul King and Tony Wang was not due to commence until two o'clock, the stands had been filled almost to capacity since the clock on the scoreboard had read 13 30. At a comparatively early stage in the championships this was quite unprecedented. It seemed that many of the spectators, mainly French, had decided to relinquish going for lunch in favour of supporting their new-found homebred superstar, from the moment that the umpire would call *'play"*. Now, within a matter of minutes prior to the players taking to the court, several VIP's were being ushered through to their seats. Amongst these dignitaries was the French President himself, normally this diligent statesman would only perhaps donate his precious time to attend the final. He smiled and waved to the gathering, who applauded his unexpected and unofficial appearance. Three rows behind the President and joining in with the hand clapping, Agnazzio Bennetti sat, flanked by two Arabian business associates, who were his guests for the day, and later when the match was over, the three had plans to talk business, in private quarters at Bennetti's hotel. Although Bennetti had been blackballed from the drugs underworld, he was quite philosophical about the fact, after all, he often would reassure himself, '*the slave trade was booming*'.

The crowd cheered from the stands, as the two players entered the arena in readiness to do battle. The clicking and flashing of cameras was abundant, and the shrill of screaming young females emanated from several quarters, resembling to Bennetti, the sound of fingernails scraping down a blackboard. He could relate though, with their foolish infatuation, for the devilish good looks, supported by Jean Paul King's strapping frame, caused the ageing homosexual's heart to beat with a flurry. '*The boy's father was not as handsome by half*' Bennetti reflected, he then leaned forward in his seat to afford a glance along the row. Sitting not ten metres away, he once again surveyed the woman that earlier he had observed along with a round faced black woman making a pathway through the crowd to their designated places. He had never actually met Danielle Marie King, but the time for an introduction he concluded, was long overdue.

Just a stone's throw away, in another part of the stadium, while the two players warmed up Ace, along with his brother, Helen and his coach were assembled in readiness for the event. Earlier in the day, Ace had taken part in a two hour practice session with Tony Wang. Where after, Wang's coach and Ace had agreed that their man, was in great shape for the match, both physically and mentally. He was beginning to return to his very best form, and enjoying playing on his favourite playing surface, clay. Indeed, the general consensus was that today, Tony Wang would be a very tough nut to crack. But, crack he did, much to Ace's dismay, the first set saw the progressively perturbed Hong Kong man fall 6-2. Then by the completion of the next set of games Tony Wang appeared to be running out of ways to cope, with the Frenchman's superior groundstrokes and the discriminate enthusiasm of the Parisian faithful. Then, at 3-0 in the third, Ace was infuriated to witness Jean Paul whipping the home crowd into a frenzy by audaciously choosing to serve underarm to a by now, bedraggled opponent who careered headlong towards the net, failing then to play the return.

"That's totally out of order!" Ace chided.

"To serve underarm is perfectly legal." Fenton reasoned.

"All the same, it's not exactly sportsmanlike is it?"

"The guy's a showman, the crowd love it, look at them!"

"He needs a lesson in manners!"

"Hey, what's got into you Ace?"

"I just don't like seeing my friend being humiliated by such a big headed son ..... that's all!"

"That's all? ... If you want my opinion, he can afford to have a big head, he's a bonzer of a player."

"I didn't ask for your opinion Greg, anyway I'm out of here, I'll meet you at the player's entrance later."

This was only the second time since becoming Ace's coach that the Australian had recognised this uncharacteristic side of Ace's disposition. That was, he recalled when Jean Paul was playing, and winning the match against the world number one, Emerson, in the final of the Italian Open. At that time, Fenton put it down simply to professional jealousy, now he was not so sure, '*something much deeper ... but what?*' He brooded.

On witnessing his brother's premature departure, Jack leaned over towards Fenton and asked,

"What's Ace uptight about, is he OK?"

"Yeah, he's fine, he's just peeved at losing his pound bet, that's all." He answered drolly, though for the remainder of the match, which resulted in an admirable victory for Jean Paul King, Fenton's concentration over the proceedings had been fractured.

One of Jean Paul's major sponsors was holding a corporate get together after the match, though an all ticket affair, one or two outsiders had been allowed in to join in with the festivities. Along with two of his aides, the French President gladly accepted an invitation. Ensconced in another corner, Agnazzio Bennetti plucked a glass of champagne from the salver that was being conveyed around the room by a leggy waitress. He had sent his Arabic friends on to the hotel, with the promise of joining them within the next hour or so, there they would resume their business, after which he would be taking a short flight to London. An elegantly dressed woman within earshot, was making conversation with a man that he understood to be Managing Director of the Company playing host. He wished at this moment that his sister was here with him, her linguistic talents were so much greater than his own. Although, if needs be he could get by, his French was not good, but yes, he had always managed to struggle through in the past. The Managing Director excused himself, explaining that he felt obliged to mingle, Bennetti strolled over toward the woman.

"Bonjour Madame Danielle King, no?"

"Oui!?"

"Pardon Madame ... my name is Agnazzio Bennetti." Albeit in a clumsy manner, he continued with his attempts to converse in French. Promptly spotting the Italian's uneasiness with the language, Danielle reciprocated by speaking slowly and precisely in her native tongue. Only long enough though to realise the hopelessness of the situation. As politely as her growing displeasure would allow, she interrupted him mid-sentence, '*the man might as well be speaking Eskimo*' she mused, but said.

"Signor Bennetti .... do you speak English?"

The relief in his tone in return was unmistakable.

"Yes ... yes, I am infinitely better with English than I am with French, no!?"

Her smile was agreeable and succeeded in concealing her actual thoughts, because in response to her invitation to make conversation in a language that they both might understand, she had sincerely hoped that his answer would have been a negative one. He now proceeded with a bombardment of inconsequential questions, to which she answered with the odd yes and no, while as subtly as she could contrive, her eyes fleetingly explored the cleverly embellished enclosure for someone, indeed anyone whom with a little luck might rescue her from her one-to-one scenario with this man who, at first sight and, for some unaccountable reason had provoked her intuition, dealing with her misgivings. *'Where has Floss got to? .. Must be a long line of women waiting to use the ladies' rest room,'* she brooded.

"You understand what I am saying?" Bennetti said, piercing her contemplation.

"Pardon ... I am sorry, I was .."

"I am saying, your boy Jean Paul, he is very talented."

"Yes he is, and thank you."

"He graces the courts, in the same way that you grace this marquee on this splendid occasion Madame."

Danielle was disdainful of this latest superficial remark for she had caught sight of her son's coach, Brad Holding, who on making his entrance through the main ingress, was greeted by the sponsors and their guests with an enthusiastic round of applause. She waved a hand in an effort to attract his attention, on his noticing her, Danielle made a motion for him to join her. He heeded her request, gesturing a thumb in the air then forming words through soundless lips he said.

"Give me five minutes, OK?"

"OK." She heard herself say despondently.

"You must be very proud of him." The Italian was saying.

"Who?"

"Your son ... you must be proud."

"Yes, immensely so."

"Your boy ... he has many of your attributes, no!?"

"People do say this is so."

"I do hope though, he does not have any of his father's treacherous nature!"

"Pardon me!?"

"This time I think you hear what I say."

"I do not think that this is the time or the place to be discussing my dead husband."

"Please ... today I have much to do, so I will get straight to the point Madame, are you aware that you are not the beneficiary to Irwin King's estate?"

"Legally I have not got around to dealing with these affairs, until recently I have been unwell and ..."

"You were never acquainted with these facts relating to your financial status no?"

"With my husband?"

"Yes."

"He was most secretive about everything." She explained, while the crude grin on his face ignited further uneasiness inside her.

"I will explain, until not so long ago, I had outright control of yours and your husband's assets, until the filthy bastard, he disappear with a hoard of my merchandise."

"Disappeared, but..."

"You don't think that the headless body they found in the London River was Irwin, do you? I tell him no-one fucks with Agnazzio Bennetti, and what does he do ... as God is my judge he will pay for this!" He chided. Floss on her return from the ladies' room approached them with a tentative stride on witnessing, along with several other guests, the Italian's animated outburst.

"Madame Danielle, are you alright?" Floss asked.

"Yes Floss, thank you I am fine, please leave us for a while will you."

With a wary expression, Floss complied with Danielle's instruction and made her way over towards the buffet.

"I will ask you please Signor Bennetti, to conduct yourself in a more fitting manner." Danielle affirmed and was amazed how swiftly his composure had returned, *'as if in the blink of an eye'* she mused. In a matter-of-fact pitch he said.

"If I so desire I could foreclose your account at the bank, repossess your home and leave you without a franc."

She looked the Italian in the eye and, in an impassive tone said,

"I do not know what your intentions are, but if you think that your threats intimidate me, then you are greatly mistaken Signor Bennetti. You see, unlike my husband, money is not so important to me, it is not something that I worship like a God!"

"Good ... good, this is just the response I believed that I would receive from you, I am happy for you."

If Danielle was confused by now at this peculiar Latin man's behaviour, his ensuing deed underlined his eccentricity. With his forefinger he summoned over a tall smartly dressed man, whom Danielle guessed to be one of Bennetti's aides. He carried with him a Gucci briefcase, which on reaching Bennetti's side he was ordered to open. Bennetti took out from inside the case a brown folder and handed it to Danielle.

"What is this?" She frowned.

"Documents."

"Documents, for what?"

"The house, the money, everything."

"I do not understand."

"Everything is now in your sole name, from today you are a wealthy lady, in your own right!"

"Why should you do this?"

"Because I know your husband, when he learns of this, like the slimy worm he is, he will wriggle out from his hiding place, and we will be ready for him."

Chapter Thirty Five

Sonya had tuned in and viewed Jean Paul's flamboyant performance live on the small screen in the sitting room at Allan House. After which, she surmised that, aside from his gamesmanship, his display of formidable talent on court today, would by now, be sending shock waves through each competitor remaining in the championships.

Two evenings past, Sonya had returned to the apartment, following her first discouraging evening as an escort to find Danielle in a mood of great elation, galvanised by her sudden recollection of a number of significant episodes from her personal history. Her excitement had been so contagious that before the three flat-mates knew it, the dawn was breaking. In those hours, before the sun had started to slowly filter through the kitchen window, Danielle's emotions fluctuated as the fragmented images from here and there intermittently replayed in her mind's eye. She had been especially enthusiastic when re-establishing instances akin to Jean Paul. Indeed, thanks to Sonya and Floss' constant encouragement, the majority of the time had been taken up recapturing the years that Danielle had spent grooming her boy for the future. The conversation was rounded off by Danielle expressing her thorough intent to establish a reunion with her son as soon as possible.

It was five in the morning, Sonya's bed was calling, Floss' eyes had become heavy by then also. They both made their excuses and retired, leaving Danielle alone with her thoughts. She was so fired up, that rest, even a couple of hours, had been the last thing on her mind.

Now, thirty hours later, and twenty four hours subsequent to making her excuses not to join Danielle and Floss on their trip to Paris, Sonya sat alone with her own thoughts. It was time to return to the States she had decided, she had made up her mind to quit chasing her own tail, in the hope of ever finding her kid sister. Yes, she was going to go home and get her own life into some kind of order. The telephone suddenly ringing fractured through her deliberations.

"Yeah, hello?"

Ah, hello could I speak to Sonya Kennedy please?"

"Yeah, speaking, who's this?"

"Ms Peterson at the agency, I have your fee for accompanying Lord Bucknall the other evening, it's here at my office."

"My fee?"

"Less my commission of course, would you like to collect it personally or would you prefer me to mail it to you?"

"I ... er ... I'll collect, if that's OK?"

"Perfectly, now I have had an enquiry from a gentleman, who was rather impressed with your appearance on the Internet."

"Oh?"

"He will be calling me back shortly, can I tell him that you will be delighted to partner him this evening?"

"Er, yeah sure!"

"Excellent, obviously the camera likes you dear, I only released your promotion video into the Internet yesterday, and I have had a rather overwhelming response already, so have your diary handy when I call you back within the hour, goodbye for now."

"Oh, Ms Peterson!?"

"Yes?"

"Before you go ... about the other evening ... the guy I was supposed to meet."

"Yes?"

"The Lord Bucknall guy, well he called off our arrangement."

"Oh!?"

"What's more, I found out later that the guy was a phoney."

"A phoney?"

"Yeah, I called the hotel later, only to be told that there was nobody by that name registered."

"I see, well at least his money wasn't phoney as you put it. As with all new clients, I demand payment into my bank account in advance of an introduction to an escort, and well ... he has not been back on the phone to complain, so as far as I am concerned we kept our side of the bargain, and even if the man did call me demanding a refund, I would tell him to go and whistle for it!" She declared, and at this moment Ms Peterson went up one hundred percent in Sonya's estimation.

"Let's hope that the gentleman that you meet up with this evening." Ms Peterson continued, "Is not so discourteous!"

"I couldn't agree more."

"I will speak to you again shortly, goodbye."

"OK, bye."

The short telephone conversation now put an entirely new complexion on her scenario. She was going to give the escort undertaking another shot, but first, she would give Don Lawrence a call, and in no uncertain terms tell him to back off, and if Lawrence asked her where she was going to meet with the client, she simply would not tell him.

Irwin King had reviewed her winning performance via the internet several times, before deciding to telephone Ms Peterson, then enquiring about the availability of the tall brunette.

"Sonya is one of our most recent recruits here at the agency, and already one of our most popular young ladies." Ms Peterson had rendered.

"With looks like hers I don't wonder." King had agreed smoothly.

"Have you requested an appointment with any of our hostesses before ... Mr er...?"

"Le Saux, Claude Le Saux, and no, I have not had that pleasure."

"In that case Mr Le Saux, I will depend upon you to provide us with payment in advance, you understand!?"

"Yes, perfectly."

"I take it then, that you are here in London on business?"

"Yes, flew in only yesterday." King lied skilfully, as he did with the remainder of his telephone interview, in which, Ms Peterson appraised him with her customary mini-barrage of personal questions. Since making the call earlier in the day, his thoughts had progressively grown in anticipation of his meeting with Sonya. He sat back in his chair, satisfied that before long, he would have the answers to one or two questions that his inquisitive nature challenged him to find out. *'It simply had to be done,'* King told himself. Now, his mouth curled into a smile, he pressed the appropriate buttons, allowing access once more into the internet. The screen readily presented him once more with the image of Sonya. Wearing a short summer dress, she was sitting on a tall stool, her long shapely legs crossed in front of her. In an effortless manner her beguiling demeanor conveyed itself through the TV, her intelligent eyes penetrating the viewer's gaze, she leaned slightly forward now, towards the camera, the observer espied the alluring crevice of her cleavage, and as Sonya's full lips mouthed and delivered her dialogue, his eagerness heightened towards his imminent encounter with her, and the dimensions of the erection in his groin further confirmed King's expectations.

As promised, Ms Peterson had called Sonya back within an hour, relaying to her the necessary details and information relating to her rendezvous that evening. She arrived outside the meeting point in Maida Vale, W9 with time to spare, enough time in fact to ponder about telling the cab driver to turn the car around and make a hasty retreat. The taxi's engine idled, Sonya remained seated in the back with her thoughts, anxiety gripping her guts.

"We're there Miss, Ronaldo's Restaurant!?" The driver announced through the glass partition that separated them.

"What ... oh yeah, thanks." She said, willing herself to step out of the car. After paying the fare, she stood motionless for a moment, surveying the restaurant's exterior. In contrast, Ronaldo's was a comparatively modest establishment to the one which she had been sent to for her initial venture. In an odd sort of way, that fact served to put her at her ease somewhat. Besides, she had hardly eaten anything since breakfast, and was by now quite hungry. With that thought in mind she walked briskly towards the entrance, and an appointment with the stranger within. She motioned a hand towards the polished handle, though before she made contact the door swung open and a tall, dark haired man, smartly dressed in evening attire greeted her with a smile.

"Miss Sonya?"

"Yes."

"Please come this way."

She stepped inside, breathing in the delightful aroma of cooking drifting from the kitchens, serving to further tantalise her appetite. The interior of the restaurant was dimly lit, pleasantly illuminated though, by the flickering candles that burned on each individual table throughout. Classical music played softly in the background, favouring the establishment with an agreeable warmth. Although, as the man she guessed to be a waiter walked ahead of her towards the farthest end of the room, the fact that there was nobody dining at any of the tables, apart from that is, just one man seated in the far corner, instantly presented her with an unwelcome chill. By the time that Sonya had reached the table, the assigned date was on his feet, gesturing a hand towards the chair across the table from him. She noted that his powerful build carried with it an equally potent air. The glow given off by the three candles in the centre of the table danced and illuminated his tanned features, the frosty grey of his hair gave him a bearing of middle-aged distinction and as he crouched down to once again take his seat, the candlelight cast an ominous dark shadow onto the wall behind him.

"Bring the young lady an aperitif!" He said to the man that had greeted her at the door.

"Thanks, that would be nice." Sonya said.

"I am happy that you agreed to join me here this evening."

"I'm pleased to be here." She corresponded, telling herself to '*come on .. relax*'. After all this very afternoon, as a precaution, prior to instructing Don Lawrence to 'back off', she had mentioned to him that she would be obliged if he would go on a fact finding mission to find out as much as he could about the guy who was presently smiling at her through the candlelight. The gumshoe had phoned back a couple of hours later assuring her that, she had nothing to worry about.

"I saw your presentation on the internet, you came across very well." He said with a wry smile.

"Thanks."

"I have reserved the restaurant exclusively for us tonight, as you can see!?" The man was saying now.

"Yeah ... yes, that's real nice for you, I mean ... what I mean is for you to be able to afford to do such a thing."

"Able to afford such a thing!?" There was an air of sarcasm this time in his tone.

"I did this so that we can enjoy an intimate meal together."

"Great .." She grinned, *'but that's as intimate as it gets pal!'* her thoughts rendered.

"I am sure we have much to talk about, already I know we have much in common."

"You do? .. Well I'm sure we'll get on just swell!" Sonya complied pleasantly, while actively reasoning '*anything you say buster, because you, are just one of a list of rich asshole sons of bitches that's gonna help me get home to the good old US of A, and with it a goddamn healthy bank balance to boot!*'

"Would you mind if a man of my years tells you that you are a very beautiful young woman?" He said smoothly.

"No, I don't mind at all, and thank you ...besides you're not so old anyway!" She replied. He simply smiled and shrugged his shoulders. Now, Sonya's reasoning reprimanded her for having those mercenary notions, prior to his compliment.

"I must remember to call my friend." He continued, "For making the appointment with you for me tonight, I only arrived here from Paris an hour ago."

"Excuse me .. your friend?, You say your friend made these ..."

"Yes, he is not only my friend, he is also your friend!"

"Wait a minute here, ... are you saying that we've got a mutual acquaintance?"

"Actually ... we have a few."

"What!?"

"As I said before, we have much in common."

"Then, tell me please, who these people ... these friends are? .. I'm intrigued to know!"

"Let us start with Mr Lawrence the Englishman, he is a friend of yours, no?"

"Don Lawrence!?" She gasped, unable to mask her confusion. At that moment the waiter returned with their drinks, then, after placing them in front of the two assembled diners, he turned and almost in a military fashion, bowed his head in the direction of Sonya's dining partner and then the two men proceeded to converse in what was obviously their native tongues. So puzzled had Sonya been by the disclosure from the man sitting at the table with her, that she was unable to translate one word of their brief, though extravagantly animated conversation, apart from that is, the waiter's concluding words before making his way towards the kitchen.

"Si Signor Bennetti, for you only the very best!" Bennetti thanked him, then turned his attention back to Sonya.

"I took the liberty to order the food for us both, trust me, I had my own personal chef prepare this for me."

"I must say I'm looking forward to eating."

"I forget to ask ... are you vegetarian?"

"No."

"Bene ... good, then you will enjoy my sister's excellent recipes ... now where were we?"

"Mutual friends!?"

"Ah yes, mutual friends." He agreed, then his features twisted conspicuously into a frown, "And enemies!"

"Oh?"

"As I explained, we have much in common, you like me have been hunting for the same kill for some time, no?"

"We have?" Sonya said, smiling in an effort to conceal her growing uneasiness for, in Bennetti's eyes she was sure she recognised a hint of madness.

"You see .." He went on, "Nobody ... no-one, fuck with Agnazzio Bennetti, capiche!?" His voice boomed.

"Yeah ... sure I understand."

"And this includes that traitorous shit, Irwin King!" He affirmed, trailing off his dogmatic statement with a flurry of vitriolic utterances in Italian that Sonya did not comprehend. She remained silent, somewhat numbed by the man's outburst which on reflection, reminded her of some of the old black and white footage, that witnessed a certain Adolph Hitler delivering one of his wild fanatical orations. To her surprise now his wrath abated as swiftly as it had appeared and, with the aid of his napkin, he wiped away a dribble of saliva that had escaped from the corner of his mouth and journeyed down the side of his chin. He cleared his throat and continued.

"All the time that my people, my men, search for our prey, we find ourselves one step behind you and your friend Lawrence, so I decide, why not make a ... how do you say? ... A consolidated effort, no?"

The wry smile had returned to Bennetti's face and Sonya suddenly had a hundred and one questions to hit the 'oddball Italian' with.

"So, how long have you been associated with Don Lawrence?"

"Since your escape from the French crazy house, you see, my men had been searching for Madame Danielle since King's vanishing act, with not only a fortune in my merchandise, but that traitor, he stole money from me also."

"Merchandise?"

"Si ... yes, I am a business man, that is all you need to know, you understand!?"

"OK, point taken."

"All that you need to know, is that we are on the same side ... you scratch my back, I scratch yours."

"So, what makes you think that King is still alive Signor Bennetti?"

"For the same reasons as you, and because I know him, like I know myself, trust me, he is out there somewhere."

"Somewhere in London?"

"Maybe ... maybe not, ... but between us we will find him, wherever he is!"

"Even though, as Don Lawrence and I suspect, he's got a new identity, and maybe a new face to go with it!?"

"Which begs me to ask the question, why do you take a job as an escort girl with the same agency that King always used whenever he was in London?"

"A chance in a million I guess of just maybe bumping into the son of a bitch!"

"Si ... exactly, you are very how do you say? .. Astute, I am happy for you Sonya, but like I say, I know King, I know what makes him tick, and believe me, I think that we are close to coaxing him into our web. Because, like me, King cannot turn down a challenge ... and that .... is what he gets off on!"

By the time that the food arrived at their table, Sonya had forgotten how ravenous she had felt earlier, she merely picked at the meal with her fork, while actively discussing the pros and cons involving the likelihood of trapping their foe. When their plates had been removed, and the waiter once again out of sight, Sonya said,

"Has Don Lawrence mentioned to you why I've been working my butt off for so long, trying to track down King?"

"Yes, he tells me that you are trying to find your sister, no?"

"That's right, though I guess my chances of ever finding her now are ..." Sonya halted her flow, then sighed. She combed her fingers through her hair, then shook her head in a dissenting fashion.

"Shit, goddamn it! ... What's the use anyway!?" She declared woefully. Bennetti's dark eyes contemplated her for a long moment, then, while neatly clipping off one end of a Havana cigar, he said.

"What if I was to say, maybe ... I do not promise you anything you understand!?... But, just perhaps Agnazzio Bennetti can find your sister!"

"Yeah ..? How do you propose ..."

"Let us say, I have my ways and means, remember, you scratch my back!? ..." He said raising his eyebrows, as if anticipating her response.

"I'll scratch yours." She complied. At that instant the waiter eagerly returned from the kitchen and scurried up to their table, he then flicked his Zippo lighter into life and with a slightly trembling hand, he lit Bennetti's cigar. The Italian's mouth puckered while he puffed hard on the cylindrical roll of tobacco, then satisfied that it was adequately alight, he expelled a mouthful of second-hand smoke heedlessly in Sonya's direction, its pungency almost sending her reeling. She managed though, to constrain her annoyance, '*after all*' she reflected '*this oddball, however discourteous, arrogant and even as crazy as he obviously is, just might be able to wield the apparatus necessary, to put a finish to my seemingly endless quest!*'

"Lawrence, he tells me that she was kidnapped, no?"

"That's right."

"Where ... how, I need to know these things!"

"OK."

"Take your time." He said between puffs on his cigar. "I'm listening." And as the silver-grey smoke hovered around the table's occupants, Sonya reiterated her story of the fateful day in Morocco. When Sonya had finally completed her adaptation, Bennetti greeted it with a negative clicking of his tongue.

"People they never learn, everyday individuals, they are captured, how do you say ... abducted, they ... they disappear off the face of the earth!"

"I know but ..."

"So, you think Irwin King, he had something to do with your sister's kidnapping?"

"As I say, from what my friend Larry Hickman and myself found out, yeah, sure ... King, along with other members of the ring, whoever they might be!?"

Darkness had by now fallen outside Ronaldo's Restaurant, a quarter moon glowed above, in a clear sky. On the opposite side of the street, merely forty metres away, a dark blue car was parked at the curbside, it's engine and lights switched off, enveloped beneath the shadows of one of the Avenue's tall trees. The vehicle's sole occupant was sitting behind the steering wheel, his eyes vigilantly anchored on the building that temporarily housed Sonya and the Overlord. Earlier, he had followed Sonya's taxi from Kensington, at what he considered to be a sufficient distance to guarantee that his pursuit would not be noticed by the cab driver, or indeed, his passenger. Although, at the junction of Park Lane and Marble Arch, he had almost lost them amidst the hectic bustle of cars, buses and a throng of London cabs, identical to the one that he had been trailing. Fortunately for him, after weaving a way through the traffic he had once again caught sight of Sonya's mode of transport stationary, at a set of lights not far from Little Venice.

He looked at his wristwatch now, impatience was beginning to meld in with his growing anxiety regarding his imminent conquest. The alteration to his desired programme for this evening, had been quashed by the brief telephone conversation that had taken place between Ms Peterson and himself that afternoon although, if everything was to go to plan tonight, he, Irwin King, would be forever grateful to the escort agent, whom he considered to be a pompous bitch. King had phoned her shortly after reviewing Sonya's internet video. His growing inquisitiveness boosted by basic sexual lust, had prompted him to propose that, if he offered to pay the agency twice the usual fee, then Ms Peterson might perhaps consider bringing his appointment with Sonya forward to this very evening. After all, it had worked when he had posed as Lord Bucknall's personal secretary.

"I'm awfully sorry, I'm afraid that would be out of the question!" Ms Peterson had responded to King's request.

"Treble ... I will pay you treble!?" King had then bid.

"My goodness Mr Le Saux, I must say, you're remarkably keen."

"I know this must seem kind of impulsive of me." King had reasoned in a friendly tone, "But I am indeed keen to meet her!"

"Well, I'm terribly sorry to disappoint you, but I'm afraid I will have to be firm on this, and say no, I do have one or two young ladies though, very popular girls they are too, if you would like me to I will ...."

"No ... no ... that won't be necessary, thanks all the same."

"You must understand, and I'm sure that, as a business man yourself, you will agree, for me to do such a thing, as to, for want of a better word, gazump a client, would be simply unethical!?"

King had, at that point in the conversation been sorely tempted to tell the 'bitch to go fuck herself!' though he had muzzled his annoyance amply, continuing skilfully in a composed, if not amicable fashion, he said.

"Believe me Ms Peterson, if you would just grant the young lady a chance to be in my company tonight, I would indulge her with anything that she might wish for, squander a fortune on her. I would treat the girl like a princess!"

The revelation that had ensued in Ms Peterson's reply, came by way of an error on her part.

"Mr Le Saux, I expect ... no indeed it is a precondition and I insist upon it that, all my girls are treated with the utmost respect, and yes, treated as you say, like princesses. Therefore, although Signor Bennetti is a new client, I'm sure ..."

Her voice wavered off, suddenly mindful of her heedless blunder. She began saying something about another unwritten rule, and that she herself had been stupid enough to have just broken it by accidentally uttering a client's name. King was oblivious to her ramblings for, the mention of the Italian's name had hit him like a sledgehammer..

"Would that be Agnazzio Bennetti?" He asked.

"Really, Mr Le Saux ... for the very reasons I've just mentioned, I cannot divulge names."

"But you just did!"

"I know but ..."

"Come on, Agnazzio is an old friend of mine."

"I'm sorry."

"Do you have a phone number where I can reach him?"

"Mr Le Saux, what do you take me for!?"

"I see, so you're not denying that it is the same man?"

"There surely must be a thousand and one males ..."

"What, with the name Agnazzio Bennetti? ... In London?" King had interjected. Ms Peterson was aware, that the hole that she had been digging for herself, was becoming bigger, unable by this time to conceal her growing exasperation, she retaliated.

"Look ... this particular gentleman's engagement was in fact arranged for him this evening by a third party!"

"A third party you say?"

"That sir ... is as much as I am willing to divulge, I'm afraid that I have let slip quite enough already."

"OK ... my apologies." King had said in a frivolous tone, "Let's forget we even had this conversation, it really doesn't matter in any case."

"Your apologies I accept, and thank you, I take it though that you will still be keeping your appointment with Sonya on the date that we primarily agreed?"

"Yes, oh yes, as I've already said I'm very keen to meet her."

"Very well, then I will wish you good day." Ms Peterson had said in conclusion. King had then placed the phone back in its cradle and muttered aloud his thoughts at that moment.

"Go fuck yourself, you bitch!"

He was now certain that, inside Ronaldo's, the girl that he had followed here was in the company of Agnazzio Bennetti. He had recognised the guy that had opened the door to the restaurant for Sonya when earlier, he had slowly driven by. It was Dino, one of the Overlord's personal aides. He wondered to himself, how many other attendants and bodyguards might be on duty inside, although what freaked him somewhat more presently was, what was a middle-aged homosexual racketeer, doing wining and dining an escort girl? King's eyes studied the row of shops on either side of the restaurant, all of which were closed down for the night.

Bennetti on his part tonight, had done something that he very rarely did, he had instructed his three regular personal bodyguards to take some time off and take in some sightseeing. They had, albeit reluctantly complied with the Overlord's order. Bennetti had considered that, the sight of three burly guards might well have motivated Sonya into unnecessary apprehension. Tonight he did not want that, he simply wanted to acquire a new ally. The sound of his mobile phone fractured Sonya and Bennetti's current conversation. He picked the small appliance up from the table, then spoke into the mouthpiece.

"Si ... si, cinque minutos." He said, then promptly switched the phone off, turning his attention back to his guest.

"My car will be here in five minutes to take you home Miss Kennedy."

"To take me home?" Sonya replied in surprise.

"Yes, I take it that you want to go home, when I say home I mean to your apartment here in London!?"

"Yeah sure."

"Our business here I think is complete, no?"

"Yeah, that is I mean ..."

"Bene, good, so there is little more to be said, but remember, I scratch your back, you scratch mine!"

King crouched lower into his seat when he observed the Daimler Limousine pulling up outside Ronaldo's. He squinted over the dashboard and watched the three broad shouldered men as they climbed out from the luxury vehicle, each of them surveying the vicinity with cautious eyes. King's heart somersaulted for an instant, when one of the men gazed over suspiciously in King's direction, for what seemed to him like an eternity, before turning and joining his fellow henchmen and entering the restaurant. King had instantly recognised the hostile gaze, he went by the name of Pedro Garoz, whose nick-name was 'hands', a truly malicious being who, would often brag about the men that he had killed by using nothing more to accomplish his condemnable exploits than his bare hands. King's plans for this evening, were by now changing, along with the changing circumstances that he had witnessed. He had several alternatives in mind, one of which presently was becoming more than likely his best option. That was simply to fire up the car's engine, speed away and draw up a more conceivable plot.

Chapter Thirty Six

Sonya was not surprised by the prompt arrival of the three bodyguards, each bearing physiques of Herculean proportions. For, she had surmised by now that, Agnazzio Bennetti must be a fairly well established member of some elitist organisation. But, no matter who, or what the guy might be, she was thankful that he was on her side. She leaned forward in her chair.

"Can I use your phone Signor Bennetti?"

"Be my guest."

She thanked him and pressed in the appropriate number then waited for an answer.

"Yes, Don Lawrence speaking." Came the voice from the other end of the line.

"Ah, Don, glad I caught you at home."

"Excuse me, after being requested to ... how did you put it? ... Ah yes, back off, where else did you think that I'd be?"

"Very funny Don, I'm falling about here!"

"I apologise, they do say that sarcasm is the lowest form of wit, forgive me."

"Cut the shit Don, listen, are you free for the rest of the evening?"

"Is everything going well at your end?"

"Swimmingly, goddamn it Don, just answer the question!" "I have no engagements as such, although I was just about to paint my toe nails." He said, though his second rare attempt at humour fell on stony ground.

"I'll see you at the apartment in half an hour!"

"Yes, very well I'll be there."

"Good, see you then and, by the way."

"Yes?"

"Ciou!"

She hung up and passed the mobile back to its owner, who smiled and asked.

"Is Signor Lawrence well?"

"Sure is, why he's as perky as a dog with two dicks, though the way he's going I might just have to get him spayed."

Bennetti did not quite understand Sonya's little quip and continued.

"Give him my regards when you see him, no!?"

"You bet!"

"Now when you are ready, two of my men here will escort you back to your apartment, they are good boys, trust me, you will be safe in their hands." He assured her, now his face displayed a look of concern, he said.

"For tonight, you are under my protection."

Sonya was taken somewhat by surprise by this statement.

"Protection?" She frowned.

"Si, yes, remember you are the bait we use to catch the fish."

"What ... do you figure that King's onto our little game already?"

"No, no, I am not saying that, but after tonight me and my people, we will keep our distance."

"Jeeze thanks ... so what you are saying is, tonight I'm safe and tomorrow!?..."

"Understand, King, he knows my people, if he catches sight of the hook, we lose our fish, capiche?"

"So how do you propose that I get in touch with you, if and when I land the catch?"

"Our friend Signor Lawrence, he will fill you in with the details of our plan."

"I don't believe this ... shit, I'm the first one in line in all this and it seems to me always the last to know what's going on!" Sonya sighed, then as an afterthought asked.

"Besides, who's paying Lawrence for his part?"

"This is something that you do not need to worry about, I pay him handsomely for his services."

"Yeah!? ... Well let me tell you, I've got a whole lot of things to say to that mercenary son of a bitch!"

Bennetti got up from his seat, then, realising that for now at least, their business had reached its conclusion, Sonya also got to her feet. Bennetti handed out his orders in a stern tone to his three henchmen, who despite possessing features liken to that of reinforced concrete, responded with such a level of subservience that Sonya thought they resembled a trio of obedient students desperate to please their tutor. '*I wonder which one of these apes brought teacher the apple today?'* Sonya mused lightly to herself. She and Bennetti shook hands. Before she turned to leave Bennetti said,

"Good luck with the fishing, remember a good angler, he ... I mean she should always be well prepared."

King glanced at his wristwatch again for the umpteenth time, deciding that the time had come to give up the ghost. He was poised to turn the ignition key on the dark blue Toyota when he saw Sonya stepping out through the door of the restaurant, flanked by the two bodyguards. Instantly, he slid down low in his seat and held his breath, watching the three of them walk towards the Daimler. One of the Overlord's men opened the rear offside door, at the same time, his practised eyes searched around the area surrounding them for anything remotely suspicious. He then stood to one side, allowing Sonya to manoeuvre her shapely figure through the opening then make herself comfortable on the back seat.

Remaining perfectly still, King waited until the luxury vehicle eased away, then at the crossroads further along the tree lined avenue it turned and disappeared from view.

"Perfect." King told himself, while once more getting himself upright in his seat. There was never, or indeed ever going to be, a more opportune time for him to resolve his differences once and for all with Agnazzio Bennetti. Seemingly, tonight the Overlord was being unusually complacent with the deployment of his personal guard. In the time that had passed, subsequent to his vigilant watch over Ronaldo's, King had witnessed several potential customers being turned away at the door and he had put two and two together concluding that, the Overlord had been throwing his own private little party. Because, coupled with the fact that he was aware the Italian did not like to be surrounded by strangers, he had not seen any other people, apart from Sonya and the muscle-bound minders vacate the premises. He opened the glove compartment, reached inside and took out the .38 calibre revolver. The cool metallic weight of the gun felt good in his hand as, in a steady unflustered fashion, he screwed the silencer onto the barrel. Satisfied, he pulled his dark bomber jacket to one side and pressed the weapon inside his waistband. Aside from the occasional passing motorist or pedestrian all was quiet. He got out of the car, his eyes moving about with the hungry intensity of a wild cat. Above him, the moon was now hidden behind a large cover of dark cloud from which, descended the first drops of rain and delivering with it, a warning to the stalker of the deluge that would imminently follow. He walked across the street with a casual stride, though now his heart was beating as if he had been running, sweat beaded his brow and upper lip beneath his moustache. Another fifteen metres and he would be on the threshold of the restaurant. Again he carefully scanned the length of the avenue, on the lookout for anyone who could possibly witness the impending deed, there was nobody within sight, although had there been, they would be running to take cover, for now the heavens opened and the rain pelted down hard onto the pavement. King was delighted with the sudden downpour, knowing that it would serve to blanket the commotion and clamour that would inevitably come about the moment he forced his intrusion upon the unsuspecting prey.

The establishment's owner Ronaldo, had just come out from the kitchen, after spending most of the evening in attendance with Bennetti's sister, playing kitchen porter for the most part and was presently involved in light-hearted conversation with, to date his most prized and opulent customer. Their amiable banter was abruptly severed when the gatecrasher, burst through the unguarded front door. The owner was about to make clear his protestations and reprimand the uninvited intruder when, before he even had the chance to comprehend that the man was aiming a gun at him, he had been shot, just above the upper lip, the impact lifted him momentarily off the floor, forcing him to stagger backwards. The bullet had gone straight through his tongue and lodged in the back of his throat, shocked and bleeding he tried to beg for his life, but the only sound that emanated from his shattered voice-box was a hideous gurgle. Then like a falling chimney, he fell face first onto the marble floor. Pedro 'hands' Garoz had gone for the gun which was tucked inside his shoulder holster, as he drew it, King's next shot found its target, his bullet entered through Pedro's left cheek zigzagging through his brain and exiting through the back of his head. The final few beats of his heart pumped blood out onto the wall behind where his body quaked. To the left of where Pedro had just keeled and dropped, the door to the kitchen suddenly swung open, Dino, the aide that King had spotted earlier had appeared at the doorway armed with a revolver, though, before he had had the opportunity to take aim and fire, King maintaining a combat position shot the tall Italian through the heart, sending him reeling backwards through the door, which only a second ago he had impetuously entered through. Intent on not staying around any longer than necessary and to guarantee no more intrusions from any of the Overlord's would-be pawns left in the game, he walked at a steady pace towards the kitchen, his eyes flitting spasmodically over towards the table under which he knew Bennetti was hiding. He pushed the kitchen door ajar, Dino's body lay a quarter of the way inside the clinically tiled area, the front of his once pristine white shirt now glistening crimson under the bright lights.

"Peek-a-boo ... anyone else want to come and play?" King said, his mocking tone reverberating around the walls. He fell silent for a moment listening for the slightest movement. Now, from underneath the table where earlier he had been dining and, more recently been cowering, Bennetti saw his chance and made a desperate dash for the gun that lay on the floor by the side of his dead bodyguard. King's voice chided across the room, putting an abrupt halt to his bid for salvation.

"Freeze!" He bellowed, then in a calmer though firm tone added, "Don't even fucking think about it! ... Now get down on your knees and put your hands on your head!"

Bennetti did not comply swiftly enough to his command, so he raised his voice once more.

"Fucking do it!"

Bennetti, no longer master of himself or situation, did as he was ordered to do and sank to his knees, his hands shaking uncontrollably before coming to rest on his crown. The tan on his face appeared to fade, the skin now grey with fright, his eyes wide and dilated, staring up towards the man, he now scolded himself for foolishly underestimating. He had recognised the intruder the moment that he had fired the first shot, slaying Ronaldo and causing himself to dive for cover. Even under the subdued lighting and the man's cleverly adjusted facial appearance he knew without doubt that this crazed killer was Irwin King. The fleeting nervous tic that carried with it that subtle arrogance, just a moment ago confirmed Bennetti's belief. Twitch or no twitch, King's eyes remained mean and as steady as the aim of the .38. He walked forward toward his captive and stepped over Garoz's bloody lifeless bulk, he then crouched down, gun levelled in his right hand with his free hand he scooped up the weapon that only a matter of seconds ago, the Overlord had made his last ditch attempt at avoiding his fast approaching death. King remained in the squatting posture, his features creased into a contemptuous grin, his long awaited triumph over the Overlord rapturously swelling his ego.

"Now, before you leave us ..." He began, breaking off mid-sentence to make way for a peel of obnoxious laughter, while Bennetti could only glare back in defiance, for now frustration fuelled by hatred, began to build with each remaining beat of his doomed heart. King's laughter subsided, his voice stern once more.

"Before I blow you away, I have some questions and I want some answers!"

She carefully took off her shoes and stepped out from behind the door that King had left ajar and where she had in desperation hidden herself. In her hand, the stainless steel blade of the eight inch calving knife glistened as she crept silently up behind the man who was sitting on his heels and pointing a gun at her beloved brother. She had been tempted to go for Dino's revolver which lay on the floor, where it had fallen. But she knew that the slightest noise would rouse the gunman and she could not risk that. Remaining with his broad back to her, she was thankful of Pavarotti's powerful larynx, though even with the volume turned down to its minimum, it was enough to camouflage her stealthy approach.

"I do not intend hanging around here much longer." King was saying, "But, the more that you co-operate the longer you might live."

Bennetti's contemptuous retort was delivered the second that he had gathered together as much saliva as his arid, nervous mouth could muster, he then spat in his captor's eye. Repulsed and furious, King cussed venomously while affording himself room to rise up from his crouched position. To his absolute surprise, his progress towards stretching to his full height was momentarily halted by, what he guessed to be a malicious fist striking powerfully home, between his shoulder blades. Instinctively, he swung around and pistol whipped his assailant, sending her crashing into a nearby table and unconsciousness. Shocked, though unaware that a knife had been thrust some way into his back, King turned himself and his attention back towards the Overlord, intent on now finishing his gruesome night's work.

His intentions though were abruptly undermined by his adversary who, recognising another opportunity to secure a future for himself, had caught King unawares, launching himself bodily at him. The impetus of the Italian's crunching tackle, sent the two men grappling and scurrying over the slick marble surface. King tripped over the dead bodyguard's legs, he felt himself stumbling backwards and the momentum would bring Bennetti's full weight down on top of him. On their way to the floor, King pressed the .38 hard against the Overlord's temple, pulled the trigger and sent Agnazzio Bennetti into oblivion. The bullet left the opposite side of his head, only a fraction of a second before the sleek silver blade pierced cleanly through Irwin King's right ventricle on its rapid journey through his torso. Together they had fallen into death's final embrace. Damnation alone, now awaiting their imminent calling.

Chapter Thirty Seven

The next day Sonya had risen from her bed at the crack of dawn and in accord with the bright sunlit morning, her mood conveyed an air of optimism. She hummed a cheerful tune to herself, while gathering up the morning paper from the welcome mat inside the hallway. She bit into a piece of toast that she held in one hand, while employing the other to manipulate the tabloid to afford a glimpse of the front page headlines. In bold black print the journal declared 'Train crash carnage claims fourteen – fifty-two injured.' Sonya clicked her tongue woefully and turned to make her way back towards the kitchen, telling herself that she would reserve absorbing that particular communiqué for later, wishing not to digest the details of such an awful tragedy along with her breakfast. She turned swiftly to the sportspage, there, taking up fully three quarters of the back cover, was a colour photograph of Jean Paul. He had been pictured embracing an attractive young woman, amongst an army of other Jean Paul female devotees. His lips were puckered and he was playfully pecking the girl's blushing cheek. The banner quotation above the merrymaking image caused Sonya to smile.

'French Kissing!' it declared. The column itself praised the young Frenchman's devastating performance and outright win over the Hong Kong man, placing him as odds on favourite now along with every French maiden's choice to become this year's champion in Paris. After perusing the glowing report, she smiled again, this time at his photograph. Her skin tingled, aroused in recollection of their first night of fervent passion. Re-entering the kitchen she thought about pouring herself a fresh cup of coffee, in advance of doing so she paused, closing her eyes, granting her imagination a moment to recapture some of the sensual magic that she and Jean Paul shared together on that balmy night in Monaco. They had feverishly fondled and toured each other initially, with craving hands and enthusiastic mouths, she had known that it was pure animal attraction that had galvanised the basis of this unison. She could almost sense presently, the stimulating aroma of the fragrant perspiration that emerged between them and, there, through the open window, moonlight shafted onto their graceful, naked bodies and limbs, illuminating them both with a silver oily radiance, serving to accentuate her womanly curves and highlight his vigorous structure. She could taste him now.

"Stop it!" Sonya said aloud. Instantly her eyes snapped open, she reprimanded herself, *'you've gone without for too long that's all''* she brooded, and went about the mundane task of pouring coffee, while filling her cup an inner voice enquired *'if it was so good between you two guys how come ...?'* The answer to that question was simple. *'We both got aspirations, sure kinda diverse goals, but all the same we neither of us want anything to get in the way!'* she reflected.

"It was mutual." Sonya heard herself say to the empty walls. Carrying the coffee and the newspaper she made her way over to the large oak table and sat down in one of the adjoining chairs. Then while sampling the aromatic drink, she turned the pages of the paper, allowing her eyes to browse over the printed contents. A particular advertisement caught her eye momentarily, it read, 'Visit Blackpool Pleasure Beach this summer and take a ride on the Big One!' Inadvertently her thoughts wandered once more to that night only last year. They were locked together as one, manoeuvring harmoniously over the sumptuous silk bedcovers. She could feel the immense proportions of his manhood inside her, his 'big one'. Sonya pondered now, as she had done that night in Monaco, whether Jean Paul had inherited this particular attribute from his father. His father, the man who if still alive, stood to make her dream of being re-united with her kid sister a reality, the man who, so far, had eluded her every step. She pushed these thoughts to the back of her mind now, returning her concentration to the morning news. It was when she turned to page four that her mouth gaped open and the coffee cup fell from her grip, bouncing off the table then smashing into a multitude of pieces on the kitchen floor. The photograph underneath the headline, was of Ronaldo's restaurant in its former glory. Sonya's confounded eyes scanned the large print above. 'Five die in restaurant blaze' it declared. The small accompanying article was unable to elucidate very much upon the cause of the fire, though it did name some of the victims. The Police were treating its occurrence with suspicion and were poised to question the sole survivor, whom the article said, was thought to be a relative of one of the men killed in the inferno. She got up from the chair and in utter frustration, kicked a fragment from the broken cup across the floor. It was now surely beyond the bounds of possibility that she would ever see her sister again. The whole fruitless experience had been plagued by ill-fortune, heartache and the spilling of blood. She inadvertently, had become enveloped in a living nightmare right from the start. She sighed and walked slowly over to where she knew that the dustpan and brush was stored, the earthenware crunched under the soles of her shoes and as she brushed up the broken debris her thoughts went back to the last time that, in a moment of absolute shock she had dropped a cup. The lucidity of the never-to-be forgotten picture in her mind's eye of her friend Larry Hickman, hanging from the beam, his eyes bulging, tongue hanging grotesquely out from the side of his mouth, replenished her heart with pain and anger. The sudden clamorous ring on the front door bell startled her, causing an ominous feeling in her already anxious stomach.

She had refused to make a statement without first seeking advice. The Detective Sergeant with the large red face, who had acted on a tip-off from a taxi driver, had repeatedly explained that she was not under suspicion but merely brought in to answer a few questions that might draw some light on the case. He finally decided to comply with Sonya's request to make a phone call. Don Lawrence arrived at the station twenty minutes later. A WPC opened the door to the interview room, then ushered Sonya and Lawrence through before taking a position guarding the doorway. The red-faced Detective Sergeant popped his head round and said.

"Take a seat won't you, I'll be with you in a moment." Sonya looked around the cheerless walls and sat down next to Lawrence on one side of the basic wooden table. In a whispered tone Lawrence said.

"What in heaven's name is going on, why have you been brought here?"

"You mean you don't know? Haven't you read the papers this morning?"

"I had only just got out of bed when you called."

"There was a barbecue at the restaurant I was at last night, ... according to the cops here, the carcasses they later found inside were burned to a crisp. There was only one survivor, it's my guess the fire was started by a lighted candle."

"Started by a candle you say, how come ..."

"They didn't escape?"

"Yes."

"Let's say, I know why the paper said that police were treating the incident with suspicion, truth is I reckon ..."

The Detective Sergeant's reappearance through the door interrupted her flow. He was followed in by another plain clothed officer, the two men quickly took their seats at the other side of the table.

"Now can we get on, we have wasted enough time as it is, wouldn't you agree Miss Kennedy!?"

"Just taking good care of my rights."

"Is this gentleman your solicitor?"

"No, he's a friend, Detective Sergeant Wilson, this is Don Lawrence." Sonya announced, then once the formalities were out of the way, DS Wilson turned his attention to Sonya and proceeded with the questioning, Sonya in return duly collaborated frankly to the verbal bombardment which lasted for twenty minutes and before DS Wilson was content to bring the interview to a close. He said.

"Thank you Miss Kennedy for your co-operation, I take it that you will be staying at the address, ... at Allan House if we need you?"

"Need me, for what?"

"Further questioning."

"But I've told you all I know."

"Yes, but there may be one or two things that we have overlooked."

"Hell, goddamn it, I was planning on going home."

"Home, to America?"

"Yeah, so you're telling me I can't leave London, is that what you're saying?"

"Let us just say, we would like you to postpone your journey, until we have a clearer picture of this particular felony."

"OK, can I go now?" Sonya said, rising from her chair.

"We will be in touch."

Two minutes subsequent to their departure from the Interview Room, DS Wilson was still in a quandary as to where he had seen Don Lawrence before. Then, the penny dropped, causing him to wonder, what an intelligent young woman like Miss Kennedy might be doing using a fraudulent ex-solicitor as her confidant.

Sonya leaned back in the passenger seat, closing her eyes against the bright late morning sun while Lawrence steered the car at a dawdling pace amongst the heavy London traffic.

"If the fire had been caused by an incendiary device," she said, "Then you could understand why Bennetti, along with whoever else was in there, had been powerless to avoid being turned into over-cooked meat, but ..."

"Fumes perhaps, asphyxiation!?" Lawrence offered. She opened her eyes and turned to him with a hint of irritation in her tone.

"Fumes ..? Come on Don, bullshit!"

"What?"

"Jeeze, you call yourself a private eye!?"

"You have a theory then?"

"Yeah."

"Better than the lighted candle I hope."

"Don't mock me Don."

"Go ahead, I'm listening."

"OK ... I figure that those guys were dead before the fire got started."

"That, if you don't mind me saying, is a rather credulous assertion."

"And that, if you don't mind me saying, is a contradiction in terms!"

"Possibly, though what I am saying is that at this stage we should not jump to conclusions."

"Really Don, sometimes you are one patronising son of a bitch!"

"I'm merely suggesting that we keep our composure, wouldn't you agree?"

She looked at him for a long moment, Lawrence's self-righteous attitude had always to some extent grated on her. Today though, following the meeting that had taken place when arriving home last night and his, seemingly uninspired conduct on her behalf with the police, had succeeded in heightening displeasure to the point of exasperation.

"OK Mr Smart-Ass." she continued, "What do you think of this credulous assertion, the cops back there called it a felony yeah? ... well, I figure that our infamous friend, Irwin King, has been a step or two in front all the time and ..."

"Now you're being paranoid."

"Goddamn it, whose side are you on?!"

"And irrational I might add."

"Are you trying to antagonise me?"

"Certainly not."

"Well, you sure as hell are from where I'm sitting."

"Please don't raise your voice, it really doesn't become you."

"If my voice is being raised, it's because my words, it seems, keep falling on deaf ears."

"All the same, I would appreciate it if you would kindly refrain from taking your frustration out on me, and may I say, I think that you are being extremely unreasonable."

"Maybe so ... hey and sure ... sure I'm frustrated, I have got a kidnapped sister somewhere out there and I'm no closer to finding her than when I damn well started. Let me tell you what I think is unreasonable. The way I see it, there's only one person who's benefited from all the shit along the way ... and that's you mister!"

"I would say that that was rather unwarranted."

"What's more, I guess that since your main benefactor, Signor Bennetti has bit the dust, your motivation with regard to my accomplishing my goal will no doubt wane now. Oh and let me add a postscript here, my financial resources are running a little low now, so it's gonna be kinda hard to pay your wage bill." She folded her arms in front of her, awaiting a response that did not transpire. His expression remained composed, almost aloof, as if he was treating her reproach with contempt. This did much to irritate her further.

"You're nothing more than a bad ass parasite!" She heard herself say through tightened lips. He shifted slightly in his seat, then in his typically monotone manner said.

"I sincerely regret that our association should terminate in such an acrimonious fashion ..."

"So you're quitting." She declared, releasing a wheeze of sardonic laughter, prior to adding, "Well screw you Don Lawrence!"

Her anger was now almost fuelled to its pinnacle and no doubt, had she been capable of reading Lawrence's thoughts at this time, she would surely have slapped the habitually smug expression clean off his face. For in his ignorance regarding women in general and their fundamental characteristics, his ill-considered notion imagined that Sonya's delirious behaviour as he saw it, was due to pre-menstrual tension. On catching sight of the small revolver that she had produced from inside her shoulder bag, he wondered for an instant how unsound the mind of a female suffering from that condition might become. To his relief, Sonya opened up the glove compartment and said.

"I believe this gun belongs to you." She deposited the weapon inside the compact opening, adding somewhat cynically.

"If you wasn't sitting on your butt right now Don, I sure could have found a better home for it."

She closed the small compartment once more then said.

"Thanks for the ride Don, this I think is as far as we two go, so would you be good enough to stop the car and let me out."

Later that day, equipped with a bouquet of flowers, Don Lawrence had made his third attempt in as many hours, to pay a visit to Margarita Bennetti, inside the hospital where she was being treated for shock and minor burns. This time she had finally agreed to meet with him at her bedside, with the strict instruction that she would allow him no more than ten minutes of her time. Standing outside the private hospital room, a WPC and her male colleague, asked Lawrence a few pertinent questions, and before allowing him to enter, insisted that because Signorina Bennetti was presently helping the police with their enquiries, he should undergo a body search. To his slight embarrassment, it was the female police officer that set about this task, prior to accompanying him through the door, which she closed behind her and stood guard. Bennetti's sister did not correspond with Lawrence's cordial approach, with a stern expression and a tone of voice to match, she said.

"Put them over there."

"What?"

"The flowers, put them on the table over there, say what you have to say and leave me to grieve alone."

"Yes ... may I offer my deepest sympathy on the loss of your brother."

"The police they say the same, like you their words are empty, then they pester me asking the questions, anyway, how did you know where to find me?"

"I'm a private detective remember!?"

"And if you had done your job properly, then none of this would have happened, Agnazzio would still be alive!"

"I'm afraid that Irwin King outsmarted us once again."

"No, he did not outsmart me Signor Lawrence, I killed him and if it means that I am locked away for life as my punishment, so be it, it will be worth it, I have no regrets."

"Yes, I can understand."

"So, what do you want to speak to me about?"

"You and Agnazzio ..."

"Signor Bennetti to you!"

"Yes ... er ... you and your brother, you were very close, yes?"

"We were partners in life, in business, we never hid any secrets from each other, it was a relationship built on trust."

"Yes, I can appreciate that, and I have no wish to pry into your personal and business affairs ..."

"To do that, might be dangerous for you Signor Lawrence! So I think we have nothing more to talk about."

"Very well, but before I go, may I ask if you were privy to the agreement that your brother and I had in way of payment for my services?"

"To supply you with the whereabouts of a certain young woman, no?"

"Yes, my friend's sister, Karen Kennedy."

"My brother was a man of his word Signor Lawrence." She said, then angled herself around, wincing slightly as she opened the bedside cabinet, from which she plucked a large white envelope.

"You will find all the information you need inside this, now take it and go."

Once outside the room, the two police officers opened the envelope and perused its contents before allowing Lawrence to leave the hospital, with the newly acquired information safely tucked in his inside coat pocket.

Chapter Thirty Eight

In a fiercely competitive clash and enduring five gruelling sets, Jean Paul King had snatched another famous victory over the American Carl Emerson, in the final of the French Open Championships. Unashamedly proud of her son's achievement, Danielle had returned with Floss by her side to Allan House. On greeting them, Sonya was delighted to observe a considerable improvement in Danielle's overall demeanour. She appeared to be well rested and in excellent spirits. Sonya remarked on the fact and Danielle responded brightly, saying.

"My dear Sonya, I am walking on air, much of my memory has thankfully returned to me. It is like being born again, come let us sit down, I will tell you more, no!?"

For the next thirty minutes, the three women chatted at the table, Danielle with her new found zest for life, monopolised the majority of the conversation. The very last thing that Sonya wished to be by this time was a kill-joy, though her apprehension obviously displayed itself on her face, for Danielle halted her flow presently and said.

"Sonya, are you .... is there something wrong?"

"No ... I mean, well yeah I guess so."

"Please, tell me about it."

Sonya sighed, then, with a mindful approach painstakingly described her rendezvous with Bennetti and, the events that took place following her departure. It was time now to enlighten Danielle with the most recent disclosures appertaining to the tragedy. Sonya looked at Danielle for a long moment then said.

"Floss here was right, the body they found in the River Thames was not your husband's."

"How do you know this?" Danielle frowned.

"Because an anonymous woman, that was apparently the only survivor there that night, has come forward and wants to take responsibility for killing the guy, who she said, had burst into the place and cold-bloodedly plugged Bennetti and his gang full of bullets, just before the place went up in flames."

"So you are saying ..."

"What I'm saying is that the guy, who was doing the Al Capone impersonation was your husband!"

The room fell unexpectedly silent, Sonya's eyes lingered on her friends and, for the first time since her return, the vitality seemed to drain from Danielle's body. Sonya felt that she should apologise for the manner in which she had broken the news, after all, she considered that whatever dark iniquitous force drove Irwin King, he had been the woman's husband and albeit long ago, together they surely had shared at times, moments of tenderness and passion. Before her words of remorse had had the opportunity to pass through her lips and, to Sonya's astonishment, Floss ran from the room sobbing noisily. Consequently, though a little confused, Sonya got to her feet in readiness to pursue and offer Floss some comfort, but Danielle's words halted her progress.

"Sonya, please, leave her to grieve on her own, believe me I know that this is what she would desire, for the time being at least."

"I don't get it Danielle ... I mean, the way that bastard .... I'm sorry I ..."

"Do not be sorry, you are right my husband was a bastard."

"I know he was your husband, but I hope you don't mind me saying, I'm glad that you acknowledge the fact."

"Yes, though I would not recommend that you use such narratives in front of Floss, she is ... well, very loyal."

"But why should Floss be so upset, I mean the way that the guy apparently treated her, the way in which he treated you, the goddamn mind games he played, the oppression ... and the rest, hell I don't need to tell you, but why should Floss ... to me it just don't make any sense."

"There was a time Sonya, not long before my accident, that I too would have been confused by dear Floss' response to the news of Irwin's death. Although due now to my new-found knowledge of much of my past, I can understand her pain at this time, but I'm afraid that I cannot share with you the reasons, for it would challenge my discretion."

Sonya was naturally intrigued, but instead of pressing for an answer, or jumping to conclusions, she simply said,

"I understand."

"Thank you Sonya, I appreciate your prudence."

"Sure thing." Sonya agreed, and the two women granted each other an appreciative smile. Sonya then turned and poured two fresh cups of coffee from the percolator. In the short space of time that it took to accomplish this small task, Danielle's collectedness had fragmented, teardrops fell liberally from her doleful eyes. Sonya placed the cups on the table and sat down next to her. Danielle turned and like the sun breaking through on a gloomy day, she smiled through her tears and said.

"Perhaps now, my father .... my dear Papa can rest in peace!"

"Amen to that." Sonya agreed lifting her cup high. Danielle then raised her own cup aloft.

"Let us drink to my father's memory, and to my departed husband ... may he rot in hell!"

"Real slowly." Sonya agreed. Then, using a couple of soft tissues, Danielle mopped away the tears from her cheek and declared.

"Did I mention to you that I also met with Agnazzio Bennetti in Paris?"

"No!?"

"As it has turned out, for me it was very fortunate that I did."

The ensuing ten minutes was taken up by Danielle's description of the whole curious scenario and its extraordinary outcome. When she had concluded with her interpretation of events, Sonya said.

"I guess now that you will be packing your bags, and going home to Monaco!?"

"Not just yet, I promised Jean Paul that I would remain in London until the end of the Wimbledon Championships."

"An excellent idea."

"And I would like you Sonya, to be my guest here for the duration, and tomorrow I will treat us both to a shopping spree, to celebrate my new-found fortune, no!?"

"And freedom!"

"Yes, and freedom!"

"I think I might have to turn down your generous offer, as the police are now through with needing me for questioning I ..."

"But my dear Sonya, Jean Paul is looking forward to seeing you once again."

"What? Danielle, have you been playing cupid while you were away?"

"Yes, and I am not ashamed to admit it."

"Honestly." Sonya declared with a wry smile.

"And I am not ashamed to admit, that I told my son that you were without doubt, the most remarkable and courageous young woman that I have had the pleasure of knowing."

"Well ... wow, thank you … I don't know what to say."

"Moreover, it is I that should be thanking you Sonya, please allow me to show my appreciation of your friendship, and say yes."

"OK... yeah, yes let's drink to that!"

"Oh dear, I'm afraid that the coffee has gone cold."

"Then let's make some fresh."

Chapter Thirty Nine

Wimbledon, June 24

Yesterday, Ace had visited the All England Lawn Tennis and Croquet Club for the first time in the company of his coach, without whom, owing to him being a long time member, he would not have been allowed access. His eyes wide with anticipation had surveyed the buildings swathed in ivy. He had breathed in the aromatic scent emanating from the white, pink and blue blossom of the garden's hydrangeas, and absorbed himself in the genteel atmosphere, enlightened by the sound of birdsong. This, he knew was the lull before the storm. With eleven and a half months of meticulous preparation in place, it was as if the venue had been shored up against a foreign invasion. A fraction of the three hundred thousand invaders that would be passing through the gates over the next fortnight, had already began to form a line outside the periphery fencing, in the hope of playing spectator on the opening day of the most famous tennis tournament in the world. TV cameras had already been strategically installed overlooking six of the premier courts, all set to send out 466 hours of match coverage to networks in 145 countries. Ace had been unable to conceal his excitement when he and Fenton were accompanied by a security man for a tour of the illustrious Centre Court and the new Number One. They later paid a visit to the court where, on the opening day, Ace would be competing for a place in the second round. Coach and player surveyed Court Fourteen, while a groundsman with the aid of a mobile piece of machinery, was carefully marking out the white lines over the superbly cultivated grass.

"How are you feeling Ace?" Fenton had asked.

"Never better."

"From tomorrow you'll be just six matches away from your dream coming true."

"Sounds easy when you put it like that Greg."

"On paper it's as simple as that, demolish six guys and you're in the final on Centre Court, thing is though, there are a hundred and twenty seven other eager wannabes turning up with the same dream!"

"Do I detect a hint of defeatism from my coach!?"

"No mate, just being realistic, but believe me Ace I reckon that on grass, you're going to be a handful for any one of those hundred and odd guys, and that includes the big guys, the seeds."

"Well, I'm up for it!"

"But, if providence doesn't prevail for us this year,...."

“Hey coach, I’ve got a feeling in my guts, that we are not going to have to wait too long before I make my mark!” Ace declared. Fenton smiled back at his young protégé.

“Keep that belief and you can’t go wrong.”

Today, in preference to joining Fenton in an official courtesy car, that had been provided by the tournament organisers, Ace had chosen to ride in on his pushbike from their small hotel in Morden, situated a few miles from Wimbledon. His journey so far, had been a pleasant one and had served to warm his muscles up in readiness for his practice session with Tony Wang and his coach, prior to his Wimbledon debut. Pleasant that is, until being almost knocked off his bicycle at a small roundabout by a *‘bloody idiot’* as Ace had called after the rider of the large Harley Davidson motorbike. Fortunately for Ace, he managed to recapture control of the bicycle in time to avoid possible injury which would no doubt have wrecked his Wimbledon chances before they had even got started. The incident had shook him up somewhat and, it was not until dismounting the bicycle on his arrival at the all England Club’s Aarongi Park practice courts, that his indignation had subsided. The identity tag pinned to his tracksuit top ensured his entry to the training sector without posing any problems. En route to joining Fenton, Wang and his brother Jack, Ace caught sight of the powerful motorcycle that, only five minutes earlier had been just inches away from causing him inevitable injury, he also recognised the owner, garbed in brightly coloured motorcycle leathers.

The moment that he and the shapely brunette, who had been riding pillion, removed their helmets, they were immediately surrounded by a posse of media people. Photographers fervently jockeyed for position, while the columnists directed questions towards the long-haired male motorcyclist.

A rush of uninvited jealousy invaded Ace’s reasoning and, although he rebuked himself for being susceptible to these irrational feelings, he had to fight off the urge to walk up to Jean Paul King and punch his lights out. Fortunately, he succeeded in repressing his indignation and set about the task of securing his bicycle, using a lock and chain. While engaged in this mundane undertaking, he listened in on the interview.

“You won the Italian Open, and of course more recently you were crowned French Champion, are you up to the challenge of making Wimbledon your third Grand Slam title this year?”

“Losing is not an alternative.” Jean Paul replied with a self-assured air. Another journalist then asked.

“Maybe so Jean Paul, although you did experience something of a hiccough at Queens in the Stella Artois Tournament, crashing out in the early stages, would you say that your game does not lend itself to the grass surface?”

“This question I have answered many times, once more I will explain that, maybe because of my elation at winning in Paris, I was suffering from fatigue on that day at Queens, besides Monsieur, when I lift the golden trophy on Centre Court, you my friend will eat your words!”

Then, amidst a volley of somewhat more pertinent questions and, while Ace, harnessed his bag of equipment onto his shoulder, he was suddenly aware of

Jean Paul's companion staring at him openly. At first he thought that it was simply his imagination, although when she granted him a friendly smile, he was rather confused and felt a tinge of self-consciousness sweep over him, nonetheless intuition told him that it was his job now to get to his nominated court, although to get there, he realised he would have to walk through the gathering, '*so what?!"* he mused, marching purposefully forward and when he got within earshot of the tall dark-haired young woman, he said.

"Do me a favour would you, tell your big-headed, long-haired boyfriend to get some lessons in the art of riding a motorbike!"

Before Sonya could react to Ace's cutting remark, Jean Paul declared sourly.

"What did you just say Monsieur?"

"I was just telling this lovely lady that you're pretty good at tennis, but you're crap at riding a motorbike!"

"You will take that back if you do not want a thorough beating!" Jean Paul hissed.

"Bloody hell, I'm shaking in my shoes." Ace teased.

Recognising the onset of an apparent altercation, the flock of news-people fell quiet, some of the cameramen though, were poised to capture the potential fracas. Sonya took hold of Jean Paul's arm.

"Hold it, come on the pair of you, are you guys crazy or something!?"

Ignoring her plea, Jean Paul shrugged her aside and stepped arrogantly towards Ace. With only a yard or so between them now, he came to a halt, both men glaring defiantly into one another's eyes, searching for weaknesses.

"I demand that you apologise." Jean Paul maintained.

"I reckon it's you that should be apologising to me, mister big time."

"Say that you are sorry to Mademoiselle Kennedy and myself and we will forget that this happened."

"Bollocks."

"Say ... you are sorry!"

"No bloody chance, kermit!"

"Kermit?"

"As in ... frog!?"

"Now you're both being totally childish, stop this won't you." Sonya interrupted, sensing the growing animosity between them. Again, Jean Paul pushed her away.

"Keep out of this." He said.

"For God's sake ... you are brothers!" She yelled, in a vain attempt to be heard, though alas she was not, for as her words were dispatched, so too was Jean Paul's staff-straight right hand punch. Such was the swiftness of his hand speed, Ace did not see it until it was too late, and although he managed to ride the strike, which caught him just below his left eye, the impact sent him staggering backwards, some onlookers gasped in horror that such an unseemly spectacle should take place, here, on the boundary of the bastion of the genteel sport of lawn tennis. Ace was oblivious to the consequences that his retaliation might bring about presently, and adopted a southpaw boxing style, which he had practised many times during his gymnasium training. He sprang back on his toes towards his tormentor, then fired a long snapping jab, punching nothing but air. Jean Paul had been alert enough to avoid it, the Frenchman then countered with another solid right, catching Ace square in the mouth and splitting his bottom lip. However, with a nimble spring in his legs, Ace managed to avoid yet another forceful looking blow. But, by missing his target, Jean Paul stumbled marginally off balance and dropped his guard just enough for Ace to seize the chance to land his first punch. His left hook travelled no more than six inches before making solid contact with Jean Paul's angular jaw. A chorus of white light went off behind the recipient's eyes and his legs turned to soup. At this juncture and unexpectedly for Ace, a pair of sturdy arms now encircled him from behind, pinning his own arms to his torso, instinctively he struggled to free himself, then suddenly another man's hands were upon him, clutching so vehemently at his tracksuit that the garment and the shirt beneath it ripped away from his chest. The dazzle from the photographer's flashbulbs caused Ace to flinch and cuss through blooded lips and, with his hands still clinched in fists of rage, he glared at his disputant, while the familiar voices that accompanied the stalwart grip they held, pleaded with Ace to calm himself. Albeit reluctantly to begin with, Ace succumbed to their wishes.

He stood there breathing heavily, through a combination of exertion and anger, not only towards the Frenchman, but the realisation of what his own petulant actions may bring about. These things, along with the metallic taste of his own blood, made him want to vomit.

Through glazed eyes, the last thing that Jean Paul observed, prior to Fenton and Jack escorting their man away, was the gleaming talisman that hung on Ace's naked chest.

Chapter Forty

Fate had dealt Ace a catalogue of new and formidable challenges during the first week of the Wimbledon campaign. At the outset, though he had been overjoyed and proud after winning his opening match on court fourteen, against a highly rated German opponent, the press had not exactly endeared themselves to him. Overnight fame came to Ace not by way of his tenacious show on court that day, but rather his by now, infamous embroilment with Jean Paul King. In fact, some quarters of the Games Ruling Body had called for Ace's banishment from the competition. Although, at the last hour, thanks to the respected British Davis Cup Captain, along with Greg Fenton's fervent appeal on Ace's behalf, the majority succumbed and motioned that the young man could continue, albeit under their watchful eye.

By the time that the championships had reached the eighth day of competition, those same watchful eyes had come to recognise that, although Ace had been extremely competitive and occasionally rather animated on court, his behaviour had been unquestionable. Indeed, having witnessed the young Briton's progressive victories in the 2nd, 3rd and 4th rounds against eminently regarded opposition, many of the less starchy members of the media and the aforementioned organisation, actually believed that this 'young upstart' as he was initially tagged, could go all the way. To further amplify his unprecedented success so far, the Wimbledon crowds by now, had taken Ace to their hearts.

Jean Paul's Wimbledon to date, had been punctuated with a string of uncharacteristically inconsistent performances. On day one, a packed crowd had sat around the number one showcourt, rather disenchanted by the number two seed's opening account, which, thanks to a combination of luck and, his lowly ranked opponent's comparatively moderate racket skills, saw him scrape his way through by a narrow margin in the deciding set. Contrarily, against much stiffer opposition in the next round, he silenced any scepticism with a display of outstanding brilliance on the famous centre court. But, like the British weather, Jean Paul's game fluctuated. Another languid performance in the third round, once again saw him go through by the skin of his teeth. His coach had not concealed his concern after that particular display.

"What the hell happened out there today!?" Holding had said.

"Tired ... I just felt tired Brad."

"Again?"

"Yes, do not worry yourself I am fine."

"You sure?"

"Trust me."

"What ... did you sleep badly last night or what? Do you want me to change your accommodation maybe?"

"No, my accommodation suits me very well."

"OK, I guess then, it must be that dusky broad of yours Sonya, that's keeping you awake at night."

The two men had laughed at this suggestion though the joviality was severed by Holding's following words.

"All the same, I think you should undergo a physical, it's the third ..."

"No Brad," Jean Paul had intervened, "Trust me, I am fine and, when I win Wimbledon this year, we will look back on this and smile."

"But if you play like you did today in the next match against Zenovka, I'm afraid that the fourth round's as far as we will go!"

"Would you care to have a wager with me coach?"

"What!?"

"Believe me, I will annihilate Zenovka!"

"Way to go Jean Paul, way to go!"

As the two men vacated the locker rooms, Brad Holding had offered another proposition.

"Maybe after Wimbledon, I'll make arrangements for you to have a little vacation, it's been a long hard year, what do you say?"

"I have no time for vacations." Jean Paul had replied impatiently.

Forty six hours subsequent to this conversation, court number three witnessed Jean Paul King thrashing the Russian, Zenovka, in three straight sets, 6-2, 6-3 and 6-1, earning him a place in the quarter finals.

31st June

Jean Paul had made arrangements with Sonya and his mother to meet inside his main sponsor's marquee three hours prior to his quarter final match on centre court. On their arrival, the handsome French star greeted the two women warmly then, while envious female eyes looked on, he escorted them through to a cordoned area marked VIP's only. Around the interior of the large tent, TV screens relayed footage from recent matches. Jean Paul glanced up at the screen nearest to them for a moment, Danielle studied what she thought to be dark circles beneath her son's eyes, hoping at the same time that it was just a trick of the light.

"So Jean Paul, are you well?" She asked.

"Oui, yes very well Ma ma, I am fit and raring to go." He lied, for again today, he felt somewhat fatigued and, on recognising in her a look of maternal concern, he swiftly made an effort to quell any further talk regarding his well-being.

"Later today, I will make you proud of your son, trust me. For now though, let us relax, come Ma ma, Sonya, let us have a drink and toast success."

With that, he gestured a hand and a waitress scurried coyly over to his side.

"Oui monsieur?"

"I will have a fresh orange juice please, and Sonya, what would you care for to drink?"

"It's a little early in the day but, to hell with it! I'll have a small martini."

"And you Ma ma?"

"Vodka over ice." Danielle heard herself unwittingly say, then for a brief moment, pondered why the words '*vodka over ice*' should stir a niggling feeling deep inside her. Later in the day she would scold herself for not taking heed of this intuition.

Before leaving the marquee for the practice courts and his pre-match warm up, Jean Paul paid a visit to the men's room. Once inside the small cubicle, he locked the door, then from down inside his sock, he carefully pulled out a small polythene bag within which, the white powder he assured himself, would soon serve to alleviate his lethargy. As an athlete, he had always been in harmony with his anatomy. He knew that something within his physical structure was not quite right presently but, he had convinced himself that, if he was to win the Wimbledon title this year and by doing so, achieve his dream of becoming number one in the world, then, for that accolade he was prepared to take risks. He rolled up a twenty pound note, forming a tube, '*if I am found out*' his thought reasoned, '*I will hold up my hands and tell the truth, the truth being that I have never, ever before used any enhancement substances in competition or before any championship ... never!... and that I only took this to relieve myself from feelings of exhaustion ... after all, it is not steroids that I have been taking!?*' With these thoughts in mind he stooped down and proceeded to snort the white line.

At the end of his first practice session of the day, Ace spotted a familiar face in the small crowd, assembled on the viewing platform, with a broad smile he waved a hand then gestured to her, to come over and join him. She acknowledged the invitation and Ace greeted her with a warm embrace.

"Lorna Davies, as I live and breathe, let me look at you, how's things?"

"Well, you know ..."

"No I don't know, tell me, better still, let's go and find a little corner somewhere, you can tell me then, OK?

"Sure, that is if you have the time ..."

"For you Lorna, I have got the time."

"OK, great."

"I'll just take a quick shower and meet you in fifteen minutes at the tea lawn."

"But won't you get hassled, you know, by people ... after all, you're a big star now and all!?"

"Take it easy, Ace here has got to carry that head of his onto number one later!" Fenton said, as he and Jack approached.

"Greg ... how nice to see you, how's things?.. And Jack, how are you?" Lorna said brightly.

"I will leave you three to reminisce, but I'll see you Lorna in fifteen minutes, OK?" Ace said, making a swift exit for the showers.

The number of people in attendance, inside the red, white and blue canvas walls of the marquee had doubled within the last hour, stimulating the agreeable light-hearted atmosphere. But, amidst the waves of frivolous chatter Danielle's head was beginning to swim. She wished at this moment, that she had accepted

Brad Holding's earlier invitation, as Sonya had done, to join him in viewing Jean Paul's final preparations at the practice courts. However, the temptation of having another drink or two had, for some unknown reason to her, been a more inviting alternative. To amplify her growing displeasure, a middle-aged man had just a few minutes earlier, introduced himself and was holding a one-way conversation with her. Out of courtesy, she managed to respond with the odd yes and no. She drained the remnants of her vodka, then stifled what she thought might come out sounding like an inane giggle.

"Would you like another?" The man asked.

"Pardon?"

"Another drink?"

"Yes .. er no .. I mean I .." She managed to stutter, through a mouth that was now agape, her eyes were fixed in a dilated stare on the TV screen. The image from which, had unexpectedly uncovered another shrouded part of her mind's encumbered memories.

Danielle needed desperately to vacate the marquee.

"Are you alright? .. You look like you've seen a ghost." The man had said, but the sudden recollection had rendered her speechless. Once outside, she took in several deep breaths of fresh air, in the hope that it might stimulate her lungs and somehow strengthen her reasoning. Although to her horror, this undertaking had only contributed in making her head even fuzzier than before. She had given herself a minute, before turning and making her way towards the practice courts, though in all honesty at this moment, her sense of direction had deserted her and her legs felt as though they were wading through syrup. '*Pull yourself together!*' her inebriated thoughts chided. She almost laughed out loud at the absurdity of her inner voice's next command, *'rational thinking, that is what we need right now Danielle!'* She came to a halt and closed her eyes, swaying like a tree in the breeze, oblivious now to her surroundings, she tried to review and evaluate the reasons for her consternation earlier inside the marquee.

She had been paying little attention to the TV which was showing a recording from a fourth round match. The players had taken to their seats between games and the camera had zoomed in on a head and shoulder shot of one of the young male athletes, whose fingers were busily searching inside the collar of his shirt. It was the glimmer of the metal talisman that had in that split second, fractured the viewer's disinterest.

"The Gemini twins." She said aloud to herself, and was now abruptly conscious of the sound of people giggling nearby. She opened her eyes and frowned, *'one day at a time.!?'* her inner voice declared and she cussed, this latest skeleton to have fallen out of her memory closet.

Due to his journey on foot being obstructed several times along the way by friendly well-wishers and starry-eyed youngsters requesting autographs, Ace had taken longer than he had anticipated to join Lorna at the tea lawn. When he got there, she was seated at a table beneath a colourful parasol, actively polishing off the remains of a bowl of fresh strawberries.

"Lorna .... sorry I took so long I ..."

"Like I said Ace, you'll get no peace parading around the place, for all to see."

He sat down in the seat opposite, then with a smile he said.

"I know that it's kind of naive, but this recognition thing, I'm enjoying it, besides, I want to grab every minute of this, my first Wimbledon and relish it."

"I don't think that you're naive, on the contrary, you said that you would compete here one day and by God ... you did it, I'm so pleased for you Ace!"

"Thanks Lorna, but if it wasn't for you introducing me to Greg, then ..."

"I reckon you would have done it one day anyway, it was meant to be!"

"Excuse me Mr Sharpe?" A young voice said over Ace's shoulder.

"Yes!?"

"Would you sign my programme please?"

He turned around to face the young female fan. Then while obliging her with his signature, he chatted cheerfully with her for a moment or two before handing the official magazine back to her. She thanked him and walked away with a beaming smile on her face. A man passing by, made known his good wishes regarding Ace's forthcoming match. Ace thanked him, gesturing a thumb in the air.

"You haven't changed one iota Ace." Lorna said sincerely, "None of this fantastic new success seems to have affected you in any way."

"Thanks Lorna, you always did have a way of inflating my ego."

"Talking of inflation, have you seen the price of the strawberries here!?"

"So what happened?"

"What do you mean?" Lorna said slightly bemused.

"I looked up your name, it was the first thing I did when I got here last week, your name wasn't on the list of entries."

"I didn't qualify, I even tried for a wildcard, but it seems that, apart from watching your progress of course, the only taste of Wimbledon for me is going to be through eating their strawberries."

"So how come ... I mean what about your time spent in America?"

"Oh that ... well, it all went pear-shaped."

"I'm sorry, I thought ..."

"Please, don't be sorry, it just didn't work out, it's as simple as that."

"That explains it then."

"What?"

"The letters, the calls, they stopped coming."

"Wounded pride I'm afraid."

At this moment the conversation was breached, while their attention was momentarily diverted, towards a nearby table, where a woman had accidentally clattered into an unoccupied chair. When she once again found her footing, Ace was suddenly uncomfortably aware, that she was staring directly at him. Lorna leaned over and whispered.

"Fasten your seatbelt Ace, this one looks like she's had one over the eight and I've got a feeling, she's going to want more than just your autograph!"

Amidst the progressively growing numbers of expectant Wimbledon patrons, Sonya and Brad Holding were strolling past the museum shop on their way to the tea lawn, the American coach looked up towards the early afternoon sky and said.

"Looks like the centre court's gonna be a hot spot today Sonya!"

"That's what the forecast says."

"It's like playing tennis in four different seasons in two weeks over here."

"OK Brad, you asked me to take a walk with you for a reason, so let's cut the small talk eh!? What's on your mind?"

"Well ... Jean Paul tells me he's in the best shape he has ever been in."

"He sure looked in great shape in practice back there."

"Bright as a button."

"Well?"

"Have you noticed anything unusual, in his general behaviour of late?"

"He's been a little pensive I guess, but that's understandable, considering the stress that the guy has had to burden over the last year or so."

"Sure thing, and I've handled a lot of pro-players in my time, now I can tell you, I've never known anyone that handles stress remotely as well as Jean Paul, he uses tension like a tool."

"I guess that's one of the reasons he's such a good tennis player."

"A great tennis player!"

"Sure."

"And I know how that dynamic engine inside of him works, everything from the balls of his feet, to his biorhythmic cycles. I may well be exaggerating a little here, but lately ..."

"Are you saying that you think he has something wrong with him, physically I mean?"

"Hell no ... I mean I don't know, it's just that in the last month, one day he's kinda low and lethargic, next he's firing off all cylinders, if I didn't know better, I'd say he was on something."

"You can't mean that Brad!?"

"No, no I'm kidding of course."

"Yes .... of course." She agreed, although her mind flashed back in time, to the day that she and Jean Paul had taken a voyage around Port De Monaco on board his luxury speed boat. '*Surely not*' she mused '*he wouldn't be snorting that shit while being involved in a major competition!?*' These rather disturbing thoughts were severed, as on her approach to the tea lawn, she caught sight of a woman nearby, stumble against a chair, then move unsteadily towards a table which, to Sonya's surprise was occupied by Ace and a young female. Now, to her utter dismay, she was abruptly aware that the somewhat intoxicated woman was in fact Danielle, who, with a belly full of Dutch courage, had by this time approached the table where the young couple were sitting and appeared to be talking to Ace, who in response to this intrusion gave the impression of being both uncomfortable and fairly puzzled. '*Oh my God, she knows, and this is surely not the time or the place.*' Sonya brooded and on realising the possible implications that this untimely meeting might present, Sonya hollered her friend's name in an effort to attract her attention, but Danielle did not respond. Sonya hastily stepped up her pace, leaving Brad Holding following in her wake. On reaching the table, she discovered to her relief, that Danielle was rattling on to a bewildered listener in her native tongue. Sonya took a hold of Danielle's arm and said.

"What are you doing!?"

"Pardon?"

"Come with me Danielle!"

"Where ... where are we going?"

"We are going home."

"Home?"

"I think you need to sleep this one off, goddamn it!"

"Everything OK?" Holding asked on approaching the two women.

"Take Danielle's arm please Brad, like I say, we're taking a ride home."

Holding complied with Sonya's request and without any further fuss, Danielle allowed herself to be escorted away. Sonya called after them.

"I'll catch you guys up, OK?" She said, then turned her attention towards Ace.

"Are you OK, I apologise for my friend, I've never seen her .. well you know? .. See, she's just getting over a nasty accident and ..."

"It's fine don't worry about it." He said with a broad reassuring smile.

"Thanks."

"Seems to me though, trouble kind of follows you around, what with my fight with your boyfriend and things."

"Yeah, trouble's been my middle name lately ... anyway, thanks once again for being so understanding on my friend's behalf."

"Just one thing before you go ... did your friend think that I was French or something, I mean, why was she speaking to me in French?"

"I don't know, but I guess I'm kinda relieved that that's what happened." She said, then excused herself and walked away. Ace watched on as she disappeared amongst the swarm of Wimbledon patrons. Lorna turned to Ace now and said.

"Did I ever tell you Ace, that I can speak French?"

"No."

"Well, I can!"

"Really?"

"Quite fluently in fact. Would you like to know what that French woman was saying to you?"

"Sure."

"I warn you now, it's a little unnerving, and even rather sad, from whatever angle you look at it."

"What do you mean?"

"Well, if it's true that she recently met with an accident as we were led to believe, then in that mishap, she may have bumped her head, which subsequently left her a bit crazy. Now if we look at it from your point of view then ..."

"Then what Lorna?"

"Ace ... that white woman said that you were her long lost son!"

Chapter Forty One

Following her markedly unbecoming conduct at Wimbledon, a despondent Danielle on her premature return to Allan House, had been quite reluctant to comply with Sonya and Floss' advice and retire to bed to sleep off her ordeal, although her liquored up body did eventually surrender to the notion. Consequently, she slept the afternoon away, while the other two women viewed the quarter final matches on television.

As Brad Holding had predicted that it would be, the centre court that afternoon, became a hot bed of excitement. Jean Paul and his German opponent had embellished the famous old stadium, with an exhibition fuelled with emotion, skill and unremitting determination. By the time that this compelling engagement had neared its conclusion, the mesmerised crowd had reached fever pitch. At advantage against him in the extended fifth and final set and 6-7 down, Jean Paul's courageous opposition had lost his service game, to a succession of superbly executed winning groundstrokes, which had succeeded in bringing the crowd to its feet and, the brave crestfallen German to his knees.

Later on that day, out on court number one, a match that was looked upon as being reasonably less enthralling, a jubilant Ace had won through against an out of sorts Czech seed, who throughout the match, had complained of stomach cramps. Incredibly, nonetheless Ace was now in the semi- finals. That evening he had invited Lorna and his brother Jack along for a quiet celebratory dinner, at a small secluded restaurant located fairly close to his lodgings. Throughout the meal, conversation between the three had been pleasant and light-hearted, which had in effect, certainly helped Ace relax, after the heady excitement of his most recent Wimbledon victory. Within the compact, though popular establishment it had been obvious that Ace's presence had not gone unnoticed. For once that it had become evident that he, along with his small party had finished their meals and looked probably set to vacate the scene, their table was suddenly surrounded by people requesting the young tennis star's signature and for a chance to pose for a photograph with him. To their delight he had accommodated their wants and needs amicably. Though, when the fuss had eventually abated, Ace let go a subtle sigh. With a proud grin Jack had then said to him.

"That's the price of fame Bro!"

"I guess."

"And the way that things are going, it's going to get worse!"

"I'll cope."

"I suppose it's the nutters you've got to be on your guard against Ace!?"

"I've had a couple of those already Jack."

"Oh?"

"Sure, there was one today that said she was my mother."

"What?" Jack said with a chortle.

"It's true, to look at her you would say that she was kind of chic .. you know, she was wearing stylish clothes and looked as if she was loaded."

"Loaded, she certainly was!" Lorna had concurred.

"You can never judge a book by its cover."

"Jack ... I think what Lorna means is that the woman was pissed, and to top that she rambled on to me in French, obviously I didn't understand a word she was saying."

"So how did you come to the conclusion, that this woman claimed to be your mother?"

"Because Lorna here, is not just a pretty face, she's also a bit of a linguist."

Ace and Jack had then been all ears, while Lorna explained in detail, what the stranger had said. Lorna's concluding translated words had then caught the attentive pair abruptly by surprise.

"You never mentioned that the woman had claimed to have sent me a talisman." Ace had said.

Two Days Later

Ace's semi- final was against Rod Devereux, an Australian player who, in the last round had swept aside the number one seed, Carl Emerson, with a display that saw power and aggression winning that day, over skill and agility. Consequently some parts of the media had billed the Devereux Vs Sharpe match today as 'the clash of the titans', which evidently, was proving to be an apt description of their swashbuckling encounter out on centre court. The first three sets had gone to tie-breaks, with Ace holding on grimly to narrowly achieve a two sets to one lead. Now, as the blow for blow meeting progressed towards its climax and with neither man having broken the others serves in any of the games so far, Ace, at 5-4 up for the match, braced himself to receive another blistering service from the man at the other side of the net. With a raucous grunt, the Australian delivered the shot deep and hard, but Ace's forehand return was equal to it, sending the ball fizzing past the advancing aggressor, who could only watch Ace's effort land just a fraction inside the baseline. The crowd yelled and cheered their approval and Ace punched the air with a clenched fist. When the umpire was satisfied that the excited clamour inside the stadium had subsided sufficiently to continue, he announced the present score.

"Thirty forty." The voice said. Ace sucked in a deep breath of the electrifying air before taking up his position, a good three metres behind the baseline. Now, he angled himself in readiness to anticipate the route that Devereux's next bullet-like service might take. With a degree of disguise, the Australian hammered the shot down the centre line and the receiver's backhand side. A fault was called late by a linesman who adjudged the ball to have landed beyond the six metre line and, within the tiny fragment of time that the speeding yellow ball took to reach Ace's end of the court he had already committed himself at full stretch in the endeavour to make good his return, albeit with a little too much exuberance for his own good. Consequently, he slipped and lost his balance, then in trying to remain on his feet, his right foot landed awkwardly beneath his weight. He felt a searing pain tear through the fibrous tissue around his ankle. Then after falling in a heap on the hollowed turf, his mind instantly reflected with trepidation, that this might be the final act in his Wimbledon dream. *'No way, it was only a twinge!'* a positive part of him chided. With a certain amount of caution, he slowly got to his feet, the crowd showered him with their approval by cheering and clapping noisily while he walked somewhat tentatively towards the baseline to continue. He took up position hoping earnestly that Devereux's next shot would be the last of the day, for he now believed that without treatment, his damaged ankle would probably not withstand another tie-break situation, let alone survive the pounding, that a further full set would incur should he not win his deciding point. The umpire appealed for *'quiet please'* from the excited gathering in the stands. Satisfied now that the crowd had taken heed of the official's plea, the Australian stepped up to the baseline. Then, as the audience held its breath, the service was hammered in and Ace's forehand return initiated what was to be the longest rally of the match, during which, with gritted teeth Ace had put his newly acquired injury to the back of his mind. The overhead backhand smash that finally decided the match, had succeeded in bringing the centre court crowd to their feet.

Jean Paul watched the proceedings on TV in the player's lounge and, although he had not played his semi-final match yet, he now knew who he would be facing in the final two days from now.

Chapter Forty Two

Wimbledon Men's Final Day

Basking beneath the warm afternoon sunshine, a capacity crowd waited patiently to welcome the players onto the centre court stage. Above the stadium an appointed TV camera zoomed in onto the legendary door, from behind which at any given moment now, the two finalists would emerge in readiness to brandish their talent before the watching world and, indeed for the opportunity to gain immortality in the annals of lawn tennis history. Presently, unseen by the millions of viewers, Ace and Jean Paul stood with only a few metres separating them, neither man uttered a word, nor did they attempt to make eye contact. The door suddenly opened a quarter of the way and the referee, equipped with the customary walkie-talkie and official green jacket, leaned through the opening.

"You have one minute gentlemen." He announced, then promptly closed the door again. As if the administrator's words had been a cue, the two men, for the first time since their ugly fracas a fortnight earlier, allowed their eyes to meet and become engaged in a frosty psychological battle. Although, through his audacious glare, Ace hoped fervently that the Frenchman did not recognise his growing apprehension. But inside the cool confines of the room, it was the sweat exuding through his pores which caused Ace to admit that he had unwittingly conceded an own goal. It was to his relief then, that Jean Paul fractured this unspoken game of cat and mouse, when he said wryly.

"Today Monsieur, it strikes me that you are not half as bold as you were the last time we crossed swords!"

"Oh really?"

"Which reminds me .... I am still waiting for an apology."

"Screw you Mr Big Time!" Ace snapped, while inadvertently his fingers toyed with the piece of jewellery around his neck.

"Where did you get that from?" Jean Paul probed.

"What?"

"That talisman you have there."

"That, is none of your bloody business!" Ace affirmed and their brief conversation was interrupted when the door once again swung open and the referee entered, then said.

"Your presence is needed on court gentlemen, may I take this opportunity of wishing you both the best of luck. Furthermore, I sincerely hope that we can all enjoy a sportsmanlike match, now if you are ready!?"

The two statuesque contenders followed the main official along through the provisional cordon and into the heat of the great arena, where the crowd greeted them with thunderous applause and in the thick of this enthusiastic reception,

Sonya, Danielle and Floss hailed their arrival and Danielle's heart skipped a beat, on beholding the siblings walking side-by-side. On sensing her friend's evident apprehension Sonya said.

"You OK?"

"This is very hard for me Sonya."

"Yeah, I know, but really I think you've made the right decision."

"Yes ... yes, you are quite right."

"To have enlightened the guys about their true circumstances could have proved to be a big mistake. This is a big day for them both."

"Yes, and I am so very proud." She said earnestly. Sonya looked at her for a long moment, then enquired.

"Do you intend to let the situation be known to them both, once today is over and out of the way, I mean?"

"No Sonya ... I think the time has come to bury the past no!?"

In another section of the stadium, Jack and Greg Fenton were nestled into their seats, trying hard to conceal their tension, with respect to their protégés' impending crusade.

At number 46 Argyle Street, Mrs Sharpe wiped away a prideful tear, while viewing the scenes on television in the company of her husband. The elderly couple concentrated now on listening to the commentator and his colleague's active exchange of views, on the two players pictured warming up for the match.

"I read in one of the popular tabloids, that it might be a good idea to temporarily re-name the centre court for today's final."

"Oh?"

"The columnist suggested that, the theatre of hate might be more apt."

"Tactless and rather melodramatic wouldn't you agree?"

"Probably so, but all the same, it's no secret that these two individuals of unquestionable genius, have little regard for each other."

"Yes this is unusual, it's the norm that players on the tour, although very competitive, always hold a measure of respect for fellow pros."

"If this was a boxing match, who would your money be on?"

"Well ... I didn't get to see the first fight, but from what I can gather, the Frenchman won on points."

"That's not what I heard."

"Enough frivolity now, seriously, this is the Wimbledon tennis final, who do you see lifting the trophy later today?"

"Statistically speaking, you and I know that Sharpe shouldn't have a chance, but his astonishing ascent here this year has been nothing short of miraculous."

"You haven't answered my question my friend!?"

"The grass surface suits Sharpe's powerful serve and volley game, he'll certainly make Jean Paul King work hard for his points today."

"You still haven't answered the question!"

"OK ... as a Brit, my heart says Ace Sharpe. But my head tells me, he's up against the world's best all round player."

"So you're saying that the title will go to France?"

"I can't honestly see it going anywhere else."

In Another Part Of The Capital

Short sleeved shirts and summer dresses were the order of the day for the vast majority of Sunday afternoon shoppers along Oxford Street. Most of the people amongst this busy throng that happened to share the same sidewalk, looked upon the tramp with an air of disdain. On his part, the vagrant did not give a monkey's toss and told them as much, as with a laboured stride, he searched for an unguarded shop doorway where he might get a few moments respite from the sun. Beneath his ragged duffel coat, his insipid body's stale odour had joined forces with an alcohol based drenching of new sweat, disfavouring the man with a foul acrid stench. He finally found refuge on a porch belonging to Dixons, an electrical, TV and video store. There, he took time to remove his woolly hat, then pressed his weather-beaten brow against the invigorating coolness of the large window pane, on the other side of which, a host of televisions of various sizes, broadcasted identical pictures of the live coverage from Wimbledon. The tramp watched the scenes with little interest, for his sole thought at the present moment was, where he might get his trembling hands on some booze. His befuddled brain, a maze of cloudy confusion, now brought to mind a day long ago, when a benevolent stranger had pressed a ten pound note into his grubby palm. That had been a fine day indeed, he had been able to buy a large bottle of his favourite cider and three special brew, oh yes, and not forgetting the scratch card that won him another tenner, enabling him to return to the mini-market the next day and repeat the purchase. Yes, what a great fucking day that was!

Another close-up shot of Ace's features filled the numerous television screens and, for one split second, the tramp thought that he actually recognised the face before him. He mumbled a string of unintelligible words and waited for somebody, anybody to respond, though as usual an exchange of views never came his way. Instead, the words that over the years had become all too familiar now filled his ears.

"On your way mate!" The store detective asserted, as he emerged through the automatic doors, then added what he believed to be a touch of waggish humour, saying.

"Strewth you smell like something that's just dropped out of the arse end of a dog!"

The tramp paid his respects to the man with a two-fingered salute, before making his way to another destination on the streets of London.

Ten Kilometres Outside Kuwait

On his arrival at the palace, Don Lawrence was greeted at the large double doors by an Englishman, who introduced himself as his highness' butler, before escorting the guest inside and through several extensive and magnificently furnished rooms, all of which were unoccupied. Lawrence could not help wondering where in this huge abode, the billionaire Prince might entertain his assemblage of beautiful women, though he kept these thoughts to himself. They came to a halt outside a door which Lawrence was informed, led to the private cinema and TV room. Inside the Prince and host was currently watching live televised pictures from London.

"You will wait outside, while I advise his highness of your presence." The butler said, before knocking twice on the door and entering. Two minutes later, Don Lawrence was introduced to the Arabian, who was gowned in an immaculate white robe, serving to enhance the man's dark, handsome features. He was a young man, in his mid-twenties Lawrence guessed and by virtue of his six foot frame, cut a commanding presence, he gestured with a hand, then in impeccable Etonian English said.

"Take a seat Mr Lawrence, I appreciate the fact that you have travelled half-way around the world and, I will be delighted to accommodate your needs, when I can contribute my full attention on your behalf. Although in the meantime, I sincerely hope that like myself you might be partial to watching a spot of tennis."

"Your highness, who am I to argue?"

"Exactly." The Arabian said, then employing the remote control in his right hand, he turned the interior lights down low. The two men now looked towards the huge screen and Lawrence, on observing the present score, wondered what the possibilities might be of Ace clawing his way back into the match. He then concluded that the odds of that happening, were probably as vague as he himself leaving this palace with Sonya's sister.

From the chair, the umpire relayed the score to the players and their audience.

"Game and second set to King, by six games to two ... King leads by two sets to love!"

Jean Paul sat down in his appointed seat, thoroughly satisfied with his day's work so far. Everything was going to plan and his opponent's hard hitting stratagem, had proved to be far less troublesome than he had originally expected. To further encourage the young Frenchman's confidence, his recent bouts of listlessness appeared to have receded over the last forty eight hours and, his usual vigour had returned with a vengeance. Furthermore, today he had at no time prior to the match, felt the need to pep himself up artificially for this final, he was clean and, on this form, he knew that he was unbeatable.

Sitting not five metres away, Ace reflected on his unconvincing performance and was oblivious to the TV camera homing in on his troubled features, while the pundits analysed his circumstances to their viewers.

"He really hasn't been able to settle today has he?"

"No, he appeared to be very nervous at the outset and we haven't seen him playing with the zing, that we've got used to seeing this past two weeks."

"Without wishing to sound patronising, Sharpe's inexperience has been very much in evidence today also."

"We mustn't forget though, this is a Grand Slam final, this is Wimbledon, this is the centre court and if he has choked, as an ex-professional myself, I can wholeheartedly sympathise with him!"

"But looking on the bright side, at least Sharpe appears to be showing no sign of discomfort from the injury that he sustained in his semi-final match!"

As if he had heard the commentator's words at this moment, Ace simultaneously leaned forward in his chair and adjusted the strapping around his damaged ankle, which he knew that, without agreeing to undergo some exceptionally unorthodox treatment just twenty four hours earlier, the chances were, that all his courageous endeavours and dreams would have been dashed at the final hurdle. Nevertheless, at first Ace had been reluctant to consent to the medication which would be administered to him through a needle. Assembled at Ace's lodgings and behind closed doors, Jack, Fenton and the player had held a rather anxious debate.

"Is it legal Greg?" Ace had asked.

"No ... no mate, I'm afraid it's not."

"What is it then ... the drug I mean?"

"It's called Nandroline."

"Nandroline?"

"Look mate, do you think I want to pump the crap into your bloodstream, it's unethical, foolhardy and against everything that we all believe in but,... it's vital if you want to play in the final tomorrow!"

"Shit ... I don't know Greg ... what do you think Jack?"

"Way I see it bro, you're hardly able to walk with the injury at the moment, let alone run around a tennis court."

"And will this Nandroline work, I mean will it ease the pain?"

"Sure thing!" Fenton had declared, beating Jack to the answer and, that promise had been a valid one so far today. That is to say, physically he had suffered very little from the contusion around his ankle. Although, the fact that Ace had taken the drug to enable him to compete, had had a rather bruising effect on him psychologically and consequently, he knew that he was playing well below his best. He took a sip of cool water and allowed it to dance on his tongue, before gratefully swallowing it down. '*How much do you want to win this?*' his thoughts now chided, '*forget the bloody Nandroline, think positive ... let's get back in this match, and do the job you came here to do!!*'

The man in the chair called time, prompting the players to proceed towards their respective ends of the court. The camera remained on Ace, while he accepted two balls from a young ballboy, the analysts continued with their commentary.

"Well, this is Sharpe's chance to prove his metal!"

"Yes indeed ... so it will be Sharpe to serve, in this third set and to stay in this final."

Ace studied his opponent at the other end of the court, he bounced the ball three times on the somewhat worn surface that ran alongside the length of the baseline. He then put his substantial weight behind a serve that rendered him only his second ace of the match so far, but delivered with it to Jean Paul, a reminder that if he thought that this match was in the bag, then he was very much mistaken.

For the last forty minutes or so, there had been very little dialogue between the two men, apart from the odd bit of banter regarding the tennis that was being displayed on the big screen in front of them and, although Don Lawrence was seated upon an assortment of richly embroidered silk cushions, he could not remember ever feeling quite so uncomfortable. The English butler knocked on the door, then entered delivering silver trays laden with spices and bitter tasting tea. He then went about the task of maintaining the fire in the hookah, from which the Arabian inhaled smoke through a long tube, the host then invited Lawrence to once again indulge himself in this middle eastern custom. The westerner accepted the offering with a smile that masked his repugnance towards this undertaking and he sincerely hoped, that this time he could sustain a modicum of protocol, having almost choked in his last effort to inhale the hookah's sweet scented smoke.

"It appears that the young British player is turning the match around, wouldn't you agree?" The Arabian said, although Lawrence was unable to respond, as he was too busy trying to stifle an imminent coughing fit. Suddenly, from somewhere within the palace walls, a high pitched wailing shrill pierced the air. The Arabian got to his feet and said something in his native tongue to the English butler, who responded in the same language then bowed his head. Without another word, the host briskly left the room. Rather unhinged by the Prince's sudden departure, Lawrence looked up from where he was sitting towards the butler, then said.

"What is it ... did I upset him?"

"His highness has been called to prayer."

"Oh I see, gone to bow to Mecca has he?" Lawrence said with a hint of sarcasm and instantly wished that he had not been so tactless. Then on recognising the scornful expression on the butler's face said.

"I'm sorry, I didn't intend to sound so impertinent, I'm rather like a fish out of water."

"It would be better for you to respect the ways of the east Mr Lawrence!"

"Yes, quite right."

"Might I ask, what exactly your business is here presently, with his highness?" The butler asked. Instinctively Lawrence saw an opportunity now, in the Arabian's absence, to prise some information for himself via the prince's servant. But he knew that he would have to tread carefully to win over the man's confidence, in the space of time he had left before his master returned.

"I am here representing a friend of mine." Lawrence began, "a very dear friend."

"Why couldn't your friend have come here personally?"

"Well I appreciate that I appear rather unenlightened by the eastern way of life, though, for my friend to have come here, might have met with the prince's disapproval I fear."

"Oh, why?"

"My friend is a female." Lawrence explained and, was somewhat taken by surprise by the butler's jocular reaction to what he believed to be a rational explanation.

"Is his highness not a magnificent specimen of manhood?" The butler said between hoots of laughter. "Women adore him, his sexual appetite and prowess are legendary amongst the Arab Royals, even more so amongst his beautiful devoted wives!"

Lawrence laughed albeit nervously, then said.

"I have it through a reliable source that his highness knows the whereabouts of a young lady ... an American lady who, during a shopping spree in Tangier, some time ago went missing."

"Missing?"

"I have been employed by the missing girl's sister ... my friend, to find her and, with a little luck, take her home with me."

The butler's face was stern again now.

"I sincerely hope Mr Lawrence, that you are not insinuating that his highness has had any connection with an abduction!?"

"No ... no, I'm aware that this is a very sensitive situation, I certainly have no wish to insult the prince in any way, after all, when all is said and done, I could have taken this matter to the US Embassy in London and have them deal with it." Lawrence hinted, now wishing that he had done just that.

"Who told you that you might find this young American woman here?"

"As I told you when I got in contact by telephone ... it was you, that organised my appointment with his highness, wasn't it?"

"Most of his highness' appointments are arranged through myself."

"Then you must be acquainted with the name Agnazzio Bennetti!?"

"No ... I'm afraid not."

"What about Irwin King, does that name ring a bell?"

"Irwin King you say ... no, I'm not familiar with that name either." The butler prevaricated, for it was he who, on several occasions in the past had dealt with the ring, in obtaining valuable merchandise to satisfy his master's extravagant needs. He knew too, that one particular delivery, was of a beautiful young American girl, who, after becoming his sixth wife, had blessed the prince with a healthy son. The butler vowed to himself at this moment in time, that he would do everything in his power to avoid his master suffering the least amount of distress, on their part. He had hidden these thoughts and others skilfully from Lawrence, who continued for some time to probe as tentatively as he could, in an effort to maintain the dialogue on course.

"Forgive my ignorance once again." Lawrence was saying now, "the prince ... he has a harem does he?"

"He does indeed, and as I say, his wives adore and worship him."

"I'm sure they do, after all, as well as being extremely attractive to the opposite sex, he's an extremely wealthy man too. All the same, I have been led to believe, that although very well educated and so forth, I understand that his highness is rather shy and something of a recluse."

"What are you getting at Mr Lawrence?"

"I'm simply curious to know that, if this is the case and, he rarely leaves the confines of the palace, then how does he woo these beautiful women in the first place?"

"Allah brings them to me on the warm desert winds." The Arabian's voice declared behind where Lawrence was sitting, causing him to flinch slightly.

"So tell me Mr Lawrence, how have things progressed in the tennis final while I've been away?" The Arabian then asked lightly. But, before Lawrence could collect himself enough to reply, the butler said.

"I'm afraid your guest has had little time to digest the goings on at Wimbledon, it seems that he chose the time while you were at prayer to pry into your highness's personal affairs!"

"Now just a minute, I was merely trying to establish ..."

"And I, Mr Lawrence!" The Arabian interjected in a stern tone, his dark surly eyes regarding the investigator for a long moment, before continuing, "I, Mr Lawrence, was merely trying to establish how the tennis was going on."

To Lawrence's relief, he turned his attention toward the screen, the anger in his voice subsided now.

"Goodness ... the match looks as though it's going to go into a fifth and deciding set!" He said, then held a brief conversation with the butler in Arabic. As Lawrence did not understand a word that they were saying, he wanted to object strongly to their rudeness, but told himself to bite his tongue, which through his growing uneasiness, felt as if it had absorbed a mouthful of Sahara sand.

The TV screen was now showing a slow-motion action replay of the two finalists, vigorously contesting for the point that dramatically clinched the fourth set for Ace, by winning another tie-break. To further capture some of the suspense inside the stadium, a camera specifically employed to film the crowd's reaction and that of the competitor's coaches, family and friends, homed in on Fenton and Jack, whose faces displayed a mixture of joy and utter relief. Then, in an instant, it zoomed in on Jean Paul's party and finally held the frame solely on Sonya's beguiling features, a visage that Lawrence had fallen in love with, from the moment that she had first walked through the door of his London office. Now, his eyes toured the contours of her exquisite face, a face that, unfortunately for Don Lawrence PI, he would never see again.

As with past great Wimbledon champions, who, over the years had graced the centre court, this year's contenders were embellishing the old stadium with a show befitting the final's splendid history. Now, surrounding the grunts and groans, that emanated from the players saturated and seemingly tireless bodies, the capacity crowd was a cauldron of excitement after witnessing Ace, stubbornly claw his way back into the match after winning his two sets on tie-breaks. Naturally, with the score at two sets all and 3-3 in the final set, a large proportion of people in the stands, on sensing a possible British victory, had started to vent their support and encouragement to their man loudly between games, the latest of which, saw a spectacular rally involving a pulsating array of exquisite groundstrokes, which finally reached its conclusion, when, with a overhead forehand, Ace smashed home the winner. This was greeted with an ear-splitting cheer that seemed to rock the stadium's very foundations. From the chair, the umpire had to almost shout down the microphone in order to convey the score, amidst the hubbub of excited chatter that followed.

"Fifteen ... forty!" The official announced, then "Quiet please!"

Ace had now not only stolen the initiative, but was on the brink of breaking the Frenchman's serves for the first time in the match. At the other end of the court, Jean Paul waited for the slowly decreasing noise around him to ebb away to a reasonable hush. Satisfied, he stepped up to the baseline, positioned himself and sucked in a deep breath of the electrifying air, before priming himself for his next sortie. He looked over the net towards his opponent, then, excavating as much energy as his by now, tiring limbs would allow, he launched himself into the serve, the momentum from which took him towards the net in readiness to attack the return. Ace saw the ball early and let fly with a full blooded forehand drive, which although only marginally out of the Frenchman's reach, had flashed by him and landed plumb on the baseline. The crowd went positively wild and in pure frustration Jean Paul threw his racket to the ground, then mouthed a stream of expletives, which fortunately for him, could not be heard amid the clamour. To the vast majority witnessing this rather petulant act, it appeared that the first cracks in Jean Paul King's veneer were beginning to show. In contrast, Ace looked poised and confident, as he made his way to his seat. On the other side of the umpire's chair the young Frenchman slumped into his own designated seat, grateful for the opportunity to rest and take stock of his predicament. For, during the past two games, albeit to a small degree, his entire body seemed to have lost some of its zeal, as if he was in need of sustenance to build up his energy levels. But the reason for his outburst at the completion of the last set, was not born out of poor sportsmanship, it was simply a case of knowing without doubt, that ordinarily he would have got his racket to the ball on Ace's service return and made the backhand volley count. Although to his utter bewilderment, his normally strong dependable legs had suddenly become rebellious, he rubbed his arms down with a towel, while his eyes searched the stands for his coach, who he had to concede now, had been justified to have recommended him to undergo a physical examination. But, what perturbed him immeasurably more at this moment, was that for him to fulfil his dream today, he would have to dig deeper into his resolve than ever before, as his reasoning told him that, this slight impairment would no doubt not be recognised by the eye of an unskilled observer. But, his adversary at the opposite end of the court would be perceptive enough, to lock onto the very tiniest sign of weakness and feed off it like a parasite.

The umpire called '*time*', prompting Jean Paul's disciplined mind to cast aside these and any other negative notions. *'It is your destiny to become the world number one'* he reflected, while getting up from his seat. *'By the time that this match reaches its climax, it will be you Jean Paul King that will be holding your hands aloft in sweet victory'* his thoughts pressed now and, as he stepped back out onto the court, where he was spontaneously engulfed by vigorous applause from the stands, he declared aloud to himself.

"For the love of glory, this is your destiny!"

Now, it was Ace's turn to receive the crowd's acclaim on his return in readiness to continue. The reception that he received was somewhat excessive, bordering from some quarters on fanatical, amplifying the fact that he was on home soil. In truth, Ace had never felt more at home than at this moment in time. At the baseline, he accepted two balls from a ballboy, above where he stood, the scoreboard illuminated by yellow figures displayed the present score, it read; 6-2 6-2 6-7 6-7 3-4. His senses by now were at their peak, he knew that all he needed to do was to keep himself focused and simply hold on to his service games, then victory would be his. He was aware also, that his opponent's endurance had in recent games debilitated to some degree. With that in mind, he hammered home his first serve with unmerciless venom, the ball landed spot on the centre line on the other side of the court at an astounding 139 mph, making it quite impossible for Jean Paul to administer a return, instead his flailing racket waved helplessly at fresh air, much to the approval of the captivated partisan crowd. The next serve saw Jean Paul going for the ball at full stretch, though once again to no avail. With a rush of adrenaline pumping through him, Ace demonstrated his elation by punching the air with a vehement fist. He was surely now on an unstoppable roll towards clinching a famous triumph. His third service assault though, did not have quite the same impetus and was returned with interest, consequently wrong-footing the Briton on his approach to the net, accordingly, his backhand shot flew high and lamely over the net, where his rapidly advancing opposition seized the golden opportunity to win the point, by savagely pounding the ball back with an overhead smash. From such short range, Ace's lightening reflexes for once were not quite in evidence, as he was unable to avoid the imminent impact from the speeding sphere, which with a stomach-turning clout smashed into his right eye. The pain was instantaneous and excruciating, the crowd gasped in horror at bearing witness to this awful accident, they then looked on anxiously as the young hero writhed about on the floor in agony. Sensing a possible emergency, the umpire called for the referee, who arrived on the scene accompanied by a paramedic and a doctor, who escorted the injured player to his seat.

In the stands, his anxious coach fidgeted in his seat, frustrated by the fact that he was powerless to communicate with Ace in any way. But, by the time that ten torturous minutes had elapsed, while the doctor tended to his injured player, Fenton's patience was beginning to crack under the strain of knowing, that as incredibly coincidental as it might be, his own career had been left in ruins, by similar circumstances. To his relief now, Ace was back on his feet, although he looked to all the world far from comfortable. At this moment, Fenton wished that he could hear the conversation that was presently taking place between the doctor and the officials, who encircled his dispirited looking player.

"What do you advise doctor?" The referee was saying.

"That we get him to a hospital as soon as we can."

"Are you saying that he's unable to continue?"

"I have not been able to thoroughly examine the injury because he can't open the eye for long enough, but I have been able to ascertain that the cornea, which is the transparent layer of tissue covering the front of the eye, has been quite severely damaged. He tells me that his vision is very blurred, which infers that perhaps he has wounded other more vital parts ..."

"I want to play on." Ace said, interrupting the doctor's flow.

"As a doctor, I would advise you not to participate in any further exertion."

"I appreciate your concern, but I came here to do a job and I intend to finish it!"

"Then, on your head be it, if that is your decision."

"Bet your arse!"

Two minutes later, having covered the injured eye with a patch, he was ready to continue with the challenge, much to the crowd's delight and sheer admiration. The players wasted little time in warming up once more, following the interruption in play and when they were suitably prepared to proceed with the match, the umpire reiterated the score. Jean Paul took up his position to receive, aware by this time that the delay had had a beneficial effect on him. It had given him time to recoup some of his strength although to an even greater degree than before, he sensed that from now until the match's conclusion, the crowd would be avidly yearning for his undoing at the hands of his opponent. But, such one sided support he had told himself, would not serve to discourage or intimidate him in any way, this was his destiny and nothing was going to get in the way of that.

At the other end of the court, amidst the mood of compassion and anticipation, that emanated from the packed stands, Ace stepped up towards the baseline and geared himself up to resume. He tossed the ball up and thrashed his service a good three metres beyond the line, his second service was not quite so wayward, having landed inside the targeted area, although the inadequate potency from the shot, was cold-bloodedly met with a top spin forehand, that left Ace floundering. Beneath the patch, Ace's eye throbbed insufferably with every beat of his heart, a heart that, although valiant in its attempt to beat his newly acquired handicap, would soon be broken at the hands of his accomplished opponent, before the millions of people observing the scenes on the legendary grass court. Later, even more anguish though would imminently come his way inside the locker room, where in front of an audience of just three, he would suffer the indignation of failing a drug test, prior to being whisked away for treatment for his painful injury.

Chapter Forty Three

Much to the indignation of a number of haughty party-goers, Jean Paul had made his excuses and left the official Wimbledon celebration ball early. Then, making use of the hotel room provided for him, he and Sonya had changed into more appropriate clothing to enable them to pursue a more personal style of celebrating. That is to say that, Sonya had simply complied with his somewhat bizarre arrangements. While the two made their way to where their mode of transport awaited them, Sonya had asked.

"Why the Harley?"

"What do you mean?"

"I mean, you could have had your pick of ritzy limousines, to take us anywhere we chose to go."

"My bike, releases in me a feeling of liberty."

"Sure I guess I understand what you're saying Jean Paul, but dressed in these leathers, who's gonna give us the liberty to enter a restaurant, or club come to that?"

"Trust me, I have everything under control and besides ... am I not now the World's number one tennis player!? .. This is my ticket to gain entry anywhere I choose, no?"

"In that case, as we've got time to play with, what say we pay Ace a visit at the hospital?"

"What, are you crazy!?"

"I just thought ..."

"If the press are hanging around there, they might misconstrue my motives for making such a visit."

"In what way?"

"There are some people, who might say that I hit the ball at him on purpose out there today."

"What kind of moron would suggest such a thing?" Sonya had said, suppressing a chortle at the notion that he could be guilty of such a diabolical deed. To her dismay, a brief awkward breach in their discussion had then followed and, she thought for a moment, that in his eyes she recognised a tinge of agitation.

"Do you want to talk about it?"

"Talk about what?"

"Jeez, I know that winning out there today meant a lot to you, but, am I reading this right, did you smash the ball with the intention of hitting him?" She asked apprehensively.

"I did not aim to hit him in the eye, if that is what you mean?"

"Truth is though, you had the whole of his side of the court to target the ball."

"It is a shot that I have played many times before, I hit the ball hard down at the opponent's feet ..."

"His feet you say!?"

"Yes, but unfortunately I mistimed the shot, I did not mean to cause him harm, it was an accident, you believe me don't you?" He had said in conclusion, now, half an hour after that rather disturbing conversation, in which at no time had she recognised an ounce of remorse from him. She was honestly not sure that she did believe him. Seated on the pillion, Sonya tried hard to muffle these nagging doubts, as her companion weaved the huge motorcycle through the busy London streets.

With the aid of a street light and, using his long grimy thumb nail, the ill-favoured tramp meticulously removed as much as he could of the cigarette ash, along with any other unwelcome debris from the remains of a half eaten cheese and tomato pizza which, following a slight altercation with a ravenous canine stray, he had gratefully seized from a dustbin at the back of a bistro. This would be the first morsel of food that he had eaten in two days. Satisfied now with his scouring exercise, he sunk his yellow stained teeth into his evening meal, then flinched as a hard baked part of the savoury crust scraped against his receding gums and caused them to bleed. Cussing loudly, he spat the offending particle out onto the pavement then, with an unsteady gait, he continued on his way along the Tottenham Court Road.

The effects from the ethanol that he had guzzled down earlier were by now beginning to subside and his benumbed joints would soon be aching and he himself screaming in need for a top up. Through bloodshot eyes, he saw a boisterous stag party five strong, leaving a Greek taverna just a few metres ahead of him. In noisy inebriated tones they were discussing which pub they might descend upon next, when one of the youths took an instant unkindly interest in the approaching vagrant and decided to set upon him with a barrage of abusive remarks. Recognising the chance of a good laugh, the other members of the party joined in with their friend's vulgar teasing. In an attempt to side-step these newly acquired adversaries, the unfortunate man found himself suddenly surrounded and, amidst their guffawing, they pushed his ungainly form around from one to the other. One rowdy hoodlum on his turn to render a shove, for good measure thrust a knee up hard into the vagrant's long forsaken testicles. The impact made his decrepit body shudder and his knees buckle, he fell to the floor holding his injured groin. He rolled over now onto his back, his mouth agape, desperately bidding to suck new air into his choking lungs. With eyes wide with trepidation, he watched as the thug that had instigated this hideous assault excitedly told one of the assemblage to hold the 'scruff-bag's' head still. The loud spotty-faced youth then unzipped his trousers and yanked out his penis. Now, to a peel of laughter from his accomplices, he relieved his bladder. The torrent of yellow tinted urine splashed down over the wretched man's face, and in his desperate attempts to breathe the tramp swallowed some of the foul tasting liquid causing him to cough and splutter raucously and then vomit. One of the thugs punished this unsavoury act as he saw it, by kicking him hard in the ribs. Then, following another string of expletives from the callous horde, he turned over onto his side, curling into a ball, in a pathetic attempt to cover himself up against another deluge of blows which, to his relief did not come his way. Thereafter, just how long he had remained in the foetus position he had no idea, for he had evidently passed out. He awoke from this state of unconsciousness somewhat confused. However, the vile metallic taste of his own blood, along with the aches and pains emanating from his ribs and injured groin, served as a brisk reminder of his recent beating. With a huge amount of effort, the tramp got to his feet with his eyes frantically searching his surroundings, fearful that he might catch sight of his assailants. Thankfully, amidst the by now fairly busy pavement, taken up by theatre goers and the like, there was no sign of them. Satisfied, the down-an-out turned to continue his journey, to who knows where. It was approximately fifteen minutes later, that the tramp cussed his misfortune when, to his utter dismay he espied the same gang of youths staggering out from another pub doorway then proceeded to walk towards him. Shocked and filled with panic the tramp stepped heedlessly out onto the road. There, he collided head on with an oncoming motorcycle. Jean Paul had hit the breaks, but was unable to avoid smashing into him. On impact, one of the unfortunate man's arms became ensnared in the front forks and succeeded in causing the front wheel to lock, the repercussions from which catapulted the rider and his travelling companion high over the top of the handlebars.

Epilogue

Over the past few days, Ace had received a large number of cards and letters from well-wishers and new-born advocates of his, from a wide spectrum of individuals. Replies to these though, along with numerous invitations to take part in media interviews and so on, were being put to one side for the time being. While, on tenterhooks he awaited news from the international tennis federation appeals committee and the results of his recent optical tests, which would determine whether or not he still had a future as a professional tennis player. Naturally therefore, he had been a less than enthusiastic recipient of a telephone call that he had received a couple of hours earlier on this day. Although he had been rather taken by surprise on learning who it was, that had actually called him.

"Hi Ace, it's Sonya Kennedy ... remember me?" She had said.

"Yes I remember, trouble's your middle name, what can I do for you?"

"It's not what you can do for me Ace, look I know you've got enough problems of your own right now ..."

"Sure, it seems though, we've both had our share, how are you after that motorbike accident?"

"Thank you for asking, I'm fine, the hospital kept me in overnight, but apart from a busted arm and a few cuts and bruises, I was lucky ... you probably know though, that Jean Paul wasn't quite so fortunate!?"

"I told you he was a crap rider."

"I guess I can forgive you for such a flippant remark but ..."

"If I sound bitter, it's because I am!"

"Sure, it's understandable."

"Tell me, are Jean Paul King's injuries career threatening?"

"The doctors say it's a fifty-fifty chance that he might have to quit the game, due to the injuries he sustained in the accident, but in the long term, he's got a much bigger problem than that to contend with."

"What do you mean, what could be bigger than that?"

"I can't tell you over the phone ... look can I meet up with you?"

"Well, I'm not sure I ..."

"Listen Ace, I beg of you, it's imperative that we meet!"

"Imperative?"

"You might be able to save a guy's life!"

"Who ... what guy?"

"Meet me at the Landmark Hotel, inside the Winter Gardens, and all will be made clear to you, will you do that!?"

"The Landmark Hotel?"

"It's on the Euston Road, by the train station, how does four pm suit you, can I count on you to be there ... please!?"

Sonya sat down at the same table that she had been sitting on the night that, as an escort she had waited in vain to meet with the elusive Lord Bucknall. As on that evening the pianist dextrously played a selection of tunes by Debussy. Around the elaborate dome with its eight palm trees and flourishing tropical foliage, there were only a few small parties of people gathered together, all of whom were to Sonya's satisfaction, beyond earshot of her imminent conversation with Ace. Now, to her relief she caught sight of his tall athletic figure entering the spacious restaurant gardens. She got up from her seat and with her good arm, waved to attract his attention. When he arrived at the table she smiled and said.

"Thanks for coming Ace, please rest your butt, hey, would you like a drink?"

"No I won't, thanks all the same." He said coolly and Sonya instantly picked up on his sombre vibes.

"OK ... hope you don't mind if I have one ... I guess before we're through, I'm sure gonna need one." She said as lightly as her newly acquired nervousness would allow.

"Look ... before I begin I want you to be completely open minded."

"I think I can do that." He said wryly. She took in a deep breath then, with the knowledge that she had obtained from Danielle and Floss, along with information that had come her way via Larry Hickman and Don Lawrence, she set about the task of conveying her comprehensive belief, that he and Jean Paul were long lost brothers.

Throughout the thirty minutes that followed, since embarking on her sensitive mission, Sonya could not help wondering what might be going through Ace's mind. For, to her surprise he appeared indifferent, even bored at times in response to the revelations that she had carefully enlightened him with. She suppressed her growing annoyance now and with a sigh, said.

"OK ... I guess that's as much as I know, you don't seem to have much to say for yourself, if you don't mind me saying. We've been here all this time and you ain't so much as asked one question."

Ace did not respond immediately, his fingers fidgeted around his eye patch, while he asked himself, how much longer he would be able to continue with this display of impartiality, for inside his now turbulent thoughts grappled, to comprehend the unbelievable claims that Sonya made. In as composed a manner as he could muster he said.

"What hospital did this kid ... this twin get dumped at?"

Withington ... yeah, Withington Hospital in Manchester, Floss was quite clear on that one."

"But I imagine that lots of babies are abandoned on hospital steps!?"

"Withington recorded only one that year."

"Just a minute ... I was under the impression that my coming here, was a matter of life or death, that's what you told me on the phone!?"

"That's right."

"But instead you sit me down here and give me some far-fetched tale about ..."

"OK Ace, prove me wrong why don't you!?"

"What?"

"Prove to me that, everything that I've told you is nothing more than horse shit!"

"How ... or better still, why should I do that?"

"Because ... if you were to take up the challenge, you just might be able to save Jean Paul King from a certain slow and painful death." She affirmed. A long agonising silence prevailed between them before Sonya broke the deadlock.

"Let me explain," she began, "The hospital did a few tests on Jean Paul and ... well to cut a long story short, they found that he was in the early stages of CLL."

"What's CLL?"

"Chronic Lymphatic Leukaemia," she explained, noting at the same time, that Ace looked positively stunned. She continued.

"When they think he's recovered sufficiently enough from his injuries from the accident, then they are going to transfer him to London's Royal Marsden Hospital. That's where you come in Ace. You OK this far?" Sonya asked. No words came from his gaping mouth. She went on explaining.

"I've got a hunch that your bone marrow's gonna match up with his and, if it does, I can assure you Ace, that the operation, ... your operation that is, will entail a maximum of two days in hospital and leave you with just a few aches and pains. The procedure involves a couple of needles being inserted into the hip bone under general anaesthetic ... I know this all sounds pretty gruesome and, well maybe a little too much for you to take in right now, but ... well we know that you both share the same rare blood group .."

"We do?"

"Sure, and like I say, the hope is that your bone marrow will also be compatible."

There was another long silence, which once again was fractured by Sonya, she continued.

"Well ... I guess it's up to you now, will you go through with it?" She asked. But the wry smile on his face now, she thought, was rather disturbing.

"You'll do it ... won't you?"

The smile on his face suddenly became broader, then he gave her his answer.

"No, I don't think I'm going to do that!"